L.A. Confidential

The Big Nowhere

The Black Dahlia

Silent Terror (Killer on the Road)

Suicide Hill

Because the Night

Blood on the Moon

Clandestine

Brown's Requiem

WHITE JAZZ

WHITE JAZZ

a novel by

JAMES ELLROY

ALFRED A. KNOPF
New York
1992

THIS IS A BORZOI BOOK
PUBLISHED BY ALFRED A. KNOPF, INC.

Copyright © 1992 by James Ellroy
All rights reserved under International and Pan-American
Copyright Conventions. Published in the United States by
Alfred A. Knopf, Inc., New York, and simultaneously in
Canada by Random House of Canada Limited, Toronto.
Distributed by Random House, Inc., New York.
Published in Great Britain by Century Hutchinson Ltd.

Library of Congress Cataloging-in-Publication Data
Ellroy, James, [date]
White jazz : a novel / by James Ellroy. — 1st American ed.
p.   cm.
ISBN 0-679-41449-5
I. Title.
PS3555.L6274W45   1992
813'.54—dc20   92-52890
                                                              CIP

Manufactured in the United States of America
First American Edition

TO

Helen Knode

In the end I possess my birthplace
and am possessed by its language.

—Ross MacDonald

WHITE JAZZ

All I have is the will to remember. Time revoked/fever dreams—I wake up reaching, afraid I'll forget. Pictures keep the woman young.

L.A., fall 1958.

Newsprint: link the dots. Names, events—so brutal they beg to be connected. Years down—the story stays dispersed. The names are dead or too guilty to tell.

I'm old, afraid I'll forget:

I killed innocent men.

I betrayed sacred oaths.

I reaped profit from horror.

Fever—that time burning. I want to go with the music—spin, fall with it.

L.A. *Herald-Express,* 10/17/58:

BOXING PROBE IN PROGRESS; FEDERAL GRAND JURY TO HEAR WITNESSES

Yesterday, a spokesman for the U.S. Attorney's Office in Los Angeles announced that Federal agents are probing the "gangland infiltrated" Southland prize fight scene, with an eye toward securing grand jury indictments.

U.S. Attorney Welles Noonan, former counsel to the McClellan Rackets Committee, said that Justice Department investigators, acting on information supplied by unnamed informants, are soon to question colorful Los Angeles "mob fringe character" Mickey Cohen. Cohen, now thirteen months out of prison, is rumored to have attempted contract infringement on a number of local prizefighters. Currently being questioned under hotel guard are Reuben Ruiz, bantamweight contender and regular attraction at the Olympic Auditorium, and Sanderline Johnson, former ranked flyweight working as a croupier at a Gardena poker establishment. A Justice Department press release stated that Ruiz and Johnson are "friendly witnesses." In a personal aside to Herald reporter John Eisler, U.S. Attorney Noonan said: "This investigation is now in its infancy, but we have every hope that it will prove successful. The boxing racket is just that: a racket. Its cancerous tentacles link with other branches of organized crime, and should Federal grand jury indictments result from this probe, then perhaps a general probe of Southern California mob activity will prove to be in order. Witness Johnson has assured my investigators that boxing malfeasance is not the only incriminating information he has been privy to, so perhaps we might start there. For now, though, boxing is our sole focus."

POLITICAL STEPPINGSTONES HINTED

Some skepticism greeted news of the prize fight probe. "I'll believe it when the grand jury hands down true bills," said William F. Degnan, a former FBI agent now retired in Santa Monica. "Two witnesses do not make a successful investigation. And I'm wary of anything announced in the press: it smacks of publicity seeking."

Mr. Degnan's sentiments were echoed by a source within the Los Angeles District Attorney's Office. Queried on the probe, a prosecuting attorney who wishes to remain anonymous stated: "It's politics pure and simple. Noonan's friends with [Massachusetts Senator and presidential hopeful] John Kennedy, and I've heard he's going to run for California Attorney General himself in '60. This probe has to be fuel for that run, because Bob Gallaudet [interim Los Angeles District Attorney expected to be elected to a full term as DA ten days hence] might well be the Republican nominee. You see, what a *Federal* probe implicitly states is that *local* police and prosecutors can't control crime within their own bailiwick. I call Noonan's grand jury business a political steppingstone."

U.S. Attorney Noonan, 40, declined comment on the above speculation, but a surprise ally defended him with some vigor. Morton Diskant, civil liberties lawyer and Democratic candidate for Fifth District City Councilman, told this writer: "I distrust the Los Angeles Police Department's ability to maintain order without infringing on the civil rights of Los Angeles citizens. I distrust the Los Angeles District Attorney's Office for the same reason. I especially distrust Robert Gallaudet, most specifically for his support of [Fifth District Republican Councilman] Thomas Bethune, my incumbent opponent. Gallaudet's stand on the Chavez Ravine issue is unconscionable. He wants to evict impoverished Latin Americans from their homes to procure space for an L.A. Dodgers ballpark, a frivolity I deem criminal. Welles Noonan, on the other hand, has proven himself to be both a determined crimefighter and a friend of civil rights. Boxing is a dirty business that renders human beings walking vegetables. I applaud Mr. Noonan for taking the high ground in combatting it."

WITNESSES UNDER GUARD

U.S. Attorney Noonan responded to Mr. Diskant's statement. "I appreciate his support, but I do not want partisan political comments to cloud the issue. That issue is boxing and the best way to sever its links to organized crime. The U.S. Attorney's Office does not seek to supersede the authority of the LAPD or to in any way ridicule or undermine it."

Meanwhile, the boxing probe continues. Witnesses Ruiz and Johnson are in protective custody at a downtown hotel, guarded by Federal agents and officers on loan from the Los Angeles Police Department: Lieutenant David Klein and Sergeant George Stemmons, Jr.

"Hollywood Cavalcade" Feature, *Hush-Hush* Magazine, 10/28/58:

MISANTHROPIC MICKEY SLIPS, SLIDES, AND NOSEDIVES SINCE PAROLE

Dig it, hepcats: Meyer Harris Cohen, the marvelous, benevolent, malevolent Mickster, has been out of Federal custody since September, '57. He did 3 to 5 for income tax evasion; his ragtag band dispersed, and the former mob kingpin's life since then has been one long series of skidmarks across the City of the Fallen Angels, the town he used to rule with bullets, bribes and bullspit bonhomie. Dig, children, and smell the burning rubber of those skids: off the record, on the Q.T. and *very* Hush-Hush.

April, '58: former Cohen henchman Johnny Stompanato is shanked by Lana Turner's daughter, a slinky 14 year old who should have been trying on prom gowns instead of skulking outside Mommy's bedroom with a knife in her hand. Too bad, Mickster: Johnny was your chief strongarm circa '49–'51, maybe *he* could have helped curtail your post prison tailspin. And tsk, tsk: you *really shouldn't* have sold Lana's sin-sational love letters to Johnny—we heard you raided the "Stomp Man's" Benedict Canyon love shack while Johnny was still in the meat wagon on his way to Slab City.

More sin-tillating scoop on the Mickster:

Under the watchful eye of his parole officer, Mickey has since made attempts to straighten up and skid right. He bought an ice cream parlor that soon became a criminal haven and went bust when parents kept their children away in droves; he financed his own niteclub act, somnambulistic shtick at the Club Largo. Snore City: bum bits on Ike's golf game, gags about Lana T. and Johnny S., the emphasis on "Oscar," the Stomp Man's Academy Award size appendage. And—Desperation City—the Mickster salaamed for Jesus during Billy Graham's Crusade at the L.A. Coliseum!!!! The chutzpah of Mickey renouncing his Jewish heritage as a P.R. ploy!!!! For shame, Mickster, for shame!!!!! And now the scenario darkens.

Item:

Federal agents are soon to scold Mickey for infringing on the contracts of local prizefight palookas.

Item:

Four of Mickey's goons—Carmine Ramandelli, Nathan Palevsky, Morris Jahelka and Antoine "The Fish" Guerif—have mysteriously disappeared, presumably snuffed by person or persons unknown, and (very strangely, hepcats) Mickey is keeping his (usually on overdrive) yap shut about it.

Rumors are climbing the underworld grapevine: two surviving Cohen gunmen (Chick Vecchio and his brother Salvatore "Touch" Vecchio, a failed actor rumored to be *très* lavender) are planning nefarious activities outside of Mickey's aegis. Get in on the ground floor, Mickster—we've heard that your sole source of income is Southside vending and slot machines: cigarettes, rubbers, french ticklers and one-armed bandits stuffed into smoky back rooms in Darktown jazz clubs. For shame again, Mickey! Shvartze exploitation! Penny ante and beneath you, you the man who once ruled the L.A. rackets with a paralyzingly pugnacious panache!

Get the picture, kats and kittens? Mickey Cohen is Skidsville, U.S.A., and he needs moolah, gelt, the old cashola. Which explains our most riotous rumor revelation, raffishly revealed for the frenetically foremost first time!

Digsville:

Meyer Harris Cohen is now in the movie biz!!

Move over C. B. DeMille: the fabulous, benevolent, malevolent Mickster is now sub-rosa financing a horror cheapie currently shooting in Griffith Park! He's saved his negro exploited nickels and is now partners with Variety International Pictures in the making of *Attack of the Atomic Vampire*. It's sensational, it's non-union, it's a turkey of epic proportions!

Further Digsville:

Ever anxious to parsimoniously pinch pennies, Mickey has cast lavender loverboy Touch Vecchio in a key role—and the Touchster is hot, hot, hotsville with the star of the movie: limpwristed lothario Rock Rockwell. Off-camera homo hijinx! You heard it first here!

Final Digsville:

Enter Howard Hughes: Mr. Airplane/Tool Magnate, lascivious luster after Hollywood lovelies. He used to own R.K.O. Studios; now he's an independent producer known for keeping wildly well-endowed wenches welded to "personal service contracts"—read as bit roles in exchange for frequent nighttime visits. Dig: we've heard that Mickey's leading lady left the mammary-mauling mogul spinning his own propeller—she actually amscrayed on a Hughes contract and car hopped until Mickey materialized at Scrivner's Drive-In dying for a chocolate malt.

Are you smitten, Mickster?

Are you heartbroken, Howard?

Hollywood Cavalcade shifts gears with an open letter to the Los Angeles Police Department.

Dear LAPD:

Recently, three wino bums were found strangled and mutilated in abandoned houses in the Hollywood area. *Very* Hush-Hush: we've heard the still-at-large killer snapped their windpipes post-mortem, utilizing great strength. The press has paid these heinously horrific killings scant attention; only the sin-sation slanted L.A. Mirror seems to care that three Los Angeles citizens have met such nauseatingly nasty nadirs. The LAPD's Homicide Division has not been called in to investigate; so far only two Hollywood Division detectives are working the case. Hepcats, it's the pedigree of the victims that determine the juice of investigation—and if three squarejohn citizens got choked by a neck-snapping psychopath, then LAPD Chief of Detectives Edmund J. Exley would waste no time mounting a full scale investigation. Often it takes a catchy tag name to bring dirty criminal business into the public's consciousness and thus create a clamor for justice. Hush-Hush hereby names this anonymous killer fiend the "Wino Will-o-the-Wisp" and petitions the LAPD to find him and set him up with a hot date in

San Quentin's green room. They cook with gas there, and this killer deserves a four-burner cookout.

Watch for future updates on the Wino Will-o-the-Wisp, and remember you heard it first here: off the record, on the Q.T. and *very* Hush-Hush.

I

STRAIGHT LIFE

he job: take down a bookie mill, let the press in—get some ink to compete with the fight probe.

Some fruit sweating a sodomy beef snitched: fourteen phones, a race wire. Exley's memo said show some force, squeeze the witnesses at the hotel later—find out what the Feds had planned.

In person: "If things get untoward, don't let the reporters take pictures. You're an attorney, Lieutenant. Remember how clean Bob Gallaudet likes his cases."

I hate Exley.

Exley thinks I bought law school with bribe money.

I said four men, shotguns, Junior Stemmons as co-boss. Exley: "Jackets and ties; this will end up on TV. And no stray bullets—you're working for me, not Mickey Cohen."

Someday I'll shove a bribe list down his throat.

Junior set it up. Perfect: a Niggertown street cordoned off; bluesuits guarding the alley. Reporters, prowl cars, four jackets and ties packing twelve-gauge pumps.

Sergeant George Stemmons, Jr., snapping quick draws.

Hubbub: porch-loafing jigs, voodoo eyes. My eyes on the target—closed curtains, a packed driveway—make a full shift inside working bets. A cinderblock shack—figure a steel plate door.

I whistled; Junior walked over twirling his piece.

"Keep it out, you might need it."

"No, I've got a riot gun in the car. We go in the door, we—"

"We *don't* go in the door, it's plated. We start banging on the door, they burn their paper. You still hunt birds?"

"Sure. Dave, what—"

"You got ammo in your car? Single-aught birdshot?"

Junior smiled. "That big window. I shoot it out, the curtain takes the pellets, we go in."

"Right, so you tell the others. And tell those clowns with the cameras to roll it, Chief Exley's compliments."

Junior ran back, dumped shells, reloaded. Cameras ready; whistles, applause: wine-guzzling loafers.

Hands up, count it down—

Eight: Junior spreads the word.

Six: the men flanked.

Three: Junior window-aiming.

One: "Now!"

Glass exploded *ka*-BOOM, loud loud loud; recoil knocked Junior flat. Cops too shocked to yell "TRIPLE AUGHT!"

Window curtains in rags.

Screams.

Run up, jump the sill. Chaos: blood spray, bet slip/cash confetti. Phone tables dumped, a stampede: out the back door bookie fistfights.

A nigger coughing glass.

A pachuco minus some fingers.

"Wrong Load" Stemmons: "Police! Stop or we'll shoot!"

Grab him, shout: "This was shots fired inside, a fucking criminal alter-cation. We went in the window because we figured the door wouldn't go down. You talk nice to the news guys and tell them I owe them one. You get the men together and make fucking-A sure they know the drill. *Do you understand me?"*

Junior shook free. Foot thumps—window-storming plainclothesmen. Cover noise: I pulled my spare piece. Two ceiling shots, a wipe—evidence.

Toss the gun. More chaos: suspects kicked prone, cuffed.

Moans, shouts, shotgun wadding/blood stink.

I "discovered" the gun. Reporters ran in; Junior spieled them. Out to the porch, fresh air.

"You owe me eleven hundred, Counselor."

Make the voice: Jack Woods. Mixed bag—bookie/strongarm/contract trigger.

I walked over. "Did you catch the show?"

"I was just driving up—and you should put that kid Stemmons on a leash."

"His daddy's an inspector. I'm the kid's mentor, so I've got a captain's job as a lieutenant. Did you have a bet down?"

"That's right."

"Slumming?"

"I'm in the business myself, so I spread my own bets around for good will. Dave, you owe me eleven hundred."

"How do you know you won?"

"The race was fixed."

Jabber—newsmen, the locals. "I'll get it out of the evidence vault."

"C'est la guerre. And by the way, how's your sister?"

"Meg's fine."

"Say hi for me."

Sirens; black & whites pulling up.

"Jack, get out of here."

"Good seeing you, Dave."

Book the fuckers—Newton Street Station.

Rap sheet checks: nine outstanding warrants total. Missing Fingers came up a sweetheart: rape, ADW, flimflam. Shock pale, maybe dying—a medic fed him coffee and aspirin.

I booked the plant gun, bet slips and money—minus Jack Woods' eleven hundred. Junior, press relations: the lieutenant owes you a story.

Two hours of pure shitwork.

4:30—back to the Bureau. Messages waiting: Meg said drop by; Welles Noonan said the guard gig, six sharp. Exley: "Report in detail."

Details—type them out, more shitwork:

4701 Naomi Avenue, 1400 hours. Set to raid a bookmaker's drop, Sgt. George Stemmons, Jr., and I heard shots fired inside the premises. We did not inform the other officers for fear of creating a panic. I ordered a shotgun round directed at the front window; Sgt. Stemmons misled the other men with a "birdshot assault" cover story. A .38 revolver was found; we arrested six bookmakers. The suspects were booked at Newton Station; the wounded received adequate first aid and hospital treatment. R&I revealed numerous extant warrants on the six, who will be remanded to the Hall of Justice Jail and arraigned on felony charges 614.5 and 859.3 of the California Penal Code. All six men will be subsequently interrogated on the shots fired and their bookmaking associations. I will conduct the interrogations myself—as Division Commander I must personally guarantee the veracity of all proffered statements. Press coverage of this occurrence will be minimal: reporters at the scene were unprepared for the rapid transpiring of events.

Sign it: Lieutenant David D. Klein, Badge 1091, Commander, Administrative Vice.

Carbons to: Junior, Chief Exley.

The phone—

"Ad Vice, Klein."

"Davey? Got a minute for an old gonif buddy?"

"Mickey, Jesus Christ."

"I know, I'm supposed to call you at home. Uh . . . Davey . . . a favor for Sam G.?"

G. for Giancana. "I guess. What?"

"You know that croupier guy you're watchdogging?"

"Yeah."

"Well . . . the radiator's loose in his bedroom."

ockabye Reuben Ruiz: "This is the tits. I could get used to this."

The Embassy Hotel: parlor, bedrooms, TV. Nine floors up, suite service: food and booze.

Ruiz belting Scotch, half-assed restless. Sanderline Johnson watching cartoons, slack-jawed.

Junior practicing quick draws.

Try some talk. "Hey, Reuben."

Popping mock jabs: "Hey, Lieutenant."

"Hey, Reuben. Did Mickey C. try to infringe on your contract?"

"He what you call strongly suggested my manager let him buy in. He sent the Vecchio brothers out to talk to him, then he punked out when Luis told them, 'Hey, kill me, 'cause I ain't signin' no release form.' You want my opinion? Mickey ain't got the stones for strongarm no more."

"But you've got the *cojones* to snitch."

Jabs, hooks. "I got a brother deserted the army, maybe lookin' at Federal time. I got three bouts coming up at the Olympic, which Welles Noonan can fuck up with subpoenas. My family's what you call from a long line of thieves, what you call trouble prone, so I sorta like making friends in what you might call the law-enforcement community."

"Do you think Noonan has good stuff on Mickey?"

"No, Lieutenant, I don't."

"Call me Dave."

"I'll call you Lieutenant, 'cause I got enough friends in the law-enforcement community."

"Such as?"

"Such as Noonan and his FBI buddy Shipstad. Hey, you know Schoolboy Johnny Duhamel?"

"Sure. He fought in the Gloves, turned pro, then quit."

"You lose your first pro fight, you better quit. I told him that, 'cause Johnny and me are old friends, and Johnny is now *Officer* Schoolboy Johnny Duhamel, on the fuckin' LAPD, on the righteous Mobster Squad, no less. He's tight with the—what you call him?—legendary?—Captain Dudley Smith. So I got enough fuck—"

"Ruiz, watch your language."

Junior—pissed. Johnson goosed the TV—Mickey Mouse ran from Donald Duck.

Junior killed the volume. "I knew Johnny Duhamel when I taught at the Academy. He was in my evidence class, and he was a damn good student. I don't like it when criminals get familiar with policemen. *Comprende, pendejo?*"

"*Pendejo,* huh? So I'm the *stupido,* and you're this punk cowboy, playin' with your gun like that sissy mouse on fuckin' television."

Necktie pull, signal Junior: FREEZE IT.

He froze—fumbling his gun.

Ruiz: "I can always use another friend, *Dave.* There something you want to know?"

I boosted the TV. Johnson stared, rapt—Daisy Duck vamping Donald. Ruiz: "Hey, *Dave.* You wangle this job to pump me?"

Huddle close, semi-private. "You want to make another friend, then give. What's Noonan have?"

"He's got what you call aspirations."

"I know that. *Give.*"

"Well . . . I heard Shipstad and this other FBI guy talking. They said Noonan's maybe afraid the fight probe's too limited. Anyway, he's thinking over this backup plan."

"And?"

"And it's like a general L.A. rackets thing, mostly Southside stuff. Dope, slots, you know, illegal vending machines and that kind of shit. I heard Shipstad say something about the LAPD don't investigate colored on colored homicides, and like all this ties to Noonan making the new DA—what's his name?"

"Bob Gallaudet."

"Right, Bob Gallaudet. Anyway, it all ties to making him look bad so Noonan can run against him for attorney general."

Darktown, the coin biz—Mickey C.'s last going stuff. "What about Johnson?"

Snickers. "Look at that mulatto wetbrain. Can you believe he used to be forty-three, zero and two?"

"Reuben, *give.*"

"Okay, give he's close to a fuckin' idiot, but he's got this great memory. He can memorize card decks, so some made guys gave him a job at the Lucky Nugget down in Gardena. He's good at memorizing conversations, and some guys weren't so what you call discreet talking around him. I heard Noonan's gonna make him do these memory tricks on the stand, which—"

"I get the picture."

"Good. I quit my own trouble-prone ways, but I sure got a trouble-prone family. I shouldn't of told you what I did, so since you're my friend I'm sure this ain't getting back to the Federal guys, right, *Dave?*"

"Right. Now eat your dinner and get some rest, okay?"

Midnight—lights out. I took Johnson; Junior took Ruiz—my suggestion.

Johnson, bedtime reading: "God's Secret Power Can Be Yours." I pulled a chair up and watched his lips: glom the inside track to Jesus, fight the Jew-Communist conspiracy to mongrelize Christian America. Send your contribution to Post Office Box blah, blah, blah.

"Sanderline, let me ask you something."

"Uh, yessir."

"Do you believe that pamphlet you're reading?"

"Uh, yessir. Right here it says this woman who came back to life said Jesus guarantees all gold-star contributors a new car every year in heaven."

JESUS FUCK.

"Sanderline, did you catch a few in your last couple of fights?"

"Uh, no. I stopped Bobby Calderon on cuts and lost a split decision to Ramon Sanchez. Sir, do you think Mr. Noonan will get us a hot lunch at the grand jury?"

Handcuffs out. "Put these on while I take a piss."

Johnson stood up—yawning, stretching. Check the heater—thick pipes—nix ballast.

Open window—nine-floor drop—this geek half-breed smiling.

"Sir, what do you think Jesus drives himself?"

I banged his head against the wall, threw him out the window screaming.

**3**

LAPD Homicide said suicide, case closed.

The DA: suicide probable.

Confirmation—Junior, Ruiz—Sanderline Johnson, crazy man.

Listen:

I watched him read, dozed off, woke up—Johnson announced he could fly. He went out the window before I could voice my disbelief.

Questioning: Feds, LAPD, DA's men. Basics: Johnson crash-landed on a parked De Soto, DOA, no witnesses. Bob Gallaudet seemed pleased: a rival's political progress scotched. Ed Exley: report to my office, 10:00 A.M.

Welles Noonan: incompetent disgrace of a policeman; pitiful excuse for an attorney. Suspicious—my old nickname—"the Enforcer."

No mention: 187 PC—felonious homicide.

No mention: outside-agency investigations.

No mention: interdepartmental charges.

I drove home, showered, changed—no reporters hovering yet. Downtown, a dress for Meg—I do it every time I kill a man.

10:00 A.M.

Waiting: Exley, Gallaudet, Walt Van Meter—the boss, Intelligence Division. Coffee, pastry—fuck me.

I sat down. Exley: "Lieutenant, you know Mr. Gallaudet and Captain Van Meter."

Gallaudet, all smiles: "It's been 'Bob' and 'Dave' since law school, and I won't fake any outrage over last night. Did you see the *Mirror,* Dave?"

"No."

" 'Federal Witness Plummets to Death,' with a sidebar: 'Suicide Pronouncement: "Hallelujah, I Can Fly!" ' You like it?"

"It's a pisser."

Exley, cold: "The lieutenant and I will discuss that later. In a sense it ties in to what we have here, so let's get to it."

Bob sipped coffee. "Political intrigue. Walt, you tell him."

Van Meter coughed. "Well . . . Intelligence has done some political operations before, and we've got our eye on a target now—a pinko lawyer who has habitually bad-mouthed the Department and Mr. Gallaudet."

Exley: "Keep going."

"Well, Mr. Gallaudet should be elected to a regular term next week. He's an ex-policeman himself, and he speaks our language. He's got the support of the Department and some of the City Council, but—"

Bob cut in. "Morton Diskant. He's neck and neck with Tom Bethune for Fifth District city councilman, and he's been ragging me for weeks. You know, how I've only been a prosecutor for five years and how I cashed in when Ellis Loew resigned as DA. I've heard he's gotten cozy with Welles Noonan, who just might be on my dance card in '60, and Bethune is our kind of guy. It's a very close race. Diskant's been talking Bethune and I up as right-wing shitheads, and the district's twenty-five percent Negro, lots of them registered voters. You take it from there."

Play a hunch. "Diskant's been riling the spooks up with Chavez Ravine, something like 'Vote for me so your Mexican brothers won't get evicted from their shantytown shacks to make room for a ruling-class ballpark.' It's five–four in favor on the Council, and they take a final vote sometime in November after the election. Bethune's an interim incumbent, like Bob, and if he loses he has to leave office before the vote goes down. Diskant gets in, it's a deadlock. We're all civilized white men who know the Dodgers are good for business, so let's get to it."

Exley, smiling: "I met Bob in '53, when he was a DA's Bureau sergeant. He passed the bar and registered as a Republican the same day. Now the pundits tell us we'll only have him as DA for two years. Attorney General in '60, then what? Will you stop at Governor?"

Laughs all around. Van Meter: "I met Bob when he was a patrolman and I was a sergeant. Now it's 'Walt' and 'Mr. Gallaudet.' "

"I'm still 'Bob.' And you used to call me 'son.' "

"I will again, Robert. If you disown your support of district gambling."

Stupid crack—the bill wouldn't pass the State Legislature. Cards, slots and bookmaking—confined to certain areas—taxable big. Cops hated it—say Gallaudet embraced it for votes. "He'll change his mind, he's a politician."

No laughs—Bob coughed, embarrassed. "It looks like the fight probe is down. With Johnson dead, they've got no confirming witnesses, and I got the impression Noonan was just using Reuben Ruiz for his marquee value. Dave, do you agree?"

"Yeah, he's a likable local celebrity. Apparently Mickey C. made some kind of half-baked attempt to muscle his contract, so Noonan probably wanted to use Mickey for *his* marquee value."

Exley, shiv shot: "And we know you're an expert on Mickey Cohen."

"We go back, Chief."

"In what capacity?"

"I've offered him some free legal advice."

"Such as?"

"Such as 'Don't fuck with the LAPD.' Such as 'Watch out for Chief of Detectives Exley, because he never tells you exactly what he wants.' "

Gallaudet, calm: "Come on, enough. Mayor Poulson asked me to call this meeting, so we're on his time. And I have an idea, which is to keep Ruiz on our side. We use him as a front man to placate the Mexicans in Chavez Ravine, so if the evictions go down ugly, we have him as our PR guy. Doesn't he have some kind of burglary jacket?"

I nodded. "Juvie time for B&E. I heard he used to belong to a burglary gang, and I know his brothers pull jobs. You're right—we should use him, promise to keep his family out of trouble if he goes along."

Van Meter: "I like it."

Gallaudet: "What about Diskant?"

I hit hard. "He's a pinko, so he has to have some Commie associates. I'll find them and strongarm them. We'll put them on TV, and they'll snitch him."

Bob, head shakes: "No. It's too vague and there's not enough time."

"Girls, boys, liquor—give me a weakness. Look, I screwed up last night. Let me do penance."

Silence: long, *loud*. Van Meter, off a sigh: "I heard he loves young women. He supposedly cheats on his wife very discreetly. He likes college girls. Young, idealistic."

Bob, a smirk fading: "Dudley Smith can set it up. He's done this kind of thing before."

Exley, weird emphatic: "No, not Dudley. Klein, do you know the right people?"

"I know an editor at *Hush-Hush.* I can get Pete Bondurant for the pix, Fred Turentine for bugging. Ad Vice popped a call house last week, and we've got just the right girl sweating bail."

Stares all around. Exley, half smiling: "So do your penance, Lieutenant."

Bob G.—diplomat. "He let me study his crib sheets in law school. Be nice, Ed."

Exit line—he waltzed, Van Meter walked hangdog.

Say it: "Will the Feds ask for an investigation?"

"I doubt it. Johnson did ninety days observation at Camarillo last year, and the doctors there told Noonan he was unstable. Six FBI men canvassed for witnesses and got nowhere. They'd be stupid to pursue an investigation. You're clean, but I don't like the way it looks."

"You mean criminal negligence?"

"I mean your longstanding and somewhat well-known criminal associations. I'll be kind and say you're 'acquainted' with Mickey Cohen, a focus of the investigation your negligence destroyed. Imaginative people might make a slight jump to 'criminal conspiracy,' and Los Angeles is filled with such people. You see how—"

"Chief, listen to—"

"No, you listen. I gave you and Stemmons that assignment because I trusted your competence and I wanted an attorney's assessment of what the Feds had planned in our jurisdiction. What I got was 'Hallelujah, I Can Fly' and 'Detective Snoozes While Witness Jumps Out Window.' "

Quash a laugh. "So what's the upshot?"

"You tell me. Assess what the Feds have planned past the fight probe."

"I'd say with Johnson dead, not much. Ruiz told me Noonan had some vague plans to mount an investigation into the Southside rackets—dope, the Darktown slot and vending machines. If that probe flies, the Department could be made to look bad. But *if* it goes, Noonan will announce it first—he's headline happy. We'll get a chance to prepare."

Exley smiled. "Mickey Cohen runs the Southside coin business. Will you warn him to get his stuff out?"

"I wouldn't dream of it. Off the topic, did you read my report on the bookie house?"

"Yes. Except for the shots fired, it was salutary. What is it? You're looking at me like you want something."

I poured coffee. "Throw me a bone for the Diskant job."

"You're in no position to ask favors."

"After Diskant I will be."

"Then ask."

Bad coffee. "Ad Vice is boring me. I was passing through Robbery and saw a case that looked good on the board."

"The appliance store heist?"

"No, the Hurwitz fur warehouse job. A million in furs clouted, no leads, and Junior Stemmons popped Sol Hurwitz at a dice game just last year. He's a degenerate gambler, so I'd bet money on insurance fraud."

"No. It's Dudley Smith's case, and he's ruled insurance out. And you're a commanding officer, not a case man."

"So stretch the rules. I tank the Commie, you throw me one."

"No, it's Dudley's job. The case is three days old and he's already been assigned. Beyond that, I wouldn't want to tempt you with saleable items like furs."

Shivved—deflect it. "There's no love lost between you and Dud. He *wanted* chief of detectives, and you got it."

"COs always get bored and want cases. Is there any particular reason why you want this one?"

"Robbery's clean. You wouldn't be suspicious of my friends if I worked heist jobs."

Exley stood up. "A question before you go."

"Sir?"

"Did a friend tell you to push Sanderline Johnson out the window?"

"No, sir. But aren't you glad he jumped?"

I slept the night off, a room at the Biltmore—figure reporters had my pad staked out. No dreams, room service: 6:00 P.M. breakfast, the papers. New banners: "U.S. Attorney Blasts 'Negligent' Cop"; "Detective Voices Regret at Witness Suicide." Pure Exley—*his* press gig, *his* regret. Page three, more Exley: no Hurwitz-job leads—a gang with toolmaking/electronics expertise boosted a million plus in cold fur. Pix: a bandaged-up security guard; Dudley Smith ogling a mink.

Robbery, sweet duty: jack up heist guys and boost their shit.

Work the Commie: phone calls.

Fred Turentine, bug man—yes for five hundred. Pete Bondurant—yes for a grand—and he'd pay the photo guy. Pete, *Hush-Hush* cozy—more heat on the smear.

The Women's Jail watch boss owed me; a La Verne Benson update cashed her out. La Verne—prostitution beef number three—no bail, no trial date. La Verne to the phone—suppose we lose your rap sheet—yes! yes! yes!

Antsy—my standard postmurder shakes. Antsy to itchy—drive.

A run by my pad—reporters—no haven there. Up to Mulholland, green lights/no traffic—60, 70, 80. Fishtails, curve shimmy—slow down, think.

Think Exley.

Brilliant, cold. In '53 he gunned down four niggers—it closed out the Nite Owl case. Spring '58—evidence proved he killed the wrong men. The case was reopened; Exley and Dudley Smith ran it: *the* biggest job in L.A. history. Multiple homicides/smut intrigue/interlocked conspiracies— Exley cleared it for real. His construction-king father killed himself non sequitur; now Inspector Ed got his money. Thad Green resigned as Chief of Detectives; Chief Parker jumped Dudley to replace him: Edmund Jennings Exley, thirty-six years old.

No love lost—Exley and Dudley—two good haters.

No Detective Division reforms—just Exley going iceberg cold.

Green lights up to Meg's house—just her car out front. Meg in the kitchen window.

I watched her.

Dish duty—a lilt to her hands—maybe background music. Smiling—a face almost mine, but gentle. I hit the horn—

Yes—a primp—her glasses, her hair. A smile—anxious.

I jogged up the steps; Meg had the door open. "I had a feeling you'd bring me a gift."

"Why?"

"The last time you got in the papers you bought me a dress."

"You're the smart Klein. Go on, open it."

"Was it terrible? They had this clip on TV."

"He was a dumb bunny. Come on, open it up."

"David, we have to discuss some business."

I nudged her inside. *"Come on."*

Rip, tear—wrapping paper in shreds. A whoop, a mirror dash—green silk, a perfect fit.

"Does it work?"

A swirl—her glasses almost flew. "Zip me?"

Shape her in, tug the zipper. Perfect—Meg kissed me, checked the mirror.

"Jesus, you and Junior. He can't stop admiring himself either."

A swirl, a flash: prom date '35. The old man said take Sissy—the guys hounding her weren't appropriate.

Meg sighed. "It's beautiful. Just like everything you give me. And how is Junior Stemmons these days?"

"Thank you, you're welcome, and Junior Stemmons is half smart. He's not really suited for the Detective Bureau, and if his father didn't swing me the command at Ad Vice I'd kick his ass back to a teaching job."

"Not a forceful enough presence?"

"Right, with a hot-dog sensibility that makes it stand out worse, and itchy nerves like he's raiding the dope vault at Narco. Where's your husband?"

"Going over some blueprints for a building he's designing. And while we're on the subject . . ."

"Shit. Our buildings, right? Deadbeats? Skipouts?"

"We're slumlords, so don't act surprised. It's the Compton place. Three units in arrears."

"So advise me. You're the real estate broker."

"Two units are one month due, the other is two months behind. It takes ninety days to file an eviction notice, and that entails a court date. And *you're* the attorney."

"Fuck, I hate litigation. And will you sit down?"

She sprawled—a green chair, the green dress. Green against her hair—black—a shade darker than mine. "You're a good litigator, but I know you'll just send some goons down with fake papers."

"It's easier that way. I'll send Jack Woods or one of Mickey's guys."

"Armed?"

"Yeah, and fucking dangerous. Now tell me you love the dress again. Tell me so I can go home and get some sleep."

Counting points—our old routine. "One, I love the dress. Two, I love my big brother, even though he got all the looks and more of the brains. Three, by way of amenities, I quit smoking again, I'm bored with my job and my husband and I'm considering sleeping around before I turn forty and lose the rest of my looks. Four, if you knew any men who weren't cops or thugs I'd ask you to fix me up."

Points back: "I got the Hollywood looks, you got the real ones. Don't sleep with Jack Woods, because people have this tendency to shoot at him, and the first time you and Jack tried shacking it didn't last too long. I do know a few DAs, but they'd bore you."

"Who do I have left? I flopped as a gangster consort."

The room swayed—frazzled time. "I don't know. Come on, walk me out."

Green silk—Meg stroked it. "I was thinking of that logic class we took undergrad. You know, cause and effect."

"Yeah?"

"I . . . well, a hoodlum dies in the papers, and I get a gift."

Swaying bad. "Let it go."

"Trombino and Brancato, then Jack Dragna. Honey, I can live with what we did."

"You don't love me the way I love you."

4

eporters at my door, wolfing take-out.

I parked out back, jimmied a bedroom window. Noise—newsmen gabbing *my* story. Lights off, crack that window: talk to defuse Meg's bomb.

Straight: I'm a kraut, not a Jew—the old man's handle got clipped at Ellis Island. '38—the LAPD; '42—the Marines. Pacific duty, back to the Department '45. Chief Horrall resigns; William Worton replaces him—a squeaky-clean Marine Corps major general. Semper Fi: he forms an ex-Marine goon squad. Espirit de Corps: we break strikes, beat uppity parolees back to prison.

Law school, freelance work—the GI Bill won't cover USC. Repo man, Jack Woods' collector—"the Enforcer." Work for Mickey C: union disputes settled strongarm. Hollywood beckons—I'm tall, handsome.

Nix, but it leads to *real* work. I break up a squeeze on Liberace—two well-hung shines, blackmail pix. I'm in with Hollywood and Mickey C. I make the Bureau, make sergeant. I pass the bar, make lieutenant.

All true.

I topped my twenty last month—true. My Enforcer take bought slum pads—true. I shacked with Anita Ekberg and the redhead on "The Spade Cooley Show"—false.

Bullshit took over; talk moved to Chavez Ravine. I shut the window and tried to sleep.

No go.

Lift that window—no newsmen. TV: strictly test patterns. Turn it off, run the string out—MEG.

It was always there scary wrong—and we touched each other too long to say it. I kept the old man's fists off her; she kept me from killing him. College together, the war, letters. Other men and other women fizzled.

Rowdy postwar years—"the Enforcer." Meg—pal, repo sidekick. A fling with Jack Woods—I let it go. Study ate up my time—Meg ran wild solo. She met two hoods: Tony Trombino, Tony Brancato.

June '51—our parents dead in a car wreck.

The guts, the will—

A motel room—Franz and Hilda Klein fresh buried. Naked just to see. On each other—every taste half recoil.

Meg broke it off—no finish. Fumbles: our clothes, words, the lights off.

I still wanted it.

She didn't.

She ran crazy with Trombino and Brancato.

The fucks messed with Jack Dragna—the Outfit's number-one man in L.A. Jack showed me a picture: Meg—bruises, hickeys—Trombino/Brancato verified.

Verified—they popped a mob dice game.

Jack said five grand, you clip them—I said yes.

I set it up—a shakedown run—"We'll rob this bookie holding big." August 6, 1648 North Ogden—the Two Tonys in a '49 Dodge. I slid in the backseat and blew their brains out.

"Mob Warfare" headlines—Dragna's boss torpedo picked up quick. His alibi: Jack D.'s parish priest. Gangland unsolved—let the fucking wops kill each other.

I was paid—plus a tape bonus: a man raging at the scum who hurt his sister. Dragna's voice—squelched out. My voice: "I will fucking kill them. I will fucking kill them for free."

Mickey Cohen called. Jack said I owed the Outfit—the debt kosher for a few favors. Jack would call, I'd be paid—strictly business.

Hooked.

Called:

June 2, '53: I clipped a dope chemist in Vegas.

March 26, '55: I killed two jigs who raped a mob guy's wife.

September '57, a rumor: Jack D.—heart disease bad.

I called him.

Jack said, "Come see me."

We met at a beachfront motel—his fixing-to-die-fuck spot. Guinea heaven: booze, smut, whores next door.

I begged him: cancel my debt.

Jack said, "The whores do lez stuff."

I choked him dead with a pillow.

Coroner's verdict/mob consensus: heart attack.

Sam Giancana—my new caller. Mickey C. his front man: cop favors, clip jobs.

Meg sensed something. Lie away her part, take all the guilt. Sleep—restless, sweaty.

. . .

The phone—grab it—"Yes?"

"Dave? Dan Wilhite."

Narco—the boss. "What is it, Captain?"

"It's . . . shit, do you know J. C. Kafesjian?"

"I know who he is. I know what he is to the Department."

Wilhite, low: "I'm at a crime scene. I can't really talk and I've got no-body to send over, so I called you."

Hit the lights. "Fill me in, I'll go."

"It's, shit, it's a burglary at J.C.'s house."

"Address?"

"1684 South Tremaine. That's just off—"

"I know where it is. Somebody called Wilshire dicks before they called you, right?"

"Right, J.C.'s wife. The whole family was out for the evening, but Madge, the wife, came home first. She found the house burgled and called Wilshire Station. J.C., Tommy and Lucille—that's the other kid—came home and found the house full of detectives who didn't know about our . . . uh . . . arrangement with the family. Apparently, it's some goddamn nutso B&E and the Wilshire guys are making pests of themselves. J.C. called my wife, she called around and found me. Dave . . ."

"I'll go."

"Good. Take someone with you, and count it one in your column."

I hung up and called for backup—Riegle, Jensen—no answer. Shit luck—Junior Stemmons—"Hello?"

"It's me. I need you for an errand."

"Is it a call-out?"

"No, it's an errand for Dan Wilhite. It's smooth J.C. Kafesjian's feath-ers."

Junior whistled. "I heard his kid's a real psycho."

"1684 South Tremaine. Wait for me outside, I'll brief you."

"I'll be there. Hey, did you see the late news? Bob Gallaudet called us 'exemplary officers,' but Welles Noonan said we were 'incompetent free-loaders.' He said that ordering room-service booze for our witnesses con-tributed to Johnson's suicide. He said—"

"Just be there."

Code 3, do Wilhite solid—aid the LAPD's sanctioned pusher. Narco/J.C. Kafesjian—twenty years connected—old Chief Davis brought him in.

Weed, pills, H—Darktown trash as clientele. Snitch duty got J.C. the dope franchise. Wilhite played watchdog; J.C. ratted rival pushers, per our policy: keep narcotics isolated south of Slauson. His legit work: a dry-cleaning chain; his son's work: muscle goon supreme.

Crosstown to the pad: a Moorish job lit up bright. Cars out front: Junior's Ford, a prowl unit.

Flashlight beams and voices down the driveway. "Holy shit, holy shit"—Junior Stemmons.

I parked, walked over.

Light in my eyes. Junior: "That's the lieutenant." A stink: maybe blood rot.

Junior, two plainclothesmen. "Dave, this is Officer Nash and Sergeant Miller."

"Gentlemen, Narco's taking this over. You go back to the station. Sergeant Stemmons and I will file reports if it comes to that."

Miller: " 'Comes to that'? Do you *smell* that?"

Heavy, acidic. "Is this a homicide?"

Nash: "Not exactly. Sir, you wouldn't believe the way that punk Tommy What's-His-Name talked to us. *Comes to—*"

"Go back and tell the watch commander Dan Wilhite sent me over. Tell him it's J.C. Kafesjian's place, so it's not your standard 459. If that doesn't convince him, have him wake up Chief Exley."

"Lieutenant—"

Grab a flashlight, chase the smell—back to a snipped chain-link fence. Fuck—two Dobermans—no eyes, throats slit, teeth gnashing chemical-soaked washrags. Gutted—entrails, blood—blood dripping toward a jimmied back door.

Shouts inside—two men, two women. Junior: "I shooed the squad-room guys off. Some 459, huh?"

"Lay it out for me, I don't want to question the family."

"Well, they were all at a party. The wife had a headache, so she took a cab home first. She went out to let the dogs in and found them. She called Wilshire, and Nash and Miller caught the squeal. J.C., Tommy and the daughter—the two kids live here, too—came home and raised a ruckus when they found cops in the living room."

"Did you talk to them?"

"Madge—that's the wife—showed me the damage, then J.C. shut her up. Some heirloom-type silverware was stolen, and the damage was some strange stuff. Do you feature this? I have never worked a B&E job like this one."

Yells, horn bleats.

"It's not a job. And what do you mean 'strange stuff'?"

"Nash and Miller tagged it. You'll see."

I flashed the yard—foamy meat scraps—call the dogs poisoned. Junior: "He fed them that meat, then mutilated them. He got blood on himself, then trailed it into the house."

Follow it:

Back-door pry marks. A laundry porch—bloody towels discarded—the burglar cleaned up.

The kitchen door intact—he slipped the latch. No more blood, the sink evidence tagged: "Broken Whiskey Bottles." Cabinet-drawers theft tagged: "Antique Silverware."

Them:

"You whore, to let strange policemen into our home!"

"Daddy, please don't!"

"We always call Dan when we need help!"

A dining room table, photo scraps piled on top: "Family Pictures." Sax bleats upstairs.

Walk the pad.

Too-thick carpets, velvet sofas, flocked wallpaper. Window air coolers—Jesus statues perched beside them. A rug tagged: "Broken Records/Album Covers"—*The Legendary Champ Dineen: Sooo Slow Moods; Straight Life:* The Art Pepper Quartet; *The Champ Plays the Duke.*

LPs by a hi-fi—stacked neat.

Junior walked in. "Like I told you, huh? Some damage."

"Who's making that noise?"

"The horn? That's Tommy Kafesjian."

"Go up and make nice. Apologize for the intrusion, offer to call Animal Control for the dogs. Ask him if he wants an investigation. Be nice, do you understand?"

"Dave, he's a criminal."

"Don't worry, I'll be brown-nosing his old man even worse."

"DADDY, DON'T!"—booming through closed doors.

"J.C., LEAVE THE GIRL ALONE!"

Spooky—Junior *ran* upstairs.

"THAT'S RIGHT, GET OUT"—a side door slamming—"Daddy" in my face.

J.C. close up: a greasy fat man getting old. Burly, pockmarked, bloody facial scratches.

"I'm Dave Klein. Dan Wilhite sent me over to square things."

Squinting: "What's so important he couldn't come himself?"

"We can do this any way you want, Mr. Kafesjian. If you want an invesligation, you've got it. You want us to dust for prints, maybe get you a name, you've got it. If you want payback, Dan will support you in anything within reason, if you follow—"

"I follow what you mean and I clean my own house. I deal with Captain Dan strictly, not strangers in my parlor."

Two women snuck by. Soft brunettes—nongrease types. The daughter waved—silver nails, blood drops.

"You see my girls, now forget them. They are not for you to know."

"Any idea who did it?"

"Not for you to talk about. Not for you to mention business rivals who might want to hurt me and mine."

"Rivals in the dry-cleaning biz?"

"Not for you to make jokes! Look! Look!"

A door tag: "Mutilated Clothing." "Look! Look! Look!"—J.C. yanked the knob—"Look! Look! Look!"

Look: a small closet. Spread-legged, crotch-ripped pedal pushers tacked across the walls.

Stained—smell it—semen.

"Now it is not to laugh. I buy Lucille and Madge so many nice clothes that they must keep some down in the parlor. Perverted degenerate wants to hurt Lucille's pretty things. *You look.*"

Tijuana whore stuff: "Pretty."

"Not so funny now, Dan Wilhite's errand boy. Now you don't laugh."

"Call Dan. Tell him what you want done."

"I clean my own house!"

"Nice threads. Your daughter working her way through college?"

Fists clenching/veins popping/face-rips trickling—this fat greasy fuck pressing close.

Shouts upstairs.

I ran up. A room off the hall—scope the damage:

Tommy K. up against the wall. Reefers on the floor, tough guy Junior frisking him. Jazz posters, Nazi flags, a sax on the bed.

I laughed.

Tommy smiled nice—this skinny nongreaser.

Junior: "He *flaunted* that maryjane. He *ridiculed* the Department."

"Sergeant, apologize to Mr. Kafesjian."

Half pout, half shriek: "Dave . . . God . . . *I'm sorry.*"

Tommy lit up a stick and blew smoke in Junior's face.

J.C., downstairs: "Go home now! I clean my own house!"

ad sleep, no sleep.

Meg's call woke me up: get our late rent settled, no silk-dress talk. I said, "Sure, sure"—hung up and pitched Jack Woods: twenty percent on every rent dollar collected. He jewed me up to twenty-five—I agreed.

Work calls: Van Meter, Pete Bondurant, Fred Turentine. Three green lights: La Verne's pad was bugged; a photo man was stashed in the bedroom. Diskant—tailed and overheard: drinks at Ollie Hammond's Steakhouse, 6:00 P.M.

The bait stood ready: *our* Commie consort. Pete said *Hush-Hush* loved it: pinko politico trips on his dick.

I called Narco—Dan Wilhite was out—I left a message. Bad sleep, no sleep—the nightmare Kafesjians. Junior last night, comic relief: "I know you don't think I rate the Bureau, but I'll show you, I'll really show you."

5:00 P.M.—fuck sleep.

I cleaned up, checked the *Herald*—Chavez Ravine bumped my dead man off page one. Bob Gallaudet: "The Latin Americans who lose their dwellings will be handsomely compensated, and in the end a home for the L.A. Dodgers will serve as a point of pride for Angelenos of all races, creeds and colors."

Knee-slapper stuff—it doused my Kafesjian hangover.

Ollie Hammond's—stake the bar entrance, wait.

Morton Diskant in the door, six sharp.

La Verne Benson in at 6:03—tweed skirt, knee sox, cardigan.

6:14—Big Pete B., sliding the seat back.

"Diskant's with his friends, La Verne's two booths down. Two seconds in and she's giving him these hot looks."

"You think he'll tumble?"

"I would, but then I'm a pig for it."

"Like your boss?"

"You can say his name—Howard Hughes. He's a busy guy—like you."

"He was a dumb fuck. If he didn't jump, I probably would have pushed him."

Pete tapped the dashboard—huge hands—they beat a drunk-tank brawler dead. The L.A. Sheriff's canned him; Howard Hughes found a soulmate.

"You been busy?"

"Sort of. I collect dope for *Hush-Hush,* I keep Mr. Hughes out of *Hush-Hush.* People try to sue *Hush-Hush,* I convince them otherwise. I scout pussy for Mr. Hughes, I listen to Mr. Hughes talk this crazy shit about airplanes. Right now Mr. Hughes has got me tailing this actress who jilted him. Dig this: this cooze blows out of Mr. Hughes' number-one fuck pad, with a three-yard-a-week contract to boot, all to act in some horror cheapie. Mr. Hughes has got her signed to a seven-year slave contract, and he wants to get it violated on a morality clause. Can you feature this pussy pig preaching morality?"

"Yeah, and you love it because you're—"

"Because I'm a pig for the life, like you."

I laughed, yawned. "This could go on all night."

Pete lit a cigarette. "No, La Verne's impetuous. She'll get bored and honk the Commie's shvantz. Nice kid. She actually helped Turentine set up his microphones."

"How's Freddy doing?"

"He's busy. Tonight he compromises this Commie, next week he wires some fag bathhouse for *Hush-Hush.* The trouble with Freddy T. is he's a booze pig. He's got all these drunk-driving beefs, so the last time the judge stuck him with this service job teaching electronics to the inmates up at Chino. Klein, look."

La Verne at the bar door—two thumbs up. Pete signaled back. "That means Diskant's meeting her after he ditches his friends. See that blue Chevy, that's hers."

I pulled out—La Verne in front—right turns on Wilshire. Straight west—Sweetzer, north, the Strip. Curvy side streets, up into the hills—La Verne stopped by a stucco four-flat.

Ugly: floodlights, *pink* stucco.

I parked a space back—room for the Red.

La Verne wiggled up to her door. Pete sent out love taps on my siren.

Foyer lights on and off. Window lights on—the downstairs-left apartment. Party noise: the pad across from La Verne's.

Pete stretched. "You think Diskant's got the smarts to make this for an unmarked?"

La Verne opened her curtains, stripped to peignoir and garters. "No, he's only got one thing on his mind."

"You're right, 'cause he's a pig for it. I say one hour or less."

"Twenty says fifteen minutes."

"You're on."

We settled in, eyes on that window. Lull time, party noise: show tunes, voices. Bingo—a tan Ford. Pete said, "Forty-one minutes."

I slid him twenty. Diskant walked up, hit the door, buzzed. La Verne, window framed: bumps and grinds.

Pete howled.

Diskant walked in.

Ten minutes ticking by slow . . . lights off at La Verne's love shack. Hold for the photo man's signal: flashbulb pops out that front window.

Fifteen minutes . . . twenty . . . twenty-five—a Sheriff's unit double-parking.

Pete nudged me. "Fuck. That party. 116.84 California Penal Code, Unlawfully Loud Assembly. *Fuck.*"

Two deputies walking. Nightstick raps on the party-pad window.

No response.

"Klein, this is not fucking good."

Rap rap rap—La Verne's front window. Flashbulb pops—*the bedroom window*—big-time-bad-news improvisation.

Screams—our Commie hooker.

The deputies kicked the foyer door down—I chased the fuckers, badge out—

Across the lawn, up the steps. Topsy-turvy glimpses: the photo man dropping out a window sans camera. Through the lobby—party kids mingling—La Verne's door snapped clean. I pushed through, punks tossing drinks in the face.

"Police! Police officer!"

I jumped the doorway dripping Scotch—a deputy caught me. My badge in his face: "Intelligence Division! LAPD!"

The dipshit just gawked me. Bedroom shrieks—

I ran in—

Diskant and La Verne floor-tumbling—naked, flailing, gouging. A camera on the bed; a dumbfuck shouting: "Hey! You two stop that! We're the Sheriff's!"

Pete ran in—Dumbfuck grinned familiar—old-deputy-acquaintance recognition. Fast Pete: he hustled the clown out quicksville. La Verne vs. the pinko: kicks, sissy punches.

The camera on the bed: grab it, pop the film out, seal it. Hit the button—flashbulb light in Diskant's eyes.

One blind Commie—La Verne tore free. I kicked him and punched him—he yelped, blinked and focused—ON THE FILM.

Shakedown:

"This was supposed to be some kind of setup, but those policemen broke it up. You were heading for the scandal sheets, something like 'Red Politician Blah Blah Blah.' You come across and that won't happen, because I sure would hate for your wife to see this film. Now, are you sure you want to be a city councilman?"

Sobs.

Brass knucks on. "Are you sure?"

More sobs.

Kidney shots—my knucks tore flab.

"Are you sure?"

Beet-red bawling: "Please don't hurt me!"

Two more shots—Diskant belched foam.

"You drop out tomorrow. Now say yes, because I don't like this."

"Y-yes p-p-p—"

Fucked-up shitty stuff—I hit the living room quashing shakes. No cops, La Verne draped in a sheet.

Pete, dangling bug mikes: "I took care of the deputies, and Van Meter called on your two-way. You're supposed to meet Exley at the Bureau right now."

Downtown. Exley at his desk.

I pulled a chair up, slid him the film. "He's pulling out, so we won't have to go to *Hush-Hush.*"

"Did you enjoy the work?"

"Did you enjoy shooting those niggers?"

"The public has no idea what justice costs the men who perform it."

"Which means?"

"Which means thank you."

"Which means I have a favor coming."

"You've been given one already, but ask anyway."

"The fur robbery. Maybe it's insurance fraud, maybe it's not. Either way, I want to work cases."

"No, I told you it's Dudley Smith's assignment."

"Yeah, you and Dud are such good buddies. And what's with this 'already' favor?"

"Besides no reprimand or interdepartmental charges on Sanderline Johnson?"

"Chief, come on."

"I destroyed the autopsy report on Johnson. The coroner noted a non sequitur bruise with imbedded paint fragments on his forehead, as if he banged his head against a windowsill before he jumped. I'm not saying that you're culpable; but other people, notably Welles Noonan, might. I had the file destroyed. And I have a case for you. I'm detaching you from Ad Vice immediately to start working on it."

Weak knees: "What case?"

"The Kafesjian burglary. I read the Wilshire Squad occurrence report, and I've decided I want a major investigation. I'm fully aware of the family's LAPD history, and I don't care what Captain Wilhite wants. You and Sergeant Stemmons are detached as of now. Shake the family, shake their known associates. J.C. employs a runner named Abe Voldrich, so lean on him while you're at it. I want a full forensic and the files checked for similar B&Es. Start tomorrow—with a show of force."

I stood up. "This is fucking insane. Lean on *our* sanctioned Southside dope kingpin when the U.S. Attorney just might be planning a rackets probe down there. Some pervo kills two dogs and jacks off on some—"

Exley, standing/crowding: "Do it. Detach canvassing officers from Wilshire Patrol and bring in the Crime Lab. Stemmons lacks field experience, but use him anyway. *Show of force*. And don't make me regret the favors I've done you."

6

SHOW OF FORCE.

8:00 A.M., 1684 South Tremaine. Personnel: lab crew, print team, four bluesuits.

The blues deployed: house-to-house witness checks, trashcan checks. Traffic cops standing by to shoo the press off.

Show of force—Exley's wild hair up the ass.

Show of force—short-shrift it.

A compromise with Dan Wilhite—one edgy phone call. I said Exley pure had me; he called the job crazy—J.C. and the Department: twenty years of two-way profit. I owed Dan; he owed me—favors backlogged. Wilhite, scared: "I retire in three months. My dealings with the family won't stand up to outside-agency scrutiny. Dave . . . can you . . . play it easy?"

I said, "My ass first, yours second."

He said, "I'll call J.C. and jerk his leash."

8:04—showtime.

Black & whites, a lab van. Patrolmen, tech men. Gawkers galore, little kids.

The driveway—I walked the lab guys back. Ray Pinker: "I called Animal Control. They told me they got no dead dog reports from this address. You think the people planted them in some pet cemetery?"

Garbage day—trashcans lined up in the alley. "Maybe, but check those cans behind the back fence. I don't think Old Man Kafesjian's so sentimental."

"I heard he was a real sweetheart. We find the dogs, then what?"

"Take tissue samples for a make on what they were poisoned with. If they're still chewing on washcloths, get me a make on the chemical—it smelled like chloroform. I need ten minutes to talk up J.C., then I want you to come inside and bag fibers in the kitchen, living room and dining room. Send the print guys in then, and tell them just the downstairs—I don't think our burglar went upstairs. He jerked off on some pedal pushers, so if Pops didn't throw them out you can test the semen for blood type."

"Jesus."

"Yeah, Jesus. Listen, if he did dump them, they're probably in those garbage cans. Pastel-colored pedal pushers ripped at the crotch, not everyday stuff. And Ray? I want a nice fat summary report on all this."

"Don't shit a shitter. You want me to pad it, say it."

"Pad it. I don't know what Exley wants, so let's give him something to chew on."

Madge at the back door, looking out. Heavy makeup—Pan-Cake over bruises.

Ray nudged me. "She doesn't look Armenian."

"She's not, and their kids don't look it either. Ray—"

"Yeah, I'll pad it."

Back to the street—rubberneckers swarming. Junior and Tommy K. locking eyes.

Tommy, porch loafer: bongo shirt, pegger pants, sax.

Junior sporting his new look: whipped dog with a mean streak.

I braced him—avuncular. "Come on, don't let that guy bother you."

"It's those looks of his. Like he knows something I don't."

"Forget about it."

"You didn't have to kowtow to him."

"I didn't disobey my CO."

"Dave . . ."

"Dave nothing. Your father's an inspector, he got you the Bureau, and my Ad Vice command was part of the deal. It's a game. You owe your father, I owe your father, I owe Dan Wilhite. We both owe the Department, so we have to play things like Exley's off the deep end on this deal. Do you understand?"

"I understand. But it's your game, so just don't tell me it's right."

Slap his fucking face—no—don't. "You pull that idealistic shit on me and I'll hand your father a fitness report that will bounce you back to a teaching job in record goddamn time. *My game got you where you are.* You play along or you see 'ineffectual command presence,' 'overly volatile' and 'poor composure in stress situations' on Daddy's desk tonight. You call it, Sergeant."

Punk bravado: *"I'm playing.* I called the Pawnshop Detail and gave them a description of the silverware, and I got a list of Kafesjian's dry-cleaning shops. Three for you, three for me, the usual questions?"

"Good, but let's see what the patrolmen turn first. Then, after you hit your three, go downtown and check the Central burglary files and Sheriff's files for 459s with similar MOs. You turn some, great. If not, check homicide unsolveds—maybe this clown's a goddamn killer."

A stink, fly swarms—lab men hauled the dogs out, dripping garbage.

"I guess you wouldn't tell me these things if you didn't care."

"That's right."

"You'll see, Dave. I'll prove myself on this one."

Tommy K. honked his sax—spectators clapped. Tommy bowed and pumped his crotch.

"Hey, Lieutenant! You come and talk to me!"

J.C. on the porch, holding a tray out. "Hey! We have an eye opener!"

I walked up. Bottled beer—Tommy grabbed one and guzzled. Check his arms: skin-pop tracks, swastika tattoos.

J.C. smiled. "Don't tell me too early for you."

Tommy belched. "Schlitz, Breakfast of Champions."

"Five minutes, Mr. Kafesjian. Just a few questions."

"I say all right, Captain Dan said you okay, this thing is not your idea. You follow me. Tommy, you go offer the other men Breakfast of Champions."

Tommy dipped the tray à la carhop. J.C. bowed, follow-me style.

I followed him into the den: pine walls, gun racks. Check the parlor—print men, carhop Tommy hawking beer.

J.C. shut the door. "Dan told me you just going to go through the motions."

"Not quite. This is Ed Exley's case, and his rules are different than ours."

"We do business, your people and mine. He knows that."

"Yeah, and he's stretching the rules this time. He's the Chief of Detectives, and Chief Parker lets him do what he wants. I'll try to go easy, but you'll have to play along."

J.C.: greasy and ugly. Face scratches—his own daughter clawed him. "Why? Exley, he's crazy?"

"I don't know why, which is a damn good question. Exley wants the major-case treatment on this one, and he's a better goddamn detective than I am. I can only bullshit him so far."

J.C. shrugged. "Hey, you smart, you got more juice. You a lawyer, you tight with Mickey Cohen."

"No. I fix things, Exley *runs* things. You want smart? Exley's the best detective the LAPD's ever seen. Come on, help me. You don't want regular cops nosing around, I understand that. But some piece-of-shit burglar breaks in here and rips up—"

"I clean my own house! Tommy and me, we find this guy!"

Easy now: "No. *We* find him, then maybe Dan Wilhite gives you a shot. No trouble, nice and legal."

Head jerks no-no. "Dan says you got questions. You ask, I answer. I play ball."

"No you'll cooperate, no you won't?"

"I cooperate."

Notebook out. "Who did it? Any ideas?"

"No"—deadpan—no read.

"Enemies. Give me some names."

"We got no enemies."

"Come on, you sell narcotics."

"Don't say that word in my home!"

EASY NOW: "Let's call it business. Business rivals who don't like you."

Fist shakes no-no. *You* make the rules, we play right. We do business fair and square so we don't make no enemies."

"Then let's try this. You're what we call a suborned informant. People like that make enemies. Think about it and give me some names."

"Fancy words for snitch and fink and stool pigeon."

"Names, Mr. Kafesjian."

"Men in prison can't break into nice family houses. I got no names for you."

"Then let's talk about Tommy and Lucille's enemies."

"No enemies, my kids."

"Think. This guy breaks in, breaks phonograph records and mutilates your daughter's clothing. Did those records belong to Tommy?"

"Yes, Tommy's long-play record albums."

"Right. And Tommy's a musician, so maybe the burglar had a grudge against him. He wanted to destroy his property and Lucille's, but for some reason he didn't get upstairs to their bedrooms. So, *their* enemies. Old musician buddies, Lucille's old boyfriends. *Think.*"

"No, no enemies"—soft—say his brain just clicked on.

Change-up: "I need to fingerprint you and your family. We need to compare your prints against any prints the burglar might have left."

He pulled a money clip out. "No. It's not right. I clean my own—"

I squeezed his hand shut. "Play it your way. Just remember it's Exley's show, and I owe him more than I owe Wilhite."

He tore his hand free and fanned out C-notes.

I said, "Fuck you. Fuck your whole greasy family."

Rip, tear—he trashed two grand easy.

I waltzed before it got worse.

Shitwork time.

Pinker labbed the dogs. The print guys got smudges, partials. The crowd dwindled; blues canvassed. Junior logged reports: nothing hot that night, archetypal Kafesjian rebop.

Dig: epic family brawls, all-night sax noise. J.C. watered the lawn in a jock strap. Tommy pissed out his bedroom window. Madge and Lucille: wicked tantrum shouters. Bruises, black eyes—standard issue.

Slow time—let it drag.

Lucille and Madge took off—adios in a pink Ford Vicky. Tommy practiced scales—the lab men popped in earplugs. Beer cans out the windows—Lunch of Champions.

Junior fetched the *Herald*. A Morton Diskant announcement: press conference, 6:00 tonight.

Time to kill—I hit the lab van, watched the techs work.

Tissue slicing, extraction—our boy jammed the dogs' eyes down their throats. Back to my car, a doze—bum sleep two nights running stretched me thin.

"Dave, rise and shine"—Ray Pinker, too goddamn soon.

Up yawning. "Results?"

"Yes, and interesting. I'm not a doctor and what I did wasn't an autopsy, but I think I can reconstruct some things conclusively."

"Go. Tell me now, then route me a summary report."

"Well, the dogs were poisoned with hamburger laced with sodium tryctozine, commonly known as ant poison. I found leather glove fragments on their teeth and gums, which leads me to believe that the burglar tossed them the meat, but didn't wait for them to die before he mutilated them. You told me you smelled chloroform, remember?"

"Yeah. I figured it was the washrags in their mouths."

"You're close so far. But it wasn't chloroform, it was stelfactiznide chloride, a dry-cleaning chemical. Now, J.C. Kafesjian owns a string of dry-cleaning shops. Interesting?"

The man broke in, stole and destroyed. A psycho, but precise—no disarray. Bold: and time-consuming. Psycho-crazy shit: *and* neat, precise.

"You're saying he might know the family, might work in one of the shops."

"Right."

"Did you find the girl's pants?"

"No. We found charred fabric mounds in that garbage can with the dogs, so there's no way to test the semen for blood type."

"Shit. Fried pedal pushers sounds just like J.C."

"Dave, listen. This verges on theory, but I like it."

"Go ahead."

"Well, the dogs were chemically scalded right around their eyes, and the bones in their snouts were broken. I think the burglar debilitated them with the poison, clamped down on their snouts, then tried to blind them while they were still alive. Stelfactiznide causes blindness when locally applied, but they flailed too much and bit him. They died from the poison, then he gutted them postmortem. He had some strange fix on their eyes, so he carefully pulled them out, stuffed them down their throats and stuffed the washrags soaked in chemical in their mouths. All four eyeballs were saturated with that chloride, so I rest my case."

Junior and a bluesuit hovering. "Dave—"

Cut him off: "Ray, have you *ever* heard of watchdog torture on a 459?"

"Never. And I'll go out on a limb for motive."

"Revenge?"

"Revenge."

"Dave . . ."

"What?"

"This is Officer Bethel. Officer, tell the lieutenant."

Nervous—a rookie. "Uh, sir, I got two confirmations on a prowler on this block the night of the burglary. Sergeant Stemmons, he's had me checking on the houses where nobody was home earlier. This old lady told me she called the Wilshire desk, and this man, he said he saw him too."

"Description?"

"J-just a young male Caucasian. No other details, but I called the desk anyway. They did send a car out. No luck, and no white prowlers got arrested or FI carded anywhere in the division that night."

A lead—shove it at Junior. "Call Wilshire and get four more men to hit the not-at-home addresses, say from six o'clock on. Have them go for descriptions on possible prowlers. Check those files I told you to and go by the first three Kafesjian shops on your list. Ray?"

"Yeah, Dave."

"Ray, tell Stemmons here your chemical angle. Junior, hit that angle with the employees at the shops. If you get a rabbit, don't do something stupid like kill him."

"Why not? Live by the sword, die by the sword."

"You dumb shit, I want to hear this guy's take on the Kafesjians."

Three E-Z Kleen shops—1248 South Normandie closest. I drove over—the pink Ford stood out front.

I double-parked; a guy ran out looking anxious. Make him: Abe Voldrich, Kafesjian high-up.

"Please, Officer. They don't know anything about this goddamn break-in. Call Dan Wilhite, talk to him about the . . . uh . . ."

"Ramifications?"

"Yeah, that's a good word. Officer—"

"Lieutenant."

"Lieutenant, let it rest. Yes, the family has enemies. No, they won't tell you who they are. You could ask Captain Dan, but I doubt if he'd tell you."

Smart little hump. "So we won't discuss enemies."

"Now we're cooking with gas!"

"What about stelfactiznide chloride?"

"What? Now you're talking Greek to me."

"It's a dry-cleaning chemical."

"That end of the business I don't know from."

Walking in: "I want an employee list—all your shops."

"No. We hire strictly colored people for the cleaning and pressing work, and most of them are on parole and probation. They wouldn't appreciate you asking questions."

Jig crime—no—it played wrong. "Do you have colored salespeople?"

"No, J.C. doesn't trust them around money."

"Let me check your storeroom."

"For that what you call it chemical? Why?"

"The watchdogs were burned with it."

Sighing: "Go, just don't roust the workers."

I skirted the counter. A small factory in back: pressers, vats, darkies folding shirts. Wall shelves: jars, bottles.

Check labels—two run-throughs, a catch: stelfactiznide chloride, skull and crossbones.

I sniffed a jug—foul/familiar—my eyes burned. Put it back, dawdle—the women might show. No luck—just darting slave eyes. I walked back up front popping sweat.

Lucille at the counter, hanging shirts. Bump bump—ass grinds to a radio beat. Bump, flash: a vamp smile.

I smiled back. Lucille zipped her mouth, threw away a pretend key. Outside: Voldrich and Madge. Mama K.: wet makeup, tears.

I walked out to the car. Whispers—I couldn't hear shit.

I hit a pay phone—fuck the E-Z Kleen shops.

I called Ad Vice and left a message for Junior: buzz Dan Wilhite, bag a Kafesjian snitch list. Probably futile—he'd refuse, hot to placate J.C. A message *from* Junior: he'd checked around, learned stel-what-the-fuck was a standard dry-cleaning chemical used worldwide.

Back to South Tremaine—one black & white in front. Bethel waved me over. "Sir, we got two more confirmations on that prowler night before last."

"More details on his description?"

"No, but it looks like he's a peeper too. We got that same 'young, white' make, and both people said he was peeping in windows."

Think: burglary/mutilation tools. "Did they say he was carrying anything?"

"No, sir, but I think he could have secreted the B&E stuff on his person."

"But the people didn't call in complaints."

"No, sir, but I got a lead that might tie in."

Coax him: "So tell me, Officer."

"Well, the woman in the house directly across the street told me that sometimes Lucille Kafesjian dances naked in her bedroom window. You know, with the lights on behind her at night. She said she does it when her parents and her brother are out for the evening."

Guesswork:

Exhibitionist Lucille, peeper/prowler/B&E man hooked on the family.

"Bethel, you're going places."

"Uh, yessir. Where?"

"In general. Right now, though, you stick here. You keep going back to the addresses where no one was home earlier. You try to flesh out the description of the peeper. Got it?"

"Yessir!"

Rolling shitwork:

Wilshire Station, paper checks: arrest rosters, MO files, FI cards. Results: window-peeping young white men—zero. Dog-slashing burglars—zero.

University Station, arrest/MO—buppkis. FI cards, three recent: a "youngish," "average build" white man was reported peeping whore motels. *My* eyeball man?—maybe—but:

No motel addresses—just "South Western Avenue" listed. No complainant names or badge ID numbers listed.

No place to go right now.

I called 77th Street Station. The squad boss, bored:

No dog snuffs. A young white peeper spotted roof-prowling: fuck-pad motels, jazz clubs. No arrests, no suspects, no FI cards—the squad had a new card system pending. He'd route me the club/motel locations—if and when he found them.

Tommy K.'s *jazz* records smashed?

More calls: Central Jail, LAPD/Sheriff's R&I. Results: no dog-snuff arrests this year; zero on young white peeper/prowlers. 459 pops post-Kafesjian: no Caucasian perps.

Calls—a pay phone hogged three hours—every LAPD/Sheriff's squad room tapped. Shit: no young white peepers in custody; two wetback dog slashers deported to Mexico.

Waiting: the Bureau pervert file.

I rolled downtown. An office check—no messages, a report on my desk:

CONFIDENTIAL
10/30/58
TO: LIEUTENANT DAVID D. KLEIN
FROM: SERGEANT GEORGE STEMMONS, JR.
TOPIC: KAFESJIAN/459 P.C.
947.1 (HEALTH & SAFETY CODE—ANIMAL MAYHEM)

SIR:

As ordered, I checked the Central Bureau and Sheriff's Central Burglary files for 459's similar to ours. None were listed. I also cross-checked 947.1 offenders (very few were listed) against the 459 files and found no crossover names. (The youngest 947.1 offender is currently 39 years old, which contradicts the prowler lead that Officer Bethel gave us.) I also checked local/statewide homicide files back to 1950. No 187's/187's collateral to burglaries similar to our perpetrator's MO were listed.

Re: Captain Wilhite. I "diplomatically" asked him to supply us with a list of pushers/addicts informed on by the Kafesjians, and he said that their snitches were never tallied, that no records were kept to protect the family. Captain Wilhite offered one name, a man recently informed on by Tommy Kafesjian: marijuana seller Wardell Henry Knox, male negro, employed as a bartender at various jazz clubs. Captain Wilhite's officers could not locate Knox. Knox was recently murdered (unsolved). It was a negro on negro homicide that presumably recieved only a cursory investigation.

Re the E-Z Kleen shops: at all three locations the staff flatly refused to talk to me.

Returning to Captain Wilhite. Frankly, I think he lied about the Kafesjian's snitches never being tallied. He expressed displeasure over your argument with J.C. Kafesjian and told me he has heard rumors that the Federal rackets probe will be launched, centering on narcotics dealings in South-Central Los Angeles. He expressed concern that the LAPD's suborning of the Kafesjian family will be made public and thus discredit both the Department and the individual Narcotics Division officers involved with the family.

I await further orders.

Respectfully,
Sgt. George Stemmons, Jr.
Badge 2104
Administrative Vice Division

Junior—half-ass smart when he tried. I left him a note: the peeper, stripper Lucille updates. Orders: go back to the house, run the canvassers, avoid the family.

Keyed up—glom the pervert file. Dog stuff/B&E/Peeping Tom, see what jumped:

A German shepherd–fucking Marine. Doctor "Dog": popped for shooting his daughter up with beagle pus. Dog killers—none fit my man's specs. Dog fuckers, dog suckers, dog beaters, dog worshipers, a geek who chopped his wife while dressed up as Pluto. Panty sniffers, sink shitters, masturbators—lingerie jackoffs only. Faggot burglars, transvestite break-ins, "Rita Hayworth"—Gilda gown, dyed bush hair, caught blowing a chloroformed toddler. The right age—but a jocker cut his dick off, he killed himself, a full-drag San Quentin burial. Peepers: windows, skylights, roofs—the roof clowns a chink brother act. No watchdog choppers, the geeks read passive, caught holding their puds with

a whimper. Darryl Wishnick, a cute MO: peep, break, enter, rape
watchdogs subdued by goofball-laced meat—too bad he kicked from
syph in '56. One flash: peepers played passive, my guy killed badass
canines.

No jumps.

5:45—keyed up, hungry. Rick's Reef the ticket—maybe Diskant on TV.

I drove over, wolfed bar pretzels. TV news: Chavez Ravine, traffic
deaths, the Red.

Boost the volume:

". . . and so I'm withdrawing for personal reasons. Thomas Bethune
will be re-elected by default, which I fervently hope will not guarantee the
facilitation of the Chavez Ravine land grab. I will continue to protest this
travesty as a private citizen. I . . ."

No more appetite—I took off.

Nowhere to go—just a cruise. South—some magnet pulled me.

Figueroa, Slauson, Central. A gray cop Plymouth behind me—say IAD,
Exley ordered. I gunned it—adios, maybe tail car.

Peeper turf—nightclubs, fuck flops. Bido Lito's, Klub Zamboanga,
Club Zombie—low roofs, good for climbing. Lucky Time Motel, Tick Tock
Motel. Easy peeping: roof access, weeds shoulder high. A brain click:
catch Lester Lake at the Tiger Room.

U-turn, check the rearview, shit—a gray Plymouth cut off.

IAD or Narco? Goons keeping tabs?

Side streets—dawdling evasive—Lester's set closed at 8:00 sharp.
Lester Lake: tenant, informant. Snitch duty cheap—he owed me.

Fall '52:

A call from Harry Cohn, movie kingpin. My "Enforcer" tag intrigued
him; he figured "Klein" made me a Jewboy. A shvartze crooner was banging his girlfriend—clip him for ten grand.

I said no.

Mickey Cohen said no.

Cohn called Jack Dragna.

I knew I'd get the job—no refusal rights. Mickey: a taste for light poon
don't rate death—but Jack insists.

I called Jack: this is petty shit, don't set a standard. Muscle Lester
Lake—don't kill him.

Jack said *you* muscle him.

Jack said take the Vecchio brothers.

Jack said take the nigger someplace, cut his vocal cords—

Gulp—one split second—

"Or I'll nail you for Trombino and Brancato. I'll drag your whore sister's name through the mud."

I grabbed Lester Lake at his crib: get cut or get killed—you call it. Lester said, cut, fast, please. The Vecchios showed—Touch packed a scalpel. A few drinks to loosen things up—knockout drops for Lester.

Anesthesia—Lester moaned for Mama. I hustled a disbarred doctor over—surgery in exchange for no abortion charge. Lester healed up; Harry Cohn found a new girlfriend: Kim Novak.

Lester's voice went baritone to tenor—he chased jig poon strictly now. Touch brought boyfriends to hear him.

Lester said he owed me. Our deal: a flop at my shine-only dive—reduced rent for good information. Success: he talked spook to the spooks and snitched bookies.

The club—a tiger-striped facade, a tiger-tux doorman. Inside: tiger-fur walls, tiger-garb drink girls. Lester Lake on stage, belting "Blue Moon."

I grabbed a booth, grabbed a tigress—"Dave Klein to see Lester." She zipped backstage—slot machines clanged out the doorway. Lester: mock-humble bows, bum applause.

House lights on, dig it: jungle bunnies sprawled in tiger-fur booths. Lester right there, holding a plate.

Chicken and waffles—popping grease. "Hello, Mr. Klein. I was gonna call you."

"You're short on the rent."

He sat down. "Yeah, and you slumlords cut a man no slack. Could be worse, though. You could be a Jew slumlord."

Eyes our way. "I always meet you in public. What do people figure we're doing?"

"Nobody never asks, but I figure they figure you still collect bets for Jack Woods. I'm a betting man, so I'd say that's it. And speaking of Jack, he was collecting your rents this afternoon, which made me want to call you before he leaned on me like he leaned on that poor sucker down the hall."

"Help me out and I'll let you slide."

"You mean you asks, I answers."

"No. First you get rid of that slop, then I ask and you answer."

A tiger girl passed—Lester dumped his plate and swiped a shot glass. A gulp, a belch: "So ask."

"Let's start with burglars."

"Okay, Leroy Coates, out on parole and spending money. Wayne

Layne, boss pad creeper, pimping his wife to make the nut on his habit. Alfonzo Tyrell—"

"My guy's white."

"Yeah, but I keep to the dark side of town. Last time *I* heard of a white burglar was never."

"Fair enough, but I'd call this guy a psycho. He cut up two Dobermans, stole nothing but silverware, then trashed some family-type belongings. Run with it."

"Run with it nowheres. I know nothing 'bout a crazy man like that, 'cept you don't have to be Einstein to figure he's bent on that family. Wayne Layne shits in washing machines, and he's as crazy a B&E man as I care to be acquainted with."

"Okay, peepers then."

"Say what?"

"Peeping Toms. Guys who get their kicks looking in windows. I've got peeper reports nailed at my burglary location *and* all over the Southside—hot-sheet motels and jazz clubs."

"I'll ask around, but you sure ain't getting much for your month's rent."

"Let's try Wardell Henry Knox. He sold mary jane and worked as a bartender at jazz joints, presumably down here."

"Presumably, 'cause white clubs wouldn't hire him. And *was* is correct, 'cause he got hisself snuffed a few months ago. Person or persons unknown, just in case you wants to know who did it."

Jukebox blare close—jerk the cord—instant silence. "I know he was murdered."

Indignant niggers mumbling—fuck them. Lester: "Mr. Klein, your questions are getting pretty far afield. I'll guess a motive on Wardell, though."

"I'm listening."

"Pussy. Ol' Wardell had hound blood. He was the righteous fuckin' pussy hound supreme. If it moved, he'd poke it. He'd ream it, steam it, banana cream it. He must've had a million enemies. He'd fuck a woodpile on the off chance there was a snake inside. He liked to taste it and baste it, but he'd never waste it. He—"

"Enough, Jesus Christ."

Lester winked. "Ask me something I might know something about."

In close. "The Kafesjian family. You've got to know more than I do."

Lester talked low. "I know they're tight with your people. I know they only sell to Negroes and what you'd call anybody but square white folks, 'cause that's the way Chief Parker likes things. Pills, weed, horse, they are *the* number-one suppliers in Southside L.A. I know they lend money and take the vig out in snitch information, you know, independent pushers they can rat to the LAPD, 'cause that is part of their bargain with your people. Now, I *know* J.C. and Tommy hire these inconspicuous-type Negro guys to move their stuff, with Tommy riding herd on them. And you want crazy?—try Tommy the K. He hangs out with the suedes at Bido Lito's and gets up and plays this godawful tenor sax whenever they let him, which is frequently, 'cause who wants to refuse a crazy man, even a little skinny twerp like Tommy? Tommy is craaazy. He is bad fuckin' juju. He is the Kafesjian muscle guy, and I heard he is righteous good with a knife. I also heard he will do anything to ingratiate hisself with Narco. I heard he clipped this drunk driver who hit-and-ran this Narco guy's daughter."

Craaazy. "That's all?"

"Ain't it enough?"

"What about Tommy's sister, Lucille? She's a geek, she parades around naked at her pad."

"I say say what and so what. Too bad Wardell's dead, he'd probably want to poke her. Maybe she likes it dark, like her brother. I'd poke her myself, 'cept last time I tried white stuff I got my neck sliced. You should know, you was there."

Jukebox trills—Lester himself—somebody put the plug back in. "They let you put your own songs in there?"

"Chick and Touch Vecchio do. They're more sentimental 'bout that old neck-slicin' time than slumlord Dave Klein. Long as they run the Southside slots and vending shit for Mr. Cohen, Lester Lake's rendition of 'Harbor Lights' will be on that jukebox. Which gives me pause, 'cause the past two weeks or so these new out-of-town-lookin' guys been working the hardware, which might bode bad for ol' Lester."

"Those haaarbor lights"—pure schmaltz. "Mickey should watch it, the Feds might be checking out the machinery down here. And did anyone ever tell you you sound like a homo? Like Johnnie Ray out of work?"

Howling: "Yeah, my ladyfriends. I make them think I gots queer tendencies, then they works that much harder to set me straight. Touch V. comes in with his sissy boys, and I studies his mannerisms. He brings in this bottle-blond sissy, it was like getting a righteous college degree in fruitness."

I yawned—tiger stripes spun crazy.

"Get some sleep, Mr. Klein. You look all bushed."

. . .

Fuck sleep—that magnet was still pulling me.

I zigzagged east and south—no gray Plymouths on my ass. Western Avenue—peeper turf—whore motels, no addresses to work off. Western and Adams—whore heaven—girls jungled up by Cooper's Donuts. Colored, Mex, a few white—slit-leg gowns, pedal pushers. Jump start: Lucille's hip huggers, slashed and jizzed on.

Brain jump:

Western and Adams—University Division. University Vice, hooker ID stashes there: alias files, john lists, arrest-detention reports. Lucille smiling whorish, Daddy's blood on her claws—jump to her selling it for kicks.

Big jump—odds against it.

I rolled anyway—

Uny Station, brace the squad whip—that whore stuff, a mishmash:

Loose mug shots, report carbons. Names: whores, whore monikers, men detained/booked with whores. Three cabinets' worth of paper in no discernable order.

Skimming through:

No "Kafesjian," no Armenian names—an hour wasted—no surprise—most hookers got bailed out behind monikers. Punch line: if Lucille whored, *if* she got popped—she'd probably call Dan Wilhite to chill things. 114 detention reports, 18 white girls—no physical stats matched Lucille. A half-ass system—most cops let whore reports slide, the girls always repeated. John lists: no Luce, Lucille, Lucy white girl listed—no Armenian surnames.

More mugs—some with neckboard numbers and printing: real names, john names, dates. Shine girls, Mexicans, whites—99.9 percent skank. Goosebumps: Lucille—profile, full face—no neckboard, no printing.

Go, do it: recheck all paper. Three go-rounds—zero, zilch, buppkis. No clicks back to Lucille.

Just one mug strip.

Call it lost paperwork.

Say Dan Wilhite yanked the paper—the mugs got overlooked.

Guess burglar = peeper = Lucille K. john.

I wrote it up, a note to Junior:

Check all stationhouse john/prostie lists—try for information on Lucille's tricks.

Goosebumps: that godawful family.

I hit the Bureau, dropped the note on Junior's desk. Midnight: Ad Vice empty.

"Klein?"

Dan Wilhite across the hall. I called him over—*my* squadroom.

"So?"

"So, I'm sorry for the run-in with Kafesjian."

"I'm not looking for apologies. I'll say it again: so?"

"So it's a tight situation, and I'm trying to be reasonable. I didn't ask for this job, and I don't want it."

"I know, and your Sergeant Stemmons already apologized for your behavior. He also asked for a tally of perpetrators J.C. and his people have informed on, which I refused to give him. Don't ask again, because all notations pertaining to the Kafesjians have been destroyed. *So?*"

"So it's like that. And the question should be 'So what does Exley want?' "

Wilhite crowded up, hands on hips. "Tell me what you think this 459 is. I think it's a dope mob warning. I think Narco is best suited to handle it, and I think you should tell Chief Exley that."

"I don't think so. I think the burglar's hinked on the family, maybe Lucille specifically. It might be a window peeper who's been working Darktown lately."

"Or maybe it's a crazy-man act. A rival mob using terror tactics."

"Maybe, but I don't think so. I'm not really a case man, but—"

"No, you're a thug with a law degree—"

FROST/EASY/DON'T MOVE.

"—and I regret calling you into this mess. Now I've heard that that Fed probe *is* going to happen. I've heard Welles Noonan has auditors checking tax returns—my own and some of my men. That probably means that he knows about Narco and the Kafesjians. We've all taken gratuities, we've all got expensive items we can't explain, so—"

Sweating on me, hot tobacco breath.

"—you do your duty to the Department. You've got your twenty in, I don't and my men don't. You can practice law and suck up to Mickey Cohen, and we can't. *You* owe us, because *you* let Sanderline Johnson jump. Welles Noonan has got this Southside hard-on because *you* compromised his prizefight job. The heat on my men is because of *you,* so *you* square things. Now, J.C. and Tommy are crazy. They've never dealt with hostile police agencies, and if the Feds start pressing them they'll go out of control. I want them quieted down. Stall this bullshit investigation of yours, feed Exley whatever you have to. Just get out of that family's way as quick as you can."

Crowded, elbowed in. "I'll try."

"Do It. Make like it's a paying job. Make like I think you pushed Johnson out the window."

"Do you?"

"You're greedy enough, but you're not that stupid."

Crowd him back, walk—my legs fluttered. A clerk's slip on my desk: "P. Bondurant called. Said to call H. Hughes at Bel-Air Hotel."

8

" • • • and my man Pete told me about your splendid performance vis-à-vis the Morton Diskant matter. Did you know that Diskant is a member of four organizations that have been classified as Communist fronts by the California State Attorney General's Office?"

Howard Hughes: tall, lanky. A hotel suite, two flunkies: Bradley Milteer, lawyer; Harold John Miciak, goon.

7:00 A.M.—distracted, a plan brewing: frame some geek for the Kafesjian job.

"No, Mr. Hughes. I didn't know that."

"Well, you should. Pete told me your methods were rough, and you should know that Diskant's record justified those methods. Among other things, I'm seeking to establish myself as an independent motion picture producer. I'm planning on producing a series of films depicting aerial warfare against the Communists, and a major theme of those films will be the end justifies the means."

Milteer: "Lieutenant Klein is also an attorney. If he accepts your offer, you'll receive an additional interpretation of the contractual aspects."

"I haven't practiced much law, Mr. Hughes. And I'm pretty busy right now."

Miciak coughed. Tattooed hands—zoot gang stuff. "This ain—*isn't* a lawyer job. Pete Bondurant's got his plate full, so—"

Hughes, interrupting: " 'Surveillance' sums this assignment up best, Lieutenant. Bradley, will you elaborate?"

Milteer, prissy: "Mr. Hughes has a young actress named Glenda Bledsoe signed to a full-service contract. She was living in one of his guest homes and was being groomed to play lead roles in his Air Force films. She infringed on her contract by moving out of the guest home and by leaving script sessions without asking permission. She's currently playing the female lead in a non-union horror film shooting in Griffith Park. It's called *Attack of the Atomic Vampire,* so you can imagine the quality of the production."

Hughes, prissy: "Miss Bledsoe's contract allows her to make one non-Hughes film per year, so I cannot violate the contract for that. There is, however, a morality clause that we can utilize. If we can prove Miss Bledsoe to be an alcoholic, criminal, narcotics addict, Communist, lesbian, or nymphomaniac, we can violate her contract and get her black-balled from the film industry on that basis. Our one other avenue is to secure proof that she knowingly took part in publicizing non-Hughes performers outside of her work for this ridiculous monster film. Lieutenant, your job would be to surveil Glenda Bledsoe with an eye toward securing contract-violating information. Your fee would be three thousand dollars."

"Have you explained the situation to her, Mr. Milteer?"

"Yes."

"How did she react?"

"Her reply was 'Fuck you.' Your reply, Lieutenant?"

Close to "No"—freeze it—think:

Hush-Hush said Mickey C. bankrolled that movie.

"Guest home" meant "fuck pad" meant Howard Hughes left to choke his own chicken.

Think:

Glom some Bureau guys for tail work. Glom a slush fund: Kafesjian frame cash.

JEW HIM UP.

"Five thousand, Mr. Hughes. I can recommend cheaper help, but I can't neglect my regular duties for any less than that."

Hughes nodded; Milteer whipped out a cash roll. "All right, Lieutenant. This is a two-thousand-dollar retainer, and I'll expect reports at least every other day. You can call me here at the Bel-Air. Now, is there anything else you need to know about Miss Bledsoe?"

"No, I'll find an in on the movie crew."

Hughes stood up. I laid on the glad hand: "I'll nail her, sir."

A limp shake—Hughes wiped his hand on the sly.

New money—spend it smart. Think smart:

Nail Glenda Bledsoe fast. Let Junior carry some Kafesjian weight—hope his fuck-up string ended. Figure out that Darktown tail, stay tailless.

Instinct: Exley wouldn't rat me on Johnson. Logic: he destroyed the coroner's file; I could rat him for a piece of Diskant. Instinct: call his Kafesjian fix PERSONAL. Instinct—call me bait—a bad cop sent out to draw heat.

Conclusions:

Number one: Call Wilhite and Narco more dangerous; call me a bent cop juking their meal ticket. Maybe the Fed grand jury blues upcoming: true bills, indictments. Rogue cops out of work then, one scapegoat: a lawyer-landlord with a sure police pension. Out-of-work killers, one target: me.

Number two: Find a burglar/pervert confessor—some geek to take my 459 fall. Palm squadroom bulls for leads; keep Junior on the case legit. No legit B&E man?—Joe Pervert buys the dive.

I drove over to Hollywood Station. No file-room clerk—I boosted "459 Cleared," "False Confessions," '49–'57. A 187 sheet on the board—the "Wino Will-o-the-Wisp." Perv stuff, nice—I grabbed a carbon.

Conclusion number three:

Call me still short of scared.

Griffith Park, the west road up—streams, small mountains. Steep turns, scrub-hill canyons—Movieland.

I pulled into a makeshift lot—vehicles parked tight. Shouts, picket signs bobbing way back. I hopped a flatbed, scoped the ruckus.

Union placard shakers—Chick Vecchio facing them off—the stiff-arm fungoo up close. A clearing, trailers, the set: cameras, a rocket ship half Chevy.

"Scab!" "Scab scum!"

Over, buck the line—"Police officer!" Punk pickets—they let me through, no grief. Chick greeted me—smiles, back slaps.

"Scab scum!" "Police collusion!"

We walked over to the trailers. Catcalls, no rocks—sob sisters. Chick: "You looking for Mickey? I'll bet he's got a nice envelope for you."

"He told you?"

"No, it's what my brother would call an 'inescapable conclusion to the cognoscenti.' Come on, a witness flies out the window with Dave Klein standing by. What's a card-carrying cogno supposed to think?"

"I think you almost did some union thumping."

"Hey, we should have called the old Enforcer. Seriously, you got ideas? Mickey's got a bad case of the shorts. You know any boys who won't cost us an arm and a leg?"

"Fuck it, let them picket."

"Uh-uh. They yell when we're shooting, which means scenes have to be redubbed, which costs money."

Someone, somewhere: "Cameras! Action!"

"Serious, Dave."

"Okay, call Fats Medina at the Main Street Gym. Tell him I said five sparring partners and a roadblock. Tell him you'll go fifty a man."

"For real?"

"Do it tonight, and you won't have union trouble tomorrow. Come on, I want to check out this movie."

Up to the set. Chick held a finger to his lips—scene in progress.

Two "actors" gesticulating. The spaceship close up: Chevy fins, Studebaker grille, Kotex-box launching pad.

Touch Vecchio: "Russian rocket ships have dropped atomic waste on Los Angeles—a plot to turn Angelenos into automatons susceptible to Communism! They have created a vampire virus! People have turned into monsters who devour their own families!"

His co-star—blond, padded crotch: "Family is the sacred concept that binds all Americans. We must stop this soul-usurping invasion whatever the cost!"

Chick, cupping a whisper: "The hoot is my brother's killed eight men, and he takes this noise serious. And feature—him and that bottle-blond fruitcake are porking in trailers every chance they get, *and* chasing chicken down at the Fern Dell toilets. You see that guy with the megaphone? That's Sid Frizell, the so-called director. Mickey hired him on the cheap, and to me he reads ex-con who couldn't direct a Mongolian cluster fuck. He's always talking to that guy Wylie Bullock, the cameraman, who at least has got a place to live, unlike most of the bums Mickey's hired. Feature: he hired the crew out of the slave markets down on skid row. They sleep on the set, like this is some kind of fucking hobo jungle. And the dialogue? Frizell—Mickey shoots him an extra sawbuck a day to be scriptwriter."

No Mickey, no women. Touch: "I would slay the highest echelon of the Soviet Secretariat to protect the sanctity of my family!"

Blondie: "I of course empathize. But first we must isolate the atomic waste before it seeps into the Hollywood Reservoir. Look at these wretched victims of the vampire virus!"

Cut to werewolf-mask extras hip-hopping. Hip, hop—T-Bird popped out of back pockets.

Sid Frizell: "Cut! I told you people to leave your wine back with your blankets and sleeping bags! And remember Mr. Cohen's order—no wine before your lunch break!"

A geek lurched into the spaceship. Touch squeezed Blondie's ass on the QT.

Frizell: "Five-minute break and no drinking!" Background noise: "Scab scum! Police puppets!"

No Glenda Bledsoe.

Touch oozed by the camera slow. "Hi, Dave. Looking for Mickey?"

"People keep asking me that."

"Well, it's an inescapable conclusion of the cognoscenti."

Chick winked. "He'll show up. He goes by this bakery to get week-old bread to make sandwiches with. Feature the cuisine we get: stale bread, stale doughnuts and this lunch meat sold out the back door at this slaughterhouse out in Vernon. I quit eating on the set when I caught fur on my baloney and cheese."

I laughed. Script talk: Blondie and an old geek dressed like Dracula.

Touch sighed. "Rock Rockwell is going to be such a big star. Listen, he's actually telling Elston Majeska how to interpret his lines. What does that imply to the cognoscenti?"

"Who's Elston Majeska?"

Chick: "He was some kind of silent-movie star over in Europe, and now Mickey gets him passes from this rest home. He's a junkie, so Mickey pays him off in this diluted H he gets cheap. Old Elston says his lines, shoots up and goes on a sugar jag. You ought to see him snarf those stale doughnuts."

Pops peeled a Mars Bar, weaving—Blondie grabbed his cape.

Touch, swooning: "One man sandwich with the works!"

Frizell: "Glenda to the set in five minutes!"

"When I met Mickey, he was clearing ten million a year. From that to this, Jesus Christ."

Chick: "Things come and go."

Touch: "The torch passes."

"Bullshit. Mickey got out of McNeil Island a year ago—and *nobody* has grabbed his old action. Is he scared? Four of his guys have gotten clipped, all unsolveds—and I mean *nobody* knows who did it. You guys are all the muscle he's got left, and I can't feature why you stick around. What's he got left, the Niggertown coin business? How much can he be turning on that?"

Chick shrugged. "So feature we been with Mickey a long time. Feature we don't like change. He's a scrapper, and scrappers get results sooner or later."

"Nice results. And Lester Lake told me some out-of-town guys are working the Southside coin."

Chick shrugged. Wino cheers and wolf whistles—Glenda Bledsoe in a pom-pom-girl outfit.

Feature:

Tall, lanky, honey blond. All legs, all chest—a grin said she never bought in. A little knock-kneed, big eyes, dark freckles. Pure something—maybe style, maybe juice.

Touch shot me details: "Glamorous Glenda. Rock and me are the only males on the set immune to her charms. Mickey discovered her working at Scrivner's Drive-In. He's smitten, Chick's smitten. Glenda and Rock play brother and sister. She's been infected with the vampire virus, and she puts the make on her own brother. She turns into a monster and sends Rock running off into the hills."

Frizell: "Actors on their marks! Camera! Action!"

Rock: "Susie, I'm your big brother. The vampire virus has stunted your moral growth, and you've still got two years to go at Hollywood High."

Glenda: "Todd, in times of historic struggle, the rules of the bourgeoisie don't apply."

A clinch, a kiss. Frizell: "Cut! It's a take! Print it!"

Rock broke the clinch. Whistles, cheers. A wino booed; Glenda flipped him the finger. Mickey C. ducked in a trailer, lugging groceries.

I eased around the set and tapped the door.

"Wine money not disbursed until six o'clock! The tsuris you stumblebums inflict! This is a motion picture location, not the Jesus Saves Rescue Mission!"

I opened the door, caught a flying bagel. Stale—I tossed it back.

"David Douglas Klein, the 'Douglas' a dead giveaway you are not of my kindred blood, you farshtinkener Dutch fuck. Refuse my food, but I doubt you will refuse the money Sam Giancana has transmitted to me for you."

Mickey tucked a wad under my holster. "Sammy says thank you. Sammy says damn good job on such short notice."

"It was too close to home, Mick. It caused me lots of trouble."

Mickey plopped into a chair. "Sammy doesn't care from your troubles. You of all people should know the ethos of that farshtinkener crazy cocksucker."

"He's supposed to care about *your* trouble."

"Which in his brutish spaghetti-bender fashion he does."

Glenda cheesecake—four walls' worth. "Let's say he miscalculated this time."

"As the song goes, 'I should care?' "

"You should care. Noonan's prizefight probe went out the window too, so now he's hot to get something going in Niggertown. If the Feds hit the Southside, they'll raid your coin locations. If I get a line on it I'll tell you, but I might not know. Sam put your last going business in real trouble."

Chick V. by the doorway; Mickey, cheesecake eyes. "David, such tsuris you predict, such tsuris I am nonplussed by. My desires are strictly to see district gambling get in, then retire to Galapagos and watch turtles fuck in the sun."

Laugh it out. "District gambling will never pass the State Legislature, and if it did, you'd never get a franchise. Bob Gallaudet is the only reputable politician who supports it, and he'll change his mind if he makes attorney general."

Chick coughed; Mickey shrugged. A permit on the door: "Parks-Recreation, Approval to Film." I squinted—"Robert Gallaudet," small print.

Laugh *that* out. "Bob let you film here for a campaign contribution. He's about to make DA, so you think a grand or two gets you the inside track on district gambling. Jesus, you must be shooting dope like old Dracula."

Pinups galore—Mickey blew them kisses. "The prom date I never had in 1931. I could guarantee her a corsage and many fine hours of Bury the Brisket."

"She reciprocate?"

"Tomorrow, maybe yes, but today she breaks my heart. Dinner tonight was already finalized, then Herman Gerstein called. His company is set to distribute my movie, and he needs Glenda to accompany his faygeleh heartthrob Rock Rockwell on a publicity date. Such tsuris— Herman is grooming that rump ranger for stardom apart from me, he's terrified the scandal rags will discover he takes his pleasure Greek. Such duplicity to lose her company, my comely brisketeer."

"Publicity date"—contract breaker. "Mickey, watch your coin biz. Remember what I told you."

"Go, David. Take a bagel for the road."

I walked out; Chick walked in. I checked my envelope—five G's.

A pay phone, two dimes: the DMV cop line, Junior.

Stats: Glenda Louise Bledsoe, 5'8", 125, blond/blue, DOB 8/3/29, Provo, Utah. California license since 8/46, five moving violations. '56 Chevrolet Corvette, red/white, Cal. DX 413. Address: 2489½ N. Mount Airy, Hollywood.

Junior at the Bureau—no luck—the Ad Vice clerk said he didn't check in. I left a message: buzz me at Stan's Drive-in.

I dawdled over, grabbed a space by the phone booth. Coffee, a burger—scan those file carbons.

Burglars, confessors—physical stats/MO/priors—I took notes. The Wino Will-o-the-Wisp—shit, still at large. Names, names, names—candidates for a psycho framee. Scribbling notes—distracted—flirty carhops, new money. Nagging me: a frame meant no payoff—no way to match Lucille and the burglar to WHY?

The phone—I ran, grabbed it. "Junior?"

"Yeah, the clerk said to call you."

Wary—not his style. "You got that note I left you, right?"

"Right."

"Right, and did you check the stationhouse whore files for paper on Lucille Kafesjian?"

"I'm working on it. Dave, I can't talk now. I'll—look, I'll call you later."

"The fuck later, you *jump* on that work—" CLICK—dead air.

Home, paperwork. Pissed at Junior—an erratic punk getting worse. Paperwork: Exley's Kafesjian report padded up fat. Lists next: potential Glenda tailers, potential pervert framees. Calls in: Meg—Jack Woods glommed our back rent. Pete B: do Mr. Hughes solid, I convinced him you're not a Hebe. Calls out: Ad Vice, Junior's pad, no luck—find him, ream his insubordinate heart. My tailer list, bum luck holding—no men to start tonight. *My* job by default—a publicity date meant contract breaker.

Back to Hollywood: side streets, the freeway. No tails on me: dead sure. Up Gower, Mount Airy, left turn.

2489: courtyard bungalows—peach stucco. A carport—with a red and white Corvette snuggled in.

5:10—just dark. I parked close—courtyard/carport view.

Time dragged—the stakeout blues—piss in a cup, toss it, doze. Auto/foot traffic—light. 7:04—three cars at the curb.

Doors open, flashbulbs popping: Rock Rockwell—tuxedo, bouquet. A jog to the courtyard, back with Glenda—nice—a tight sweater dress. Bulb glare caught her patented Look—it's a joke and I know it. Zoom: all three cars U-turned southbound.

Rolling stakeout—four cars long—Gower, Sunset west. The Strip, Club Largo, three-car pile-out.

Valets swooped in, servile. More photos—Rockwell looked bored. I parked in the red and fixed my windshield: "Official Police Vehicle." The entourage hit the club.

I badged in, badged a Shriner off a bar stool. Turk Butler on stage— bistro belter supreme. Ringside: Rock, Glenda, scribes. Photo men by the exit—zoom lenses zoomed in.

Break that contract.

Dinner: club soda, pretzels. Easy eyeball work: Glenda talked, Rock sulked. The reporters ignored him—snore city.

Turk Butler off stage, chorus girls on. Glenda smoked and laughed. Big lungs on the dancers—Glenda pulled her sweater up for chuckles. Rock hit the sauce—whiskey sours.

A club hop at ten sharp—across Sunset on foot to the Crescendo. Another bar stool, eyeball surveillance: pure Glenda. Showstopper Glenda—odd wisps of Meg, and her own SOMETHING.

Midnight—a dash for the cars—I tailed the convoy brazen close. Back to Glenda's pad, sidewalk arc lights: a dud goodnight kiss caught on film.

The newsman took off; Glenda waved. Quiet out—voices carried.

Rock: "Hell, now I've got no wheels."

Glenda: "Take mine, and bring Touch back with you. Say two hours?"

Rock grabbed her keys and ran—gleeful. The Vette peeled out burning rubber—Glenda winced. "Bring Touch back with you" hit funny—tail him.

Gower south, Franklin east. Sparse traffic—still no tails on *me*. North on Western, say a movie set run—Mickey's permit kept the park road open.

Los Feliz, left turn, Fern Dell—streams and glades before the Griffith Park hills. Brake lights blinked—fuck—Fern Dell—Vice cops called it Cocksuckers' Paradise.

He parked—rush hour—cigarette tips red in the dark. I swung right and stopped—my beams on Rock and a cute young quiff.

I killed my lights, cracked the window. Close—I caught the proposition:

"Hi."

"Hi."

"I . . . I think fall is the best time in L.A., don't you?"

"Yeah, sure. Listen, I just borrowed a *really* nice car. We could maybe make last call at the Orchid Room, then go someplace. I've got some time to kill before I pick my boy—I mean somebody up."

"You don't mince words."

"I don't mince period. Come on, say yes."

"Nix, sweetie. You're big and brusque, which I like, but the last big brusque guy I said yes to turned out to be a deputy sheriff."

"Oh, come on."

"Nix, nyet, nein and no. Besides, I heard Administrative Vice has been operating Fern Dell."

Wrong—Ad Vice never popped fruits. Outside chance—gung-ho Junior, Vice cowboy.

Rock—"Thanks for the memories"—match flare, his cigarette lit. Prowling now—easy to track—I watched the tip glow queer to queer.

Time wheezed, a bum soundtrack: sex moans out in the woods. An hour, an hour ten—Rock walked back zipping his fly.

Zoom—the Vette peeled. I followed slow—no traffic—call the set his destination. A roadblock out of nowhere—baseball-bat men waved him through.

Truck headlights approaching—I backed up and watched.

Brake squeals—a big flatbed—picket clowns in back. A spotlight flashed—bright white blindness on the target.

Goons hit the truck swinging—nail-studded Louisville Sluggers. The windshield exploded—a man stumbled out belching glass. The driver ran—a nail shot took his nose off.

The bed gate crashed—goons went in close—ribcage work. Fats Medina dragged a guy by the hair—his scalp came off.

No screams—wrong—why no sound—

Back to Fern Dell, down to Glenda's. No screams—weird—then my pulse quit banging my ears so I could hear.

Wait the boys out: "Rock," "Touch"—the nance type, this eight-notch killer. Suspicious: 2:00 A.M., a B-movie siren set for hostess.

One courtyard light on—hers. I tapped the two-way, flipped bands to kill boredom. Dispatch calls—the Bureau frequency—voices.

Hurwitz fur-job talk—Robbery men. Make the voices: Dick Carlisle, Mike Breuning—Dudley Smith strongarms. No trace on the furs; Dud wanted fences braced *hard.* Crackle: station-to-station interference. Breuning: Dud pulled Johnny Duhamel off the Mobster Squad—a scary kick-ass ex-fighter. More static—I flipped dials—a liquor-store heist on La Brea.

The Vette hit the carport; the boys hit Glenda's pad nuzzled up.

One ring—the door open and shut.

Figure access.

The courtyard proper—too risky. Nix the roof—no way to get up. Behind the bungalows—maybe a window to peep.

Risk it—worth it—juicy hearsay.

I walked over, counted back doors down—one, two, three—hers locked tight. One window—curtains cracked—eyes to the glass:

A dark bedroom, a connecting door ajar.

Press the glass, slide it up. Open—no shimmy, no squeak. Vault the sill: up and in.

Smells: cotton, stale perfume. Dark going gray—I saw a bed and bookshelves. Voices—hug the door—listen:

Glenda: "Well, there is a precedent."

Touch: "Not a successful one, sweetie."

Rockwell: "Marie 'the Body' McDonald. A from-nowhere career, then this kidnapping out of nowhere. The papers smelled publicity stunt quicksville. I think—"

Glenda: "It wasn't realistic, that's why. Her hair wasn't even mussed. Remember, Mickey Cohen is bankrolling our movie. He's hot for me, so the press will think gangland intrigue right off. Howard Hughes used to keep me, so we've got him for a supporting play—"

Touch: " 'Keep,' what a euphemism."

Rock: "What's a euphemism?"

Touch: "Lucky you're gorgeous, 'cause you'd never make it on brains."

Glenda: "Cut it out, and listen. I'm wondering what the police will think. It's not a kidnapping for ransom, because frankly nobody would pay good money to get Rock and I out of trouble. What I'm think—"

Touch: "The police will think revenge on Mickey or something, and Mickey won't know a thing. The police love to bother Mickey. Bothering Mickey is a favorite activity of the Los Angeles Police Department. And you two will be *good*. Georgie Ainge will slap you around just a little bit more than a smidgin, for realism's sake. The police will buy it, so just don't worry. You'll both be kidnap victims, and you'll both get lots of publicity."

Rock: "Method acting."

Glenda: "It compromises Howard, the creep. He'd never violate the contract of a beautiful kidnap victim."

Touch: "Tell true, sweetie. Was he hung?"

Glenda: "Hung like a cashew."

They all howled. The real howler: fake kidnaps *always* bombed.

A doorway crack—I pressed up, squinted. Glenda—robe, wet hair:

"He talked about airplanes to get himself excited. He called my breasts my propellers."

More laughs—Glenda edged out of my light. Needle scratches, Sinatra—wait the tune out for one more look.

No luck—just "Ebb Tide" done very slow. Through the bedroom, out the window, thinking crazy: *Don't snitch her.*

onsters:

Charles Issler, confessor—front-page-hot female snuffs. "Hit me! Hit me!"—known to bite Homicide bulls who wouldn't oblige.

Michael Joseph Krugman, confessor—the Jesus Christ 187. His motive—revenge—Jesus fucked his wife.

Swirling:

Beaucoup confessors—find a patsy in LAPD file print. Some INSTINCT working through—

Donald Fitzhugh—queer snuff confessor; Thomas Mark Janeway—kiddie molestations strictly. That INSTINCT THING worked me over—almost a taunt. The Wino Will-o-the-Wisp: strangler/mutilator/stumblebum slayer. No hard candidates—

I woke up. THAT INSTINCT big:

The Kafesjians *knew* who trashed their pad—if I framed some geek they'd fuck things up.

Sweaty sheets/sweaty files/that rap sheet I glommed late:

George Sidney Ainge, aka "Georgie." White male, DOB 11/28/22. Pimp convictions '48, '53—fourteen months County time total. Gun sale rousts '56, '7, '8—no convictions. Last known address 1219 S. Dunsmuir, L.A. Vehicle: '51 Caddy Eldo, QUR 288.

Touch to Glenda: "Georgie Ainge will slap you around just a little bit more than a smidgin."

I shaved, showered, dressed. Glenda smiled, saying stall things for now.

The Bureau, an Exley memo waiting: "Kafesjian/459—report in full." 8:00, no daywatch men in yet—no potential Georgie Ainge skinny.

Coffee—overdue. Some DA called—that botched bookie raid—I shitted him lawyer to lawyer. Junior walking: up the side stairs, furtive. I whistled—long and shrill.

He walked over. I shut the door, shut my voice in: "Never hang up on me or get cute like that again. One more time and I'm submitting a transfer request that will ruin you in the Bureau so fast—"

"Dave—"

"Dave shit. Stemmons, you fucking toe the line. You obey my orders, you do what I tell you to do. *Now,* did you check the stationhouse files for paper on Lucille Kafesjian?"

"N-no listings, I ch-checked all around"—nervous, hinky.

Change-up: "Have you been hotdogging queers in Fern Dell Park?"

"W-what?"

"Some quiff said Ad Vice was operating the park, which we both know is bullshit. I repeat, were you—"

Hands up—placating me. "Okay, okay, guilty. I owed a favor to this old student of mine at the Academy. He's working Hollywood Vice and he's swamped, the squad boss has him detached to that wino-killing job. I just made a few collars and let him do the booking. Look, I'm sorry if I didn't go by the rules."

"Learn the fucking rules."

"Sure, Dave, sorry."

Shaky, sweaty—I gave him a handkerchief. "Have you heard of a pimp named Georgie Ainge? He sells guns on the side."

Head bobs, eager to please. "I heard he's a rape-o. Some squadroom guy told me he likes gigs where he gets to hurt women."

"Wipe your goddamn face, you're sweating up my floor."

Junior quick-drawed—the gun bobbed at *me.* Quick—slap him—my law school ring drew blood.

White knuckles on his piece. Brains—he pointed it down.

"Stay angry, tough guy. We've got an outside job, and I want you pissed."

Separate cars, let him stew with half the picture: good guy/bad guy, no arrest. Stay pissed: I've got a moonlight gig going, a fake kidnap might deep-six it. Junior—"Sure, Dave, sure"—eager beaver.

I got there first—a mock chateau—four floors, maybe ten units per. A '51 Eldo at the curb—a match to the Ainge rap sheet.

I checked the mail slots: G. Ainge, 104. Junior's Ford hit the curb—two wheels on the sidewalk. I beelined down the hall.

Junior caught up. I winked; he winked—half twitch. I pushed the buzzer.

The door opened a crack. Ear tug—cue the bad guy.

Junior: "LAPD, open up!"—wrong—I signaled kick it in.

The door swung wide. Right there: a fat lowlife, arms raised. Old tracks—hold for the "I'm Clean" pitch.

"I'm clean, Officers. I got me a nice little job, and I got me Nalline test results that prove I don't geez no more. I'm still on County probation, and my PO knows I switched from horse to Silver Satin."

I smiled. "We're sure you're clean, Mr. Ainge. May we come in?"

Ainge stood aside; Junior closed the door. The flop: Murphy bed, wine bottles tossed helter-skelter. TV, magazines: *Hush-Hush,* girlie stuff.

Junior: "Kiss the wall, shitbird."

Ainge spread out. I scoped a *Hush-Hush* cover: Marie "the Body" McDonald, fake kidnap supreme.

Georgie ate wallpaper; Junior frisked him slow. Page two: some boyfriend drove Marie to Palm Springs and stashed her in an old mining shack. A ransom demand—her agent called the FBI. Satire: stage your own publicity kidnap, five easy steps.

Junior dropped Ainge—a kidney shot—not bad.

Georgie sucked wind. I skimmed the mags—bondage smut—women gagged and harnessed.

Junior kicked Ainge prone. A blonde looked sort of like Glenda.

Out loud: " 'Lesson number one: call Hedda Hopper in advance. Lesson number two: don't hire kidnappers from Central Casting. Lesson number three: don't pay your publicist with marked ransom money.' Whose idea, Georgie? You or Touch Vecchio?"

No answer.

I flashed two fingers: GO FULL. Junior slammed kidney shots; Georgie Ainge drooled bile.

Kneel down close. "Tell us about it. It's not going to happen, but tell us anyway. Tell us nice and we won't tell your PO. Stay snotty and we'll pop you for possession of heroin."

Gurgles, "Fuck you."

Two fingers/GO FULL.

Rabbit shots—strong—Ainge curled up fetal-style. A punch hit the floor—Junior yelped and grabbed his piece.

I snatched it, worked the chamber, popped the clip.

Junior—"Dave, Jesus!" —farewell, tough guy.

Ainge groaned—Junior kicked him—ribs cracked.

"OKAY! OKAY!"

I hauled him into a chair; Junior grabbed his gun back. Silver Satin on the bed—toss it over.

Chugalug—Ainge coughed, burped blood. Junior crawled for his clip—hands and knees.

"Whose idea?"

Ainge—"How'd you tumble?"—wincing.

"Never mind. I asked you, 'Whose idea?' "

"Touch, Touch V., his idea. The deal was to goose his bun boy's career, with that blond cooze along for some cheesecake. Touch said three hundred and no rough stuff. Listen, I just took the job to get a taste."

Junior: "A taste of horse? I thought you were clean, shitbird."

" 'Shitbird' went out with vaudeville. Hey, you get your badge in a cereal box?"

I held Junior back. "A taste of what?"

Giggles. "I don't sell guns no more, I don't procure females for purposes of prostitution. I switched from H to jungle juice, so my tastes are none of—"

"A taste of what?"

"Shit, I just wanted to bust up that Glenda cooze."

I froze—Ainge kept talking—rank wine breath.

". . . you know, I just wanted to put the hurt on something Howard Hughes put the boots to. I got fired at Hughes Aircraft during the war, so you could maybe call that Glenda cunt my payback. Va-va-voom, that is some fine piece of—"

I kicked his chair over, threw the TV at his head. He ducked—tubes popped, exploded. I grabbed Junior's gun—aimed, fired—clicks, no fucking clip, fuck me.

Ainge snaked under the bed. Soft, talking nice:

"Look, you think that Glenda woman's My Fair Lady? Look, I *know* her, she used to whore for this pimp Dwight Gilette. I can hand her up to you on a *guaranteed gas-chamber bounce."*

"Gilette"—vague—a 187 unsolved. I unloaded my own piece—safety valve.

Ainge, soft: "Look, I sold guns then. Glenda knew that. Gilette was slapping her around, so she bought a .32 to protect herself. I don't know, something happened, so Glenda shot Gilette. She shot him, and she ended up taking his knife away from him. She fucking cut him too, and then she sold me the gun back. I've got it stashed, you know, I figured maybe some day, some reason, maybe it's got prints on it, I was gonna threaten her with it on the kidnap thing. Touch, he don't know about it, *but you can make this a fucking gas-chamber job."*

Make the case:

'55, '56—Dwight Gilette, mulatto pimp, dead at his pad. Highland Park dicks handled it: fatal shots, no gun found—the stiff stabbed post-mortem. Knife man Gilette—aka "Blue Blade." Forensics: two blood types made; female hair and bone chips found. Hypothesis: knife fight with a whore, some hooker shot/shanked a skilled blade freak.

Bugs up my spine.

Ainge kept talking—gibberish—I didn't hear it. Junior scribbled up his notebook fast.

Fast—don't think why—find the gun.

One room—an easy toss—closet, dresser, cupboards. Ainge blabbing non-stop—Junior coaxing him out from under the bed. Tossing hard, tossing zero: skin mags, probation forms, rubbers. Topsy-turvy glimpses: evidence prof Junior stacking pages.

No gun.

"Dave."

Ainge cozied up—a fresh bottle half guzzled. Junior: "Dave, we've got ourselves a homicide."

"No. It's too old, and there's just this geek's word."

"Dave, come on."

"No. Ainge, where's the gun?"

No answer.

"Tell me where the gun is, goddamn it."

No answer.

"Ainge, give up the fucking gun."

Junior, quick hand signals: LET ME WORK HIM.

Work shit—grab his notebook. Skim it—Georgie's pitch down—details, approximate dates. No locate on the gun—call odds on latent prints thirty to one.

Junior, flexing his mean streak: "Dave, give me my notebook back."

I shoved it at him. "Wait outside."

This X-ray stare—not bad for a punk.

"Stemmons, wait outside."

Junior eeeased out, tough-guy slow. I locked the door and fixed on Ainge.

"Give up the gun."

"Not on your life. I was talking scared then, but now I figure different. You want my interpretation?"

Brass knucks, get ready.

"My interpretation is the kid thinks a murder beef for the Glenda cooze is a good idea, but for some reason you don't. I also know that if I give up that gun it's a probation violation vis-à-fucking-vis harboring contraband items. You know what a 'hole card' is? You know—"

On him—knucks downstairs/upstairs—flab rippers/broken face bones/fear-of-God time:

"No kidnapping. Not a word to Touch or Rockwell. You don't talk about Glenda Bledsoe, you don't go near her. You don't give that gun up to my partner or anyone else."

Coughs/moans/sputters trying to yes me. Bloody phlegm on my hands; shock waves up my knuck arm. I kicked through TV rubble getting out.

Junior on the sidewalk, smoking. No preamble: "We pop the Bledsoe woman for Gilette. Bob Gallaudet will grant Ainge immunity on the gun charge. Dave, she's Howard Hughes' ex-girlfriend. This is a big major case."

Head throbs. "It's shit. Ainge told me the gun story was a lie. What we've got is a three-year-old homicide with one convicted-felon hearsay witness. *It's shit.*"

"No, Ainge lied *to you.* I think there is a gun extant."

"Gallaudet would never file. I'm an attorney, you're not. Believe me."

"Dave, just listen."

"No, forget it. You were damn good in there, but it's over. We came to break up an impending felony, and—"

"And protect this moonlight job of yours."

"Right, which I'll kick back to you on."

"Which is unreported income in violation of departmental regs."

Seeing red: "There's no case. We're on the Kafesjian job, which is a major case, because Exley's got a hard-on for it. If you want juice, play tight with me on that. Maybe we soft-pedal it, maybe we don't. We have to work angles on that case to protect the Department, and I don't want you going off half-cocked on some stale-bread pimp snuff."

"A homicide is a homicide. And you know what I think?"

Smug little shitbird. "What?"

"That you want to protect that woman."

Seeing red, seeing black.

"And I think that for a cop on the take, you take pretty small. If you want to steal, steal big. If I ever broke the regs, I wouldn't start at the bottom."

PURE BLACK—knucks out.

Pure rabbit—Junior tripped into his car. Pulling out, window down:

"You owe me for the way you patronize me! You owe me! And I might collect damn soon!"

RED BLACK RED.

Junior fishtailed straight through a red light.

I drove to the set just to see her; I figured one look would say yes or no.

Big blue eyes looked right through me—I couldn't even guess. She acted; she laughed; she talked—her voice gave nothing away. I stuck to the trailers and framed her in longshots—Miss Vampire/maybe pimp slasher. A change of costume, demure stuff to low-cut gown—

Shoulder-blade scars. ID them: slash marks, one puncture wound/ bone notch. Call it à la *Hush-Hush:*

HOOKER/ACTRESS MURDERS HALF-BREED PIMP! AIRPLANE MOGUL SMITTEN! ROGUE COP STEPS FROM CLOVER TO SHIT!

I watched her act, watched her subtle-goof the whole silly business. Dark came on, I just watched, no one bugged the skulking stage-door Johnny.

Rain shut things down—I would have watched all night otherwise.

A pay-phone stint, zero luck: no Exley at the Bureau, no Junior to wheedle or threaten. Wilhite, my feelers out—not at Narco, not at home. Down to the Vine Street Hody's: paperwork, dinner.

I wrote out two Exley reports: full disclosure and whore Lucille omitted—insurance if I swung Wilhite's way. That frame brainstorm—nix it—Exley wouldn't bite, the Kafesjians made one big monkey wrench. Hard to concentrate—Junior hovered—taunting me with murderess Glenda.

Ex-whore Glenda; whore Lucille.

Rain blurred people outside. Hard to see faces, easy to imagine them—easy to make women Glenda. A brunette looked in the window— Lucille K. one split second. I banged the table getting up; she waved to a waitress, just some plain Jane.

Darktown—nowhere else to go.

Systematic:

No exact peeper locations—two divisions botched paperwork— no whore motel/jazz club addresses to work from. South on Western, driving one-handed, one hand free to jot motel names. Systematic: no tails on *me,* forty-one hot-sheet flops Adams to Florence.

Jazz clubs, more confined: Central Avenue, southbound. Nineteen clubs, count bars in, boost the tally up to sixty-odd. Rain kept foot traffic thin; neon signs hit hypnotic—half-second blips in my windshield.

Rain fizzling—try the coffee-and-donuts routine.

A Cooper's stand on Central—whore heaven—I fed the girls coffee and showed the Lucille pix. Big nos, one yes—a Western-and-Adams girl stepping east. Her story: Lucille worked "occasional"—tight pedal pushers—no street name, no truck with other whores.

Pedal pushers—slashed/jacked off on—*my* burglar.

Midnight—half the clubs shut down. Neon blipped off; I caught boss men locking their doors. Peeper/prowler questions—"Say what?"s straight across. The Lucille mugs—straight deadpans.

1:00 A.M., 2:00 A.M.—shit police work. B-girls at bus stops and cab stands—I talked Lucille with my brain revving Glenda. More nos, more rain—I ducked into a diner.

A counter, booths. Packed—all spooks. Whispers, nudges—niggers smelling Law. Two B-girl types in a front booth—hands under the table furtive quick.

I joined them. One bolted—I jerked her back by the wrist. Sitting beside me: a skanky high yellow. Bad juju percolating—I could feel it.

"Dump your purses on the table."

Slow and cool: two pseudo-snakeskin bags turned out. Felony tilt: tinfoil Benzedrine.

Change-up: "Okay, you're clean."

Darky: "Sheeeit!"

High Yellow: "Man, what you—?"

I flashed the Lucille pix. "Seen her?"

Purse debris zoomed back; High Yellow chased Bennies with coffee.

"I said, have you seen her?"

High Yellow: "No, but this other po-lice been—"

The dark girl shushed her—I felt the nudge.

"What 'other police'? And don't you lie to me."

High Yellow: " 'Nuther officer was aroun' asking questions 'bout that girl. He didn' have no photographs, but he had this, this . . . po-lice sketch, he called it. Very same girl, good picture if you asks me."

"Was he a young man? Sandy-haired, late twenties?"

"That's right. He had this big pom-po-dour that he kept playin' with."

Junior—maybe working off a Bureau likeness sheet. "What kind of questions did he ask you?"

"He ask did that mousy little white girl ho' roun' here. I say, 'I don't know.' He ask did I work the bars down here, and I say yes. He ask 'bout some Peepin' Tom, I say I don't know 'bout no jive Peepin' Tom."

Brace the dark girl: "He asked you the same questions, right?"

"Tha's right, an' I told him the same answers, which is the righteous whole truth."

"Yeah, but *you* nudged your friend here, which means *you* told her something else about that policeman, because *you* are the one acting hinky. Now spill before I find something else in your purse."

Cop-hater rumbles—the whole room. "Tell me, goddamn it."

High Yellow: "Lynette tol' me she see that po-liceman shake down a man in Bido Lito's parking lot. Colored man, an' Lynette say the pom-podour cop take money from him. Lynette say she see that same po-lice at Bido's talkin' to that pretty-boy blond po-liceman who works for that mean Mr. Dudley Smith, who jist loves to have his strongarm men roust colored people. Ain' all that whooole truth, Lynette?"

"Sho' is, sugar. The whoooole truth, if I'm lyin', I'm flyin'."

Flying:

Junior—shakedown artist?—"If you want to steal, steal big." "Pretty-boy blond cop"—??????

"Who was the colored man at Bido Lito's?"

Lynette: "I don't know, an' I ain't seen him before or since."

"What did you mean by 'shakedown'?"

"I mean he put the arm on that poor man for money, and he be usin' rude language besides."

"Give me a name for that blond cop."

"Ain' got a name, but I seen him with Mr. Smith, and he so cute I *give* it free to him."

Lynette laughed; High Yellow howled. The whole room laughed— at me.

Bido Lito's, 68th and Central—closed. Mark it: a lead on crazy man Junior.

I staked the parking lot—no suspicious shit—music out a door down the block. Squint, catch the marquee: "Club Alabam—Art Pepper Quartet Nitely." Art Pepper—*Straight Life*—a Tommy K. smashed record.

Strange music: pulsing, discordant. Distance distorted sounds—I synced a beat to people talking on the sidewalk. Hard to see faces, easy to imagine them: I made all the women Glenda. A crescendo, applause—I hit my brights to get a real look. Too bright—jigs passing a reefer—gone before I could blink.

I pulled up and walked in. Dark—no doorman/cover charge—four white guys on stage, backlit. Sax, bass, piano, drums—four beats—not music, not noise. I bumped a table, bumped a left-behind jug.

My eyes adjusted—bourbon and a shot glass right there. I grabbed a chair, watched, *listened.*

Sax solo—honks/blats/wails—I poured a shot, downed it.

Hot—I thought of Meg—juicehead parents scared us both away from liquor. Match flare: Tommy Kafesjian at ringside. Three shots quick—my breath timed itself to the music. Crescendos, no break, a ballad.

Pure beautiful: sax, piano, bass. Whispers: "Champ Dineen," "The Champ, that's his." Tommy's broken record: *Sooo Slow Moods.*

One more shot—bass notes—skipped heartbeats. Glenda, Meg, Lucille—some booze reflex warmed their faces.

Exit-door light—Tommy K. walking out. Validate this slumming, pure cop instincts:

Peeper/prowler/B&E man—all one man. Jazz fiend/voyeur—the noise fed the watching.

Noise/music—go, follow it—

Hot-sheet row—motels pressed tight—one long block. Stucco dives— bright colors—an alley behind them.

Ladder roof access: I parked, climbed, looked.

Vertigo—noise/music and liquor still had me. Slippery, careful, a perch—pure balls made me choose a high signpost. A breeze, a view: windows.

A few showing light: fuck flop rooms—bare walls—nothing else. I shivered out the booze—the music hit harder.

Lights on and off. Bare walls—no way to see faces, easy to imagine:

Glenda killing that pimp.

Glenda naked—Meg's body.

Chills—I got the car, cranked the heater, drove—

Meg's—dawn—no lights on. Hollywood—Glenda's place dark. Back to my place—a letter from Sam G. in the mailbox.

USC season tickets. A P.S.: "Thanks for proving jungle bunnies can fly." Noise/music—I smashed the mailbox two-handed.

L.A. *Times,* 11/4/58:

COUNCILMANIC RACE ANTICLIMACTIC; CHAVEZ RAVINE SWING VOTE GAINED BY DEFAULT

A down to the wire run was expected in the race for Fifth District City Councilman; today's election vote should have been nip and tuck. But while state, municipal, and judicial candidates nervously awaited poll news, incumbent Republican Councilman Thomas Bethune relaxed with his family at his Hancock Park home.

Up until last week, Bethune was hotly challenged by Morton Diskant, his liberal Democratic opponent. Diskant, stressing his credentials as a civil liberties lawyer, sought to portray Bethune as a pawn of the Los Angeles political establishment, his chief focus the Chavez Ravine issue. The Fifth Councilmanic District, which has a 25% Negro population, became a litmus test: how would voters respond when an entire campaign revolved around whether or not to relocate impoverished Latin Americans in an attempt to create space for a Los Angeles Dodgers ballpark?

Diskant pressed that issue, along with what he called "collateral matters": the allegedly overzealous enforcement measures of the Los Angeles Police Department and the "Gas Chamber Happy" Los Angeles District Attorney's Office. More than a litmus test, the Fifth District race was crucial to the passage of the Chavez Ravine bond issue: a Council straw vote showed that body currently standing 5 to 4 in favor, with all other Republican and Democratic candidates vying for Council seats also voicing their approval of the measure. Thus, only Diskant's election could force a City Council deadlock and legally postpone the wedding of Chavez Ravine and the Dodgers for some time.

But it was not to be. Last week, Diskant dropped out of the race, just as straw polls began to show him pulling ahead of his incumbent opponent. The Chavez Ravine Council vote will remain 5 to 4 in favor, and the bond issue is expected to be voted into law in mid-November. Diskant cited "personal reasons" as his motive for withdrawing; he did not elaborate further. Speculation in political circles has raged, and U.S. Attorney Welles Noonan, Chief Federal Prosecutor for the greater Southern California District, voiced this opinion to Times reporter Jerry Abrams: "I won't name names, and frankly I can't name names. But Diskant's withdrawal smacks of some sort of coercion. And I'll go on the record as a Democrat and a determined crimefighter with credentials including work for the McClellan Senate Rackets Committee: you can be both a moderate liberal and a foe of crime, as my good friend Senator John Kennedy proved by his work for the Committee."

Noonan declined to answer questions on his own political ambitions, and Morton Diskant could not be reached to voice his response. Councilman Bethune told the Times: "I hated to win this way, because I relish a good fight. Get those hot dogs and peanuts ready, [Dodger organization president] Walter O'Malley, because I'm putting in for season tickets. Play ball!"

L.A. *Mirror,* 11/5/58:

GALLAUDET ELECTED D.A.; YOUNGEST IN CITY'S HISTORY

It was no surprise: Robert "Call Me Bob" Gallaudet, 38, a former LAPD and DA's Bureau officer who went to USC Law School nights, was elected Los Angeles District Attorney yesterday, topping a six man field with 59% of the total votes cast.

His election marks a fast rising career streaked with good luck, chiefly the resignation of former DA Ellis Loew last April. Gallaudet, then Loew's favored prosecutor, was appointed interim DA by the City Council, largely, it was believed, because of his friendship with LAPD Chief of Detectives Edmund Exley. A Republican, Gallaudet is expected to run for State Attorney General in 1960. He is a staunch law and order advocate, and a frequent target of death penalty repeal groups, who consider him overzealous in his recommendations of capital punishment.

A recent barb was thrown at the new District Attorney from another angle. Welles Noonan, U.S. Attorney for the Southern California Federal District and often spoken of as Gallaudet's likely opponent in the Attorney General's race, told the *Mirror:* "DA Gallaudet's support of the District Gambling Bill currently stalled in the California State Legislature stands out as a startling contradiction to this man's supposedly bedrock anti-crime philosophy. That bill [i.e.—proposed legitimate gambling zones confined to certain areas surveilled by local police agencies, where cards, slot machines, off track betting and other games of chance will be legal, but heavily surtaxed for State revenue purposes] is a moral outrage that condones compulsive gambling under the guise of political good. It will become a magnet for organized crime, and I exhort DA Gallaudet to retract his support of the measure."

At a press conference to announce his upcoming victory gala at the Ambassador Hotel's Cocoanut Grove two nights from now, Gallaudet pooh-poohed his critics, chiefly U.S. Attorney Noonan. "Look, he's running against me for A.G. already, and I just got elected to *this* job. On my political future: no comment. My comment on my election as Los Angeles District Attorney: watch out, criminals. And take heart, Angelenos: I'm here to make this city a peaceful, safe haven for all its law-abiding citizens."

Hush-Hush Magazine, 11/6/58:

HELLO DODGERS!!!
ADIOS HUDDLED MASSES!!!

Dig it, kats and kittens, chicks and charlies: we love the national pastime as much as you do, but enough is enough. Doesn't that great lady the Statue of Liberty have some kind of rebop inscribed by her tootsies? Something like: "Give us your poor, huddled, wretched masses yearning to be free?" Look, east coast geography isn't our strong suit, and we can tell you're tired of this patriotic shtick already. Look, *everybody* wants a bonaroo home for the Dodgers, us included. *But*—iconoclasm dictates that we take a different tack, if only for the sake of our circuitously circling circulation. Social protest from *Hush-Hush!* They said it couldn't happen! Remember, dear reader, you heard it first here!

Dig: The L.A. City Council is set to boot an egregiously entrenched enclave of impecunious, impoverished, impetuously machismo mangled Mexican-Americans from their sharecropper shingle shacks in that shady, smog-shrouded Shangri-La Chavez Ravine!!! Those pennant flopper, fly ball dropper L.A. Dodgers are moving in as soon as the dust clears and a stadium is built—and they'll have a new home from which to rule the National League cellar!!! Dig it!! You're happy, we're happy!! Go, Dodgers!!! But what will happen to those dourly dispossessed, Dodger doomed delinquents: the maladroitly mismanaged Mexicans?

Digsville: The California State Bureau of Land and Way is granting shack dwellers $10,500 per family relocation expenses, roughly ½ the cost of a slipshod, slapdash slum pad in such colorful locales as Watts, Willowbrook and Boyle Heights. The Bureau is also enterprisingly examining dervishly developed dump dives preferred by rapaciously rapid real estate developers: would-be Taco Terraces and Enchilada Estates where Burrito Bandits bounced from shamefully sheltered Chavez Ravine could live in jerry-rigged slum splendor, frolicking to fleabag firetrap fandangos!

Dig, we've heard that among the sites being considered are converted horse paddock–jail cells once used to house Japanese internees during World War II, and a converted bungalow motel in Lynwood, replete with heart shaped beds and cheesy gilt-edged mirrors. Say! Those places sound like the office here at *Hush-Hush!!!*

Hey! The rent here on the sin-tillating, salivatingly sensational Sunset Strip has steadily steepened—and we've heard that several dismayingly disgusted dispossessees have put in for their money and moved back to Mexico ahead of the general eviction date, leaving behind abandoned shacks! Hey—*Hush-Hush* could move its operations into them! As a result, we could charge a lower price for this rag! If you believe that, we'll sell you a Pendejo Penthouse and a brand new Chorizo Chevrolet!

But, to close on a more serious note, it appears that the L.A. powers-that-be have a front man chatting up the many remaining Chavez Ravine dwellers, passing out trinkets and doing his best to convince them to move out before the established eviction date without seeking legal injunctions. That man: popular bantamweight battler Reuben Ruiz, currently ranked 8th by *Ring* Magazine, a man whom *Hush-Hush* hastens to charge with a checkably checkered past.

Item:

Reuben Ruiz served time at the Preston Reformatory for juvenile burglary.

Item:

Reuben Ruiz has three brothers: Ramon, Reyes and Reynaldo—!God!—alliteration to make *Hush-Hush* proud!—and all three men have burglary and/or grand theft auto convictions on their records.

Item:

Reuben Ruiz was a guarded witness during Federal bright boy Welles Noonan's recently short lived boxing probe. (You recall that probe, hepcats: another witness jumped out the window while the LAPD detective guarding him resided in Snooze City.)

Item:

Reuben Ruiz was spotted a few days ago, lunching at the Pacific Dining Car with DA Bob Gallaudet and City Councilman Thomas Bethune. A late breaking extra, on the Q.T. and *very* Hush-Hush:

Reuben Ruiz' brother Ramon was arrested for grand theft auto several days before, but now the charges have been mysteriously dropped. . . .

A captivatingly corrosive coercion conclusion to consider:

Is Reuben Ruiz a bagman–P.R. man for the DA's Office and City Council? Does Ruiz' hellacious hermano rowdy Ramon owe his freedom to Reuben's politically prudent pandering? Will Reuben's extra-curricular efforts extricate his lethal left hook when he fights tough Stevie Moore at the Olympic next week?

Remember, dear reader, you heard it first here: off the record, on the Q.T. and *very* Hush-Hush.

"Crimewatch" Feature, *Hush-Hush* Magazine, 11/6/58:

FUR FLIES FURTIVELY OUT OF FUR KING'S FREEZERS—FUR WHERE?

You all know Sol "The Fur King" Hurwitz, hepcats: he does his own commercials on TV's Spade Cooley Show. His running gag is an animated snowstorm descending on Grauman's Chinese Theatre while unprepared Angelenos shiver in Bermuda shorts. He cuts these commercials on a sound stage made up like an igloo, with his marionette mascot Maurizio Mink supplying a hard sell Greek chorus: scientists are predicting a new ice age several centuries down the line, buy your Hurwitz Fur now at rock bottom low prices, easy monthly payments, store your fur during the "off season" at our San Fernando Valley fur warehouse free of charge. Follow the drift, kats and kittens? Sol Hurwitz knows that fur is a preposterous Southern California item, and he's poking fun at himself while neglecting to mention the basic fact of his business: people buy furs for two reasons: to look good and to show off how much money they have.

Dig that especially L.A. ethos? Good, you're on our wavelength. Dig further that Hurwitz' free storage come-on is good for lots of biz. Shiver, shiver, brrrr. Your beloved Charlie Chinchilla, Mindy Mink and Rachel Raccoon are safe with Sol, right? Well, up until October 25th you weren't whistling Dixie. . . .

On that fateful night, three or four daring desperadoes presumed to have toolmaking and electronics expertise *furtively fur*thered their criminal careers by overpowering a security guard and absconding with an estimated one million dollars in "Off-Season" storaged furs. Did you read the small print on your "free" storage contracts, kool kats? If not, dig: in case of theft, Hurwitz Furs' insurance carrier reimburses you at the rate of 25% of the estimated value of your lost stole or coat, and *fur*thermore, the police have no clues as to who these *fur*shtinkener *fur*tive *fur* heisters are!

Captain Dudley Smith, head of the LAPD's Robbery Division, told reporters at Van Nuys Station: "We know that a large flatbed truck was the means of entry and escape, and the regrettably injured guard told us that three or four men wearing stocking masks disabled him. A complex freezer locking system was dismantled, giving the robbers access to the furs. Technical expertise is an obvious strong point of this gang of thieves, and I will not rest until they are apprehended."

Assisting Captain Smith are Sergeant Michael Breuning and Sergeant Richard Carlisle. A surprise addition to the celebrated crimebuster's team: Officer John Duhamel, known to So Cal fight fans as "Schoolboy" Johnny Duhamel, former middleweight Golden Gloves champ. Captain Smith, Sergeant Breuning and Sergeant Carlisle refused to talk to *Hush-Hush,* but ace *Hush-Hush* scribe Duane Tucker cornered Officer "Schoolboy" Duhamel at last week's Hollywood Legion Stadium fistfest. Off the record, on the Q.T. and *very* Hush-Hush, Officer "Schoolboy" spoke out of school.

He called the robbery a baffler, and ruled out insurance fraud, even though Sol Hurwitz is rapaciously rumored to be a dice game degenerate. "Schoolboy" then bit his tongue and offered no *fur*ther comments.

In a *fur*ther development, a score of *fur*ious *fur*meisters picketed Sol Hurwitz' Pacoima scene-of-the-crime storage facility. With a scant 25% assessed value refund coming to them, these perplexed parents impatiently importuned Mindy Mink, Rachel Raccoon and Charlie Chinchilla:

Come home! It's 80 degrees and we're freezing without you!

Look for *fur*ther developments in upcoming Crimewatch features. Remember, you heard it *fur*st here: off the record, on the Q.T. and *very* Hush-Hush!

L.A. *Herald-Express*, 11/7/58:

U.S. ATTORNEY ANNOUNCES SOUTHSIDE RACKETS PROBE

This morning, in a brief, tersely worded prepared statement, U.S. Attorney Welles Noonan announced that Justice Department investigators assigned to the Southern California District Office would soon begin a "minutely detailed, complex and far reaching" probe into racketeering in South-Central Los Angeles. He called his investigation a "gathering of evidence aimed at establishing criminal conspiracies"; he said that his goal was to present "convincing evidence" to a specially convened Federal Grand Jury, with an eye toward securing major indictments.

Noonan, 40, former counsel to the U.S. Senate's McClellan Rackets Committee, said that his investigation would encompass crimes including narcotics trafficking, jukebox, vending machine and slot machine illegalities, and that he would "thoroughly explore" rumors that the Los Angeles Police Department allows vice to rage in Southside Los Angeles and rarely investigates homicides involving both Negro victims and perpetrators.

The U.S. Attorney declined to answer reporters' questions, but stated that his task force would include four prosecuting attorneys and at least a dozen specially selected Justice Department agents. He closed his press conference stating that he fully expects the Los Angeles Police Department to refuse to cooperate with the probe.

LAPD Chief William H. Parker and Chief of Detectives Edmund Exley were informed of U.S. Attorney Noonan's announcement. They declined to comment.

II

VAMPIRA

10

cope the party:

The Cocoanut Grove, a society band. Chief Parker, Exley—smiles for our boy: Gas Chamber Bob Gallaudet.

Drink waiters, dancing—Meg brought Jack Woods so she could mambo. Dudley Smith, Mayor Poulson, Tom Bethune—no thank-you to me for the tank job.

Newsmen, Dodger execs. Gallaudet grinning, bombed by flashbulbs. Mingle, look:

George Stemmons, Sr., two Smith goons: Mike Breuning, Dick Carlisle. Read their lips: FED PROBE, FED PROBE. Parker and Exley holding cocktails—talking FED PROBE—bet money. Meg danced Jack by— hoodlums still jazzed her—my fault.

Show-up time: I owed Bob congratulations. Better to wait, get him alone—*my* bad PR lingered. I watched the crowd, matched thoughts to faces.

Exley—tall, easy to spot. He'd read my 459 report: the Lucille/peeper leads, a bogus addendum—shitcan the job, it's dead-ended. He said keep going; some part of me rejoiced—I wanted to drag that family through the gutter. Both ends against the middle: I'd told Dan Wilhite I'd go easy.

Inspector George Stemmons, Sr., by the punchbowl—Junior twenty-odd years older. Junior missing since the Georgie Ainge roust—stalemate time—he knew Glenda Bledsoe killed Dwight Gilette. *His* Kafesjian report: fluff. No john/whore file checks, my Darktown scoop made him too busy: that shakedown outside Bido Lito's; that confab with a "pretty-boy blond cop." Pretty boy's ID: Johnny Duhamel, Dud Smith's new Mobster Squad lad.

Junior: no way to trust him; no way to dump him off the case just yet.

Solo now:

I checked the stationhouse lists—luck at University—john names, no hooker names connected. I ran them through the DMV and R&I—all phonies—most Vice cops didn't press for real IDs—no heart to ream pussy prowlers. Luck crapped out—I saved the names to check against—most johns kept the same alias.

Darktown strutter:

I questioned Western Avenue whores, three nights' worth—no Lucille pic IDs. I checked with the 77th Squad—still no locate on the peeper complaints. I peeped myself: the Kafesjian pad, car-radio jazz to kill boredom. Two nights—family brawls; one night, Lucille alone—a window striptease—the radio pulsed to her movements. Three nights total, no other watchers—make *me* the only voyeur. That Big Instinct confirmed: prowler/peeper/B&E man—all one man.

Homework, two nights' worth: Art Pepper, Champ Dineen—listening to what the burglar smashed. My phonograph, the volume torqued: that Instinct solid. One session pushed me back to the house—I tailed Tommy K. down to Bido Lito's. Tommy: *in with his own key,* weed bags stashed by slot machines. I called Lester Lake: glom me skinny on Tommy's known associates.

Happy chatter—the party crowd swelling. Meg and Jack Woods talking—they'd probably start up again. Jack muscled our rent; we cut a percentage deal: his dice game, our Westside vacant. Holding hands: my sister, my hood friend. Exhausted—I shifted to Glenda Overdrive—

Hooked bad—I couldn't subcontract the Hughes job. Moonlight work: I tailed her, watched for tails on me, ditched some maybes. Movie set skulks, rolling stakeouts:

Glenda raids Hughes' fuck pads; Glenda donates stolen food to "Dracula's" rest home. Frequent Glenda guests: Touch V. and Rock Rockwell—Georgie Ainge nowhere in sight. Last night, Good Deed Glenda: foie gras for the oldsters at the Sleepy Glade dump.

R&I—Bledsoe, Glenda Louise:

No wants, no warrants, no prostitution arrests. 12/46: ten days, juvie shoplifting. A Juvenile Hall file note: Glenda beat up an amorous bull dyke.

LAPD Homicide—Dwight William Gilette, DOD 4/19/55 (unsolved)—ZERO ON GLENDA LOUISE BLEDSOE.

Fake reports to Bradley Milteer: Glenda's thefts deleted, her publicity date lied off—a "friendly outing." Glenda Overdrive driving me: good scary/scary good.

I edged up to the crowd. Gallaudet had a new haircut: that Jack Kennedy/Welles Noonan style. A nod my way, but no shake—bad-press cops rated low. Walter O'Malley sidled by—Bob almost genuflected. Chavez Ravine, ballpark, ballpark—loud, happy.

"Hello, lad."

That brogue—Dudley Smith.

"Hello, Dud."

"A fine evening, is it not? Mark my words, we are celebrating the beginning of a splendid political career."

An envelope passed: Dodger man to DA's man. "Bob was always ambitious."

"Like yourself, lad. And does the prospect of a stadium for our home team thrill you?"

"Not particularly."

Dud laughed. "Nor I. Chavez Ravine was a splendid place to purchase spic trinkets, but now I fear it will be replaced by traffic jams and more smog. Do you follow baseball, lad?"

"No."

"Not interested in athletics? Is extracurricular money your only passion?"

"It's this Jew name I got stuck with."

Howls—his suitcoat gapped. Check the ordnance: magnum, sap, switchblade. "Lad, you have the power to amuse this old man."

"I only get funny when I'm bored—and baseball bores me. Boxing's more my sport."

"Ah, I should have known. Ruthless men always admire fisticuffs. And I phrase 'ruthless' as a compliment, lad."

"No offense taken. And speaking of boxing, Johnny Duhamel's working for you, right?"

"Correct, and a splendidly fear-inducing addition to the Mobster Squad he is. I've given him work on my fur-robbery job as well, and he is proving himself to be a splendid all-around young policeman. Why do you ask, lad?"

"His name came up. One of my men used to teach at the Academy. Duhamel was a student of his."

"Ahh, yes. George Stemmons, Jr., am I correct? What a memory for students past that lad must have."

"That's him."

Exley nailed me—a curt nod. Dud caught it: "Go, lad, Chief Exley beckons from across the room. Ah, the gaze of a shark he has."

"Good seeing you, Dud."

"My pleasure entirely, lad."

I walked over. Exley, straight off: "There's a briefing day after tomorrow. Nine o'clock, all Bureau COs. Be there—we're going to discuss the Fed probe. Also, I want you to get ahold of the Kafesjian family's tax records. You're an attorney—find a loophole."

"Income tax records require a Federal writ. Why don't you ask Welles Noonan? It's his district."

White knuckles—his wineglass shook. "I read your report, and the john names interest me. I want a trick sweep on Western and Adams to-morrow night. Set it up with University Vice, and detach as many men as you need. I want detailed information on Lucille Kafesjian's customers."

"Are you sure you want to risk riling that family with the Feds around the goddamn corner?"

"Do it, Lieutenant. Don't question my motives or ask why."

Pissed—I hit the lobby steaming. A phone, a dime—buzz the Bureau.

"Administrative Vice, Officer Riegle."

"Sid, it's me."

"Hi, Skipper. You telepathic? Hollenbeck just left you a message."

"Hold on, I need you to set something up first."

"All ears."

"Call University and set up a trick sweep. Say eight men and two whore wagons. Make it eleven P.M. tomorrow night, Western and Adams, Chief Exley's authorization."

Sid whistled. "Care to explain?"

BRAINSTORM:

"And tell the squad lieutenant I need a row of interrogation rooms, and tell Junior Stemmons to meet me at the station, I want him in on this."

Scribble sounds. "It's on paper. You want that message now?"

"Shoot."

"The Pawnshop Detail turned the Kafesjian silverware. Some Mexican tried to pawn it in Boyle Heights, and the shop owner saw our bulletin and stalled him. He's in custody at Hollenbeck Station."

I whooped—heads turned. "Call Hollenbeck, Sid. Tell them to put the Mex in a sweat room. I'll be right over."

"On it, Skipper."

Back to the party—Gas Chamber Bob swamped—no way to check out graceful. A blonde swirled by—Glenda—a blink—just some woman.

11

esus Chasco—fat, Mex—not my peeper. No rap sheet, a '58 green card running out. Scared—the sweat room sweats.

"Habla inglés, Jesus?"

"I speak English good as you do."

Skim the crime sheet. "This says you attempted to sell stolen silverware to the Happytime Pawnshop. You told the officers that you didn't steal the silverware, but you wouldn't tell them where you got it. Okay, that's one felony—receiving stolen goods. You gave your car as your address, so that's a misdemeanor charge—vagrancy. How old are you, Jesus?"

T-shirt and khakis—sweated up. "Forty-three. Why you ask me that?"

"I'm figuring five years in San Quentin, then the boot back to Mexico. By the time you get back here, you might win a prize as the world's oldest wetback."

Chasco waved his arms; sweat flew. "I sleep in my car to save money!"

"Yeah, to bring your family up here. Now sit still or I'll cuff you to your chair."

He spit on the floor; I dangled my handcuffs eye-level. "Tell me where you got the silverware. If you prove it, I'll cut you loose."

"You mean you—"

"I mean you walk. No charges, no nada."

"Suppose I don't tell you?"

Wait him out, let him show some balls. Ten seconds—a classic pachuco shrug. "I do custodian work at this motel. It's on 53rd and Western, called the Red Arrow Inn. It's . . . you know, for *putas* and their guys."

Tingles. "Keep going."

"Well . . . I was fixing the sink in room 19. I found all this nice-looking silver stuck into the bed . . . you know, the sheets and the mattress all ripped up. I . . . I figured . . . I figured the guy who rented the room went crazy . . . and . . . and he wouldn't press no charges if I swiped his stuff."

Grab the lead: *"What does 'the guy' look like?"*

"I don't know—a guy. I never seen him. Ask the night clerk, she'll tell you."

"She'll tell both of us."

"Hey, you said—"

"Put your hands behind your back."

Balls—two seconds' worth—another shrug. I cuffed him up loose—keep him friendly.

"Hey, I'm hungry."

"I'll get you a candy bar."

"You said you'd cut me loose!"

"I'm going to."

"But my car's back here!"

"Take a bus."

"Pinche cabrón! Puto! Gabacho maricón!"

A half-hour run. Praise Jesus: no backseat noise, no cuff thrashing. The Red Arrow Inn: connected cabins, two rows, a center driveway. A neon sign: "Vacancy."

I pulled up to cabin 19: dark, no car out front. Chasco: "I got my master key."

I unlocked his cuffs. High beams on—he opened 19, backlit nice.

"Come look! Just like I tol' you, man!"

I walked over. Evidence: doorjamb jimmy marks—*recent*—fresh splinters. The room itself: small, linoleum floor, no furniture. The bed: slashed sheets, ripped mattress spilling kapok.

"Go get the clerk. Don't run away, you'll piss me off."

Chasco hauled. I scoped the bed close up: fork holes in the mattress, stabs down to the springs. Semen stains—my peeper screamed CATCH ME NOW. I ripped off a sheet swatch—the jizz could be tested for blood type.

"No-good ofay trash!"

I turned around—"Ofay trash dee-stroy my nice bed!"—this jig granny flapping a rent card.

Grab it—"John Smith"—predictable—ten days paid up front, checkout time tomorrow. Granny popped spit; Chasco pointed outside.

I followed him. Jesus, eager: "Carlotta don't know who rented the room. She said she thinks it's a young white guy. She said this wino rented the room for him, and the tenant guy said he had to have room 19. She ain't seen the tenant guy herself. I ain't either, but listen, I know that wino. You give me five dollars and a ride back to my car and I find him for you."

Fork it over: two fives, the Lucille pix. "One for you, one for Carlotta. Tell her I don't want any trouble and ask her if she knows this girl. *Then* you go find me that wino."

Chasco ran back, passed the five, flashed the mugs—Moms nodded yes yes yes. Jesus, back to me: "Carlotta said that girl's like a once-in-a-while—she rent short-timer and don't fill out no rent card. She said she's a prostie, and she always ask for number 18, right next to where I found that nice silver. She said the girl likes 18 'cause she got a street view case the police show up."

Think:

Room 19, room 18: the peeper peeping Lucille's trick fucks. Room 19 Jimmy marks—make some third party involved?

Granny jiggled a tin can. "For Jehovah. Jehovah get ten percent of all rent money spent on this sinful premises tithed back to him. I gots the slot-machine gambleitis myself, and I kicks back ten percent of my winnings to Jehovah. You a handsome young po-lice, so for one more dollar for Jehovah I give you more skinny on that slummin', thrill-seekin' white ho' Hay-soos showed me them pictures of."

Fuck it, fork it—Moms fed the can. "I seen that girl at Bido Lito's, where I was indulgin' my one-arm-bandit gambleitis to tithe Jehovah. This other po-lice, he was askin' people at the bar 'bout her. I tol' him what I tol' you: she jist a thrill-seekin', slummin' white ho'. Later on, after hours, I seen that girl in the pictures do this striptease with this bee-you-tiful mink coat. That other po-lice, he saw it too, but he actin' cool, like he *not* a po-lice, an' he didn' even stop her from makin' that disgraceful display, *or* act like he was too hot and bothered."

Think—don't jump yet. "Jesus, go get me that wino. Carlotta, what did that policeman look like?"

Chasco breezed. Moms: "He had light brown hair done up with pomade, an' he maybe thirty years old. Nice-lookin', but not as high-steppin' as you, Mister Po-lice."

Jump: Darktown Junior lead number two. Reverse jump: Rock Rockwell at Fern Dell—some quiff said Ad Vice was working the Park. Junior copped to it—"a favor"— he owed a pal working Hollywood Vice.

Rattle rattle—I shoved Moms some change. "Listen, have you ever seen the man staying in this room?"

"Praise Jehovah, I seen him from the back."

"Have you ever seen him *with* anyone else?"

"Praise Jehovah, no I hasn't."

"When was the last time you saw the girl in my photographs?"

"Praise Jehovah, when she did that striptease at Bido's maybe four, five days ago."

"When was the last time she brought a trick to this front room here?"

"Praise Jehovah, maybe a week ago."

"Where does she solicit her tricks?"

"Praise Jehovah, I don't know."

"Has she brought the same man more than once? Does she have regular tricks?"

"Praise Jehovah, I has taught myself not to look at the faces of these sinners."

Chasco walked a piss bum up. "I don't know, but I think maybe this guy's not so sharp with questions."

"This guy": Mex, Filipino—grime-caked—a tough call. "What's your name, sahib?"

Mumbles, hiccups—Jesus shushed him. "The cops call him Flame-O, 'cause sometimes he sets himself on fire when he's drunk."

Flame-O flashed some scars—Moms took off going "Uggh." Jesus: "Look, I asked him 'bout that guy he rented the room for, an' I don't think he remembers so good. You still gonna drive me—"

Back to room 19—my blinders on. Throw the lock, eyeball it—zoom—a connecting door.

Room 19 to room 18—Lucille's preferred fuck spot. Jamb-ledge jimmy marks—different than the front door marks.

Think:

Peeper hits or tries to hit Lucille's room.

Peeper trashes his own room, leaves the silver, moves out panicked. Or: *different* pry marks on peeper's front door. Say somebody else broke in. Make some third party involved?

I rattled the connecting door—no answer. A shoulder push—slack, give, snap—I rode loose hinges into room 18.

Just like 19—but no closet door. Something else: ripples on the wall above the bed.

Up close: buckled wallpaper, paste spackling. A square indentation—perforated drywall underneath. Peeled wallpaper—one thin strip, follow the line:

The wall to the connecting door—a drop to the crack under the door. Odds on:

A bug—planted and removed, the mike above the bed—the peeper voyeurs Lucille, basic electronics skill—

I tore up the room—empty, zero, nothing. Number 19—dump it twice, closet swag: Jockey shorts tangling up a tape spool.

Panic move-out validated.

Moms and Jesus outside pitching tantrums.

I shoved through them double time. Granny chucked her tin can at me.

The Bureau—Code 3—a lab stop, orders: test the sheet-swatch jizz for blood type. My office, my old chem kit—dust the spool.

Smudges—no latent prints. Edgy now, I glommed a tape rig from the storeroom.

Nightwatch lull—the squadroom stood quiet. I shut my door, pressed Play, killed the lights.

Listen:

Static, traffic boom, window shimmy. Outside noises: business at the Red Arrow Inn.

Spook whores talking—ten minutes of pimp/trick rebop. I could *SEE IT:* hookers outside HER window. Silence, tape hiss, a door slamming. "In advance, sweet"—pause—"Yes, that means now"—Lucille.

"Okay, okay"—a man. A pause, shoes dropped, mattress squeaks—three minutes' worth. The tape almost out, groans—his climax. Silence, garbled words, Lucille: "Let's play a little game. Now I'll be the daughter and you'll be the daddy, and if you're *reeeeal* sweet we can go again no extra."

Traffic noise, driveway noise, breath. Easy to imagine:

That wall between them.

Surveillance not enough.

My peeper breathing hard—scared to bust down that wall.

12

Static garbled dreams: Lucille talking sex jive to *me*. The lab, my wake-up call—the jizz tested out 0+. Chills off a late phone stint: Hollywood Vice called Junior's queer roust story bullshit.

"Horse pucky—whoever told you that lied through his teeth. We're too busy with the Will-o-the-Wisp to work fruits, and none of our guys have popped Fern Dell Park chicken in over a year."

Coffee—half a cup—my nerves jangled.

The buzzer—loud.

I opened up—fuck—Bradley Milteer and Harold John Miciak.

Stern looks—their cop colleague in a towel. Miciak scoped my Jap sword scar.

"Come in, gentlemen."

They shut the door behind them. Milteer: "We came for a progress report."

I smiled—servile. "I have sources on the movie set accruing information on Miss Bledsoe."

"You've been in Mr. Hughes' employ for a week, Lieutenant. Frankly, so far you haven't 'accrued' the results he hoped for."

"I'm working on it."

"Then please produce results. Are your normal police duties interfering with your work for Mr. Hughes?"

"My police duties aren't quite normal."

"Well, be that as it may, you are being paid to secure information on Miss Glenda Bledsoe. Now, Mr. Hughes seems to think that Miss Bledsoe has been pilfering foodstuffs from his actress domiciles. A criminal theft charge will violate her contract, so will you surveil her even more diligently?"

Miciak flexed his hands—no gang tattoos.

"I'll begin that surveillance immediately, Mr. Milteer."

"Good. I expect results, Mr. Hughes expects results."

Miciak—jailhouse eyes, cop-hater fuck.

"First Flats or White Fence, Harold?"

"Uh, what?"

"Those tattoos Mr. Hughes made you burn off."

"Listen, I'm clean."

"Sure, Mr. Hughes had your record wiped."

Milteer: "Lieutenant, *really.*"

The geek: "Where'd you get that scar, hotshot?"

"A Jap sword."

"What happened to the Jap?"

"I stuck the sword up his ass."

Milteer, rolled eyes oh-you-heathens: "Results, Mr. Klein. Harold, come."

Harold walked. Fist signals back at me—pure White Fence.

Movie-set bustle:

Wine call—Mickey C. doling out T-Bird to his "crew." "Director" Sid Frizell, "cameraman" Wylie Bullock—poke the head monster's eyes out with a stick or a knife? Glenda feeding extras sturgeon, read *her* eyes: "Who's *that* guy, I've seen him before."

Rock Rockwell's trailer—tap the door.

"It's open!"

I walked in. Cozy: a mattress, one chair. Rockwell cranking push-ups on the floor. THE LOOK: cop, oh fuck.

"It's not a roust, I'm friends with Touch."

"Did I hear my name?"

Touch stepped out of the bathroom. No fixtures—just TV sets stacked high. "David, you didn't see those."

"See what?"

Rockwell slid up on the mattress; Touch tossed him a towel. "Meg's my first customer. She told me she wants to put TV's in all your furnished vacancies so she can raise the rent. Oh, excuse me. Rock Rockwell, David Klein."

No hello—Rock toweled off. Touch: "Dave, what's this about?"

Eyes on Rockwell—Touch caught the drift. "He can keep police-type confidences."

"I had some questions about activities in Fern Dell Park."

Rockwell scratched the mattress—Touch sprawled beside him. *"Vice-*type activities?"

I pulled the chair up. "Sort of, and it gets tricky because I think one of my men might be pulling shakedowns in Fern Dell."

Touch tensed up.

"What? What is it?"

"David, what does this man of yours look like?"

"Five-ten, one-sixty, long sandy hair. Sort of cute—you might like him."

No laugh—Touch coiled toward Rockwell.

"Come on, tell me. We go back—you know nothing you say leaves this room."

"Well . . . since it sort of involves Mickey, and you're his friend . . ."

Coax him: "Come on—like the magazine says: 'off the record.' "

Touch stood up, threw a robe on, paced—"Last week, that guy, that . . . policeman you just described to a T, he rousted me in Fern Dell. I told him who I was, *who I knew,* including Mickey Cohen, which *he* was oblivious to. Look, I was cruising—you know what I am, David—Rock and I, we have this arrangement—"

Rockwell—BAM!—out the door pulling on pants.

"It's the way our kind of people have to be to get along, and this . . . oh shit, this *policeman* said he'd seen me installing slots and coin hardware on the Southside a while back, and he said that Fed probe would happen and he'd snitch me to it if I didn't cooperate with him, so all right, *we* both know how to do business, David, but *this policeman* was acting so hopped-up and crazy that I *knew he didn't,* so I listened. He said, 'You must know Darktown pretty well,' I said yes, I got the impression he was messed up on Bennies or goofballs *or both,* and *then* he started rambling about—and I quote you, David—this 'gorgeous'—he actually used the word 'gorgeous'—other policeman working the Mobster Squad—"

"Gorgeous" Johnny Duhamel. My head throbbed—queer lilt synchronized—

"This policeman, he just kept rambling. He wouldn't tell me *details,* he just . . . kept rambling. He told me this crazy story about a whore in a mink coat stripping and how the gorgeous Mobster Squad cop got panicky and made her stop. David, here's where it gets strange and funny and sort of . . . well . . . *incestuous,* because the crazy policeman saw that the fur-coat spiel made me just a tad suspicious. He came on strong, and he found a gun on me and threatened me with a concealment charge, and I said the fur thing spooked me because Johnny Duhamel, that sort-of-famous ex-boxer, he tried to sell Mickey a bulk load of hot furs, which Mickey refused. The crazy cop, he laughed and laughed and started muttering 'Gorgeous Johnny,' and then he just sort of warned me off and walked away, and David, that policeman, he is one of us, if you catch my

drift, dear heart, and I only told you all this because our mutual friend Mickey played just a tad of a supporting role."

Touch—hands in his robe, out with a piece—bet he almost shoved it up Junior's ass.

Think:

Junior shakes down a guy at Bido Lito's.

Hobnobs with Johnny Duhamel—Bido Lito's.

Scopes out Lucille's fur strip—Bido Lito's.

More:

Junior—Kafesjian work fluffed off.

Fern Dell Park shakedowns—faggot Junior—Touch knew the turf—call it a maybe.

Touch: "I don't want you to tell Mickey what I told you. Duhamel just approached Mickey because he's Mickey. Mickey doesn't know anything about that extortionist policeman of yours, I just know it. Dave, are you listening to me?"

"I heard you."

"You won't tell Mickey?"

"No, I won't tell him."

"You look like you've seen a ghost."

"Lots of them."

Ghost chaser—

The Observatory lot—phone work.

Dime one: Jack Woods—set to bird-dog Junior post–trick sweep. Two: Ad Vice/Sid Riegle/confirmation: everything set, Junior told to stick at University Station. Orders: walk over to Robbery, skim the fur-heist file. Riegle: sure, I'll call you back.

Tick tick tick—my pulse outran my watch. Eleven minutes, Sid with stale news:

No suspects, fences leaned on—no furs surfacing. Three to five men, a truck, solid knowhow: electronics and toolworking. Dud Smith ruled out fraud—no profit motive—Sol Hurwitz packed low payoff-rate insurance. Sid—"Why the interest?"—cut him off, work dime three—a Personnel clerk who owed me.

My offer: your debt wiped for a file check: Officer John Duhamel. He agreed; I asked one question: did Duhamel possess technical expertise?

I held the line—twenty long minutes. Results: Duhamel, cum laude grad—engineering—USC, '56. Straight-A average—rah, rah, fellow Trojan.

Duhamel—possible fur thief. Possible partners: Reuben Ruiz and his brothers—Reuben and Johnny fought amateur together. Nix it on instinct: Ruiz boosted pads, ditto his brothers—the family topped out at auto theft. More likely:

Dudley co-opts Johnny to the fur heist; Johnny gloms some solo leads and gloms some furs. Smart into dumb—he offers Mickey Cohen the goods—the kid doesn't know Mickey's scuffling.

My scuffle—rat him to Dud?—think it through. *Tick tick tick*—not yet—too circumstantial. My priority: sort Junior and Johnny out, ease Junior off Glenda.

Ghost chaser.

Glenda.

Results.

Time before the trick sweep—tail her.

The park road—wait her out.

Her routine: drive home at 2:00, pilfer later. Time to kill, time to think—

Easy: my "crush" stretched me too thin—catch her stealing and snitch her—TODAY. Kicks: get her a Commie lawyer enraged at big money—Morton Diskant, just the ticket. Arraignment, trial—Glenda pays cunthound Morty off in trade. "Guilty," State time, Dave Klein there with flowers when they boot her.

Play the radio, drift.

Bop—maybe queer cops prowling Darktown—too jangly, too frantic. Skim the dial, ballads—"Tennessee Waltz"—Meg. '51, that song, the Two Tonys—Jack Woods probably knew the whole story. Him and Meg back on; I dumped a witness and she got suspicious—and Jack wouldn't shit her. She'd know, she'd be scared, she'd forgive me. Her and Jack—I wasn't jealous—call him dangerous and safe—safer than me.

Back to bop—jangly good now—think:

Lucille on tape: "I'll be the daughter and you'll be the daddy." Lucille, nude: fleshy like this boot camp whore I had. Big-band tunes, the war, schoolgirl Glenda—*close her out*—

Noon, 1:00, 1:30—I snoozed and woke up cramped. Stomach growls, a piss in the weeds. Early: her Vette zooming by with the top down.

I rolled—a brown Chevy cut between us—weird familiar. Squint, make the driver: Harold John Miciak.

Three-car tail string—absurd.

Up to the Observatory; down to street level. Glenda carefree, her scarf billowing. Pissed: hit the siren, ream that shitbird.

Miciak gunned it—bumper-to-bumper close. Glenda looked around; he looked around—sixty miles an hour, kill the siren, hit the mike: "Police! Pull over now!"

He swerved, banged the curb, stalled out. Glenda slowed down and stopped.

I got out.

Miciak got out.

Glenda watched—see it her way:

This big goon walks up shouting; this shoulder-holster shirtsleeves guy shouts back: "This is mine! You'll get your results! Tell your fucking boss that!"

The goon stutters, kicks the ground, U-turns off.

The cop goes back to his car—his B-movie goddess is gone.

Time to kill, time to figure her route. I tried due east: Hughes' Glendale fuck pad.

I drove there. Paydirt: a Tudor mansion flanked by airplane-shaped hedges. A circular driveway—her Vette by the door.

I pulled up. Drizzling—I got out and touched the rain. Glenda walked out carrying groceries.

She saw me.

I just stood there.

She tossed me a tin of caviar.

13

estern and Adams—the whores briefed nice—quasi-deputies for the night.

Bluesuits out in force: popping tricks, impounding trick cars.

Prostie vans behind Cooper's Donuts; Vice bulls bagging IDs. Men stationed southbound and northbound—hot to foil sex prowlers hot to rabbit.

My perch: Copper's roof. Ordnance: binoculars, a bullhorn.

Dig the panic:

Johns soliciting whores—cops grabbing them. Vehicles impounded, van detainment—fourteen fish bagged so far, prelim Q&A:

"You married?"

"You on parole or probation?"

"You like it white or colored? Sign this waiver, we might cut you loose at the station."

No Lucille K.

Some clown tried to run—a rookie plugged his back tires.

Epidemic boo-hoo—"DON'T TELL MY WIFE!" Leg-shackle clangs—the prostie vans shook.

Luck—whores mixed fifty-fifty: white girls, coons. Fourteen tricks arrested—all Caucasian.

Panic down below: Shriners bagged en masse. Five men, fez hats flying—a whore grabbed one and pranced.

I hit the bullhorn: "We've got nineteen! Let's close it down!"

The station—dawdle over—let Sid Riegle work setup. Luck: Junior's Ford by the squadroom door. Headlight signals goosed me walking in: Jack Woods, contingency tail man.

Squadroom, muster room, jail. I badged the jailer—*click/whoosh*—the door opened. Down the catwalk, turn the corner: the swish tank facing the drunk tank. Drunks and tricks hooting at the floorshow: drag queens masturbating.

Riegle outside the bars, marking nametags. He shook his head—too much noise to talk.

I scanned the fish—shit—nothing peeper-aged. Fuck it—I hit the show-up room.

Chairs, a height strip stage: one-way glass lit up harsh. Rap sheets and IDs laid out for me—I checked them against my john alias list.

No crossovers—expected—I'd run the fake names through the DMV. No real-name spinoffs; driver's license ages thirty-eight and up—my peeper ten years older minimum. Six tricks misdemeanor rap-sheeted—no Peeping Toms, burglars, sex fiends. A cover note: sixteen out of nineteen men were married.

Riegle walked in. I said, "Where's Stemmons?"

"He's waiting in one of the interrogation rooms. Dave, is the scoop on this real? J.C. Kafesjian's daughter is some kind of prostie?"

"It's true, and don't ask me what Exley wants, and don't tell me how the Department doesn't need this shit with the Feds nosing around."

"I was gonna mention it, but I think I'll stay on your good side. One thing, though."

"What's that?"

"I saw Dan Wilhite in the watch commander's office. Given what he is to the Kafesjians, I'd say he's more than a little pissed."

"Shit, that's more shit I don't need."

Sid smiled. "Yeah, but it's a duck shoot—they *all* signed the false-arrest waivers."

I smiled back. "Move them in."

Riegle walked back out; I grabbed the intercom mike. Shackle clang, shackle shuffle—whore chasers lit up on stage.

"Good evening, gentlemen, and listen closely"—the speaker kicked on loud.

"You have all been arrested for soliciting for purposes of prostitution, a California Penal Code violation punishable by up to a year in the Los Angeles County Jail. Gentlemen, I can make this easy or I can make this one of the worst experiences of your life, and the way I play it depends entirely on you."

Blinks, shuffles, dry sobs—sad sacks all in a row. I read my john list and scoped reactions:

"John David Smith, George William Smith—come on, be original. John Jones, Thomas Hardesty—that's more like it. D. D. Eisenhower—come on, that's beneath you. Mark Wilshire, Bruce Pico, Robert Normandie—street names, come on. Timothy Crenshaw, Joseph Arden, Lewis Burdette—he's a baseball player, right? Miles Swindell, Daniel Doherty, Charles Johnson, Arthur Johnson, Michael Montgomery, Craig Donaldson, Roger Hancock, Chuck Sepulveda, David San Vicente—Jesus, more street names."

Fuck—I couldn't scan faces that quick.

"Gentlemen, here's where it gets either easy or very difficult. The Los Angeles Police Department wishes to spare you grief, and frankly your *illegal* extramarital pursuits do not concern us that greatly. Essentially, you have been detained to aid us in a burglary investigation. A young woman known to occasionally sell her services on South Western Avenue is involved, and I need to isolate men who have purchased those services."

Riegle up on stage, mug shots out.

"Gentleman, we can legally hold you for seventy-two hours prior to arraigning you in Misdemeanor Court. You are entitled to one phone call apiece, and should you decide to call your wives, you might tell them that you are being held at University Station on one-eighteen-dash-six-zero charges: soliciting for purposes of prostitution. I understand that you might be reluctant to do that, so listen closely, I'll only say it once."

Rumbles—breath fogged the glass.

"Officer Riegle will show you photographs of that young woman. If you have purchased her services, take two steps forward. If you have seen her streetwalking, but haven't purchased her services, raise your right hand."

Pause a beat.

"Gentlemen, *legitimate confirmations* will get all of you released within several hours, *with no charges filed.* If none of you admit to purchasing this woman's services, then I will conclude that either you are lying or simply that none of you have ever seen her or dallied with her, which means in either case that all nineteen of you will be subjected to intensive questioning, and all nineteen of you will be booked, held for seventy-two hours and arraigned on soliciting charges. You will be held during that time in the facility that we reserve here for homosexual prisoners, i.e. the queer tank, where those nigger queens were shaking their dicks at you. Gentlemen, if any of you do admit to dallying with the young lady, and your statements convince us that you are telling the truth, you will in no way be criminally charged and your disclosures will be kept in the strictest confidence. Once we are convinced, you will all be released and allowed to claim your confiscated property and impounded cars. Your cars are being held at a County lot nearby, and as a reward for your cooperation you will not be charged the standard impound fee. Again: we want the truth. You cannot lie your way out of here by claiming that you fucked her when you didn't—your lies won't wash. Sid, pass the mugs."

Handoff: Riegle to a scrawny granddad type.

Dizzy, lawyer high—David Klein, Juris Doctor.

I looked down, held a breath, looked up: one Shriner and one lounge lizard stood forward. I checked driver's license pix and matched up names:

Shriner: Willis Arnold Kaltenborn, Pasadena. Lizard: Vincent Michael Lo Bruto, East L.A. A rap sheet check, paydirt on the wop: child-support skips.

Sid walked in. "We did it."

"Yeah, we did. Stemmons is waiting, right?"

"Right, and the tape recorder's in with him. The fourth booth down, he's there."

"Put Kaltenborn in number 5, and the greaseball in with Junior. Take the rest of them back to the drunk tank."

"Feed them?"

"Candy bars. And no phone calls—a smart attorney could wangle writs. Where's Wilhite?"

"I don't know."

"Keep him away from the sweat rooms, Sid."

"Dave, he's a captain."

"Then . . . shit, just do it."

Riegle strolled out—pissed. I strolled, itchy—over to sweat box row.

Standard six-by-eights, peekaboo glass. Booth 5: fez man Kaltenborn. Number 4: Lo Bruto, Junior, a tape rig on the table.

Lo Bruto rocked his chair; Junior squirmed. Touch V.'s take: Junior doped up at Fern Dell. The Ainge roust, a late make: dope eyes. Worse now—pin slits.

Open the door, slam it. Junior nodded—half lurch.

I sat down. "What do they call you—Vince? Vinnie?"

Lo Bruto picked his nose. "The ladies call me Mr. Big Dick."

"That's what they call my partner here."

"Yeah? The nervous, silent type. He must get a lot."

"He does, but we're not here to discuss his sex life."

"Too bad, 'cause I got time. The old lady and the kids are in Tacoma, so I coulda done the whole seventy-two hours, but I figured, why spoil it for the other guys? Look, I fucked her, so why beat around the bush, no pun intended."

I slid him cigarettes. "I like you, Vinnie."

"Yeah, then call me Vincent. And save your money, 'cause I quit on March 4, 1952."

Junior stripped the pack. Shot nerves: three swipes at a match.

I leaned back. "How many times did you go with that girl?"

"Once."

"Why just once?"

"Once qualifies as strange. More than once you might as well pop your old lady for all the surprises you get with whoo-ers."

"You're a smart guy, Vincent."

"Yeah, then why am I a security guard for a buck twenty an hour?"

Junior smoking—huge drags. I said, "You tell me."

"I don't know—I get to choke my mule on the Mighty Man Agency's time. It's a living."

Hot—I took off my jacket. "So you solicited that girl just once, right?"

"Right."

"Had you seen her around before?"

"No."

"Have you seen her since?"

"There hasn't been no since. Jesus Christ, I get paid, I go cruising for some strange and some punk kid cop strongarms me. Jesus fucking—"

"Vincent, what attracted you to that girl?"

"She was white. I got no taste for nigger stuff. I'm not prejudiced, I just don't dig it. Some of my best friends are nig—I mean Negroes, but I don't go for dark cooze."

Junior smoking—hot—he kept his coat on.

Lo Bruto: "Your partner don't talk much."

"He's tired. He's been working undercover up in Hollywood."

"Yeah? Wow, now I know why he's such a pussy bandit. Man-oh-Manischewitz, they say the snatch grows fine up there."

I laughed. "It does, but he's been working fruits. Say, partner, remember how you popped those queers in Fern Dell? Remember—you helped out that Academy pal of yours?"

"Sure"—dry-mouthed, scratchy.

"Jesus, partner, it must have made you sick. Did you stop for some poon on the way home, just to get rid of the TASTE?"

Sweaty knuckle pops—his sleeves dropped. WRIST TRACKS—he tugged his cuff links to hide them.

Lo Bruto: "Hey, I thought this was my show."

"It is. Sergeant Stemmons, any questions for Vincent?"

"No"—dry, fretting those cuff links.

I smiled. "Let's get back to the girl."

Lo Bruto: "Yeah, let's do that."

"Was she good?"

"Strange is strange. She was better than the wife, but not as good as the amateur stuff handsome here probably gets."

"He likes them *blond* and *gorgeous.*"

"We all do, but I'm lucky to get it plain old Caucasian."

Junior stroked his gun, spastic-handed.

"So how was she better than your wife?"

"She moved around more, and she liked to talk dirty."

"What did she call herself?"

"She didn't tell me no name."

Lucille's window striptease—use it. "Describe the girl naked."

Fast: "Chubby, low-slung tits. Big brown nipples, like she maybe had some *paisan* blood."

Tilt—he knew. "What was she wearing when you picked her up?"

"Hip huggers—you know, pedal pushers."

"Where did you screw her?"

"In the snatch, where else?"

"The location, Vincent."

"Oh. I . . . uh . . . I think it was a dive called the Red Arrow Inn."

I tapped the tape rig. "Listen close, Vincent. There's a man on this, but I don't think it's you. Just tell me if the girl talked up any similar stuff."

Lo Bruto nodded; I punched Play. Static hiss, "Now I'll be the daughter and you'll be the daddy, and if you're *reeeeal* sweet we can go again no extra."

I hit Stop. Junior—no reaction. Lo Bruto: "Boy, that sick kitten is just full of surprises."

"Meaning?"

"Meaning she didn't make me wear a safe."

"Maybe she uses a diaphragm."

"Nyet. Trust Mr. Big Dick, these girls *always* go the rubber route."

"And she didn't?"

"What can I tell you, she let this jockey ride bareback. And let me tell you, *paisan,* my big sausage *works*. Witness the goddamn offspring that got me slaving to feed them."

A guess: scrape jobs made Lucille sterile. "What about that tape?"

"What about it?"

"Did the girl talk up any of that daddy-daughter stuff with you?"

"No."

"But you said she talked dirty."

Tee-hee. "She said I was the biggest. I said they don't call me Mr. Big

Dick for nothing. She said she's liked them big since way back when, and I said, 'Way back when to a kid like you means last week.' She said something like 'You'd be surprised.' "

Junior tugged his cuff links. Tweak him: "This Lucille sounds like a Fern Dell Park faggot, partner. Big dicks, that's a queer fixation. *You've* worked fruits more than me, wouldn't you say so?"

Hot seat—Junior squirmed.

"Wouldn't you say so, Sergeant?"

"Y-yeah, s-sure"—hoarse.

Back to Big Dick. "So the girl wore pedal pushers, right?"

"Right."

"Did she mention a guy perved on her, maybe peeping her trick assignations?"

"No."

"And she wore pedal pushers?"

"Yeah, I told you that already."

"What else did she wear?"

"I don't know. A blouse, I think."

"What about a *fur coat?*"

Hophead nerves—Junior twitched a cuff link clean off.

"No, no fur coat. I mean, Christ, she's a Western Avenue whoo-er."

Change-up: "So you said the girl talked dirty to you."

"Yeah. She said Mr. Big Dick sure deserved his nickname."

"Forget about your dick. Did she talk dirty besides that?"

"She said she was screwing some guy named Tommy."

Tingles/goosebumps. "Tommy who?"

"I don't know, she didn't say no last name."

"Did she say he was her brother?"

"Come on, that's crazy."

" 'Come on'? You remember that tape that I just played you?"

"So that was a game. Daddy and daughter don't mean brother, and white people don't do that kind of stuff. It's a sin, it's an *infamia,* it's—"

Hit the table. *"Did she say he was her brother?"*

"No."

"Did she say his last name?"

"No"—soft—scared now.

"Did she say he was perved on her?"

"No."

"Did she say he was a musician?"

"No."

"Did she say he sold narcotics?"

"No."

"Did she say he paid her for it?"

"No."

"Did she say he was a burglar?"

"No."

"A peeper, a voyeur?"

"No."

"Did she say what he did?"

"No."

"Did she talk about her family?"

"No."

"Did she describe this guy?"

"No."

"Did she say he chased colored girls?"

"No. Officer, look—"

I slapped the table—Big Dick crossed himself.

"Did she mention a man named Tommy Kafesjian?"

"No."

"Fur coats?"

"No."

"Fur-coat robberies?"

Junior squirming, scratching his hands.

"Officer, she just said she was banging this guy Tommy. She said he wasn't that good, but he turned her out, and you always pack a torch for the guy who took your cherry."

I froze.

Junior jumped bolt upright—that cuff link rolled under the door.

Itchy scratchy nerves—he jerked the door open. Standing outside: Dan Wilhite. Hall speaker blinks—he'd heard.

"Klein, come here."

I stepped forward. Wilhite jabbed my chest—I bent his hand back. *"This is my case. You don't like it, take it up with Exley."*

Narco goons right there—I let him go. Junior tried to waltz—I pulled him back.

Wilhite—pale, popping spit bubbles.

His boys flushed—wicked pissed, spoiling to trash me.

Lo Bruto: "Jesus, I'm hungry."

I shut the door.

"Hey, I'm starved. Can I have a sandwich or something?"

I hit the intercom. "Sid, bring the other man in."

Lo Bruto out, Kaltenborn in: this fat geek wearing a fez. Junior sulked and hid his eyes.

The geek—"Please, I don't want any trouble"—his voice half-ass familiar.

I hit Play.

Lucille: "In advance, sweet." Pause. "Yes, that means *now*."

Kaltenborn winced—hot potato.

Pause, "Okay, okay"—*more* familiar. Mattress squeaks, grunts— Fats sobbed along.

Lucille: "Let's play a little game. Now I'll be the daughter and you'll be the daddy, and if you're *reeeeal* sweet we can go again no extra."

Big sobs.

I pushed Stop. "Was that you, Mr. Kaltenborn?"

Sobs, nods. Junior squirmed—junkie shitbird.

"Quit crying, Mr. Kaltenborn. The sooner you answer my questions, the sooner we'll let you go."

His fez slid down cockeyed. "Lydia?"

"What?"

"My wife, she won't . . ."

"This is strictly confidential. *Is* that you on the tape, Mr. Kaltenborn?"

"Yes, yes it is. Did . . . did the police record that . . ."

"That *illegal* extramarital assignation? No, we didn't. Do you know who did?"

"No, of course not."

"Did you play the daddy?"

Muffled, sob-choked: "Yes."

"Then tell me about it."

Fretting the fez—twisting it, stroking it. "I wanted to go again, so the girl put on her clothes and begged me to rip them off. She said, 'Rip my clothes off, Daddy.' I did it, and we went again, and that's all. I don't know her name—I never saw her before and I haven't seen her since. This is all just a terrible coincidence. That girl was the only prostitute I ever trafficked with, and I was at a meeting with my Shrine brothers to discuss our charity fish fry when one of them asked me if I knew where prostitutes could be procured, so I—"

"Did the girl talk about a man named Tommy?"

"No."

"A *brother* named Tommy?"

"No."

"A man who might be following her, or tape-recording her or eaves-dropping on her?"

"No, but I—"

"But what?"

"But I heard a man in the room next to us crying. Maybe it was my imagination, but it was as if he was listening to us. It was as if what he heard disturbed him."

Peeper bingo.

"Did you *see* the man?"

"No."

"Did you hear him say or mutter specific words?"

"No."

"Did the girl mention other members of her family?"

"No, she just said what I told you and what you played me on that tape. Officer . . . where did you get that? I . . . I don't want my wife to hear—"

"Are you *sure* she didn't mention a man named Tommy?"

"Please, Officer, you're shouting!"

Change-up: "I'm sorry, Mr. Kaltenborn. Sergeant, do you have any questions?"

Sergeant—this gun-fondling hophead—"N-no"—watch his hands.

"Mr. Kaltenborn, did the girl wear a FUR COAT?"

"No, she wore tight toreador pants and some sort of inexpensive wrap."

"Did she say she dug STRIPTEASE?"

"No."

"Did she say she frequented a Negro club named BIDO LITO'S?"

"No."

"Did she say that peeling off a HOT FUR COAT was ecstasy?"

"No. What are you—?"

Junior dropped his hands—watch for a quick draw.

"Mr. Kaltenborn, did she say she knew a GORGEOUS BLOND POLICE-MAN who used to be a boxer?"

"No, she didn't. I . . . I don't understand the thrust of these questions, Officer."

"Did she say she knew a shakedown-artist cop with a THRUST for young blond guys?"

RABBIT—

Out the door, down the hall—Junior, his piece unholstered. Outside, chase him, sprint—

He made his car—heaving breathless. I grabbed him, pinned his gun hand, bent his head back.

"I'll let you slide on all of it. I'll pull you off the Kafesjian job before you fuck things up worse. We can trade off right now."

Greasy pomade hair—he thrashed his head free. Stray headlights hit this dope face oozing spittle: "That cunt killed Dwight Gilette, and you're suppressing it. Ainge left town, and maybe I got the gun she fired. You're queer for that cunt and I think you pushed that witness out the window. *No trade,* and you just *watch* me take you and that cunt down."

I grabbed his neck and dug in to kill him. Obscene—his breath, his lips curled to bite. I edged back—slack—a knee slammed me. Down, sucking wind, kicked prone—tires spinning gravel.

Headlights: Jack Woods in tail pursuit.

West L.A., 3:00 A.M. Junior's building—four street-level units—no lights on. No Junior Ford parked nearby—pick the lock, hit the lights.

Aches groin to ribcage—hurt him, kill him. I left the lights on—*let him show.*

Bolt the door, walk the pad.

Living room, dinette, kitchen. Matched wood—fastidious. Neatness, grime: squared-off furniture, dust.

The sink: moldy food, bugs.

The icebox: amyl nitrite poppers.

Butt-filled ashtrays—Junior's brand—lipstick-smudged.

Bathroom, bedroom: grime, makeup kit—the lipstick color matched the butts. A waste basket: red-lip-blotted tissue overflowing. An unmade bed, popped poppers on the sheets. I flipped the pillow: a silencer-fitted Luger and shit-caked dildo underneath.

Paperbacks on the nightstand: *Follow the Boys, The Greek Way, Forbidden Desire.*

A padlocked trunk.

A wall photo: Lieutenant Dave Klein in LAPD dress blues. Track queer thinking, zoooom:

I'm not married.

No woman heat pre-Glenda.

Meg—he *couldn't* know.

The Luger smiling—"Go ahead, shoot something."

I fired, point-blank silent: shattered glass/ripped plaster/ripped ME. I shot the trunk—splinters/cordite haze—the lock flew.

I tore in. Neat paper stacks—fastidious Junior. Slow, inventory them pro—

Carbons:

Johnny Duhamel's Personnel file. Dudley Smith fitness reports—all Class A. Co-opt requests—Johnny to the fur job—fur-heist references checkmarked. Strange: Johnny *never* worked Patrol—he moved straight to the Bureau post-Academy.

More Duhamel—boxing programs—beefcake deluxe. Academy papers, Evidence 104—Junior told Reuben Ruiz he taught Johnny. Straight A's, blind fag love—Duhamel's prose style stunk. More fur-job paper: Robbery reports, figure Junior scooped Dudley—*he* made Johnny as the thief and Dud never tumbled.

A formal statement: Georgie Ainge rats Glenda on the Dwight Gilette 187. Lieutenant D. D. Klein suppresses the evidence; Junior tags the motive: lust. Grab those pages, safe-deposit-box info underneath: figure Junior had backup statements stashed at some bank. No mention of the gun or Glenda's prints on a gun—maybe Junior stashed the piece as a hole card.

Plaster dust settling—my shots grazed some pipes. Miscellaneous folders, file cards:

Folder number one—Chief Ed Exley clippings—the Nite Owl job. Number two—odd Exley cases '53–'58. Concise—the *Times, Herald*—fastidious.

WHY?

The cards—LAPD FIs—four-by-six field questioning forms. "Name," "Location," "Comments"—filled in shorthand. I read through them and interpreted:

All locations "F.D.P."—make that Fern Dell Park. Initials, no names. Numbers—California Penal Code designations—lewd and lascivious behavior.

Comments: homo coitus interruptus, Junior levies on-the-spot fines—cash, jewelry, reefers.

Sweaty, close to breathless. Three cards clipped together—initials "T.V." Comments: the Touch Vecchio roust—credit Junior with extortion skill:

Touch calls Mickey C. power-broke and desperate. He's hot to do something "on his own"; he's got his own shakedown gig brewing. Feature: Chick Vecchio to pork famous women; Touch to pork celebrated fruits. Pete Bondurant to take pix and apply the strongarm: cough up or *Hush-Hush* gets the negatives.

Chills—bad juju. The phone—once, stop, once—Jack's signal.

I grabbed the bedside extension. "Yeah?"

"Dave, listen. I tailed Stemmons to Bido Lito's. He met J.C. and Tommy Kafesjian in this back room they've got there. I saw them shake him for a wire, and I caught a few words before they shut the window."

"What?"

"What I heard was Stemmons talking. He offered to protect the Kafesjian family—he actually said 'family'—from you and somebody else, I couldn't catch the name."

Maybe Exley—that clip file. "What else?"

"Nothing else. Stemmons walked out the front door counting money, like Tommy and J.C. just palmed him. I tailed him down the street, and I saw him badge this colored guy. I think the guy was selling mary jane, and I think he palmed Stemmons."

"Where is he now?"

"Heading your way. Dave, you owe me—"

I hung up, dialed 111, got Georgie Ainge's listing. Dial it, two rings, a message: "The number you have reached has been disconnected." Junior's story held: Ainge blew town.

Options:

Stall him, threaten to rat him as a homo. Maim him, trade him: depositions and print gun for no exposé.

Shit logic—psychos don't barter.

I doused the lights, packed the Luger. Kill him/don't kill him. Pendulum: if he walks in on the wrong swing he's dead.

Think—queer pinup fever—psycho Junior hates heartthrob Glenda.

Time went nutso.

My ribs ached.

The morning paper hit the door—I shot a chair. Bullet logic: this grief for a woman I never even touched.

I walked outside. Dawn—milkman witnesses nixed murder.

I dropped the Luger in a trashcan.

I primped—don't think, just do it.

14

knocked; she answered. My move—she moved first. "Thanks for yesterday."

Set ready: gown and raincoat. My move—she moved first. "It's David Klein, right?"

"Who told you?"

She held the door open. "I saw you on the set, and I saw you following me a few times. I know what unmarked police cars look like, so I asked Mickey and Chick Vecchio about you."

"And?"

"And I'm wondering what you want."

I walked in. Nice stuff—maybe fuck-pad furnished. TVs by the couch— Vecchio stash.

"Be careful with those televisions, Miss Bledsoe."

"Tell your sister that. Touch told me he sold her a dozen of them."

I sat on the couch—hot Philcos close by. "What else did he tell you?"

"That you're a lawyer who dabbles in slum property. He said you turned down a contract at MGM because strikebreaking appealed to you more than acting."

"Do you know why I was following you?"

She pulled a chair up—not too close. "You're obviously working for Howard Hughes. When I left him, he threatened to violate my contract. You obviously know Harold Miciak, and you obviously don't like him. Mr. Klein, did you . . . ?"

"Scare off Georgie Ainge?"

"Yes."

I nodded. "He's a pervert, and fake kidnaps never work."

"How did you know about it?"

"Never mind. Do Touch and his boyfriend know I scared him away?"

"No, I don't think so."

"Good, then don't tell them."

She lit a cigarette—the match shook. "Did Ainge talk about me?"

"He said you used to be a prostitute."

"I was also a carhop and Miss Alhambra, and yes, I used to work for a call service in Beverly Hills. A very expensive one, Doug Ancelet's."

Shake her: "You worked for Dwight Gilette."

Stylish—that cigarette prop helped. "Yes, and I was arrested for shoplifting in 1946. Did Ainge mention anything—"

"Don't tell me things you might regret."

A smile—cheap—not *that* smile. "So you're my guardian angel."

I kicked a TV over. "Don't patronize me."

Not a blink: "Then what do you want me to do?"

"Quit stealing from Hughes, apologize to him and fulfill the stipulations of your contract."

Her raincoat slid off—bare shoulders, knife scars. "Never."

I leaned closer. "You've gone as far as you can on looks and charm, so use your brains and do the smart thing."

Smiling: "Don't *you* patronize me."

That smile—I smiled back. "Why?"

"Why? Because I was *dismissable* to him. Because last year I was carhopping and one of his 'talent scouts' saw me win a dance contest. He got me an 'audition,' which consisted of me taking off my brassiere and posing for pictures, which Mr. Hughes liked. Do you know what it's like to get screwed by a man who keeps naked pictures of you and six thousand other girls in his Rolodex?"

"Nice, but I'm not buying."

"Oh?"

"Yeah, I think you got bored and moved on. You're an actress, and the style angle of jilting Howard Hughes appealed to you. You figured you could get yourself out of trouble, because you've been in shitloads of trouble before."

"Why, Mr. Klein?"

"Why what?"

"Why are you putting yourself to such trouble to keep me out of trouble?"

"I can appreciate style."

"No, I don't believe you. And what else did Georgie Ainge say about me?"

"Nothing. What else did the Vecchio brothers say about me?"

Laughing: "Touch said he used to have a crush on you. Chick said you're dangerous. Mickey said he's never seen you with a woman, so maybe that rules out the standard reason for your being interested in me. I'm only thinking that there must be a payoff involved somewhere."

Scope the room—books, art—taste she got somewhere. "Mickey's on the skids. If you thought you traded Hughes up for a big-time gangster, you're wrong."

She chained cigarettes. "You're right, I miscalculated."

"Then square things with Hughes."

"Never."

"Do it. Get us both out of trouble."

"No. Like you said, I've been in trouble before."

Zero fear—daring me to say I KNOW.

"You should see yourself on camera, Miss Bledsoe. You're laughing at the whole thing, and it's real stylish. Too bad the movie's headed for drive-ins in Dogdick, Arkansas. Too bad no men who can help your career will see it."

A flush—one split second. "I'm not as beholden to men as you think I am."

"I didn't say you liked it, I just meant you know it's the game."

"Like being a bagman and a strikebreaker?"

"Yeah, wholesome stuff. Like you and Mickey Cohen."

Smoke rings—nice. "I'm not sleeping with him."

"Good, because guys have been trying to kill him for years, and it's the people around him who get hurt."

"He was something once, wasn't he?"

"He had style."

"Which we both know you appreciate."

This portrait on a shelf—a ghoul woman. "Who's that?"

"That's Vampira. She's the hostess of an awful horror TV show. I used to carhop her, and she gave me pointers on how to act in your own movie when you're in someone else's movie."

Shaky hands—I wanted to touch her.

"Are you fond of Mickey, Mr. Klein?"

"Sure. He had it once, so it's rough to see him diving for scraps."

"Do you think he's desperate?"

"Attack of the Atomic Vampire?"

Glenda laughed and coughed smoke. "It's worse than you think. Sid Frizell is putting in all this gore and incest, so Mickey's afraid they'll have to book it straight into drive-ins to make a profit."

I fixed the TV pile. "Be smart and go back to Hughes."

"No. Frizell's directing some stag films on the side, though. He has a place in Lynwood fixed up with mirrored bedrooms, so maybe I could get work there."

"Not your style. Does Mickey know about it?"

"He's pretending he doesn't, but Sid and Wylie Bullock have been talking it up. Mr. Klein, what are you going to do about this?"

Shelves packed tight—college texts. I opened one—comp stuff, doodling: a heart circling "G.B. & M.H."

"Yes, I stole those. What are you going—"

"What happened to M.H.?"

That smile. "He got another girl pregnant and died in Korea. David—"

"I don't know. Maybe I'll just pull out and set you up with an attorney. But the best you can hope for is a violated contract and no criminal charges."

"And the worst?"

"Howard Hughes is Howard Hughes. One word to the DA gets you indicted for grand theft."

"Mickey said you're friends with the new DA."

"Yeah, he used to study my crib sheets in law school, and Hughes put two hundred grand in his slush fund."

"David—"

"It's Dave."

"I like David better."

"No, my sister calls me that."

"So?"

"Let it rest."

The phone rang—Glenda picked up. "Hello? . . . Yes, Mickey, I know I'm late. . . . No, I've got a cold. . . . Yes, but Sid and Wylie can shoot around my scenes. . . . No, I'll try to come in this afternoon. . . . Yes, I won't forget our dinner. . . . No—goodbye, Mickey."

She hung up. I said, "M.H. took off, but Mickey won't."

"Well, he's lonely. Four of his men have disappeared, and I think he knows they're dead. Business was business, but I think he misses them more than anything else."

"He's still got Chick and Touch."

A breeze—Glenda shivered. "I don't know why they stay. Mickey has this scheme to have them seduce famous people. It's so un-Mickey it's pathetic."

"Pathetic"—Junior's notes confirmed. Glenda—shivers, goosebumps.

I grabbed her raincoat and held it out—she stood up smiling.

Touching her.

She slid the coat on; I pulled it back and touched her scars. Glenda: this slow turn around to kiss me.

· · ·

Day/night/morning—the phone off the hook, the radio low. Talk, music—soft ballads lulled Glenda sleepy. Losing her brought it ALL back.

She slept hard, stirred hungry. Yawns, smiles—open eyes caught me scared. Kisses kept her from asking; the whole no-payoff feel kept me breathless.

Pressed hard together—no thoughts. *Her* breath peaking—no thoughts. Inside her when her eyes said don't hold back—no queers, no peepers, no dope-peddler-daughter whores taunting me.

15

"**. . .** and they are out there, within our jurisdiction, superseding our jurisdiction. So far as we know, there are seventeen Federal agents and three Deputy U.S. Attorneys backstopping Welles Noonan. Noonan has not requested an LAPD liaison, so we must fully assume that this is a hostile investigation aimed at discrediting us."

Chief William H. Parker speaking. Standing by: Bob Gallaudet, Ed Exley. Seated: all stationhouse commanders and Detective Division COs. Missing: Dan Wilhite, Dudley Smith—Mike Breuning and Dick Carlisle pinch-hitting.

Eerie—*no* Narco men. Odd—no Dudley.

Exley at the mike: "The chief and I view this 'investigation' as conceived for political gain. Federal agents are not city policemen and certainly not conversant with the realities of maintaining order in Negro-inhabited sectors. Welles Noonan wishes to discredit both the Department and our colleague Mr. Gallaudet, and Chief Parker and I have agreed on measures to limit his success. I will be briefing each of you division heads individually, but before I commence I'll hit some key points you should all be aware of."

I yawned—bed-bruised, exhausted. Exley: "Division commanders should tell their men, both plainclothes and uniform: muscle and/or palm your informants and tell them not to cooperate with any Federal agents they might encounter. Along those lines, I want Southside club and bar owners visited. 'Visited' is a euphemism, gentlemen. 'Visited' means that the station COs at Newton, University and 77th Street should send intimidating plainclothesmen around to tell the owners that since we overlook certain infractions of theirs, they should overlook speaking candidly to the Feds. The Central Vagrant Squad will follow a parallel line: they will round up local derelicts to insure their silence vis-à-vis enforcement measures that quasi-liberals like Noonan might consider overzealous. The 77th Squad is to politely muscle white swells out of the area—we want no well-connected people federally entrapped. Robbery and Homicide Division detectives are currently sifting through recent Negro-on-Negro unsolved homicides, with an eye toward presenting indictment-ready evidence to Mr. Gallaudet—we want to counter Noonan's charge that we let colored 187s lie doggo. And finally, I think it's safe to say that the Feds might raid the slot and vending-machine locations controlled by Mickey Cohen. We will let them do this, and we will let Cohen take the fall. Central Vice has destroyed all the coin-hardware complaints that we've ignored, and we can always say that we didn't know those machines existed."

Implied: Mickey didn't yank his Southside coin. Warn him—again— tell Jack Woods to pull his Niggertown book.

Parker walked out; Exley coughed—crypto-embarrassed. "The chief has never liked white women fraternizing with Negroes, and he's hard-nosed the club owners down there who encourage it. Sergeant Breuning, Sergeant Carlisle—you men make sure that those club owners don't talk to the Feds."

Smirks—Dudley's boys loved strongarm. Exley: "That's all for now. Gentlemen, please wait outside my office, I'll be down to brief you individually. Lieutenant Klein, please remain seated."

Gavel bangs—meeting adjourned. A big exit; Gallaudet slipped me a note.

Exley walked over. Brusque: "I want you to stay on the Kafesjian burglary. I'm thinking of stepping it up, and I want a detailed report on the trick sweep."

"Why wasn't Narco represented at this meeting?"

"Don't question my measures."

"One last time: the Kafesjians are prime Fed meat. They're twenty years dirty with the Department. Rattling their cage is suicidal."

"One last time: don't question my motives. One last time: you and Sergeant Stemmons stay on the case full priority."

"Was there any specific reason why you wanted Stemmons on this job?"

"No, he just seemed like the logical choice."

"Meaning?"

"Meaning he works closely with you at Ad Vice, and he had excellent ratings as an evidence teacher."

Deadpan—a tough read. "I can't believe this personal-involvement routine. Not from you."

"Make it personal yourself."

Tight reins—don't laugh. "It's getting there."

"Good. Now what about the family's known associates?"

"I've got my best snitch looking into it. I spoke to a man named Abe

Voldrich, but I don't think he knows anything about the burglary."

"He's a longtime Kafesjian KA. Maybe he has some family background information."

"Yeah, but what do you want—a burglary suspect or family dirt?"

No retort—he walked. I checked Gallaudet's note:

Dave—

I understand your need to protect certain friends of yours who have Southside business dealings, and I think Chief Exley's fix on the Kafesjians is a bit untoward. Please do what you can to protect the LAPD's Southside interests, especially in light of this damn Fed probe. And please, without telling Chief Exley, periodically update me on the Kafesjian investigation.

Four days—chase evidence, get chased back. Sprint, get chased harder—pictures I couldn't outrun.

I told Mickey to pull his machines—he shrugged the whole Fed business off. Shit-for-brains Mickey—Jack Woods yanked his biz in record time. Chase Exley with paper: Kafesjian 459 PC, record detail. Covered: the peeper tape and Q&A—those two Lucille tricks.

Exley said keep going. Small talk: how's Stemmons handling the job?

I said just fine. Mental pictures: beefcake Johnny Duhamel, lipstick on cigarette butts.

Exley said keep going; I fed Bob Gallaudet information on the sly. Politics: he didn't want Welles Noonan reaping juice off the Kafesjians.

Chase, watch for chasers. No tails—near-crack-ups making sure. Exley/Hughes/Narco/the Feds: potential chasers, big resources.

Chasing evidence:

I staked the Red Arrow Inn—no Lucille, no peeper suspects. I checked 77th: no peeper FI cards found. Tri-State MO checks: zero. Lester Lake said scoop soon—"maybe." Chasing secrets, chasing pictures—

Solo trick rousts—no new Lucille fuckers confirmed. Western and Adams, points south—pressing for stories—I stayed high-octane juiced on that family.

Like Exley.

Call it lawyer style:

Disturbing the Kafesjians with a Federal narcotics probe in progress is certifiably insane. Edmund Exley is a certifiably brilliant detective with nationally recognized leadership skills. Narco was not present at Exley's Fed probe briefing. Narco is the most autonomous LAPD division. Narco and the Kafesjian family go back autonomously twenty-odd years. Exley knows that the Fed probe will succeed. Exley wants the probe diverted from the rank-and-file LAPD. Exley knows that heads must roll. Exley has convinced Chief Parker that the least damaging, most judicious move is to sacrifice Narco to the Feds—they can be portrayed as rogue cops autonomously run amok without severely damaging the overall prestige of the Department.

I didn't quite buy it—his hard-on for that family played too ugly.

Like mine, like Junior's.

George Stemmons II—*my worst pictures.*

I chased him four days—call him plain gone. Ad Vice: straight no-shows. The pad I trashed: locked tight. Darktown: no. His father's house: no. Fern Dell: no. Fag bars: no, he didn't have the guts to go that blatant. Long shot—Johnny Duhamel—his known haunts.

Personnel shot me his address. I checked it three days/nights running—no Johnny, no Junior. No way to catch Duhamel on duty—I couldn't tip Dudley Smith. An instinct said Junior's crush ran unrequited—Blond and Gorgeous didn't play fruit. Possible approach: Reuben Ruiz, Johnny's pal. Gallaudet turned him: front man set to oil the spics out of Chavez Ravine.

I fed Bob a snow job: Ruiz knew a guy I needed to lean on. Gallaudet: he's in training somewhere, check the Ravine in a few days—he'll be there working the crowd.

Tapped out.

Clay pigeon:

Junior nails Glenda dead—for Murder One. A nigger pimp victim—Gallaudet might not seek an indictment. But: Howard Hughes snaps his fingers; Gas Chamber Bob jumps. Snap—pick the judge, stack the jury—Glenda green-room bound. Accessory charges pending: on me.

The upshot:

Neutralize Junior. Hush up his Kafesjian dealings—if Exley tumbles, he'll rat Glenda to buy out. My buyout—Duhamel—feed him to Dudley, the *peak moment, work for Exley—Junior/Glenda insurance.*

I paid Jack Woods two grand: find me Junior Stemmens. My *skip trace—HER—a movie-set trailer late nights.*

Miciak kept quiet—we both made his tail strictly freelance. I wrote Milteer fake reports—Glenda fed me fake details. The set—Mickey's wino crew passed out. We talked low, made love and danced around IT.

I never said I knew; she never pressed me. Biographies, gaps: I hid Meg, she bypassed whoring.

I never said I kill people. I never said Lucille K. made me a voyeur.

She said I used people up.

She said I only bet on rigged games.

She said ranking cop/lawyer put some distance on white trash.

She said I never got burned.

I said three out of four—not bad.

III

DARKTOWN RED

irt roads, shacks. Hills trapping smog—Chavez Ravine.

Swamped—I parked long-distance and scanned it:

Geeks waving placards. Newsmen, bluesuits. Commie types chanting: "Justice, sí! Dodgers, no!"

Friendly throngs—eyes on Reuben Ruiz, gladhander. Sheriff's bulls, Agent Will Shipstad.

Ruiz—Fed witness?

I jogged into it—"Hey, hey! No, no! Don't drive us back to Mexico!" Badge out—blues eased me through.

Heckler hubbub:

Ruiz, fighting tonight—be there to cheer his opponent. The fascist Bureau of Land and Way: plans to relocate the spics to Lynwood slum pads. "Hey, hey! No, no! Justice, sí! Dodgers, no!"

Ruiz blasting bullhorn Spanish:

Move out early! Your relocation dough means Easy Street! New homes soon available! Enjoy the new Dodger Stadium YOU helped create!

Noise war—Reuben's bullhorn won. Deputies tossed tickets—spics genuflected, grabbed. I snatched one: Ruiz vs. Stevie Moore, Olympic Auditorium.

Chants, jabber—Ruiz saw me and bucked fans.

I shoved close. Reuben cupped a shout: "We should yak! Say my dressing room after my bout?"

I nodded yes—"Scum! Dodger pawn!"—no way to talk.

A quick run—the Bureau, my office.

A message from Lester Lake—meet me 8:00 tonight—Moonglow Lounge. Exley skirted Ad Vice—I gestured him over.

"I had a few questions."

"Ask them, as long as they're not 'What do you want?' "

"Let's try 'Why just two men on a case you're so hot to clear?' "

"No. Next question, and don't ask " 'Why me?' "

"Let's try 'What's in it for me?' "

Exley smiled. "If you clear the case I'll exercise a rarely used chief of detective's prerogative and jump you to captain without a civil-service listing. I'll rotate Dudley Smith into Ad Vice and give you the Robbery Division command."

Jig heaven—don't swoon.

"Is something wrong, Lieutenant? I would have expected you to express your gratitude."

"Thanks, Ed. That's a dandy carrot you just dangled."

"Given what you are, I'd say it is. Now I'm busy, so ask your next question."

"Lucille Kafesjian's the key to this thing. I've got a hunch that the family knows damn well who the burglar is, and I want to bring her in for questioning."

"No, not yet."

Change-up: "Give me the Hurwitz fur job. Take it away from Dudley."

"No, and no emphatically, and don't ask me again. Now, let's wrap this up."

"Okay, then let me lean on Tommy Kafesjian."

"Explain 'lean on,' Lieutenant."

"Lean on. Muscle. I fuck Tommy up, he tells us what we want to know. You know, outré police methods, like the time you shot those unarmed niggers."

"No direct approach on the family. Other than that, you have carte blanche."

Carte blanche shitwork, overdue: big fucking distractions.

Simple:

Lucille pix/tape rig/motel list—haul them southbound and ask questions:

Have you rented to her?

Has a man requested a room adjoining hers?

Have wino/bums rented rooms here by proxy?

Bad odds—call the Red Arrow her sole trick pad.

Southbound—Central Avenue all the way. Police intrigue, big-time:

IA cars trailing Fed cars—discreet. Bum rousts—Vag cops spread thick. Prostie wagons prowling for whores.

Feds:

License-plate checks outside bars and nightclubs.

Kibitzing a sidewalk crap game.

Staking out a swanky coon whorehouse.

Crew-cut gray suit Feds Darktown rife.

I stopped at 77th Street Station and borrowed a tape rig. Sweat box row was packed: jig-on-jig 187 "clearance." Feds outside with cameras—snapping cop IDs.

Shitwork now:

Tick Tock Motel, Lucky Time Motel—no to all my questions. Darnell's Motel, De Luxe Motel—straight nos. Handsome Dan's Motel, Cyril's Lodge—No City. Hibiscus Inn, Purple Roof Lodge—NO.

Nat's Nest—81st and Normandie. "Kleen Rooms Always"—brace the clerk.

"Yessir, I know this girl. She's a short-timer rental, an' she always ask for the same room."

I gripped the counter. "Is she registered now?"

"Nosir, an' not for maybe six, seven days."

"Do you know what she uses the room for?"

"Nosir. My motto is 'See no evil, hear no evil,' an' I adheres to that policy 'cept when they be makin' too much noise doin' whatever it is they be doin'."

"Does the girl ask for a front room with a street view?"

Shocked: "Yessir. How you know that?"

"Have you rented the room next to hers to a young white man? Did a bum request that particular room and register for him?"

Shut-my-mouth shocked—he dipped behind the counter and pulled out a rent card. "See, 'John Smith,' which in my opinion be an alias. See, he gots two days left on his rent. He ain' in right now, I seen him leave this morn—"

"Show me those rooms."

He beelined outside, fumbling keys. Two doors opened quick—good and cop scared.

Separate bungalows—no connecting door.

I caught up. Easy now—frost him with a ten spot. "Watch the street. If that white guy shows up, stall him. Tell him you've got a plumber in his room, then come and get me."

"Yessir, yessir"—genuflecting streetside—

Two doors—no mutual access. Side windows—the peeper could WATCH her. Hedges below, a loose-stone walk path.

Look:

A wire out HIS window.

Into HIS hedge, out, under the stones.

I grabbed it and pulled—

Stones flew—the wire jerked taut. Into HER room—under the carpet, yank—a spackle-covered mike snapped off the wall.

Walk the cord back:

HIS window—jam the ledge up—step in. Pull—*thunk*—a tape machine under the bed.

Empty reels.

Back outside, check the doors—no pry marks. Figure HE went in HER window.

I shut both doors and tossed HIS room.

The closet:

Soiled clothes, empty suitcase, record player.

The dresser: skivvies, jazz albums—Champ Dineen, Art Pepper. Title matchers—Tommy K.'s smashed wax duplicated.

The bathroom:

Razor, shaving cream, shampoo.

Pull the rug:

Girlie mags—*Transom*—three issues. Cheesecake, text: movie-star "confessions."

No tape.

Dump the mattress, punch the pillow—a hard spot—tear, rip—

One tape spool—rig it up for a listen fast—

Nerves—I fumbled the goods, smeared potential prints. Spastic-handed—loop the tape/push Start.

Rustles, coughs. I shut my eyes and imagined it: lovers in bed.

Lucille: "You don't get tired of these games?"

Unknown Man: "Hand me a cigarette"—pause—"No, I don't tire of them. You certainly know how to—"

Sobs—distant—motel room walls shutting *my* man out.

Trick Man: ". . . and you know that father-daughter games have staying power. Really, given our age variance, it's quite a natural bed game to play."

A cultured voice—Tommy/J.C. antithetical.

Sobs, louder.

Lucille: "These places are filled with losers and lonesome creeps."

No hink/no recognition/no surveillance fear.

Click—figure a radio—". . . chanson d'amour, ratta-tat-tatta, play encore." Blurred voices, *click,* Trick Man: ". . . of course, there was always that little dose you gave me."

"Dose": clap/syph?

I checked the reels—tape running out.

Sleepy voices jumbled—*more than a trick stand.* I shut my eyes—please, one more game.

Silent tape hiss—sleepy lovers. Hinge creak/"God!"—too close, too real—NOW. Eyes open—a white man standing by the door.

Fucked up blurry vision—I drew down, aimed, fired. Two shots—the doorjamb splintered; one more—wood scraps exploding.

The man ran.

I ran out aiming.

Screams, shouts.

Zigzags—my man bucking traffic. I fired running—two shots went wide. Aiming straight—a clear shot—this jolt: if you kill him, you won't know WHY?

Bolting traffic, sighting in on this white head bobbing. Horns, brakes—black faces on the sidewalk, my white speck disappearing.

I tripped, stumbled, ran. Losing him—black all around me.

Shouts.

Black faces scared.

My reflection in a window: this terrified geek.

I slowed down. Another window—black faces—follow their eyes:

A curbside roust—Feds and niggers. Welles Noonan, Will Shipstad, FBI muscle.

Grabbed, shoved—pinned to a doorway. Rabbit-punched—I dropped my piece.

Pinned—gray suit Fed gorillas. Welles Noonan sucker-punched me: spit in my face. His punch line: "That's for Sanderline Johnson."

17

he Moonglow—early for Lester. Jukebox tunes killed time.

Noonan, backed by music—replays still smelling his spittle:

Those Feds—cut-rate revenge. Back to Nat's Nest—prowl cars responding to shots. I chased them off and bagged evidence: records, skin mags, tape rig, tape.

Calls next:

Orders to Ray Pinker: dust both rooms, bring a sketch man—make the clerk face-detail the peeper. Mugshot checks later—pray for good eyes.

Jack Woods, glad tidings: he spotted Junior, tailed him for two hours and lost him. Busy Junior—three indy pusher shakedowns—Jack glommed descriptions and plate numbers.

Jack, verbatim: "He looked fried to the gills and fucking insane. I checked his car out while he stopped for cigarettes. You know what I saw in the backseat? A hypodermic kit, six empty tuna-fish cans and three sawed-off shotguns. I don't know what he's got on you, but in my opinion you should clip him."

The jukebox, unmistakable—Lester Lake's "Harbor Lights"—and not on my dime.

Bingo—Lester himself, oozing fear. "Hello, Mr. Klein."

"Sit down. Tell me about it."

"Tell you about what?"

"The look on your face and why you played that goddamn song."

Sitting down: "Just reassurance. Good to know Uncle Mickey keeps my tune in his Wurlitzers."

"Mickey should pull his boxes before the Feds pull him. What is it? I haven't seen you this spooked since the Harry Cohn thing."

"Mr. Klein, you know a couple of Mr. Smith's boys named Sergeant Breuning an' Sergeant Carlisle?"

"What about them?"

"Well, they workin' overtime at the Seven-Seven."

"Come on, get to it."

Breathless: "They goin' aroun' trying' to solve colored-on-colored killins, word is to forestall all this potential good Federal investigation publicity. You remember you ask me 'bout a maryjane pusher named Wardell Knox? You remember I tol' you he got hisself killed by person or persons unknown?"

Tommy K. snitched Knox to Narco—Dan Wilhite told Junior. "I remember."

"Then you should remember I tol' you ol' Wardell was a cunthound with a million fuckin' enemies. He was fuckin' a million different ladies, includin' this high-yellow cooze Tilly Hopewell that I was also climbin'. Mr. Klein, I heard them Mr. Smith boys been lookin' for me on account of some bogus rumor that I snuffed fuckin' Wardell, and it looks to me like they be measurin' me for a quick statistic. Now you want skinny on the fuckin' Kafesjians and their fuckin' known associates, so I got a real knee-slapper for you, which is that I just recently heard that crazy Tommy Kafesjian popped ol' Wardell roun' September, some kind of fuckin' dope or sex grievance, 'cause he was also climbin' that fine Tilly Hopewell on occasion."

Breathless/heaving.

"Look, I'll talk to Breuning and Carlisle. They'll lay off you."

"Yeah, maybe thas' true, 'cause ol' slumlord Dave Klein knows the right people. But Mr. Smith, he hates the colored man. An' I don' see you people pinnin' the Wardell Knox job on Tommy the K., your righteous motherfuckin' informant."

"So do you want to change the world or waltz on this thing?"

"I wants you to give me an extra month's free rent for all the fine skinny I gots on the fuckin' Kafesjian family."

"Harbor Lights" snapped on again. Lester: "And on that note, I heard the daughter's a righteous semipro hooker. I heard Tommy and J.C. beat up Mama Kafesjian and her like batting practice. I heard Madge—that's Mama—used to have a thing goin' with Abe Voldrich, he's this head guy in their dope operation, an' he runs one of their dry-cleaning joints on the side. I heard Voldrich dries up big bushels of mary jane in them big dryers they got at their plants. I heard the way they keep things copacetic with rival pushers is kickbacks from little Mickey Mouse independents that they tolerates, but no righteous organizations would ever try to infringe on the Southside, 'cause they knows the LAPD would come down hard just to keep them Armenian fucks happy. I heard the only humps they snitch to you people is the indies who won't kick back no operatin' trib-ute. I heard the family is fuckin' skin tight, even though they don't treat each other with so much fuckin' respect. I heard that outside of Voldrich an' this colored trim Tommy the K. goes for, the family only gots employees and customers, not no fuckin' friends. I heard Tommy used to be pals with some white kid named Richie, I don't know no last name, but I heard they blew these punk square horns together, like they pretended they had talent. That crazy-ass burglary you told me about—them chopped-up watchdogs an' stolen silverware an' shit—I heard jackshit 'bout that. I also heard you thinkin' 'bout raisin' the rent in my buildin', so I—"

Cut him off: "What about Tommy fucking Lucille?"

"Say what? I didn' hear nothin' like that. I said 'skin tight,' not fuckin' skin deep."

"What about this Richie guy?"

"Shit, I tol' you what I heard, no more, no less. You want me—"

"Keep asking around about him. He might connect to this peeper guy I've been chasing."

"Yeah, you mentioned that Peepin' Tom motherfucker, an' I knows how to improvise off what a man tells me. So I been askin' aroun' 'bout that, an' I ain't heard nothin'. Now, 'bout that rent increase—"

"Ask around if the Kafesjians have been looking for a peeper themselves. I have a hunch that they know who the burglar is."

"An' I got a hunch slumlord Dave Klein gonna raise my rent."

"No, and I'll carry you to January. If Jack Woods comes around to collect, call me."

"What about Mr. Smith's boys in hot pursuit of ol' Lester?"

"I'll take care of it. Do you know Tilly Hopewell's address?"

"Can my people dance? Have I strapped on at that love shack more than a few times myself?"

"Lester—"

"8491 South Trinity, apartment 406. Say, where you goin'?"

"The fights."

"Moore and Ruiz?"

"That's right."

"Bet on the Mex. I used to climb Stevie Moore's sister, an' she tol' me Stevie couldn't take it to the breadbasket."

I badged in ringside—late.

The sixth-round break—card girls strutting. Spectator chants: "Dodgers, no! Ruiz must go!" Boos, shouts: pachucos vs. Commies.

The bell—

Rockabye Reuben circling; Moore popping right-hand leads. Mid-ring clinch—Ruiz loose, the spook winded.

"Break! Break!"—the ref in and out.

Moore stalking slow—elbows up, open downstairs. Headhunter Reuben—near-miss hooks moving back.

Lazy Reuben, bored Reuben.

A snap guess: tank job.

Moore—no steam, no juice. Ruiz—lazy hooks, lazy right-hand leads.

Moore swarming and sucking in air; Reuben eating blockable shots—the coon wide open.

Ruiz—a lazy left hook.

Moore catching wind, his guard low.

Bullseye—the wrong man went down.

Pachuco cheers.

Pinko boos.

Reuben—this oh-fuck look—stalling the count. Dawdle time—he oozed over to a neutral corner slow.

Six, seven, eight—Moore up, wobbly.

Ruiz dawdling center ring. Moore backing up—shot to shit. Bomb range, Reuben bombs—wild misses. Ten, twelve, fourteen—real air whizzers.

Ruiz fake-gasping; fake-weary arms flopping dead.

Moore threw a bolo shot.

Rockabye Reuben staggered.

Moore—left/right bolos.

Reuben hit the canvas—eyes rolling, fake out. Seven, eight, nine, ten—Moore kissed Sammy Davis, Jr., at ringside.

Bleacher attack—get the Reds—spics tossing piss-filled beer cups. Placard shields—no help—the pachucos moved in swinging bike chains.

I hit an exit—coffee down the block, let things chill. Twenty minutes, back over—shitloads of prowl cars and Commies shackled up.

Back in—follow the liniment stench. Dressing rooms, Ruiz alone—wolfing a taco plate.

"Bravo, Reuben. The best tank job I've ever seen."

"Hey, and the riot wasn't so bad neither. Hey, Lieutenant, what did those back-pedal hooks tell you?"

I shut the door—noise down the hall—newsmen and Moore. "That you know how to entertain the chosen few."

Chugging beer: "I hope Hogan Kid Bassey saw the fight, 'cause the deal was Moore gets the bantam elimination shot and I move up to the feathers and fight him. I'll kick his ass, too. Hey, Lieutenant, we ain't talked since that night Sanderline jumped."

"Call me Dave."

"Hey, Lieutenant, a nigger and a Mexican jump out a six-story window the same time. Who hits the ground first?"

"I've heard it, but tell me anyway."

"The nigger, 'cause the Mexican's got to stop on the way down and spray *'Ramón y Kiki por vida'* on the wall."

Ha, ha—polite.

"So, Lieutenant, I know you saw Will Shipstad watchdogging me at the ravine. Let me reassure you and Mr. Gallaudet that I'm grateful for this what you call public-relations gig you got me, 'specially since it got my goddamn brother off another GTA bounce. So, yeah, I'm a Fed witness again, but Noonan just wants me to testify on some stale-bread bookie stuff, and I'd never snitch Mickey C. or your buddy Jack Woods."

"I always figured you knew how to play."

"You mean play to the chosen few?"

"Yeah. Business is business, so you fuck your own people to get next to the DA."

Smiling nice: "I got a trouble-prone family, so I gotta figure they're more important than Mexicans in general. Hey, I kiss a little ass, so that what you call them—slumlords?—like you and your sister can stay fat. You know, *Dave,* the fuckin' Bureau of Land and Way's been checking out these dumps in Lynwood. There's supposed to be some what you call converted whorehouse that these hard boys want to dump my poor evicted *hermanos* into, so maybe you and your goddamn slumlord sister can buy in on the ground floor."

Brains—fuck his bravado. "You know a lot about me."

"Hey, Dave 'the Enforcer' Klein, people talk about you."

Change-up: "Is Johnny Duhamel queer?"

"Are you nuts? He is the snatch hound to end all snatch hounds."

"Seen him lately?"

"We keep in touch. Why?"

"Just checking up. He's on the Hurwitz fur case, and it's a big assignment for an inexperienced officer. Has he talked to you about it?"

Head shakes—half-ass wary. "No. Mostly he talks about this Mobster Squad job he's got."

"Anything specific?"

"No, he said he's not supposed to talk about it. Hey, why you pumping me?"

"Why did you look so sad all of a sudden?"

Hooks, jabs—air whizzed. "I saw Johnny maybe a week ago. He said he'd been doing this bad stuff. He didn't, how you say, elaborate, but he said he needed a penance beating. We put on gloves, and he let me punch him around. I remember he had these what you call blisters on his hands."

Rubber-hose work—Johnny probably hates it. "Remember Sergeant Stemmons, Reuben?"

"Sure, your partner at the hotel. Nice haircut, but a punk if you ask me."

"Have you seen him?"

"No."

"Has Johnny mentioned him to you?"

"No. Hey, what's this Johnny routine?"

I smiled. "Just routine."

"Sure, subtle guy. Hey, what do you get when you cross a Mexican and a nigger?"

"I don't know."

"A thief who's too lazy to steal!"

"That's a riot."

Fondling a Schlitz: "You ain't laughing so hard, and I can tell you're thinking: at the ravine Rockabye Reuben said we should talk."

"So talk."

Pure pachuco—he bit off the bottle cap and guzzled. "I heard Noonan talking to Will Shipstad about you. He hates you like a goddamn dog. He thinks you pushed Johnson out the window and fucked up some guy named Morton Diskant. He tried to get me to say I heard you toss Johnson, and he said he's gonna take you down."

18

orensics—at my living room desk.

Dust the magazines, tape rig, spools—smudges and four identical latents. I rolled my own prints to compare—it confirmed my own fumble-hand fuck-up.

The phone rang—

"Yes?"

"Ray Pinker, Dave."

"You're finished?"

"Finished is right. First, no viable suspect latents, and we dusted every touch surface in both rooms. We took elimination sets off the clerk, who's also the owner, the janitor and the chambermaid, all Negroes. We got *their* prints in the rooms and nothing else."

"Fuck."

"Succinctly put. We also bagged the male clothing and tested some semen-stained shorts. It's O positive again, with the same cell breakdown—your burglar or whatever is quite a motel hopper."

"Shit."

"Succinct, but we had better luck on the sketch reconstruction. The clerk and the artist worked up a portrait, and it's waiting for you at the Bureau. Now—"

"What about mug shots? Did you tell the clerk we'll need him for a viewing?"

Ray sighed—half pissed. "Dave, the man took off for Fresno. He implied that your behavior disturbed him. I offered him an LAPD reimbursement for the door you shot out, but he said it wouldn't cover the aggravation. He also said don't go looking for him, because he is gone, no forwarding. I didn't press for him to stay, because he said he'd complain about that door you destroyed."

"Shit. Ray, did you check—"

"Dave, I'm way ahead of you. I asked the other employees if *they* had seen the tenant of that room. They both said no, and I believed them."

Shit. Fuck.

Half pouty: "Lots of trouble for a one-shot 459, Dave."

"Yeah, just don't ask me why."

Click—my ear stung.

Go, keep dusting:

Smudges off the album covers—grooved records themselves wouldn't take prints. Champ Dineen on my hi-fi: *Sooo Slow Moods, The Champ Plays the Duke.*

Background music—I skimmed *Transom.*

Piano/sax/bass—soft. Cheesecake pix, innuendo: blond siren M.M. craves she-man R.H.—she'll do anything to turn him around. Nympho J.M.—gigantically endowed—seeks double-digit males at Easton's Gym. Ten inches and up, please—J.M. packs a ruler to make sure. Recent conquests: B-movie hulk F.T.; gagster M.B.; laconic cowboy star G.C.

Breathy sax, heartbeat bass.

Stories—traveling-salesman gems. Pix: big-tit slatterns drooping out of lingerie. Piano trills—gorgeous.

One issue down, Dineen percolating. *Transom,* June '58:

M.M. and baseball M.M. hot—her J.D.M. torch pushed her toward hitters. The swank Plaza Hotel—ten-day/ten-night homestand.

Alto sax riffs—Glenda/Lucille/Meg, swirling.

Ads: dick enlargers, home law school. "Mood Indigo" à la Dineen—low brass.

A daddy/daughter story—a straight-dialogue intro. Photos: this skank brunette, bikini-clad.

"Well . . . you look like my daddy."

"Look? Well, yeah, I'm old enough. I guess a game is a game, right? I can be the daddy because I fit the part."

"Well, like the song says, 'My heart belongs to Daddy.' "

Skim the text:

Orphan Loretta lusts for a daddy. The evil Terry deflowered her—she crawls for him, she hates it. She sells herself to older men—a preacher kills her. Accompanying pix: the skank sash-cord-strangled.

Champ Dineen roaring—think it through:

Loretta equals Lucille; Terry equals Tommy. "Orphan" Loretta—non sequitur. Lucille lusts for Daddy J.C.—hard to buy her hot for that greasy shitbird.

Call the dialogue voyeured.

Call the peeper "author."

Transom, July '58—strictly movie-star raunch. Check the masthead—a Valley address—hit it tomorrow.

The phone rang—cut the volume—catch it.

"Glen—"

"Yes. Are you psychic or just hoping?"

"I don't know, maybe both. Look, I'll come up to the set."

"No. Sid Frizell's shooting some night scenes."

"We'll go to a hotel. We can't use your place or my place—it's too risky."

That laugh. "I read it in the *Times* today. Howard Hughes and his entourage left for Chicago for some Defense Department meeting. David, the Hollywood Hills 'actress domicile' is available, and I have a key."

Past midnight—call it safe. "Half an hour?"

"Yes. Miss you."

I put the phone down and cranked the volume. Ellington/Dineen—"Cottontail." Memory lane—'42—the Marine Corps. Meg—that tune—dancing at the El Cortez Sky Room.

Raw now—sixteen years gone bad. The phone right there—do it.

"Hello?"

"I'm glad I got you, but I figured you'd be out after Stemmons."

"I had to get some sleep. Look, slavedriver—"

"Kill him, Jack."

"Okay by me. Ten?"

"Ten. Clip him and buy me some time."

19

The hills—a big Spanish off Mulholland.

Lights on, Glenda's car out front. Twenty-odd rooms—fuck pad supreme.

I parked, beams on a '55 Chevy. Bad familiar: Harold John Miciak's.

Be sure, tweak the high beams—Hughes Aircraft decals on the back fender.

Late-night quiet—big dark houses, just one lit.

I got out and listened. Voices—his, hers—muffled low.

Up, try the front door—locked. Voices—his edgy, hers calm. Circuit the house, listen:

Miciak: ". . . you could do worse. Look, you come across for me, you pretend it's Klein. I seen him come see you in Griffith Park, and as far as that goes, you can still give it to him—I'm not possessive and I got no partners. Mr. Hughes, he's never gonna know, just you come across for me and get that money I want from Klein. I know he's got it, 'cause he's connected with some mob guys. Mr. Hughes, he told me so hisself."

Glenda: "How do I know there's just you?"

Miciak: " 'Cause Harold John's the only daddy-o in L.A. man enough to mess with Mr. Hughes and this cop who thinks he's so tough."

Around to the dining room window. Curtain gaps—look:

Glenda edging backward; Miciak pressing up, grinding his hips.

Slow walking—both of them—a knife rack behind Glenda.

I tried the window—no give.

Glenda: "How do I know there's just you?"

Glenda: one hand reaching back, one hand out come hither.

Glenda: "I think we'd be good together."

Around the back, a side door—I shoulder-popped it and ran in.

The hallway, the kitchen, there—

A clinch: his hands groping, hers grabbing knives.

Slow-motion numb—I *couldn't* move. Shock-still frozen, look:

Knives down—in his back, in his neck—twisted in hilt-deep. Bone cracks—Glenda dug in—two hands blood-wet. Miciak thrashing AT HER—

Two more knives snagged—Glenda stabbing blind.

Miciak clawing the rack, up with a cleaver.

I stumbled in close—numb legs—smell the blood—

He stabbed, missed, lurched into the knife rack. She stabbed—his back, his face—blade jabs ripped his cheeks out.

Gurgles/screeches/whines—Miciak dying loud. Knife handles sticking out at odd angles—I threw him down, twisted them, killed him.

Glenda—no screams, this look: SLOW, I've been here before.

SLOW:

We killed the lights and waited ten minutes—no outside response. Plans then—soft whispers holding each other bloody.

No dining room carpet—luck. We showered and swapped clothes—Hughes kept a male/female stash. We bagged our own stuff, washed the floor, the rack, the knives.

Blankets in a closet—we wrapped Miciak up and locked him in his car trunk. 1:50 A.M.—out, back—no witnesses. Out and back again—*our* cars tucked below Mulholland.

A plan, a fall guy: the Wino Will-o-the-Wisp, L.A.'s favorite at-large killer.

Out to Topanga Canyon solo—I drove Miciak's car. Hillhaven Kiddieland Kamp—defunct, wino turf. I flashlight-checked all six cabins—no bums residing.

I stashed the car out of sight.

I wiped it.

Kougar Kub Kabin—dump the body.

I throttled the corpse per the Wisp MO.

I rolled it through sawdust to stuff up the stab wounds. Forensic logic: impacted wounds made knife casting impossible.

Hope logic:

Howard Hughes, publicity shy—he might not push to find his man's killer.

I walked back to Pacific Coast Highway. SLOW fear speeding up—

Sporadic tails dogging me.

A tail tonight meant grief forever.

Glenda picked me up at PCH. Back to Mulholland, two cars to my place, bed just to talk.

Small talk—her will held. CinemaScope/Technicolor knife work—I pushed to know she didn't like it.

I hit the pillow by her face.

I shined the bed light in her eyes.

I told her:

My father shot a dog/I torched his toolshed/he hit my sister/I shot him, the gun jammed/these Two Tony fucks hurt my sister/I killed them/I killed five other men/I took money—what gives you the right to play it so stylish—

Hit the pillow, make her talk—no style, no tears:

She was floating, carhopping, this pretend actress. She was sleeping around for rent money—a guy told Dwight Gilette. He propositioned her: turn tricks for a fifty-fifty split. She agreed, she did it—sad sacks mostly. Georgie Ainge once—no rough stuff from him—but regular beatings from Gilette.

She got mad. She got this pretend-actress idea: buy a gun off Georgie and scare Dwight. Pretend actress with a prop now: a real pistol.

Dwight made her drive his "nieces" to his "brother's" place in Oxnard. It was fun—cute colored toddlers—their pictures on TV a week later.

Two four-year-olds starved, tortured and raped—found dead in an Oxnard sewer.

Pretend actress, errand girl. This real-actress idea:

Kill Gilette—before he sends any more kids out to be snuffed.

She did it.

She didn't like it.

You don't skate from things like that—you crawl stylish.

I held her.

I talked a Kafesjian blue streak.

Champ Dineen lulled us to sleep.

I woke up early. I heard Glenda in the bathroom, sobbing.

arris Dulange—fifty, bad teeth: "Since me and the magazine are as clean as a cat's snatch, I will tell you how *Transom* works. First, we hire hookers or aspiring actresses down on their luck for the photos. The written stuff is by yours truly, the editor-in-chief, or it's scribed by college kids who write out their fantasies in exchange for free issues. It's what *Hush-Hush* calls 'Sinuendo.' We tack those movie-star initials onto our stories so that our admittedly feeble-minded readers will think, 'Wow, is that really Marilyn Monroe?' "

Tired—I made an early Bureau run for Pinker's sketch. Exley said no all-points distribution—last night left me too fried to fight him.

"Lieutenant, are you daydreaming? I know this isn't the nicest office in the world, but . . ."

I pulled the June '58 issue out. "Who wrote this father-daughter story?"

"I don't even have to look. If it's plump brunettes hot for some daddy surrogate, it's Champ Dineen."

"What? Do you know who Champ Dineen *is?"*

"Was, because he died some time back. I *knew* the guy was using a pseudonym."

I flashed Pinker's sketch. Dulange deadpanned it: "Who's this?"

"Odds are it's the man who wrote those stories. Haven't you *seen* him?"

"No. We only talked on the phone. Nice-looking picture, though. Surprising. I figured the guy would be a troll."

"Did he say his real name was Richie? That might be a lead on his ID."

"No. We only talked on the phone once. He said his name was Champ Dineen, and I thought, 'Copacetic, and only in L.A.' Lieutenant, let me ask you. Does the Champster have a voyeur fetish?"

"Yes."

Dulange—nodding, stretching: "Say eleven months ago, around

Christmas, this pseudo-Champ guy calls me up out of the blue. He says he's got access to some good *Transom*-type stuff, something like a whorehouse peek. I said, 'Swell, send me a few samples, maybe we can do business.' So . . . he sent me two stories. There was a PO-box return address, and I thought, 'What? He's on the lam or he lives in a post office box?' "

"Go on."

"So the stuff was good. *Cash good*—and I rarely pay for text, just pictures. Anyway, it was two girlie-daddy stories, and the dialogue introductions were realistic, like he eavesdropped on this sick game stuff. The accompanying stories weren't so hot, but I sent him a C-note off the books and a note: 'Keep the fires stoked, I like your stuff.' "

"Did he send the stories in handwritten?"

"Yes."

"Did you keep them?"

"No, I typed them over, then tossed them."

"You did that every time he sent stories in?"

"That's right. Four issues featuring the Champ, four times I typed the stuff up and tossed it. That was June '58 you showed me, plus the Champ also made it in February '58, May '58 and September '58. You want copies? I can have the warehouse send them to you, maybe take a week."

"No sooner?"

"The wetbacks they got working there? For them a week's Speedy Gonzales."

I laid a card down. "Send them to my office."

"Okay, but you'll be disappointed."

"Why?"

"The Champ's a one-trick jockey. It's all quasi-incest stuff featuring plump brunettes. I think I'll start editing him and change things around. Rita Hayworth looking to bang father surrogates is spicier, don't you think?"

"Sure. Now, what about a contributors' file?"

He tapped his head. "Right here. We're cramped for space in the plush offices of *Transom* magazine."

Itchy—thinking Glenda. "Do you pay the man by check?"

"No, always cash. When we talked on the phone he said cash only. Lieutenant, you're getting antsy, so I'll tell you. Check PO box 5841 at the main downtown post office. That's where I send the gelt. It's always cash, and if you're thinking of finking me to the IRS, don't—because the Champ man is covered under various petty-cash clauses."

Hot—the A.M. sweats. "How did he sound that one time you talked to him?"

"Like a square punk who always wanted to be a hepcat jazz musician. Say, did you know that my kid brother was a suspect in the Black Dahlia case?"

PO box stakeout?—too time-consuming. Glom a writ to bag the contents?—ditto. Bust the box open?—yes—call Jack Woods.

Phone dimes:

Jack—no answer. Meg—tap our property account for ten grand cash. Okay, no "Why?", news: She and Jack were an item again. I resisted a cheap laugh: give *him* the ten—he's killing Junior for me.

Shot/shivved/bludgeoned—picture it—Junior dead.

Pincushion Miciak—seeing it/*feeling* it: knife blades snagged on his spine.

More calls:

Mike Breuning and Dick Carlisle—77th, the Bureau—no luck. Picture Lester Lake scared shitless—cops out to frame him.

Picture Glenda: "Shit, David, you caught me crying."

I drove down to Darktown—a name-tossing run. Bars and early-open jazz clubs—go.

Names:

Tommy Kafesjian, Richie—an old Tommy friend? Tilly Hopewell—consort—Tommy and the late Wardell Knox. My wild card: Johnny Duhamel—ex-fighter cop.

Names tossed to:

B-girls, hopheads, loafers, juice friends, bartenders. My tossbacks: Richie—straight deadpans. White Peeping Toms—ditto. Tilly Hopewell—junkie talk—she was an ex-hype off a recent hospital cure. Wardell Knox—"He dead and I don't know who did it." Schoolboy Johnny—boxing IDs only.

My peeper sketch: zero IDs.

Dusk—more clubs open. More name tosses—zero results—I checked slot-machine traffic on reflex. A coin crew at the Rick Rack—white/spic—Feds across the street, camera ready. Mickey slot men on film—Suicide Mickey.

Cop-issue Plymouths out thick—Feds, LAPD. Intermittent heebie-jeebies—tails on me LAST NIGHT?

I stopped at a pay phone. Out of dimes—I used slugs.

Glenda—my place, her place—no answer. Jack Woods—no answer.

Over to Bido Lito's—toss names, toss shit—I got nothing but sneers back.

Two-drink minimum—I grabbed a stool and ordered two scotches. Voodoo eyes: wall-to-wall niggers.

I downed the juice fast—two drinks, no more. Scotch warm, this idea: wait for Tommy K. and shove him outside. Do you fuck your sister/does your father fuck your sister—brass knucks until he coughed up family dirt.

The barman had drink three ready—I said no. A combo setting up—I waved the sax man over. He agreed: twenty dollars for a Champ Dineen medley.

Lights down. Vibes/drums/sax/trumpet—go.

Themes—loud/fast, soft/slow. Soft—the barman talked mythic Champ Dineen.

Dig:

He came out of nowhere. He looked white—but rumor made his bloodlines mongrel. He played piano and bass sax, wrote jazz and cut a few sides. Handsome, jumbo hung: he fucked in whorehouse peek shows and never had his picture taken. Champ in love: three rich-girl sisters, their mother. Four mistresses—four children born—a rich cuckold daddy shot the Champ Man dead.

A drink on the bar—I bolted it. *My* mythic peeper—dig *his* story, just maybe:

Whorehouse peek equals *Transom;* family intrigue equals KAFESJIAN.

I ran outside—across the street to a phone bank. Jack Woods' number, three rings—"Hello?"

"It's me."

"Dave, don't ask. I'm still looking for him."

"Keep going, it's not that."

"What is it?"

"It's another two grand if you want it. You know the all-night post office downtown?"

"Sure."

"Box 5841. You break in and bring me the contents. Wait until three o'clock or so, you'll get away clean."

Jack whistled. "You've got Fed trouble, right? Some kind of seizure writ won't do it, so—"

"Yes or no?"

"Yes. I like you in trouble, you're generous. Call me tomorrow, all right?"

I hung up. My memory jolted—*plate numbers.* Jack's work—those Junior shakedownees he spotted. I dug my notebook out and buzzed the DMV.

Slow—read the numbers off, wait. Cold air juked my booze rush and cleared my head—*pusher* shakedown victims—potential Junior/Tommy snitchers.

My readout:

Patrick Dennis Orchard, male caucasian—1704½ S. Hi Point; Leroy George Carpenter, male negro—819 W. 71st Street, #114; Stephen NMI Wenzel, male caucasian, 1811 S. St. Andrews, #B.

Two white men—surprising. Think: Lester Lake shot me Tilly Hopewell's address. There, grab it: 8491 South Trinity, 406.

Close by—I got there quick. A four-story walk-up—I parked curbside. No lift—I walked up for real. 406—push the buzzer.

Spyhole clicks. "Who is it?"

"Police."

Chain noise, the door open. Tilly: a thirtyish high yellow, maybe half white.

"Miss Hopewell?"

"Yes"—no coon drawl.

"It's just a few questions."

She walked backward—dead cowed. The front room: shabby, clean. "Are you from the Probation?"

I closed the door. "LAPD."

Goosebumps: "Narco?"

"Administrative Vice."

She whipped papers off the TV. "I'm clean. I had my Nalline test today. See?"

"I don't care."

"Then . . ."

"Let's start with Tommy Kafesjian."

Tilly backed up, brushed a chair, plunked down. "Say what, Mr. Police?"

"Say what shit, you're not that kind of colored. *Tommy Kafesjian.*"

"I know Tommy."

"And you've been intimate with him."

"Yes."

"And you've been intimate with Wardell Knox and Lester Lake."

"That's true, and I'm not the kind of colored who thinks it's all a big sin, either."

"Wardell's dead."

"I know that."

"Tommy killed him."

"Tommy's evil, but I'm not saying he killed Wardell. And if he did, he's LAPD protected, so I'm not giving away anything you don't already know."

"You're a smart girl, Tilly."

"You mean for colored I'm smart."

"Smart's smart. Now give me a motive for Tommy killing Wardell. Was it bad blood over you?"

Sitting prim—this junkie schoolmarm. "Tommy and Wardell could never get that fired up over a woman. I'm not saying Tommy killed him, but *if* he killed him, it's because Wardell was behind on some kind of dope payment. Which doesn't mean anything to you, considering the Christmas baskets Mr. J.C. Kafesjian sends downtown."

Change-up: "Do you like Lester Lake?"

"Of course I do."

"You don't want to see him get popped for a murder he didn't commit, do you?"

"No, but who says that's going to happen? Any plain fool can tell Lester's not the kind of man who could kill anybody."

"Come on, you know things don't work that way."

Getting antsy—raw off that dope cure. "Why do you care so much about Lester?"

"We help each other out."

"You mean you're the slum man Lester snitches for? You want to help him out, fix his bathtub."

Change-up: "Johnny Duhamel."

"Now I'll say 'say what' for real. Johnny who?"

Name toss: "Leroy Carpenter . . . Stephen Wenzel . . . Patrick Orchard. . . . Let's try a policeman named George Stemmons, Jr."

Cigarettes on a tray close by—Tilly reached trembly.

Kick it over, set her off—

"That Junior is trash! Steve Wenzel's my friend, and that Junior trash stole his bankroll and his speedballs and called him a white nigger! That Junior talked this crazy talk to him! I saw that crazy Junior man popping goofballs right out in the open by this club!"

Flash it—*my* bankroll. *"What crazy talk?* Come on, you're just off the cure, you know you can use a fix. *Come on, what crazy talk?"*

"I don't know! Steve just said crazy nonsense!"

"What else did he tell you about Junior?"

"Nothing else! He just said what I told you!"

"Patrick Orchard, Leroy Carpenter. *Do you know them?"*

"No! I just know Steve! And I don't want a snitch jacket!"

Twenty, forty, sixty—I dropped cash on her lap. "Tommy and his sister Lucille. Anything ugly. Tommy will never know you told me."

Dope eyes now—fuck fear. "Tommy said that sometimes Lucille whores. He said that a man in Stan Kenton's band recommended her to this Beverly Hills call-girl man. Doug something . . . Doug Ancelet? Tommy said that Lucille worked for that man for a while like several years ago, but he fired her because she gave these tricks of hers the gonorrhea."

Recoil: Glenda, ex–Ancelet girl. My peeper tape—the trick to Lucille—"that little dose you gave me."

Tilly: dope eyes, new money.

Carpenter/Wenzel/Orchard—I swung an address circuit south/northwest. Nobody home—circuit south, crack the wind wings—cold air cleared my head.

Make Junior dead or dead soon—faggot-smear him postmortem. Leak queer dirt to *Hush-Hush*—taint his Glenda dirt. Retoss his pad, dump evidence—pump his shakedown victims. Work Kafesjian 459—and tie in Junior dirty. Question mark: his Exley file.

Brain circuits:

Exley proffers my Kafesjian payoff: Robbery Division CO. It's a shiv to Dudley Smith, the fur-job boss—the perp his "protégé" Johnny Duhamel.

Johnny and Junior—heist partners?

My instinct: unlikely.

Reflex instinct: hand Johnny up to Dud—deflect Exley's shiv, curry Dud's favor.

South, hit the gas: talk had Smith working 77th. Over—newsmen outside—a captain grandstanding:

Ignore Negro-victim 187s—never!

Watch for zealous justice soon!

Door guards kept reporters out: civilians verboten, zealotry wrapped.

I badged in. Sweat box row was packed: nigger suspects, two cop teams twirling saps.

"Lad."

Smith in the bullpen doorway. I walked over; he shot me a bonecrusher shake. "Lad, was it me you came to see?"

Sidestep: "I was looking for Breuning and Carlisle."

"Ahh, grand. Those bad pennies should turn up, but in the meantime share a colloquy with old Dudley."

Chairs right there—I grabbed two.

"Lad, in my thirty years and four months as a policeman I have never seen anything quite like this Federal business. You've been on the Department how long?"

"Twenty years and a month."

"Ah, grand, with your wartime service included, of course. Tell me, lad, is there a difference between killing Orientals and white men?"

"I've never killed a white man."

Dud winked—oh, you kid. "Nor have I. Jungle bunnies account for the seven men I have killed in the line of duty, stretching a point to allow for them as human. Lad, this Federal business is damningly provocative, isn't it?"

"Yes."

"Concisely put. And in that concise attorney's manner of yours, what would you say is behind it?"

"Politics. Bob Gallaudet for the Republicans, Welles Noonan for the Democrats."

"Yes, strange bedfellows. And ironic that the Federal Government should be represented by a man with fellow-traveler tendencies. I understand that that man spat in your face, lad."

"You've got good eyes out there, Dud."

"Twenty-twenty vision, all my boys. Lad, do you hate Noonan? It's safe to say that he"—wink—"considers you negligent in the matter of Sanderline Johnson's unscheduled flight."

I winked back. "He thinks I bought him the ticket."

Ho, ho, ho. "Lad, you dearly amuse this old man. By any chance were you raised Catholic?"

"Lutheran."

"Aah, a Prod. Christianity's second string, God bless them. Do you still believe, lad?"

"Not since my pastor joined the German-American Bund."

"Aah, Hitler, God bless him. A bit unruly, but frankly I preferred him to the Reds. Lad, did your second-string faith feature an equivalent to confession?"

"No."

"A pity, because at this moment our interrogation rooms are filled with confessees and confessors, that grand custom being utilized to offset any untoward publicity this Federal business might foist upon the Department. Brass tacks, lad. Dan Wilhite has told me of Chief Exley's potentially provocative fixation on the Kafesjian family, with you as his agent provocateur. Lad, will you confess your opinion of what the man wants?"

Sidestep: "I don't like him any more than you do. He got chief of detectives over you, and I wish to hell you'd gotten the job."

"Grand sentiments, lad, which of course I share. But what do you think the man is doing?"

Feed him—my Johnny snitch prelim. "I think—maybe—he's sacrificing Narco to the Feds. It's a largely autonomous division, and *maybe* he's certain that the Fed probe will prove successful enough to require a scapegoat that will protect the rest of the Department *and* Bob Gallaudet. Exley is two things: intelligent and ambitious. I've always thought that he'll get tired of police work and try politics himself, and we know how tight he is with Bob. I think—*maybe*—he's convinced Parker to let Narco go, with his eye on his own goddamn future."

"A brilliant interpretation, lad. And as for the Kafesjian burglary itself, and your role as Exley's chosen investigating officer?"

I ticked points: "You're right, I'm an agent provocateur. Chronologically: Sanderline Johnson jumps, and now Noonan hates me. The Southside Fed probe is already rumored, and the Kafesjian burglary occurs coincident to it. Coincident to *that,* I operate a pinko politician who's enamored of Noonan. Now, the Kafesjian burglary is nothing—it's a pervert job. But the Kafesjians are scum personified and tight with the LAPD's most autonomous and vulnerable division. At first I thought Exley was operating Dan Wilhite, but now I think he put me out there to draw heat. I'm out there, essentially getting nowhere on a worthless pervert 459. It's a one—I mean *two*-man job, and if Exley *really* wanted the case cleared he would have put out a half-dozen men. I think he's running me. He's playing off my reputation and running me."

Dudley, beaming: "Salutary, lad—your intelligence, your lawyer-sharp articulation. Now, what does Sergeant George Stemmons, Jr., think of the job? My sources say he's been behaving rather erratically lately."

Spasms—don't flinch. "You mean your source Johnny Duhamel. Junior taught him at the Academy."

"Johnny's a good lad, and your colleague Stemmons should trim his disgraceful sideburns to regulation length. Did you know that I co-opted Johnny to the Hurwitz investigation?"

"Yeah, I'd heard. Isn't he little green for a case like that?"

"He's a grand young copper, and I heard that you yourself sought to command the job."

"Robbery's clean, Dud. I'm looking out for too many friends working Ad Vice."

Ho-ho, wink-wink. "Lad, your powers of perception have just won you the undying friendship of a certain Irishman named Dudley Liam Smith,

and I am frankly amazed that two bright lads such as ourselves have remained merely acquaintances all these many years."

SNITCH DUHAMEL.

DO IT NOW.

"On the topic of friendship, lad, I understand that you and Bob
Gallaudet are quite close."

Hallway noise—grunts/thuds/"Dave Klein my friend!"

Lester—sweat box row.

I sprinted over—door number 3 was just closing. Check the window—
Lester handcuffed, dribbling teeth—Breuning and Carlisle swinging saps
overtime.

Shoulder wedge—I snapped the door clean.

Breuning—distracted—huh?

Carlisle—blood-fogged glasses.

Out of breath, pitch the lie: "He was with me when Wardell Knox was
killed."

Carlisle: "Was that a.m. or p.m.?"

Breuning: "Hey, Sambo, try to sing 'Harbor Lights' now."

Lester spat blood and teeth in Breuning's face.

Carlisle balled his fists—I kicked his legs out. Breuning yelped, blood-
blind—I sapped his knees.

That brogue:

"Lads, you'll have to release Mr. Lake. Lieutenant, bless you for expe-
diting justice with your splendid alibi."

21

Dear Mr. Hughes, Mr. Milteer:

On the dates of 11/11, 11/12 and 11/13/58, Glenda Bledsoe participated in actively publicizing performers currently under contract to Variety International Pictures, a clear legal breach of her contract with Hughes Aircraft, Tool Company, Productions et al. Specifically, Miss Bledsoe allowed herself to be photographed and interviewed with actors Rock Rockwell and Salvatore "Touch" Vecchio, on matters pertaining to their acting careers outside the production/publicity confines of *Attack of the Atomic Vampire,* the motion picture all three are currently involved with. Specifics will follow in a subsequent note, but you should now be advised that Miss Bledsoe's Hughes contract is legally voided: she can be sued in civil court, dunned for financial damages and blackballed from future studio film appearances under various clauses of her Hughes contract. My continued surveillance of Miss Bledsoe has revealed no instances of actress domicile theft; if items are missing from those premises, most likely they have been stolen by local youths employing loose window access: such youths would know that the domiciles were intermittently occupied and take their thievery from there. Please inform me if you wish me to continue surveilling Miss Bledsoe; be advised that you now have enough information to proceed with all legal dispatch.

Respectfully,
David D. Klein

Dawn—the trailer. Glenda sleeping; Lester curled up outside by the spaceship.

I stepped out; Lester stirred and gargled T-Bird. Confab: the camera boss and director.

"Come on, Sid, this time the head vampire *plucks* the guy's eyes out."

"But Mickey's afraid I'm making things too gruesome. I . . . I don't know."

"Jesus Christ, you take the extra and pour some fake blood in his eyes."

"Wylie, *you* come on. Let me have coffee before I start thinking gore at six-forty-nine in the morning."

Lester weaved over—cut, bruised. "I always wanted to be a movie star. Maybe I stick aroun' an extra day or so, play the Negro vampire."

"No, Breuning and Carlisle will be looking for you. They didn't pin Wardell Knox on you, but they'll find something."

"I don't feel so much like runnin'."

"You do it. I told you last night: call Meg and tell her I said she should stake you. You want to end up dead for resisting arrest some goddamn night when you think they've forgotten about it?"

"No, I don't think I do. Say, Mr. Klein, I never thought I'd see the day Mr. Smith gave me a break."

I winked à la Dudley. "He likes my style, lad."

Lester strolled back to his bottle. The director fisheyed me—I strolled to the trailer, nonchalant.

Glenda was reading my note. "David, this could kill—I mean *ruin* me in the film business."

"We have to give them something. If they believe it, they won't press theft charges. And it diverts attention from the actress pads."

"There's been nothing on TV or in the papers."

"The more time goes by, the better. Hughes might report him missing, and the body will be found sooner or later. Either way, we might or might not be questioned. I had words with him, so I'm more likely to be a pro forma suspect. I can handle it, and I know you can handle it. We're . . . oh shit."

"We're *professionals?"*

"Don't be so cruel, it's too early."

She took my hands. "When can *we* go public?"

"We may have already. I shouldn't have stayed so late, and we should probably cool things for a while."

"Until when?"

"Until we're cleared on Miciak."

"That's the first time we've said his name."

"We haven't really talked about it at all."

"No, we've been too busy sharing secrets. What about alibis?"

"For up to two weeks you were home alone. After two weeks you don't remember—nobody remembers that long."

"There's something else bothering you. I could tell last night."

Neck prickles—I blurted it. "It's the Kafesjian job. I was questioning a girl who knows Tommy K., and she said Lucille did call jobs for Doug Ancelet."

"I don't think I knew her. The girls never used their real names, and if I knew someone similar to the way you described her, I would have told you. Are you going to question him?"

"Yeah, today."

"When did she work for Doug?"

"Doug?"

Glenda laughed. *"I* worked for Doug briefly, after the Gilette thing, and you're disturbed that I used to do what I did."

"No—I just don't want you connected to any of this."

Lacing our fingers—"I'm not, except that I'm connected to you"—squeezing tighter—"So *go*. It's Premier Escorts, 481 South Rodeo, next to the Beverly Wilshire Hotel."

I kissed her. "You make things worse, then you make them better."

"No, it's just that you like your trouble in smaller doses."

"You've got me."

"I'm not so sure. And be careful with Doug. He used to pay off the Beverly Hills Police."

I walked—lightheaded. Lester serenaded winos by the spaceship—"Harbor Lights"—the gap-toothed version.

Phone news:

Woods spotted Junior in Darktown—then lost him running a red light. Jack—irked, going back out: "It looks like he's living in his car. He had his badge pinned to his coat, like he's a fucking Wild West sheriff, and I saw him buying gas with two big automatics shoved down his pants."

Bad, but:

He hit box 5841—check under his doormat, grab the key, check his mail slot. "Four envelopes, Dave. Jesus, I thought you were sending me after jewels or something. And you owe me—"

I hung up and drove over. There: the key, the slot, four letters. Back to my car—Champ Dineen mail.

Two letters sealed, two slit. I opened the sealed ones—both from *Transom* to Champ—recent postmarks. Inside: fifty-dollar bills, notes: "Champ—Thanx mucho, Harris"; "Champ—Thanx, man!"

Two slit—left for safekeeping?—no return address, Christmas '57 postmarks. Eleven months PO box stashed—why?

December 17, 1957

My Dear Son,

I am so sad to be apart from you this holiday season. Circumstances have not been kind in the keeping us together department for several years now. The others of course do not miss you the way I do, which makes me miss you more and makes me miss the pretend happy family that we once had years ago.

The strange life that you have chosen to live is a strange comfort to me, though. I don't miss the housekeeping money I send you and it's like a secret joke when your father reads my itemized household expense lists with large "miscellaneous" amounts that I refuse to explain. He, of course, considers you just someone in hiding from the real responsibilities of life. I know that the circumstances of our family life and theirs too has done something to you. You cannot live the way other people do and I love you for not pretending to. Your musical interests must give you comfort and I always buy the records you tell me to buy even though the music is not normally the type of music I enjoy. Your father and sisters ignore the records and suspect that I buy them only to be in touch with you in this difficult absence of yours, but they don't know that they are direct recommendations! I only listen to them when the others are out and with all the lights off in the house. Every day I intercept the mailman before he gets to our house so the others will not know that you are contacting me. This is our secret. We are new to living this way, you and me, but even if we have to live this way always like long lost pen pals living in the same city I will do it because I understand the terrible things this long history of insanity both our families has endured has done to you. I understand and I don't judge you. That is my Christmas gift to you.

Love,
Mother

Neat handwriting, ridged paper—non-print-sustaining. No Richie confirmation; "Long history of insanity/both our families." My peeper: mother/father/sisters. "Circumstances of our family life and theirs too has done something to you."

December 24, 1957

Dear Son,

Merry Christmas even though I don't feel the Christmas spirit and even though the jazz Christmas albums you told me to buy didn't cheer me up, because the melodies were so out of kilter to my more traditional ear. I just feel tired. Maybe I have iron poor blood like on the Geritol TV commercials, but I think it is more like an accumulation that has left me physically exhausted on top of the other. I feel like I want it to be over. I feel more than anything else like I just don't want to know any more. Three months ago I said I was close to doing it and it spurred you to do a rash thing. I don't want to do that again. Sometimes when I play some of the prettier songs on the records you suggest to me I think that heaven will be like that and I get close. Your sisters are no comfort. Since your father gave me what that prostitute gave him I can only use him for his money, and if I had my druthers I would give you all the money anyway. Write to me. The mail gets bollixed up at Xmastime, but I'll be watching for the postman at all different times.

Love,
Mother

Sisters/music/well-heeled father.

Mother suicidal—close three months before—"it spurred you to do a rash thing."

"Your father gave me what that prostitute gave him."

The peeper tape, Trick Man to Lucille: "that little dose you gave me."

Doug Ancelet fires Lucille—"She gave these tricks of hers the gonorrhea."

Snap call:

The peeper taped Lucille and *his own father.*

"Insanity."

"Both our families."

"Our family life and *theirs* too has done something to you."

I drove home, changed, grabbed the tape rig, extra sketches and my john list. A pay-phone stop, a call to Exley—I pitched him hard, no explanation:

Leroy Carpenter/Steve Wenzel/Patrick Orchard—I want them. Send squadroom men out—*I want those pushers detained.*

Exley agreed—grudgingly. Agreed too: Wilshire Station detention. Suspicious: Why not 77th?

Unsaid:

I'm having a cop killed/I don't want Dudley Smith around—he's too close to this fur-thief cop—

"I'll implement it, Lieutenant. But I want a full report on your interrogations."

"Yes, sir!"

10:30 A.M.—Premier Escorts should be open.

Out to Beverly Hills—Rodeo off the Beverly Wilshire. Open: a ground-floor suite, a receptionist.

"Doug Ancelet, please."

"Are you a client?"

"A potential one."

"May I ask who recommended you?"

"Peter Bondurant"—pure bluff—a big-time whorehound.

Behind us: "Karen, if he knows Pete, send him in."

I walked back. A nice office—dark wood, golf prints. An old man dressed for golf, PR smile on.

"I'm Doug Ancelet."

"Dave Klein."

"How is Pete, Mr. Klein? I haven't seen him in a dog's age."

"He's busy. Between his work for Howard Hughes and *Hush-Hush* he's always on the run."

Pseudo-warm: "God, the stories that man has. You know, Pete has been both a client for several years *and* a talent scout for companions for Mr. Hughes. In fact, we've introduced Mr. Hughes to several young ladies who've gone on to become contract actresses for him."

"Pete gets around."

"He does indeed. My God, he's the man who verifies the veracity of those scurrilous stories in that scurrilous scandal rag. Has he explained how Premier Escorts works?"

"Not in detail."

Practiced: "It's by word of mouth exclusively. People know people, and they recommend us. We operate on a principle of relative anonymity, and all our clients use pseudonyms and call us when they wish to have an introduction made. That way we don't have their real names or phone numbers on file. We have picture files on the young ladies we send out on dates, and they use appropriately seductive pseudonyms themselves. With the exception of a few clients like Pete, I doubt that I know a half-dozen of my clients and girls by their real names. Those picture files on the girls also list the pseudonyms of the men they've dated, to aid us in making recommendations. *Anonymity.* We accept only cash as payment, and I assure you, Mr. Klein—I've forgotten your real name already."

Tweak him: "Lucille Kafesjian."

"I beg your pardon?"

"Another client mentioned her to me. A sexy brunette, a little on the plump side. Frankly, he said she was great. Unfortunately, he also said that you dismissed her for giving your clients venereal disease."

"Unfortunately, I've dismissed a few girls for that offense, and one of them did use an Armenian surname. Who was the client who mentioned her?"

"A man in Stan Kenton's band."

Eyeing me—copwise now. "Mr. Klein, what do you do for a living?"

"I'm an attorney."

"And that's a tape recorder you're carrying?"

"Yes."

"And why are you carrying a revolver in a shoulder holster?"

"Because I command the Administrative Vice Division, Los Angeles Police Department."

Turning florid: "Did Pete Bondurant give you my name?"

Flash the peeper sketch, dig his reaction: *"He* gave you my name? I've never seen him before, and that likeness reads much younger than the vast majority of my clients. Mr.—"

"Lieutenant."

"Mr. Lieutenant Whatever Out-of-Your-Jurisdiction Policeman, leave this office immediately!"

I shut the door. Ancelet flushed heart-attack red—baby him. "Are you in with Mort Riddick on the BHPD? Talk to him, he'll verify me. I bluffed in with Pete B., so call Pete and ask about me."

Turning beet-red/purple. A decanter set on his desk—I poured him a shot.

He guzzled it and made refill nods. I poured him a short one—he chased it with pills.

"You son of a bitch, using a trusted client of mine as subterfuge, you son of a bitch."

Refill number two—*he* poured this time.

"A few minutes of your time, Mr. Ancelet. You'll make a valuable contact on the LAPD."

"No good son of a bitch"—winding down.

I flashed the john list. "These are trick names I got out of a police file."

"I will not identify any of my client names or pseudonyms."

"Former clients, then, that's all I'm asking."

Squinting, finger-scanning: "There, 'Joseph Arden.' He used to be a client several years back. I remember because my daughter lives near the Arden Dairy in Culver City. This man trucks with common street girls?"

"That's right. And johns always keep the same alias. Now, did this man trick with that Armenian-named girl you told me about?"

"I don't recall. And remember what I told you: I don't keep client files, and my picture file on that clap-passing slut is strictly ancient history."

Lying fuck—file cabinets stacked wall-to-wall. "Listen to a tape. It'll take two minutes."

He tapped his watch. *"One minute.* I'm due on the tee at Hillcrest."

Fast: rig the spools, press Play. Squelch, Stop, Start, there:

Lucille: "These places are filled with losers and lonesome creeps."

Stop, Start, "Chanson d'Amour," the trick: ". . . of course, there was always that little dose you gave me."

I pressed Stop. Ancelet, impressed: "That's Joseph Arden. The girl sounds somewhat familiar, too. Satisfied?"

"How can you be sure? You only listened for ten seconds."

More watch taps. *"Listen,* I do most of my business on the phone, and I recognize voices. Now, follow this train of thought: I have asthma. That man had a slight wheeze. I remembered that he called me out of the blue several years ago. He wheezed, and we discussed asthma. He said he heard two men in an elevator discussing my service and got the Premier Escorts number out of the Beverly Hills Yellow Pages, where frankly I advertise my more legitimate escort business. I set the man up with a few dates and *that was that.* Satisfied?"

"And you don't recall which girls he selected."

"Correct."

"And he never came in to look at your picture file."

"Correct."

"And of course you don't keep a pseudonym file on your clients."

Tap tap. "Correct, and Jesus Christ, they'll tee off without me. Now, Mr. Policeman Friend of Pete's Who I Have Humored Past the Point of Courtesy, please—"

In his face: *"Sit down. Don't move. Don't pick up the phone."*

He kowtowed—twitching and fuming dark red. File cabinets—nine drawers—go—

Unlocked, manilla folders, side tabs. Male names—lying old whoremaster fuck. Alphabetical: "Amour, Phil," "Anon, Dick," "Arden, Joseph"—

Pull it:

No real name/no address/no phone number.

Ancelet: "This is a rank invasion of privacy!"

Assignations:

7/14/56, 8/1/56, 8/3/56—Lacey Kartoonian—call her Lucille. 9/4/56,

9/11/56—Susan Ann Glynn, a footnote: "Make this girl use a pseudonym: I think she wants clients to be able to locate her thru normal channels to avoid paying commission."

"They are on the second hole already!"

I yanked drawers—one, two, three, four—male names only. Five, six, seven—initialed folders/nude whore pix.

"Get out now, you fucking hard-on voyeur, before I call Mort Riddick!"

Yanking folders—no L.K., no Lucille pictures—

"Karen, call Mort Riddick at the station!"

I yanked *his* phone out by the cord—watch his face throb. My own throbs: fuck L.K., find G.B.—

"Mr. Ancelet, Mort's on his way!"

No L.K., files dwindling. There, G.B. paydirt—"Gloria Benson" in brackets. Glenda's movie name—she said she chose it.

I grabbed the file, grabbed the tape rig and hauled. Outside, my car—I peeled rubber—down to my jurisdiction.

Look:

Two nude snapshots dated 3/56—Glenda looked embarrassed. Four "dates" listed, a note: "A headstrong girl who went back to carhopping."

I ripped it all up.

I hit my siren out of pure fucking joy.

22

One Susan Ann Glynn DMV-listed—Ocean View Drive, Redondo Beach.

Twenty minutes south. A clapboard shack, no view—a pregnant woman on the porch.

I parked and walked up. Blond, mid-twenties—DMV stat bullseye.

"Are you Susan Ann Glynn?"

She patted a sit-down place. Expectant: cigarettes, magazines.

"You're the policeman Doug called about?"

I sat down. "He *warned* you?"

"Uh-huh. He said you looked through an old trick file that had my name on it. He said you might come to see me and make trouble like you did with him. I said I sure hope he makes it before three-thirty, when my husband gets home."

Noon now. "Your husband doesn't know what you used to do?"

A kid yelping inside—she lit a cigarette on reflex. "Uh-uh. And I bet if I cooperate with you, you won't tell him."

"That's right."

She coughed, smiled. "The baby kicked. Now, uh, Doug said the trick was Joseph Arden, so I put on my thinking cap. This isn't for murder or anything like that, is it? Because that man behaved like a gentleman."

"I'm investigating a burglary."

Cough, wince. "You know, I remember that I liked that man. I remember him good because Doug said be nice 'cause this other service girl gave him the clap, and he had to get it treated."

"Did he tell you his real name?"

"No. I used *my* real name at the service for a while, but Doug accused me of trying to recruit customers for myself, so I stopped."

"What did Joseph Arden look like?"

"Nice looking. Cultured looking. Maybe in his late forties. He looked like he had money."

"Tall, short, heavy, slender?"

"Maybe six feet. I guess you'd say he had a medium build. Blue eyes, I think. What I guess you'd call medium-brown hair."

I showed the sketch. "Does this look like him?"

"This man looks too young. The chin sort of reminds me of him, though."

Noise inside—Susan winced. Check her magazines: *Photoplay, Bride's*. "Do you know what mug shots are?"

"Uh-huh, from the TV. Pictures of criminals."

Soft: "Would you—?"

"No" shakes—emphatic. "Mister, this man was no criminal. I could look at your pictures until this new baby of mine has her sweet sixteen and never see his face."

"Did he mention a son named Richie?"

"We didn't talk much, but on like our second date he said his wife just tried to kill herself. At first I didn't believe it, 'cause lots of men tell you sad things about their wives so you'll feel sorry for them and pretend you like it more."

"You said at first you didn't believe him. What convinced you?"

"He told me he and his wife had this fight a few weeks back, and she just started screaming and picked up a can of Drano and started drinking it. He said he stopped her and fetched this doctor neighbor of his so he wouldn't have to take her to the hospital. Believe me, that story was so awful that I knew he didn't make it up."

"Did he say that she went to a hospital for follow-up treatment?"

"No. He said the neighbor doctor took care of all of it. He said he was glad, 'cause that way nobody knew how crazy his wife was."

One dead lead. "Did he tell you his wife's name?"

"No."

"Did he mention the names of any other family members?"

"No, he sure didn't."

"Did he mention any other girls who worked for Doug Ancelet?"

Nods—eager. "Some girl with one of those foreign-type I-A-N names. It seemed to me he had—"

"Lacey Kartoonian?"

"Riiight."

"What did he say about her?"

"That she loved it. That's a big thing with call-service customers. They think they're the only ones who can make you love it."

"Be more specific."

"He said, 'Do it like Lacey does.' I said, 'How's that?' He said, 'Love it.' That's all he said about her, I'm sure."

"He didn't mention her as the one who gave him a dose?"

"Uh-uh, that's all he said. And I never met that girl myself, and nobody else ever brought her up to me. And if she didn't have such a funny call name I wouldn't have remembered her at all."

Chrono links:

Christmas '57: peeper's mother with the suicide blues *again*. Susan Glynn/Joseph Arden—trick dates 9/56. Mrs. Arden, Drano drinker— private treatment. Police agencies sealed suicide files. Arden, wealthy—*if* his wife killed herself, he'd buy *extra* legal closure.

Linkage:

Letters, peeper tapes, Ancelet.

Quotes:

Joseph Arden to Lucille: "that dose you gave me."

Mom to Champ/peeper: "Your father gave me what that prostitute gave him."

Conclusive:

The peeper peeped his own father fucking Lucille.

Susan: "Penny for your thoughts."

"You don't want to know."

"Ask me one."

Try her: "When you worked for the service, did you know a girl named Gloria Benson? Her real name's Glenda Bledsoe."

Smiling, pleased: "I remember her. She quit Doug's to become a movie star. When I read she was under contract to Howard Hughes it made me so happy."

23

ilshire Station—wait, work.

I dusted the Mom-peeper envelopes—two prints surfaced. I checked Jack Woods' Vice sheet—match-up—Jack pawed the goods.

No post-Christmas letters box-stashed—why?

I buzzed Sid Riegle: check white female attempted suicides/suicides Christmas '57 up. Assume Coroner's file closure; inquire station squad to squad—City/County. Look for: middle-aged/affluent/husband/son/ daughters. Sid said I'll help you part time—*you* never show up—*I'm* running Ad Vice by default.

I called the Arden Dairy—a shot at a Joseph Arden make. Strikeout: no Arden-surname owners/employees; the founder dead, heirless.

I called University Station—4:00—nightwatch roll call in progress. Via intercom hookup:

Did any of you men trick-card Joseph Arden—white male alias?

One taker—"I *think* I carded that alias"—no real name, vehicle or description recalled.

Joseph Arden—dead for now.

A teletype check: no Topanga Canyon 187s—Pincushion Miciak decomposing.

Dinner: candy bars from a vending machine. Grab a sweat room, wait.

I tilted a chair back—sleep waves hit me. Half dreaming: Mr. Third Party says hi!

The Red Arrow Inn—peeper jimmies Lucille's door. Jimmy marks *on the peeper's door*—nonmatching. Kafesjian 459: watchdogs chopped and blinded—eyes shoved down their throats.

The peeper sobbing, listening to:

Lucille with odd tricks—and his own father.

Read the peeper passive.

Read the burglar brutal.

Silverware stolen, found: the peeper's bed stabbed and ripped. Assumed: the peeper himself. My new instinct: third party/door chopper = burglar/bed slasher =

One separate fiend.

Half dreaming—sex-fiend gargoyles chasing me. Half waking—"Double-header, Lieutenant"—Joe Plainclothes shoving two punks in.

One white, one colored. The plainclothesman cuffed them to chairs, their hands racked to the slats.

"Blondie's Patrick Orchard, and the Negro guy's Leroy Carpenter. My partner and me checked Stephen Wenzel's place, and it looked like he cleaned it out in a hurry."

Orchard—skinny, pimples. Carpenter—purple suit, this coon fashion plate.

"Thanks, Officer."

"Glad to oblige"—smile—"Glad to earn a few points with Chief Exley."

"Did you run them for warrants?"

"Sure did. Leroy's a child-support skip, and Pat's a Kern County probation absconder."

"If they cooperate, I'll cut them loose."

He winked. "Sure you will."

I winked. "Check the jail roster tomorrow if you don't believe me."

Orchard smiled. Leroy said, "Say what?" Plainclothes—huh?—back out shrugging.

Showtime.

I reached under the table—bingo—a sap taped on. "I meant what I said, and this has got *nothing* to do with you. This is about a policeman named George Stemmons, Jr. He was observed rousting you two and a guy named Stephen Wenzel, and all I want is for you to tell me about it."

Orchard—wet lips—snitch-eager.

Leroy—"Fuck you, ofay motherfuck, I know my rights."

I sapped him—arms, legs—and dumped his chair. He hit the floor sideways—no bleats, no yelps—good stones.

Orchard, snitch frenzied: "Hey, I know that Junior cat!"

"And?"

"And he shook me down for my roll!"

"And?"

"And he stole my . . . my . . ."

"And he stole your felony narcotics. *And?*"

"And he was stoned out of his fucking gourd!"

"And?"

"And he was talking this 'I'm a criminal mastermind' rebop!"

"*And?*"

"And he boosted my shit! He popped these goofballs right out in the open by the Club Alabam!"

Tilly Hopewell confirmed. *"And?"*

"An-an-an—"

I sapped his chair. "AND?"

"An-an-an' I know Steve Wenzel. St-St-Steve s-said J-Junior t-t-talked this crazy shit to him!"

Tilly confirmation ditto. I checked Leroy—too quiet—watch his fingers—

Waistband pokes, surreptitious.

I hauled his chair up and jerked his belt—H bindles popped out of his pants.

Improvise:

"Pat, I didn't find these on Mr. Carpenter, I found them on you. Now, do you have anything else to say about Junior Stemmons, Steve Wenzel and yourself?"

Leroy—"Crazy, daddy-o!"—dig the ofay.

"AND, Mr. Orchard?"

"An-an-and St-Steve s-said he c-cut a d-deal w-w-with c-crazy Junior. J-Junior p-promised Steve this b-big money to buy this b-bulk horse. C-couple days ago, Steve, he told me this. He s-s-said J-Junior n-needed twenty-four hours to get the money."

Leroy: "Sissy fink stool pigeon motherfucker."

Craaazy Junior—KILL HIM, JACK.

Twirling my sap: "Possession of heroin with intent to sell. Conspiracy to distribute narcotics. Assault on a police officer, because you just took a swing at me. *AND,* Mr. Orch—"

"Okay! Okay! Okay!"

I sapped the table. "AND?"

"A-and c-crazy Junior, he made me go with him to the club Alabam. Y-y-you know that b-boxer cop?"

"Johnny Duhamel?"

"R-right, who w-won the G-Golden Gloves. J-J-Junior, he started bothering the-the-the—"

Tongue tied bad—uncuff him, cut him slack.

Leroy: "You afraid to let *my* hands free, Mr. Po-lice?"

Orchard: "Fuck, that's better."

"AND?"

"And J-Junior, he was bugging the G-Golden Gloves guy."

"What was Duhamel doing at the Club Alabam?"

"It looked like he was eyeballing these guys back by this curtained-off room they got there."

"What guys? What were they doing?"

"It looked like they were filing numbers off these slot machines."

"And?"

"Man, you keeping saying that!"

I sapped the table hard—it jumped off the floor. "AND why did Junior Stemmons take you to the Club Alabam?"

Orchard, hands up, begging: "Okay okay okay. Junior what's-his-name was stoned out of his gourd. He buttonholed the Golden Gloves man and told him this crazy fantasy rebop that I had this big money to buy mink coats with. The boxer cop, he almost went nuts shushing Junior. They almost threw blows, and I saw these two *other* cops that I sorta knew by sight watching the whole thing sort of real interested."

"Describe the two other cops."

"Shit, mean looking. A heavyset blond guy, and this thin guy with glasses."

Breuning and Carlisle—go from there:

Duhamel scoping slot work—Mobster Squad duty? Goons scoping *him*—suspected fur thief?

Orchard: "Man, I got no more 'ands' for you. Whatever you threaten me with, I'll be feeding you bullshit from here on in."

Work the spook: *"Give,* Leroy."

"Give shit, I ain't no stool pigeon."

"No, you're a small-time independent narcotics pusher."

"Say what?"

"Say this heroin is a month's pay for you."

"An' say I got a bail bondsman ready to stand my bail an' a righteous Jew lawyer set to defend me. Say you book me, say I get my phone call. Say what, shit."

I uncuffed him. "Did Tommy Kafesjian ever muscle you, Leroy?"

"Tommy K. don't scare me."

"Sure he does."

"Horse pucky."

"You're either paying him protection, snitching for him or running from him."

"Horse pucky."

"Well, I don't think snitching's your style, but I think you're looking over your shoulder a lot waiting for some Kafesjian guy to notice you."

"Maybe that's true. But maybe the Kafesjians ain't gonna control the Southside traffic that much longer."

"Did Junior Stemmons tell you that?"

"Maybe he did. But maybe it's just loose talk pertainin' to this big Southside Federal thing. And either way I ain't no snitch."

Tough monkey.

"Leroy, why don't you tell me how Junior Stemmons muscled you."

"Fuck you."

"Why don't you tell me what you two talked about."

"Fuck your mother."

"You know, if you cooperate with me, it might help bring the Kafesjians down."

"Fuck you. I ain't no snitch."

"Leroy, were you acquainted with a maryjane pusher named Wardell Knox?"

"Fuck you, so what if I was."

"He was murdered."

"No shit, Sherlock."

"You know, there's quite a push to clear up these Negro homicides."

"No shit, Dick Tracy."

Tough and stupid.

I walked Orchard next door and cuffed him in tight. Back to Leroy—

"Give on you and Junior Stemmons, or I drive you down to 77th Street and tell Dudley Smith you killed Wardell Knox and molested a bunch of little white kids."

Coup de grace—I laid the H on the table. "Go ahead, I never saw it."

Leroy snatched his shit back. Zoooom—instant cooperation:

"All that Junior punk and me *did* was talk. Mostly he talked and I listened, 'cause he shook me down for my roll and some shit, and I knew that wasn't no crackerjack badge he showed me."

"Did he mention Tommy Kafesjian?"

"Not Tommy specific."

"Tommy's sister Lucille?"

"Uh-uh."

"A peeper spying on Lucille?"

"Uh-uh, he just said the Kafesjian family itself was going down, gonna get fucked up by the Federal business. He said LAPD Narco was gonna get neutralized by the Feds, and he was gonna be the new Southside dope kingpin—"

KILL HIM.

—"this snotnose little twerpy cop flying on a snootful of shit. He said he had the goods on the Kafesjians, and access to his boss's burglary investigation, which was full of dirty stuff to blackmail J.C. Kafesjian with—"

KILL HIM.

—"and he said he was gonna drive the Kafesjians out and steal their turf, and right about this time I'm biting my tongue to keep from laughing. Next he says he's got stuff on these brothers working for Mickey Cohen. He said they're gonna pull these sex shakedowns on movie stars—"

Junior's FI cards—Vecchio stud service—

—"and the capper is little Junior says he's gonna take over Mickey Cohen's kingdom, which as I understand it ain't such a hot kingdom no more."

"And?"

"And I was just thinking the money and dope I lost was worth it to catch this crazy motherfucker's act."

Woods' surveillance—Junior, Tommy and J.C. at Bido Lito's. Overheard: he'd protect THEM from ME. Double-agent Junior—mercy-kill him.

"Give me the dope back."

"Man, you said I could have it!"

"Give it to me."

"Fuck you, lying motherfucker!"

I sapped him down, broke his wrists, pried it free.

24

"Crazy motherfucker's act."

Junior's door—six padlocks—crazy new precautions. The dumbfuck used LAPD hardware—my master keys got me in.

Hit the lights—

Rice Krispies on the floor.

Piano wire strung ankle-high.

Closet doors nailed shut; mousetraps on the furniture.

CRAAAAZY.

Toss it slow now—the trunk distracted me last time—

I pried the closets open—nothing but food scraps inside.

Cornflakes and tacks on the kitchen floor.

Sink sludge—motor oil, glass shards; friction tape sealing the icebox. Peel it off—

Amyl nitrite poppers in an ice tray.

Reefer buds in a casserole dish.

Chocolate ice cream—plastic shoved down an open pint container. Dump it, yank—

One Minox spy camera—no film loaded in.

The hall—neck-high wires—duck. The bathroom—mousetraps, a medicine chest glued shut. Smash it open—K-Y jelly and two C-notes on a shelf.

A hamper—nailed tight—pry, pull—

Bloody hypos—spikes up—a booby trap. Dump them—a small steel strongbox underneath.

Locked—I banged it open on the wall.

Booty:

One B of A Hollywood branch passbook—balance $9,183.40.

Two safe-deposit-box keys, one instruction card. Fuck: "Box access requires password and/or visual okay."

Call it:

Evidence holes—Junior caution pre–complete CRAAAZY.

Logic:

Glenda/Klein dispositions stashed THERE—ditto the gun Georgie Ainge sold Glenda.

Find the password.

I tossed the bedroom—carpet glass spread thick—the trunk gone. The drawers—pure shit—paper scraps gibberish-scrawled.

I dumped the mattress, the couch, the chairs—no rips, no stash holes. I pulled the TV apart—mousetraps snapped. That wall section I shot out—stuffed with Kotex.

No password. No FI cards. No depositions. No Exley/no Duhamel files.

Snap, crackle, pop—Rice Krispies underfoot.

Phone *bbrinng*—

The hall extension—grab it.

"Uh, yeah?"

"It's me, Wenzel. Uh, Stemmons . . . look, man . . . I don't want any part of dealing with you."

I faked Junior's voice: "Meet me."

"No . . . I'll get your money back to you."

"Come on, let's talk about—"

"No, you're nuts!"—*click,* say it: Junior bought Wenzel's dope; Wenzel wised up later.

Bank books, box keys—mine now. I clipped the padlocks fumble-handed—kill him, Jack.

I drove to Tilly's place. Four flights up—knock—no answer.

Peep the spyhole, listen—light, TV laughs. A shoulder wedge snapped the door.

Tilly flipping channels—sprawled on the floor, hophead-dreamy.

Bindles on a chair—say a pound's worth.

Flip—Perry Como, boxing, Patti Page. Slack-face Tilly on cloud nine.

I crammed the door shut and bolted it. Tilly flipped stations, goofy-eyed: Lawrence Welk, Spade Cooley. I grabbed her, dragged her—

Clenching up, kicking—good. The bathroom, the shower, full-blast water—

Cold—soak her clothes, freeze her sober. Wet myself—fuck it.

Freezing her: big shivers, jumbo goosebumps. Teeth clicks trying to beg me—sweat her.

Hot water—fighting now—I let her hit, kick, squirm. Back to ice-cold—"All right! All right!"—no dope slur.

I pulled her out, sat her down on the toilet.

"I think Steve Wenzel left you that dope for safekeeping. He was going to give it to that policeman Junior Stemmons we talked about the other night, and Junior already paid him for it. Now he wants to give Junior his money back because Junior's crazy and he's scared. *Now you tell me what you know about that.*"

Tilly trembled—spastic shivers. I tossed her towels and tapped the heater.

She bundled up. "Are you going to tell the Probation?"

"Not if you cooperate with me."

"And what about that . . ."

"That shit in your front room that will get you a dime in some dyke farm if I decide to get ugly?"

Popping cold sweat now. "Yes."

"I won't touch it. And I know you want to geez, so the sooner you talk to me, the sooner you can."

Red coils, heat. Tilly: "Steve heard that Tommy Kafesjian's out to kill him. This seller man Pat Orchard, he knows Steve, and he was in jail this afternoon. This policeman strongarmed him—"

"That was me."

"I'm not surprised, but just let me tell you. Anyway, according to Steve, that policeman which I guess was you asked this Pat Orchard all these questions about this Junior policeman. You released him, and he went to Tommy Kafesjian and snitched that Junior man and Steve. He said that Steve sold Junior this big stash, and that the Junior policeman was talking up all this dope-kingpin jive. Steve said he moved out of his place, and he's going to try to give Junior his money back, 'cause he heard Tommy's out to get him."

"And Wenzel left his shit with you for safekeeping."

Antsy—squirming up her towels. "That's right."

"I cut Orchard loose no more than three hours ago. How did you learn all this so quickly?"

"Tommy came by here before Steve did. He told me, 'cause he knows I know Steve, and he thought I might know where he's hiding. I didn't tell him I talked to you the other night, and I said I don't know where Steve is, which is the truth. He left, then Steve came by and dropped his stash off. I told him, 'You run from that crazy Tommy and that crazy Junior.' "

Steve calls Junior—and gets me. "What else did you and Tommy talk about?"

Stifling coil heat—Tilly dripped sweat. "He wanted to do it to me, but I said no 'cause you told me he killed Wardell Knox."

"What else? The sooner I go, the sooner you can—"

"Tommy said he's looking for this guy spying on his sister, Lucille. He said he's going crazy looking for that spyer."

"What else did he tell you about him?"

"Nothing."

"Did he say his name was Richie?"

"No."

"Did he say he was a musician?"

"No."

"Did he say he had leads on where the guy was?"

"No. He said the spyer was like a f-ing phantom, and he didn't know where he was."

"Did he mention a different man, someone spying on the spyer?"

"No."

"Did he mention *any* name on the spyer?"

"No."

"Champ Dineen?"

"Do you think I'm stupid? Champ Dineen was this music writer who died years ago."

"What else did Tommy say about Lucille?"

"Nothing."

"Did he mention the name Joseph Arden?"

"No. Please, I need to—"

"Did Tommy say *he* was screwing Lucille?"

"Mister, you got an evil curiosity about that girl."

Fast: out to the front room, back with the dope.

"Mister, that belongs to Steve."

I cracked the window, looked down—a crap game in the alley dead below.

"Mister . . ."

I tossed a bindle out—dice-blanket bullseye. "What else did Tommy say about Lucille?"

"*Nothing.* Mister, please!"

Shouts downstairs—dope from heaven.

Two more bindles out—"Mister, I need that!"—four, five—alleyway roars.

"TOMMY AND LUCILLE"—six, seven, eight.

Nine, ten—"It's wrong to be thinking what you're thinking. Would you be doing that with your own sister?!"

Crap-game reveries—praise Jesus.

Eleven, twelve—I threw them at Tilly.

. . .

Downtown—R&I—a run for Steve Wenzel's rap sheet and mugshots. Wenzel—two dope falls, butt-ugly: lantern-jaw white trash. No KAs/ known haunts listed—I shifted to THEM.

A run by their house—lights on, cars out front. I parked, window reconned.

Down the driveway—dark—I watched for new dogs. Hop the fence, peep around—Madge cooking, no Lucille. Dark rooms, the den—J.C., Tommy and Abe Voldrich.

I squatted down. Closed windows—no sound. Eyeball it:

J.C. waving papers; Tommy giggling. Voldrich—read his hands—be calm.

Muffled shouts—the window glass hummed.

I squinted; J.C. kept waving those papers. He moved closer—fuck—Ad Vice forms.

No way to read the fine print.

Probably Klein-to-Exley stuff—peeper leads. Stolen, leaked—maybe Junior, maybe Wilhite.

"Tommy going crazy chasing that spyer."

I circuited back to my car. Peep surveillance—*my* eyes on *her* window. Forty minutes down—there—Lucille nonchalant naked. Her lights went out too fucking soon—I scoped the front door still hungry to watch.

Ten minutes, fifteen.

Slam—the three men ran out—over to separate cars. Tommy's Merc crunched off the sidewalk dragging sparks.

J.C. and Voldrich headed northbound.

Tommy—dead south.

Follow *him*—

La Brea south, Slauson east—this purple coon coach. *Way* east, Central Avenue south.

Peeper turf.

Light traffic—lay back, tail that jig rig. Way south—Watts—east.

Tommy, brake lights on—Avalon and 103—after-hours-party-club row.

Nigger Heaven:

Two tenements wood-plank-linked—three stories up, open windows, fire-escape access.

Tommy parked. I cruised by, backed up, watched him:

He walked over to the right-side building.

He climbed up the fire escape and stepped on the plank.

Tommy creeping—wobbly wood, rope holds.

Tommy crouching.

Tommy peeping the left-side window.

Big-time-hinky wrong: Tommy just plain looking.

I bolted my car, bolted the left-side steps. No lobby lookout—sprint.

Three floors up—bouncers at the door. Looks: who's this cop know? Instant bouncer-doormen—I walked in.

Mock-zebra walls, party geeks—white, colored. Music, party noise.

I scanned the room—no peeper-sketch look-alikes, no Tommy.

Check the window—no Tommy on the plank.

Geeks packed tight—white hepcats/snazzy niggers—hard to move.

Reefer smoke close by—lantern-jaw Steve Wenzel passing a stick.

Geeks between us.

Tommy behind him, hands in his coat.

Hands out—a sawed-off pump getting loose.

I yelled—

Some nigger hit a switch—the room went black.

Shotgun roar—full auto—one long blast. Spatter spray/random pistol shots/screams—muzzle flash lit up Steve Wenzel, faceless.

Screams.

I ripped through them out the window.

I crawled the plank, glass and brains in my hair.

25

arbor Freeway northbound, two-way squawk:

"Code 3 all units vicinity 103rd and Avalon multiple homicides 10342 South Avalon third floor ambulances responding repeat all units multiple 187s 10342 South Avalon see the building superintendent—"

Breathing blood—my raincoat cleaned me up—clean, but still smelling it.

"Repeat all units four dead 10342 South Avalon Code 3 ambulances responding."

Shell shock worse than Saipan—the road blurred.

"Traffic units vicinity 103 and Avalon Code 3 see Sergeant Disbrow Code 3 urgent."

6th Street off-ramp, down to Mike Lyman's—Exley's late dinner spot. I palmed a waiter: get the Chief *now*.

Happy people all around me—gargoyles.

"Lieutenant, this way please!"

I followed the waiter. A booth at the back—Exley standing, Bob Gallaudet sprawled—what's this?

Exley: "Klein, what is it?"

Bar seats close—I gestured him over. Bob—feelers perking, out of earshot.

"Klein, what *is* it?"

"You remember that pickup order you issued this morning?"

"Yes. Three men to be detained at Wilshire Station. You owe me an explanation on it, so start—"

"One of the men was an indie pusher named Steve Wenzel, and half an hour ago Tommy Kafesjian shotgunned him at one of those sanctioned after-hours pads in Watts. I was there, I saw it, it's all over the City air. Four dead so far."

"Explain this to me."

"It all pertains to Junior Stemmons."

"Explain it."

"Fuck . . . he's dirty past your wildest . . . fuck, he's shooting dope, he's shaking down pushers. He's a faggot, he's extorting queers in Fern Dell Park, I think he's leaking my 459 reports to you to the Kafesjians, he's driving around Niggertown like a crazy man, talking up how he's the new—"

Restraining me: "And you've been trying to take care of it yourself."

I pulled loose. "That's right. Junior bought Wenzel's stash, to quote unquote 'set himself up as the new Southside dope kingpin.' One of the other men on that pickup order, *who I questioned extensively about Stemmons and Wenzel,* snitched both of them to Tommy K. I tailed Tommy down to Watts, and I was there when he took out Wenzel."

Pure patrician frost: "I'll send an IAD team down to seal those homicides. It was Wenzel and innocent bystanders?"

"Right."

"Then I'll make sure *his* ID is kept away from the press, which will prevent that pickup order from coming back to haunt us."

"You don't want the Feds getting ahold of this, so you'd better drop a blanket on the press right now."

"Klein, you know that you can't approach—"

"I won't go near Tommy Kafesjian—*yet*—even though I saw him kill a man, even though you won't tell me why you're using me to operate that family."

No rebuke, no comeback.

"Where's Stemmons now?"

"I don't know"—KILL HIM, JACK.

"Do you think they'll . . ."

"I don't *think* they'll clip him. They might put Dan Wilhite on it, but I don't think they'd clip an LAPD man."

"I want a detailed confidential report on this within twenty-four hours."

I crowded him—Bob G. watching. *"Nothing on paper,* are you fucking insane? And while I've got you, you should know that Junior's queer for Johnny Duhamel. Next time you see Dudley, tell him he's got a fruit heartthrob working for him."

Exley blinked—simple loose talk shivved him. "There must be a reason why you didn't tell me these things about Stemmons before."

"You don't inspire friendly talks."

"No, but you're much too smart to bypass authority when it can get you what you want."

"Then help me get a bank writ. Junior has some dope stashed in safe-deposit boxes. Help me get it out before it embarrasses the Department."

"Altruistic of you to be so concerned, but *you're* the lawyer, bank writs are Fed business and Welles Noonan is the U.S. Attorney here."

"You could petition a Federal judge."

"No."

"No, *and?*"

"No, and right now I want you to go by that man Wenzel's place and toss it for evidence on his dealings with Junior Stemmons. If you find any, destroy it. *That* would be a service to the Department."

"Chief, let *me* take care of Stemmons."

"No. I'm going to call out every man in IAD. I'm going to wrap that Watts shootout up, find Stemmons and sequester him where the Feds can't find him."

Junior ratting Glenda—wide screen/VistaVision/3-D—

"Will you quash *anything* incriminating that comes out on me and mine?"

"Yes. But don't cloak your self-serving motives in respect for the Department. Given what you are, it's pitifully transparent."

Change-up: "Has IAD been tailing me sporadically since the Johnson thing?"

"No. If you've been under surveillance, it's the Feds. I forgave you for *that* murder, remember?"

X-ray eyes—the fuck made me blink.

"Clean yourself up, Lieutenant. You smell like blood."

I cruised by Wenzel's pad—J.C.'s car was parked outside. Call it: potential Tommy links snipped quick.

Shell-shock images:

The Feds bag Junior live. He plea bargains: queer exposure quashed in exchange for Dave Klein nailed. Junior, evidence-prof savant—all my killings, all my payoffs itemized.

Go—toss that insane hovel one more time—

I drove over, unlocked six padlocks to get in. Lights on, new horror:

Shotgun shells in the oven.

Cherry bombs crammed down a toaster.

Razor blades choking a heat duct.

Do it:

Bag the spy camera.

Bag the gibberish notes.

Dump the furniture again—four chairs in—loose stitching. Rip, reach—

Cash tucked away—$56.
Gilette 187 carbons—Homicide-pilfered.
A new Glenda/Klein report—more detail:

PRIOR TO HER FATAL SHOOTING AND STABBING OF GILETTE,
MISS BLEDSOE FIRED TWO NON-WOUNDING SHOTS WITH THE
AFOREMENTIONED .32 REVOLVER THAT SHE HAD PURCHASED
FROM GEORGE AINGE. (SEE BALLISTICS REPORT # 114-55 AT-
TACHED TO THE HIGHLAND PARK SQUAD CASE FILE FOR DETAILS
ON THE EXPENDED ROUNDS TAKEN FROM GILETTE'S BODY AND
FOUND EMBEDDED IN HIS LIVING ROOM WALLS.) THAT RE-
VOLVER IS NOW SAFE IN MY POSSESSION, LEFT WITH ME BY
AINGE PRIOR TO HIS DEPARTURE FROM LOS ANGELES. I HAVE
TEST FIRED SIX ROUNDS FROM IT, AND BALLISTICS ANALYSIS OF
THE ROUNDS INDICATES THAT THEY ARE *IDENTICAL* TO THE
ROUNDS TAKEN FROM BOTH GILETTE'S BODY AND THE GILETTE
PREMISES. IT IS PLASTIC WRAPPED AND THE SMOOTH PEARL
GRIPS SUSTAINED RIGHT AND LEFT THUMB PRINTS WHICH
MATCH TO ELEVEN COMPARISON POINTS THE PRINTS ON FILE
FROM GLENDA BLEDSOE'S 1946 JUVENILE SHOPLIFTING ARREST.

I ripped it up, flushed it.
"Safe"/"wrapped"/powdered = safety-box-stashed.
I tapped the walls—no hollow spots.
I unzipped cushions—mousetraps set with Cheez Whiz snapped at me.
I yanked a loose floorboard—an electric dashboard Jesus glowed up iridescent.
I laughed—
99% CRAAAZY Junior—1% sane. Sane evidence—methodical, logical, concise, succinct, plausible—assume death provisions rigged—willing the concise, logical, plausible, succinct evidence to its most logical, po-tentially vindictive heir: Howard Fucking Hughes.
Laughing—hard to breathe—Rice Krispies popping on the floor. Voices next door—why's that nice Mr. Stemmons laughing so CRAAAZY?
I grabbed the phone, fumbled it, dialed.
"Hello? Dav—"
"Yeah, it's me."
"Where are you? What happened with Doug?"
Ancelet—skewed time—ancient stuff. "I'll tell you when I see you."
"Then come over now."

"I can't."

"Why?"

"I'm waiting someplace. There's an off chance the guy who lives here might show up."

"Then leave him a note and have him call you at my place."

Don't laugh. "I can't."

"You sound very strange."

"I'll tell you about it when I see you."

Silence—line crackle—Miciak hovered.

"David, do you . . ."

"Don't say his name, and if it hasn't been in the papers or on TV, figure no."

"And when it's yes, I know what to do."

"You always know what to do."

"And you'll always push me for where I learned it."

"I'm a detective."

"No, you're this man who implements things. And everything about *me* can't be explained."

"But I'll—"

"But you'll always try—so come over and try now."

"I can't. Glenda, tell me things. Distract me."

Hear it—match flare, exhale. "Well, Herman Gerstein came by the set today and raised hell with Mickey. It seems that he's seen rushes, and he's afraid Sid Frizell's making the movie too gory. Also, quote, 'This vampire incest routine might get that goddamn goyishe Legion of Decency on our ass,' unquote. To top that off, Touch told me that Rock gave him the crabs, and Sid's been screening outtakes from this stag film he's shooting down in Lynwood. Not the most attractive performers, but the crew seemed to enjoy it."

I checked a window—dawn coming. "I should keep this line open."

"Tonight then?"

"I'll call you."

"Be careful."

"Always."

I hung up, grabbed a chair and drifted someplace. Vampires there: Tommy, Pops chasing Meg with his fly down. Blank sleep, hands on me— "Yeah, he's the boss at Ad Vice."

"Lieutenant, wake up."

Up thrashing.

Two prototype IA men, guns out.

"Sir, Junior Stemmons is dead."

26

ode 3 to Bido Lito's—
two cars—no explanation.
Spooked: Jack said he'd
lose the corpse.

Side streets, there:

Reporters, prowl cars, Plymouths—Feds snapping zoom-lens pix. Civilians milling around—no crowd ropes yet.

I parked and followed a morgue team. Feds talking—duck by, listen:

". . . and their pictures weren't in our Intelligence files. These were unknown, most likely out-of-town hoods seen servicing the coin machines here and at a dozen other Southside locations."

"Frank—"

"Please, just listen. Yesterday, Noonan got an anonymous tip on a garage down here. We hit it, and we found slot machines up the wazoo. *But*—it was just a separate garage on a dirty little street, and we can't trace the ownership to save our lives."

Slot intrigue—fuck it—

I ran inside. Heavy brass: Exley, Dudley Smith, Inspector George Stemmons, Sr. Lab men swarming, Dick Carlisle, Mike Breuning.

Voodoo eyes strafed me—Lester Lake's savior. They flipped stiff fingers surreptitious—Breuning kissed his.

Flashbulb pops. Stemmons shouting, close to tears.

Morgue jockeys pushed a gurney in. I chased them—past the bandstand, back hallways—a slot room.

FUCK—

Junior dead—fetal-curled on the floor.

Junkie-tied—an arm tourniquet—rigor-locked teeth on a sash cord.

A spike bent off a mainline; bulging eyes. Short sleeves—needle tracks and vein scars exposed.

A bluesuit, gawking: "I checked his pockets. He had a key to the front door on him."

A lab man: "The janitor got here early and found him. Jesus, this kind of grief right in the middle of the Fed thing."

The coroner, mind reader: "It's either a legitimate OD or a very skillful hotshot. Those marks are proof of the man's addiction. My God, a Los Angeles police officer."

Jack Woods—never.

Ray Pinker nudged me. "Dave, Chief Exley wants to see you out back."

I double-timed it out to the lot. Exley was standing by Junior's car. "Interpret this."

"Interpret shit. It's real or it's the Kafesjians."

"IA said they found you asleep at Stemmons' apartment."

"That's right."

"What were you doing there?"

"I drove over to Steve Wenzel's place and saw J.C.'s car in front. Junior's apartment was close, and I thought he might show up. What happened with Watts?"

"Five dead, and no eyewitnesses. It was dark when Tommy Kafesjian fired, is that correct?"

"Yeah, he had some nigger kill the lights. Did you—"

"Wenzel was the only white victim, and the state of his body precluded an early ID. Apparently, the shotgun rounds provoked a reaction from a number of independently armed men inside the club. Bob Gallaudet and I went down there and mollified the press. We told them all the victims were Negroes and promised them passes to the Chavez Ravine evictions if they soft-pedaled the story. Of course they agreed."

"Yeah, but you can bet the Feds were monitoring our radio calls."

"They were there taking pictures, but so far as they know it was just some sort of glorified Negro altercation."

"And since they're charging us with giving shine killings the go-by, you sent a dozen Homicide dicks over for appearances."

"Correct, and Bob and I spoke to an influential Negro minister. He has political aspirations, and he promised to talk to the victims' loved ones. While he's at it, he's going to urge them not to talk to the Feds."

Junior's car—grime-streaked windows, filthy. "What did you find here?"

"Narcotics, canned food and homosexual literature. IA's impounding it."

Noise inside the club. Check the window: Stemmons, Sr., kicking chairs. "What about Junior?"

"We'll tell the press it was accidental death. IA will investigate, very discreetly."

"And steer clear of the Kafesjians."

"They'll be dealt with in time. Do you think Narco could have done this?"

Stemmons sobbing.

"Klein—"

"No. Sure, they could rig a hotshot, but I don't think it's them. I'm leaning toward a legit OD."

"Why?"

"A patrolman said Junior had a front-door key in his pocket. He was a doped-up crazy fuck, and this place is a known Tommy K. dope drop and hangout. If they were going to kill him, they wouldn't have left the body here."

"What kind of condition did you find his apartment in?"

"You wouldn't believe me if I told you, and you should let me forensic it. I aced forensics undergrad, and I trashed the place and probably left prints up the ying-yang."

"Do it, then wipe it. And call Pacific Bell and get his phone records sealed. Now, last night you said Stemmons had dope stored in safe-deposit boxes."

"Yes."

"Do you know which banks?"

"I've got his bank books and the box keys."

"Good, and you're an attorney, so I'll go along with your 'dope stash' fantasy and tell you to study your law books and figure out a strategy to bypass Welles Noonan and secure a bank writ."

"Fantasy?"

Sighing: "Stemmons has dirt on you. It's most likely stored in those boxes. He was extorting you on some level, or you would have dealt with him in your inimitable strongarm fashion before this lunacy of his extended so far out of control."

NOW, SPILL IT:

"He had a clipping file on *you.* It was hidden with some Personnel forms on Johnny Duhamel. Last night I made a bullshit comment on Duhamel that jacked your blood pressure up about twenty points, so don't you fucking patronize me."

"Describe the file"—no reaction, pure frost.

"All your Bureau cases. Thorough—Junior was as good a paperwork evidence man as I've ever seen. I broke into his apartment last week and found it. *Last night* it was gone."

"Interpret."

I winked Dudley-style. "Let's just say it's nice to know that my good buddy Ed has got a personal stake in this too. And don't worry on Kafesjian 459 PC—I'm in way too deep to stop."

Window view—Papa Stemmons grieving. "You should calm him down,

Eddie. We don't want him screwing up this personal thing of ours."

"Call me after your forensic"—about-face, watch him go.

Window view:

Exley waltzing up to Stemmons—no handshake, no embrace. Crack the window, listen:

"Your son . . . forbid you to interfere or talk to the press . . . spare you the pain of his pervert tendencies made public."

Stemmons weaving, grief-crazy.

27

ar radio downtown:

KMPC: Policeman Found Dead at Southside Jazz Club—LAPD Says Heart Attack.

KGFJ: After-Hours Shootout! Five Negroes Dead!

Press blanket—Exley working fast.

Nothing on Harold John Miciak.

Police-band check—dipshit cops ID'ing Junior by name.

The Bureau, my office—a run for clean clothes. A locker-room shave and shower—keyed up, exhausted.

Down the hall to Personnel—I requisitioned Junior's print abstract. Furtive: I grabbed Johnny Duhamel's.

The lab—I bagged an evidence kit and a camera. A call to PC Bell—Exley's name dropped.

Do this:

Compile all Gladstone 4-0629 calls going back twenty days.

List the names and addresses of all people called.

Hold all George Stemmons, Jr., records—awaiting Chief Exley's court order.

Call *me* at that number—with full results—inside four hours.

Car radio back out:

Watts killings—Negro preacher blames liquor—"the enslaver of our people."

Exley press-leak fantasia:

During a hot pursuit through a closed-down Southside nightclub, Sergeant George Stemmons, Jr., suffers a fatal heart attack. The robber escapes; there will be no autopsy—it violates the dead officer's religion.

No Miciak.

No Fed stuff.

Blues guarding Junior's door—I locked them out and worked.

I took photos:

Booby traps/cornflake piles/sloth.

I bagged fibers, listed property.

Print dusting next—tedious, slow. I got Junior himself—multiple sets—ten point matched to the abstract. The living room/hallway/ kitchen—odd latents, featuring scar ridges. An easy make—me—Pops caught me stealing and burned my fingers.

Three rooms down—I wiped them clean. The inside doorway—a new set, a match: Duhamel, eight comparison points. Extrapolate it: Johnny scared to enter.

I wiped them. The phone rang—PC Bell, responding.

I copied:

10/28/58—BR 6-8499—Mr. & Mrs. George Stemmons, 4129 Dresden, Pasadena.

10/30/58—BR 6-8499—ditto.

11/2/58—MA 6-1147—Administrative Vice Division, LAPD.

11/2/58—Mom/Dad.

11/3/58, 11/3/58, 11/4/58, 11/4/58—Ad Vice.

11/5/58, 11/5/58, 11/6/58—GR 1-4790—John Duhamel, 10477 Oleander, Eagle Rock.

11/6/58, 11/6/58, 11/7/58, 11/9/58, 11/9/58—AX 4-1192—Victory Motel, Gardena.

11/9/58—MU 8-5888—pay phone, 81st/Central—Los Angeles.

11/9/58—MU 7-4160—pay phone, 79th/Central—Los Angeles.

11/9/58—MU 6-1171—pay phone, 67th/Central—Los Angeles.

11/9/58—Victory Motel.

11/9/58—ditto.

11/9/58—Duhamel's pad.

11/10/58—WE 5-1243—pay phone, Olympic/La Brea—Los Angeles.

11/10/58—Victory Motel.

11/10/58, 11/10/58, 11/11/58, 11/12/58—KL 6-1885—pay phone, Aviation/Hibiscus—Lynwood.

11/16/58—HO 4-6833—Glenda Bledsoe, 2489½ N. Mount Airy, Hollywood.

Writer's cramp—interpret the data:

Mom-Dad/work early on—straight biz. Duhamel calls next—Junior going crazy. The Victory Motel—Mobster Squad HQ—Smith's strongarm spot/Johnny on duty.

Pay phones then—Darktown locations—say dope biz, maybe talks with Steve Wenzel. A non-sequitur phone booth—Olympic and La Brea—the Kafesjian pad six blocks south. Crazy Junior—THEY said don't call the house.

11/12 to 11/16—no calls, Junior INSANE. 11/16—*my* late Glenda call. Logical, but:

Lynwood pay-phone calls = ????

Exhaustion-fried—I dusted the bed rail.

Fuck—

Interlocked hand spreads—laced fingers gripping. Sweat smears, viable latents: and *no* Johnny points. Obvious Junior prints linked with unknown prints: some ham-handed faggot.

Wipe them—*bbring bbring*—grab the phone, shut the bed out.

"Exley?"

"It's John Duhamel."

"What the—how did you know I was here?"

"I heard a radio call about Stemmons. I drove by his place, and the patrolmen told me you were inside. I—look, I need to talk to you."

ADRENALINE—my head buzzed.

"Where are you?"

"No . . . meet me tonight."

"Come on, *now.*"

"No, we'll make it eight o'clock. 4980 Spindrift. It's in Lynwood."

"Why there?"

"Evidence."

"Johnny, tell me—"

Click—dial tone—tap the button—Exley, fast.

NO.

Don't—he's hinked on Johnny—just maybe.

Option call—I dialed MA 4-8630.

"Office of the District Attorney."

"Dave Klein for Bob Gallaudet."

"I'm sorry, sir. Mr. Gallaudet is in a staff meeting."

"Tell him it's urgent."

Transfer clicks, "Dave, what can I do for you?"

"A favor."

"Name it—you've shot me a few recently."

"I need a look at an IAD personal file."

"Is this an Ed innovation? IA's very much his cadre."

"Yeah, it's an Exley thing. When a man makes the Detective Bureau, IAD does a very thorough background check. I'm meeting a man tonight, and I need more of a handle on him. It's about the Darktown trouble, and you could get a look at the file with no questions."

"You're doing this behind Ed's back."

"Yeah, like those Kafesjian reports I gave you."

A pause—seconds ticking. "Touché, so call me back in a few hours. It can't leave the Bureau, but I'll oblige you with a synopsis. What's the man's name?"

"John Duhamel."

"Schoolboy Johnny? I lost a bundle on his pro debut. Care to enlighten me?"

"When it's over, Bob. Thanks."

"Well, quid pro quo for now. And next time I see you, let me tell you about the meeting Ed and I had with this colored minister. Strange bedfellows, huh?"

That bed—laced hands. "The fucking strangest."

28

Surplus adrenaline—it jacked me up to peep the Kafesjians.

I staked their house from three doors down—no bedroom-window strip show. Nobody peeper-chasing—three cars on the lawn.

Stakeout time killer—my car radio:

Junior eulogized—LAPD chaplain Dudley Smith: "He was a grand lad. He was a dedicated crimefighter, and it is a cruel caprice of fate that so young a man should suffer cardiac arrest while chasing a common robber."

Welles Noonan on KNX: ". . . and I'm not saying that the surprising death of an allegedly healthy young policeman is connected to the other five deaths that have occurred within the past twenty-four hours in South Central Los Angeles, but it seems curious to me that the Los Angeles Police Department should be so eager to explain it all away and be done with it."

Smart Noonan—shit draws flies.

4:00—Tommy sax-honks—my cue to leave. My own music juicing me—I was closing in on SOMETHING.

Early dusk—clouds, rain. A phone booth stop—Bob out, Riegle in. Bum station check news—no suicides clicked in PEEPER'S MOTHER.

Up to the set—hard rain—no shooting in progress. Luck: her trailer light on. A sprint—in the door dodging puddles.

Glenda was smoking, distracted. Sprawled on the bed—no rush to touch me.

Easy guess: "Miciak?"

She nodded. "Bradley Milteer came by. Apparently he and Herman Gerstein know each other independent of his work for Hughes. He told Herman that Miciak's body and car were found, and that all of Hughes' contract players were going to be discreetly questioned. Mickey overheard him tell Herman that detectives from the Malibu Sheriff's Station would be by to talk to me."

"That's all you heard?"

"No. Mickey said the Sheriff's are keeping their investigation under wraps to avoid embarrassing Howard."

"Did he mention the Hollywood Division LAPD? A killer named the Wino Will-o-the-Wisp?"

Glenda blew smoke rings. "No. I thought—I mean *we* thought Hughes would just push this under the table."

"No, we *wished* it. And there's no evidence that Miciak was killed at . . ."

"At the *fuck pad* where Howard Hughes used to *fuck* me and the man I killed wanted to *fuck* me?"

Stop her/make her think. "You bought it, and now you're paying for it. Now you act your way out."

"Direct me. Tell me something to make it easy."

Touch me, tell me *things.*

"You say you were home alone that night. You don't flirt with the officers or try to charm them. You subtly drop that Hughes is a lech and you can spill the goods on it. You reach for whatever it is that you won't tell me about that gave you the stones to . . . oh shit, Glenda."

"Okay"—just like that—"Okay."

I kissed her—dripping wet. "Is there a phone I can use?"

"Outside Mickey's trailer. You know, if I could cry on cue, I would."

"Don't, please."

"You're leaving?"

"I have to meet a man."

"Later, then?"

"Yeah, I'll come by your place."

"I won't expect much. You look like you haven't slept in a week."

Raining buckets—I ducked under Mickey's trailer awning. The phone worked—I dialed Gallaudet's private line.

He picked up himself. "Hello?"

"It's me, Bob."

"Dave, hi, and quid pro quo fulfilled. Are you listening?"

"Shoot."

"John Gerald Duhamel, age twenty-five. As far as IA personal files go, not much—I checked a few others for a comparison."

"And?"

"And aside from the interesting combination of a cum laude engineering degree and an amateur boxing career, not much of note."

"Family?"

"An only child. His parents were supposedly rich, but died in a plane crash and left the kid broke while he was still in college, and under known associates we've got the somewhat dicey Reuben Ruiz and his sticky-fingered brothers, but of course Reuben's on our side now. The kid apparently has an undiscriminating appetite for poontang, which I did myself when I was twenty-five. There were unsubstantiated rumors that he tanked his one and only pro fight, and that's all the news that's fit to print."

No bells rang. "Thanks, Bob."

"I'll never high-hat you, son—I remember those crib sheets too well."

"Thanks."

"Take care, son."

I hung up, took a breath, ran—

"Dave! Over here!"

Lightning glow lit up the voice—Chick Vecchio under a tarp hang. Bums behind him, sucking T-Bird.

I dashed over—time to kill.

Chick: "Mickey's at home today."

Glenda—fifty-fifty he knew. "I should have known. Fuck, this rain."

"The *Herald* said two inches. The *Herald* also said that kid partner of yours had a heart attack. Why don't I believe the *Herald?"*

"Because your kid brother told you my kid partner shook him down in Fern Dell Park."

"Yeah, and I don't feature twenty-nine-year-old extortionist cops having heart attacks."

"Chick, *come on."*

"All right, all right. Touch told me he told you about him and Stemmons in Fern Dell, but there's something he didn't tell you."

Preempt him: "You, Touch and Pete Bondurant are planning your own shakedown gig. It's sex, and it's cough up or *Hush-Hush* gets the pictures. Stemmons got it out of Touch, so now you're afraid that *we* know."

"Hey, *you* know."

I lied: "Stemmons told me. The regular Bureau doesn't have a clue, and if they knew they'd bury it to protect the kid's reputation. Your gig's covered."

"Copacetic, but I still don't feature no heart attack."

"Off the record?"

"Uh-huh, and on the QT, like *Hush-Hush."*

I cupped a whisper. "The kid was fucking around with J.C. and Tommy Kafesjian. He was popping H, and he OD'd or took a hotshot. It's a toilet job, and it's headed for a whitewash."

Chick cupped a whisper. "Feature the K. boys are not to screw around with."

"Feature I'm starting to think that Ed Exley's going to take those humps down two seconds after the Fed heat peters out."

"Which may be a while, the way things are looking."

Wind, rain. "Chick, what's with Mickey? I saw some new guys moving slots out of the Rick Rack, with Feds right across the street taking pictures."

Chick shrugged. "Mickey's Mickey. He's this hebe hardhead you can't talk sense to half the time."

"The whole thing played funny. A couple of the slot guys were Mex, and Mickey never hires spics. I tipped him on the Feds early on, but he still won't pull his metal."

"Touch and me are staying out of all this Southside business. It sounds to me like Mickey's hiring freelance."

Winos pissing on the spaceship. "Yeah, and maybe cut-rate, like your crew here. Does he need money that bad? I know he's buffered, but sooner or later the Feds will pin those machines on him."

"Off the record?"

"Sure."

"Then feature Mickey's paying off a syndicate loan with his slot percentages, so he's got to let the machines linger a bit. I guess he knows it's risky, but he's scuffling."

"Yeah—'He's a scrapper, and scrappers always get results.' "

"I said it and I meant it."

"And he thinks he'll get a district gambling franchise."

"Feature that bill could pass."

"Feature the AG's office under Gas Chamber Bob Gallaudet? Feature him granting *Mickey Cohen* a franchise?"

Smirking: "Feature I don't think you came here to see Mickey."

Wet ground—the spaceship capsized—bums cheered. "I hope this movie makes money."

"So does Mickey. Hey, where you going?"

"Lynwood."

"Hot date?"

"Yeah, with a pretty-boy strongarm cop."

"I'll tell Touch—he'll be jealous."

Adrenaline—rain peaked it.

29

Lynwood—wind, rain—streets running crisscross and diagonal. Dark—hard to see; Aviation and Hibiscus—that pay phone on the corner.

Tombstone laughs—Jack's call reprised:

"He kicked natural or got snuffed by somebody else? Come on, let me redeem myself. Say Welles Noonan for that same ten?"

Stucco pads—quasi slums; empty bungalow courts. Spindrift—the 4900 block—I skimmed numbers.

24, 38, 74. 4980: a two-deck stucco dive, abandoned.

One light on—downstairs left, the door open.

I walked up.

An empty living room—cobwebs, dusty floor—Schoolboy Johnny standing there calm.

No jacket, empty holster—trust me.

Trust shit—watch his hands.

"Are you grieving for Junior, Johnny?"

"What do you know about Stemmons and me?"

"I know he made you for the fur heist. I know that other stuff doesn't count."

"Other stuff" made him blink. Ten feet apart—watch his hands.

"He had evidence on you, too. He felt terrible things for certain people, and he collected evidence on them to even things out."

"We can work out a deal. I don't care about the fur job."

"You don't know the half"—eye flickers craaaazy.

Footsteps behind me.

My hands pinned/my mouth cupped—smothered/my sleeves rolled up/stabbed.

Walking air—tunnel vision—peripheral grass. Tingles/flutters up my groin/toasty warm.

Side doorways, shoes, trouser legs flapping.

Elbow dipped, shoes on concrete, right turn—

A door opened—warm air, light. Mirrored walls, herringbone patterns up close. Somebody stretched me prone.

Light overhead—snowflake blurry.

Whir, click/click—cylinder noise, like a camera. Sliding on my knees—white wax paper under me.

Propped up.

Tape strips on my eyes—slapped sticky blind.

Somebody hit me.

Somebody poked me.

Somebody burned me—hot/cold sizzles on my neck.

Not so tingly/toasty warm—no flutters up my groin.

Somebody pulled the tape off—sticky red blood in my eyes.

Cylinder *click-clicks*.

Propped up on white wax paper. Something in my right hand, heavy and shiny: MY souvenir Jap sword.

Shoved, focused in:

Johnny Duhamel naked, holding MY gun.

Burned: hot/cold—my neck, my hands.

Burned raw—Johnny kneeling, glassy eyes, taunting me.

Burned—steam in my face—Johnny taunting me—blue slant eyes.

Get him, cut him—wild swings, misses.

Johnny weaving—grip down, swing two-handed.

Miss, hit, miss—pale skin ripped, tattoos gouting blood. Hit, rip, rip—an arm gone, socket spray. Johnny jabbering Jap singsong, blue slant eyes—

Miss, miss—Jap Johnny prone, twitching crazy. Sight in—this chest tattoo—split it, split him—

Miss, miss—wax paper shredding.

Hit, jerk down—spine snaps/blade drag/pull—red EVERYWHERE.

Gasping—hard to breathe—blood in my mouth.

Somebody stabbed me—I went tingly/toasty warm/flutters up my groin.

Fading out: flamethrower burns toasty nice, Jap surrender.

Floating toasty black. *Tick tick* somewhere—a clock—I counted seconds. Six thousand—drifting off—ten thou four hundred.

Jap zeros gliding, voices:

Meg: Pops never touched me—David, don't hurt him. The peeper: Daddy, Daddy. Lucille: He's *my* Daddy.

Jap zeros strafing Darktown. *Tick tick*—fourteen thousand odd.
Toasty black.

Blurry: gray herringbones, shoes.
Wall mirrors topsy-turvy; Jap zeros. I tried to wave—stupid—taped-down arms wouldn't let me.
A chair—taped in snug.
Projector clicks.
White light, a white screen.
Movie time—Pops and Meg?—don't let him grope her.
I thrashed—futile—sticky tape, no give.
A white screen.
Cut to:
Johnny Duhamel naked.
Cut to:
Dave Klein swinging a sword.
Zooming in—the sword grip: SSGT D.D. Klein USMC Saipan 7/24/43.
Cut to:
Johnny begging—"Please"—mute sound.
Cut to:
Dave Klein thrashing—stabbing, missing.
Cut to:
A severed arm twitching on wax paper.
Cut to:
Dave Klein, gutting motions—Johnny D. coughing entrails.
Cut to:
Lens glass dripping red; a finger flicking spine chips off the surface.
I screamed—
A needle stab cut me off mute.

Fading in—moving—night—windshield blur.
Niggertown—South Central.
Chest pains, neck pains. Beard stubble, no holster.
Swerving.
Sirens *whoop whoop.*
Burn aches.
Disinfectant stink—somebody washed me.
Where/what/who—Johnny Duhamel begging.
No.

Not for real.
THEY made me do it.
Please—I didn't like it.
Sirens, flames up ahead.

30

ire trucks, prowl cars. Beard stubble—say a day's worth. Smoke, fire—Bido Lito's flaming skyward.

A roadblock—swing right—I jumped the curb. Gray suit camera men right there—monsters.

Bumper crunch, this sign: "Self-Determination Is Yours With the Prophet Muhammed."

Resting now—a nice soft dashboard. Fading out: "That's Klein. Grab him."

"I think he's got a concussion."

"He looks drugged to me."

"I don't think this is legal."

"It's dicey, but it's legal. We found him blacked out near an arson homicide scene, and he's a major suspect in our overall investigation. Mr. Noonan has a source in the Coroner's Office. He told him that Klein's partner died of a heroin overdose, and just look at this man's condition."

"Jim, for the written record in case this reaches litigation."

"Shoot."

"All right. It's 3:40 A.M., November 19, 1958, and I am Special Agent Willis Shipstad. With me are Special Agents James Henstell and William Milner. We are at the downtown Federal Building with Lieutenant David Klein of the Los Angeles Police Department. Lieutenant Klein was picked up in a stuporous condition one hour ago at 67th Street and Central Avenue in South Los Angeles. He was unconscious and in a disheveled state. We brought him here to assure that he receives proper medical attention."

"That's a riot."

"Jim, strike Bill's comment. Resuming, Lieutenant Klein, whom our Intelligence records indicate to be forty-two years old, has sustained possible head injuries. His hands and neck have been burned, the scarring forensically consistent with burns caused by dry ice. There are bloodstains on his shirt and there is friction tape stuck to his jacket. He is unarmed. We properly parked his 1957 Plymouth police vehicle at the intersection where we found him. Prior to interrogation, Lieutenant Klein will be offered medical attention."

Propped up in a straight-backed chair.

Feds.

"Jim, have this typed and see that Mr. Noonan gets a carbon."

A sweat hole. Will Shipstad, two G-men. A table, chairs, a steno rig.

Shipstad: "He's coming to. Jim, get Mr. Noonan."

One Fed walked. I stretched—kinks and aches head to toe.

Shipstad: "You know me, Lieutenant. We met at the Embassy Hotel."

"I remember."

"This is my partner, Special Agent Milner. Do you know where you are?"

My Jap sword—wide screen/color.

"Do you want to see a doctor?"

"No."

Milner—fat, cheap cologne. "Are you sure? You're looking a little raggedy-ass."

"No."

Shipstad: "Witness that Mr. Klein refused medical attention. What about an attorney? Being one yourself, you know that we have the right to hold you for questioning."

"I waive."

"You're sure?"

Johnny—Jesus God.

"I'm sure."

"Bill, witness that Mr. Klein was offered and refused legal counsel."

"Why am I here?"

Milner: "Look at yourself. The question should be where have you been?"

Shipstad: "We picked you up at 67th and Central. A short time prior to that, the Bido Lito's club was arsoned. We had agents in the vicinity on general surveillance, and one of them heard a witness talking to LAPD detectives. The witness said he was walking by Bido Lito's shortly after the club closed for the night and saw a broken front window. Seconds later the place caught fire. That certainly sounds like a firebombing to me."

Milner: "Three people died in that fire. So far, we're assuming it was the club's two owners and the cleanup man. Lieutenant, do you know how to concoct a Molotov cocktail?"

Shipstad: "We're not suggesting that *you* torched Bido Lito's. Frankly, the condition we picked you up in suggests that you were incapable of lighting a cigarette. Lieutenant, look how this appears. Two nights ago, five people were killed at an after-hours club in Watts, and a somewhat reliable source told us that Ed Exley and Bob Gallaudet exerted a great deal of pressure to keep the details under wraps. *Now,* the following morning your colleague Sergeant George Stemmons, Jr., is found dead at Bido Lito's. Chief Exley feeds the press a song and dance about a heart attack, when we've heard that it was most likely a self-inflicted heroin overdose. *Now,* forty-odd hours after *that,* Bido Lito's is torched, and *you* drive by not long after in a state that indicates narcotic-induced intoxication. Lieutenant, do you see how all this appears?"

Kafesjian setup. Johnny D. gouting blood—

Milner: "Klein, are you with us?"

"Yes."

"Do you routinely use narcotics?"

"No."

"Oh, just occasionally?"

"Never."

"How about submitting to a blood test?"

"How about releasing me on a prima facie evidence writ?"

Milner: "Hey, he went to law school."

Shipstad: "Where were you coming from when we picked you up?"

"I refuse to answer."

Milner: "Sure, on the grounds that it might incriminate you."

"No, on the grounds of nonincriminating information disclosure as detailed in *Indiana* v. *Harkness, Bodine, et al.,* 1943."

"Hey, he went to law school. You got anything to add to that, hotshot?"

"Yeah, you're a fat piece of shit and your wife fucks Rin-Tin-Tin."

Cardiac red—fat shitbird. Shipstad: *"Enough.* Lieutenant, where were you?"

"Refuse to answer."

"What happened to your service revolver?"

"Refuse to answer."

"Can you explain the unkempt condition we found you in?"

"Refuse to answer."

"Can you explain the blood on your shirt?"

Johnny begging—

"Refuse to answer."

Milner: "Something getting to you, hotshot?"

Shipstad: "Where were you?"

"Refuse to answer."

"Did *you* torch Bido Lito's?"

"No."

"Do you know who did?"

"No."

"Did the LAPD do it as revenge for Stemmons' death?"

"No, you're crazy."

"Did Inspector George Stemmons, Sr., order the torch?"

"I don't—no, you're crazy."

"Did *you* torch Bido Lito's to avenge your partner's death?"

"No"—getting light-headed.

Milner: "We don't smell liquor on your breath."

Shipstad: "Were you under the influence of narcotics when we found you?"

"No."

"Do you use narcotics?"

"No"—speaker lights on the wall—listeners somewhere.

"Were you forcibly administered narcotics?"

"No"—a good guess—JOHNNY CO-STAR. The door opened—Welles Noonan stepped in.

Milner walked out. Noonan: "Good morning, Mr. Klein."

Jack Kennedy hair—reeking of hairspray. "I said, 'Good morning.' "

JOHNNY BEGGING.

"Klein, are you listening to me?"

"I heard you."

"Good. I had a few questions before we release you."

"Ask them."

"I will. And I look forward to sparring with you. I remember that precedent you upbraided Special Agent Milner with, so I think we'd be evenly matched."

"How do you get your hair to do that?"

"I'm not here to share my hairdressing secrets with you. Now, I'm going—"

"Cocksucker, you spit in my face."

"Yes. And you were at the very least criminally negligent in the matter of Sanderline Johnson's death. So far, these are—"

"Ten minutes or I call Jerry Geisler for habeas."

"He'll never find a judge."

"Ten minutes or I engage Kanarek, Brown and Mattingly to file nuisance claims that entail immediate court appearances."

"Mr. Klein, did you—"

"Call me 'Lieutenant.' "

"Lieutenant, how well do you know the history of the Los Angeles Police Department?"

"Get to it, don't lead me."

"Very well. Who initiated what I'll euphemistically describe as the 'arrangement' between the LAPD and Mr. J.C. Kafesjian?"

"What 'arrangement'?"

"Come, *Lieutenant.* You know you despise them as much as we do."

Lead him, cut him slack. "I think it was Chief Davis, the chief before Horrall. Why?"

"And this was circa 1936, '37?"

"Around then, I think. I joined the Department in '38."

"Yes, and I hope that the fact that your pension is secure hasn't given you a false sense of invulnerability. Lieutenant, Captain Daniel Wilhite is the liaison between the Kafesjian family and Narcotics Division, is he not?"

"Refuse to answer."

"I understand, brother-officer loyalty. Has Wilhite operated the Kafesjians since the beginning of your arrangement?"

"The way I understand it, Chief Davis brought the Kafesjians in and operated them until Horrall took over as chief late in '39. Dan Wilhite didn't join the Department until mid-'39, so he couldn't have been their original operator, if he has fucking indeed *ever* been their operator."

Fey aristocrat: "Oh, come, Lieutenant. You know Wilhite and the Kafesjians are near-ancient allies."

"Refuse to comment. But keep asking me about the Kafesjians."

"Yes, we've heard they've piqued your interest."

JOHNNY BEGGING.

Shipstad: "You're looking queasy. Do you want a drink of—"

Noonan: "Did you tell Mickey Cohen to remove his slot and vending machines? He was lax, you know. We've got pictures of his men servicing them."

"Refuse to answer."

"We've recently turned a major witness, you know."

Don't bite.

"A *major* witness."

"Your clock's ticking."

"Yes, it is. Will, do you think Mr. Klein torched Bido Lito's?"

"No, sir, I don't."

"He can't or won't account for his whereabouts."

"Sir, I'm not so sure he knows himself."

I stood up—my legs almost went. "I'll take a cab back to my car."

"Nonsense, Special Agent Shipstad will drive you. Will, I'm curious as to where the lieutenant has spent the past day or so."

"Sir, my guess is either a hell of a woman or a run-in with a grizzly bear."

"Aptly put, and the blood on his shirt suggests the latter. Do you know how I suggest we find out?"

"No, sir."

"We monitor Southside homicide calls and see which ones Edmund Exley tries to obfuscate."

"I like it, sir."

"I thought you would. It's empirically valid, since we both know that Dave here murdered Sanderline Johnson. I think it's a family enterprise. Dave does the scut work, sister Meg invests the money. How's this for an adage? 'The family that slays together stays—' "

I jumped him—my legs caved—Shipstad pried me off. Thumbs on my carotid, hauled across the hallway blacking out—

Locked in, snapping back fast—wide awake quick. A four-by-six space—quilt walls—no chairs, no table. A wall speaker outlet and mir-rored spyhole—adjoining-room access.

A padded cell/watching post—scope it out:

Scarred glass—some distortion. Audio squelch—I slapped the speaker—better. Check the mirror: Milner and Abe Voldrich next door.

Milner: ". . . what I'm saying is that either J.C. and Tommy will be in-dicted, or the publicity they get when we make the grand jury minutes available to the press will ruin them. Narco is going to be cut off at the knees, and I think Ed Exley knows it himself, because he has taken no measures to protect them or to sequester evidence. Abe, without Narco the Kafesjians are just a bunch of stupes running a marginally profitable dry-cleaning business."

Voldrich: "I . . . am . . . not . . . an informant."

Milner: "No, you're a fifty-one-year-old Lithuanian refugee with a green card we can revoke at any time. Abe, do you want to live behind the Iron Curtain? Do you know what the Commies would do to you?"

"I am not a snitch."

"No, but you'd like to be. You're letting hints drop. You told me you dried marijuana bales in one of the E-Z Kleen dryers."

"Yes, and I told you J.C., Tommy and Madge didn't know about it."

Cigarette smoke—blurred faces.

Milner: "You know that J.C. and Tommy are scum. You always go to lengths to differentiate Madge from them. She's a nice woman, and you're an essentially decent man who fell in with bad people."

Voldrich: "Madge is a very fine woman who for many reasons . . . well, she just needs Tommy and J.C."

Milner: "Did Tommy clip a drunk driver who killed a Narco cop's daughter?"

"I stand on that Fifth Amendment thing."

"You and the whole goddamn world—they never should have broadcast the Kefauver hearings. Abe—"

"Agent Milner, please charge me or release me."

"You got your phone call, and you elected to call your sister. If you'd called J.C., he would have found a smart lawyer to get you released on a writ. I think you want to do the right thing. Mr. Noonan explained the immunity agreement to you, and he's promised you a Federal service reward. I think you want it. Mr. Noonan wants to take three major witnesses to the grand jury, one of them you. And the nice thing is that if all three of you testify, everyone who could conceivably hurt you will be indicted and convicted."

"I am not an informant."

"Abe, did Tommy and J.C. kill Sergeant George Stemmons, Jr.?"

"No"—hoarse.

"He died from a heroin overdose. Tommy and J.C. could have faked something like that."

"No—I mean I don't know."

"Which one?"

"I mean no, I don't think so."

"Abe, you're not exactly a poker face. Now, along those lines, we know that Tommy plays his horn at Bido Lito's. Is he tight there?"

"Fifth Amendment."

"That's TV for you. Kids break a window, they plead the Fifth. Abe, how well did the Kafesjians know Junior Stemmons?"

"Fifth Amendment."

"Stemmons and a Lieutenant David Klein were bothering them about a burglary that occurred at their house two weeks ago. What do you know about that?"

"Fifth Amendment."

"Did they try to shake down the Kafesjians for money?"

"No—I mean Fifth Amendment."

"Abe, you're an open book. Come on, Stemmons was a junkie, and Klein's as dirty as cops get."

Voldrich coughed—the speaker caught static. *"No. Fifth Amendment."*

Milner: "Let's change the subject."

"How about politics?"

"How about Mickey Cohen? Do you know him?"

"I have never met the man."

"Maybe not, but you're an old Southside hand. What do you know about Mickey's coin racket down there?"

"I know buppkis. I know that slot machines play to a nickel-and-dime mentality, which explains their allure to stupid shvartzes."

Milner: "Let's change the subject."

"How about the Dodgers? If I was a Mexican, I'd be happy to leave Chavez Ravine."

"How about Dan Wilhite?"

"Fifth Amendment."

"We've looked at his tax records, Abe. J.C. gave him twenty percent of the E-Z Kleen shop on Alvarado."

"Fifth Amendment."

"Abe, every man working Narco owns unaffordable items that we think J.C. gave them. We've audited their tax returns, and when we call them in to explain those items and say 'Tell us where you got them and you'll skate,' J.C. will be sunk on twenty-four counts of bribery and suborning federal tax fraud."

"Fifth Amendment."

"Abe, I'll give you some advice: *always plead the Fifth across the board.* Conversational answers interspersed with the Fifth simply serve to single out the responses that indicate guilty knowledge."

Silence.

"Abe, you're looking a little green at the gills."

No answer.

"Abe, we heard Tommy's been looking for a guy named Richie. We've got no last name, but we've heard that he and Tommy used to play jazz together and pull B&E's."

I pressed up to the glass—smoke, distortion—"Fifth Amendment."

"Abe, you never won a dime at poker."

Pressing up—squinting, ears cocked.

"You really do want to help us out, Abe. Once you admit it you'll feel a lot better."

Door clangs—I eased off the wall.

Two Feds flanking Welles Noonan. I hit first: "You want to turn me as a witness."

Noonan patted his hair. "Yes, and my wife's pulling for you. She saw your picture in the papers, and she's quite smitten."

"Quid pro quo?"

"You're not desperate enough, but try me."

"Richie Something. Tell me what you've got on him."

"No, and I'll have to upbraid Agent Milner for leaving that speaker on."

"Noonan, we can deal on this."

"No, you're not ready to beg yet. Gentlemen, escort Mr. Klein to a taxi."

31

ido Lito's—daybreak.

Scorched rubble, the bandstand dead center. Ash heaps, shattered glass.

Sidewalk phones intact.

One dime in my pockets—be there, please.

Six rings—"Hello?" sleepy-voiced.

"It's me."

"Where are you?"

"I'm all right."

"I didn't ask you—David, where *were* you?"

Tingles—just hearing her.

"I can't—look, were you questioned?"

"Yes, two Sheriff's men. They said it was routine, that all the Hughes contract actresses were being questioned. They didn't seem to know that Howard had me under surveillance, and I didn't have to give an alibi for a specific time, because they couldn't establish the time Miciak died. They—"

"Don't say names."

"Why? Where are you calling from?"

"A pay phone."

"David, you sound frightened. Where *were* you?"

"I'll tell you if—I mean when it's over."

"Is this the Kafesjian thing?"

"How did you know that?"

"I just did. There's things you don't tell me, so—"

"There's things you don't tell me."

Silence.

"Glenda?"

"Yes, and there's things that I won't."

"Talk to me, then."

"Come over."

"I can't, I have to sleep."

"What kind of things should I tell you?"

"I don't know, good things."

Soft, sleepy-voiced: "Well, when I was seeing H.H. I pumped him for some stock tips and bought low. Those stocks are rising now, so I think I'll make a nice profit. When you stood me up night before last, I had dinner with Mickey. He's still enamored of me, and he had me critique his acting style, something to do with his making an important speech soon. My car has a loose clutch, and I—"

"Look, it's going to be all right."

"Is it *all* going to be all right?"

"Sure."

"You don't sound convinced."

"I'll call you when I can."

Vandals got my hubcaps. Movie time encore:

"PLEASE DON'T KILL ME."

"PLEASE DON'T KILL ME LIKE YOU KILLED ALL THE OTHERS."

Happytime Liquor two doors down.

I walked in, bought a pint of Scotch. Back to the car—three shots quick.

Shudders—no toasty-warm tingles.

I tossed the rest—booze was for perverts and cowards.

Meg taught me.

32

My place: neat and clean. I holstered up replacement goods: my Marine .45.

A scream then:

My Jap sword on a bookshelf—blood-flecked.

Five grand beside it.

Sleep—JOHNNY BEGGING.

Noon—I woke up reaching for the phone. A quick reflex call: Lynwood City Hall.

Inquire:

4980 Spindrift—vacant four-flat—who's it belong to? A clerk shuffle, the word:

Lynwood City foreclosed—the owner died circa '46. Abandoned for twelve years, rebuilding bids out: potential Chavez Ravine evictee housing. A title search?—impossible—storage-basement floods destroyed those records.

Lynwood—why meet there?

Duhamel: "Evidence."

Out for the papers, back for coffee. Four L.A. dailies full of Darktown:

The after-hours shootout—five dead, no clues, no suspects. Four shines ID'd—"Negro" Steve Wenzel deleted. Exley: "Experienced Homicide detectives are working this case full-time. It is a top LAPD priority."

A flash:

Movie time—mirrored walls—familiar *somehow*—

The *Herald:*

"Three Dead in Jazz Club Fire: Arson Cops Tag Blaze 'Accidental.' " Exley: "We believe that the fire at Bido Lito's is in no way connected to the tragic heart attack death of Sergeant George Stemmons, Jr., two days before on those same premises."

Instinct: Junior hotshot—by THEM.

Instinct: potential evidence torched.

The *Mirror-News*—skank-slanted:

Dead cop/niteclub inferno—what's shaking? Stemmons, Sr., quoted: "Negro hoodlums killed my son!" Exley's rebuttal: "Pure nonsense. Sergeant Stemmons died of cardiac arrest pure and simple. The Coroner's Office will release findings along those lines within twenty-four hours. And the notion that the Los Angeles Police Department set fire to Bido Lito's as revenge for Sergeant Stemmons' death is simply preposterous."

Junior RIP—a Catholic service upcoming. Officiating: Dudley Smith, lay chaplain.

Snide:

"With a Federal rackets probe in full swing down in South Central Los Angeles (and one generally believed to be aimed at discrediting the Los Angeles Police Department), Chief of Detectives Edmund J. Exley certainly is doing his best to pooh-pooh the current Southside crime wave to members of the press. Local sources say that there are as many Federal agents on the streets as there are LAPD men, which one would think bodes for diminished crime statistics. Something is fishy here, and it certainly isn't the catfish gumbo which used to be served at the recently scorched Bido Lito's Club."

Exley, L.A. *Times:* "I feel sorry for the Federal authorities currently seeking to manufacture a successful rackets investigation in Los Angeles. They will fail, because the enforcement measures employed by the Los Angeles Police Department have proven successful for many years. Apparently, Welles Noonan has targeted the LAPD's Narcotics Division for indictments, and I was recently asked why I have not sequestered the men working that division. My answer? Simply that those men have nothing to hide."

BIG instinct—Narco, Fed bait.

The *Times/Herald/Mirror*—no male DB's found. The *Examiner:* "Sewer Worker Makes Grisly Discovery."

Skim it:

A storm drain on the Compton/Lynwood border—Sheriff's turf. Found: a white male DB—tall, pale, 160—headless, no fingers, no feet. Dead for twenty-four to thirty-six hours—EVISCERATED, SPINE SEVERED.

"No identifying marks were found on the body. Sheriff's detectives believe that the killer or killers decapitated the victim and cut off his hands and feet to render a forensic identification impossible."

"If you have information regarding this man, John Doe #26-1958,

County Homicide Bulletin 141-26-1958, call Sgt. B.W. Schenkner, Firestone Sheriff's Station, TU 3-0985."

I could call that number. I could plead:

No location or exact time-frame knowledge—I was drugged and coerced.

My assumed coercers: the Kafesjians. Two-man coercion minimum—logistics dictated it.

THEM:

Dope access.

A motive—rogue cop orbits—Duhamel linked to Junior linked to me.

I could plead details:

Johnny and Junior—fur-job filthy—maybe more. Junior—would-be "Dope Kingpin"—extorting THEM. Me—this crazed peeper chaser—THEY wanted HIM.

I could plead evidence:

My Jap sword and five grand on a bookshelf.

My hit fee—common insider knowledge.

My sword—common knowledge—I killed a shitload of Japs with it and won the Navy Cross.

I could plead linkage:

I knew Junior/Junior knew Johnny/I fucked with the Kafesjians/Junior fucked with them/Johnny fucked with them directly or indirectly—directly or indirectly due to crazy faggot Junior Stemmons/Johnny called me to plead out or buy out like I'm pleading out now/the Kafesjians made me kill him—they made me a movie star.

Home movie time.

Splicing and developing time—who did the work?

Dave Klein left alive—movie killer. Time ticking, two ways it could go:

Straight coercion: desist on the peeper.

Fed/LAPD screenings: countless angles.

I could plead theories:

Say Johnny called me legit.

Say *he* kept the meet quiet.

I told Bob Gallaudet about it; I told Chick Vecchio—obliquely.

Chick knew my clip fee.

Chick knew my sword.

Chick knew THEM—or people who did.

Chick knew Junior was fucking with the Kafesjians.

Chick tips THEM off.

99% sure—I was coerced into killing Johnny Duhamel.

1% doubt—I'm a murderer.

My closing plea:

I don't like it.

I shaved and showered. Haggard, new gray hair—forty-two going on dead. Burn tickles toweling off—dry ice coaxed my performance. My sword, five grand—fear tactics.

Invest that money—

I called Hughes Aircraft—Pete picked up.

"Bondurant."

"Dave Klein, Pete."

Caught short: "You *never* call me here. This is work, right?"

"Five grand's worth."

"Split?"

"Your share."

"Then this isn't a police gig like last time."

"No, this is a muscle job on a hard boy."

"You're good at that by yourself."

"It's Chick Vecchio, and I know about that shakedown deal you're working with him and Touch. I want to play an angle on it."

"And you're not gonna tell me how you found out about it."

"Right."

"And if I say no, you're not gonna spoil it for us."

"Right."

"And you figured you by yourself, Chick might not fold, but both of us he would."

"Right."

Knuckle pops on his end—Pete thinking angles.

"Go to seven and answer a few questions."

"Seven."

Pop, pop—ugly. "So what's the beef?"

"Chick put me in shit with the Kafesjians."

"So clip him. That's more your style."

"I need a snitch."

"Chick's a tough boy."

"Seven. Yes or no."

Pop, pop—phone static—killer hands. "Yes with a condition, because I always thought Chick was essentially a greasy wop fuck, and because Mickey changed his mind and told him and Touch not to do this sex gig. I figure Mickey was always nice to me, so I'm doing him a solid he can pay back if he ever quits this movie-mogul shit and starts behaving like a white man again. Now, what's the angle?"

"Straight strongarm, with dirt on Chick himself—in case he runs to

Sam Giancana. Chick's Outfit, and the Outfit doesn't like this kind of extortion."

"So you want to catch him at it. I bring my camera, we go from there."

"Right. *If* we don't have to wait too long."

Knuckle pops—

"Pete, come on."

"I need two days."

"Fuck."

"Fuck nothing, Chick's set to bed down Joan fucking Crawford. Now *that* is worth waiting for."

Movie stars/movie time—Johnny begging.

"All right. Two days."

"There's that condition, Klein."

"What?"

"If it looks like Chick's thinking revenge, then we clip him."

"Agreed."

Walking air—tunnel vision—peripheral grass.

Side doorways.

Mirrored walls.

Gray herringbones—a coat?

I drove down to Lynwood—crowding the speed limit.

Aviation and Hibiscus first—that pay phone. Feed the slot, use it:

PC Bell said *outgoing* booth calls weren't tallied.

Sid Riegle said his suicide queries yielded zero.

4980 Spindrift—still abandoned. The downstairs-left unit—unlocked.

Four empty rooms—like Johnny never showed up there.

Rainy that night, sunny now. I made street circuits—nothing clicked. Vacant bungalow courts—whole blocks of them.

Treading air that night—like I was carried. Grass, side doorways, a right turn.

Maybe: a courtyard right-side room—movie time.

Wet that night, sunny now—maybe dried footprints on grass.

GO—

Six blocks—thirty-odd courts. Epidemic crabgrass—weedy dry, no footprints. Right-side doors—boarded/nailed/locked—dusty, no fresh entry marks.

Johnny laughed: "Why Lynwood, Dave?"

More street circuits—empty courtyards forever.

Fuck.

. . .

Downtown to Central Records. Their burglary file vault—crime sheets back to '50.

Agent Milner:

"We heard Tommy's been looking for a guy named Richie. We've got no last name, but we heard that he and Tommy used to play jazz together and pull B&E's."

Tommy's rap sheet—undoubtedly expunged. Richie Something—maybe not.

GO—

Male adults—four cabinets' worth—no "Richard"-derivation Caucasians. Juvie—seven Richards—five Negro, two white—porkers topping out 250.

"Unsolved"—adult/juvie—hodgepodge stuff. '50 and up, bad typing—I got eyestrain. Tilt—11/6/51:

Music Man Murray's, 983 N. Weyburn, Westwood Village. Trumpets stolen and recovered: traced to unnamed juvies. No arrests, two kid suspects—"Tommy," "Richie"—no surnames. The detective assigned: Sgt. M.D. Breuning, West L.A. Squad.

Three more cabinets—no Tommy/Richie extant.

Easy to extrapolate:

Strongarm Breuning works a chump 459. He blows the job and gets nudged: Tommy's J.C. Kafesjian's son.

Do it—eat dirt.

I called Robbery first—"Breuning's out." 77th ditto—try the Victory Motel.

"Mobster Squad, Carlisle."

"Sergeant, it's Dave Klein."

Breath flutters—"Yeah, what is it?"

"Look, I'm sorry about that trouble with Lester Lake."

"Sure. You side with a nigger over two . . . Shit, all right, he was your snitch. Look, you want Dudley? He's out."

"Is Breuning in?"

"He's with Dud. What is it?"

"It's an old juvie 459 Breuning worked. November '51. Have Mike call me, all right?"

"Mike? Sure, *Dave*"—slam/dial tone.

Tapping out.

My best move now—tail THEM.

My worst move—they'd spot me.

My best nightmare: THEY approach ME. Movie time explained: threats, offers—at least I'd know WHY.

Darktown by default—go, let things happen.

Familiar now—synced to music in my head. Familiar faces staring back: black, sullen. Slow cruising, two-way-radio sputter:

County calls—no Johnny John Doe talk. No Miciak, no Bido's—half-ass comforting.

I tapped the glove box—no candy—just dope stashed and forgotten. Hiss, crackle—a gang fight at Jordan High.

North—a run by THEIR house—Fed surveillance thick. Sax noise—Will Shipstad wearing earplugs.

Radio hum—my soundtrack for Johnny begging. North on instinct overdrive: Chavez Ravine.

Feds thick—I stuck to the car. Check the view:

Eviction papers tacked door to door. A face-off: Commie geeks and pachucos. Earthmovers, dump trucks—LAPD guards standing by.

More:

The main drag cordoned off: Reuben Ruiz dancing a samba. Fans pressing close, wet-eyed women. Fed bodyguards—disgusted.

Two-way boom:

"Code 3 all units vicinity 249 South ARDEN repeat 249 South ARDEN multiple homicides 249 South ARDEN Detective units Roger your locations 249 South ARDEN on-call Homicide units that vicinity Roger your locations!"

33

Rolling Code 3.

South Arden/Joseph Arden/street name/trick name. A Hancock Park address—affluent—a strong maybe.

"Request animal disposal unit 249 South Arden. Be advised all units now standing."

I hit the mike: "4-ADAM-31 to Bureau base urgent. Over."

"Roger, 4-A-31."

"Urgent. Repeat urgent. Lieutenant D.D. Klein seeking Chief Exley. Over."

"Roger, 4-A-31."

Makeshift code: "Urgent. Advise Chief Exley homicides at 249 South Arden likely *major case* connected. Request permission to seal under IA autonomy. Urgent that you find Chief Exley. Over."

"Roger, 4-A-31. State your location."

"3rd and Mariposa westbound. Over."

Dead air, speeding—

"4-A-31, please Roger."

"Roger, this is 4-A-31."

"4-A-31, assume command 249 South Arden IA autonomy. Over."

"4-A-31, Roger, over."

3rd westbound—siren earaches. Arden Boulevard—right turn, right there:

A big Tudor house swamped—prowl cars, morgue cars.

Civilian cliques on the sidewalk—nervous.

Ice cream trucks, kids.

I jammed in curbside. Two brass hats on the porch, looking queasy.

I ran up. One lieutenant, one captain—green. A hedge behind them dripping vomit.

"Ed Exley wants this sealed: no press, no downtown Homicide. I'm in charge, and IA's bagging the evidence."

Nods—queasy—nobody said, "Who are you?"

"Who found them?"

The captain: "Their mailman called it in. He had a special-delivery package, and he wanted to leave it at the side door. The dogs didn't bark like they usually do, and he saw blood on a window."

"He ID'd them?"

"Right. It's a father and two daughters. Phillip Herrick, Laura and Christine. The mother's dead—the mailman said she killed herself earlier this year. Hold your nose when you—"

In—smell it—blood. Flashbulbs, gray suits—I pushed through.

The entrance foyer floor: two dead shepherds belly-up, dripping mouth foam. Tools nearby—spade/shears/pitchfork—bloody.

Meat scraps/drool/puke trails.

Stabbed and cut and forked—entrail piles soaking a throw rug.

I squatted down and pried their jaws loose—tech men gasped.

Washrags in their mouths—stelfactiznide-chloride-soaked.

Match it up—Kafesjian 459.

Walk/look/think—plainclothesmen gave me room:

The front hallway—broken records/tossed covers. Christmas jazz wax—confirm the Mom-peeper letters.

The dining room:

Booze bottles and portraits smashed—another K.-job match. *Family pictures:* a dad and two daughters.

Mom to peeper: "Your sisters."

Suicide talk/suicide confirmation.

A tech stampede—follow it—the den.

Three dead on the floor: one male, two female.

Details:

Their eyes shot out—powder-black cheeks, exit spatter.

Ripped cushions on a chair—bullet mufflers.

Shears, chainsaw, axe—bloody, propped in a corner.

The rug—soaked bubbling.

His pants down.

Castrated—his penis in an ashtray.

The women:

Cut/sawed/snipped—limbs dangling by skin shreds.

Bloody walls, windows sprayed—kids looking in.

Artery gout red: the floor, the ceiling, the walls. Plainclothesmen oozing shell shock.

A framed photo spritzed: handsome daddy, grown daughters.

Peeper kin.

"Fuuuck"/"My God"/Hail Marys. I skirted the blood and checked access.

Rear hall, back door, steps—jimmy marks, meat scraps, drool.

One high-heel pump just inside.

Work it:

He pries in quiet, throws the meat, waits outside.

The dogs smell it, eat it, quease.

He walks in.

Shoots Herrick.

Finds the tools, kills the dogs.

The girls come home, see the door, run in. One shoe lost—scattered tools—he hears them.

CRAAAZY shooting/mutilation—leaded windows kill the noise.

Homicide/symbolic destruction—he probably didn't steal.

Snap guess: the girls showed up unexpected.

I looked outside—trees, shrubs—hiding spots. No blood drip—say he stole clean clothes.

Blues and a mailman smoking—brace them. "Did the Herricks have a son?"

The mailman nodded. "Richard. He escaped from Chino something like September of last year. He went up on dope charges."

Mom—"pen pals/same city"—lamster Richie explained it. "Spurred you/rash thing"—he waltzed minimum-security Chino.

Nervous blues jabbering: Richie caught/convicted/gassed—their instant suspect.

Killer Richie?—NO—think it through:

The Red Arrow Inn—Richie's peep spot B&E'd. His bed ripped—with Kafesjian 459 silver. Dead cert—this killer/that burglar—one man—broken bottle/smashed record/snuffed dog confirmation. Richie—passive watcher—someone watching and pressing him. Tommy K. chasing him outright, flirt with the notion: Tommy stone psycho, Tommy trashes his own house, now THIS.

Back inside:

Blood drops—dark, fading—the main hallway off the den. I followed them upstairs—red into pink, a bathroom—stop.

Floor water—the toilet bowl full—a knife floating in piss water. Pink water in the shower, bloody hair clots.

Reconstruct it:

Bloody clothes ripped and flushed—the toilet floods. A shower then?—check the towel rack—one towel sodden.

Recent—broad-daylight killings.

I checked the hallway—wet footprint indentations on the carpet. Easy tracks—straight to a bedroom.

Drawers open, clothes scattered. A wallet on the floor—turned out, no cash.

A driver's license: Phillip Clark Herrick, DOB 5/14/06. The ID pic: "Fuck me Daddy" bland handsome.

Wallet sleeves—a photo—Lucille naked. A fake license: Joseph Arden—Herrick stats, a fake address.

I checked the window: South Arden was roped off. Bluesuit cordons held reporters back.

Other bedrooms—

One hallway, three doors. Two open—girlish bedrooms—undisturbed. One door locked—I shoulder-popped it.

A snap make: Richie's room preserved.

Neat, mothball-reeking.

Jazz posters.

Books: music bios, sax theory.

Kid-type paintings: Lucille softened, demure.

A graduation pic: Richie, peeper sketch perfect.

Doors slamming—check the window—IA swarming in.

Lucille—idealized, a madonna.

Books: all jazz.

Funny—no tech stuff—and Richie *knew* bugging.

Running footsteps—Exley in my face, catching breath. "You should be downstairs. Ray Pinker briefed me, but I wanted your interpretation first."

"There's nothing to interpret. It's Richie Herrick, or it's the guy who broke into his motel room. Check my early reports, I mentioned him then."

"I remember. And you've been avoiding me. I told you to call me after you forensic'd Stemmons' apartment."

"There was nothing to report."

"Where have you been?"

"People keep asking me that."

"That's not an answer."

Bloody wing tips—he got close.

"So what now? That's a question."

"I'm issuing an APB on Richard Herrick."

"Think it over first. I don't *think* this is him."

"You obviously want me to prompt you. *So,* Lieutenant?"

"So I think we should haul in Tommy K. I've got a strong tip that he's been looking for Richie Herrick. Richie's a damn good hider, but Tommy *knows* him. He's got a better chance of finding him than we do."

"No direct approach on the Kafesjians. And I am issuing that APB, because the Kafesjians are under blanket Fed surveillance, which somewhat impedes their ability to search for Herrick. Moreover, these deaths are front-page news. Herrick will read about them and act even more furtively. We can only control the press so far."

"Yeah, which must really gall you."

"Frankly, it does. Now surprise me or anticipate me. Tell me something I don't know."

I jabbed his vest—hard. "Johnny Duhamel's dead. He's a Sheriff's John Doe down near Compton, and I think you two are dirty together. You're running me on the Kafesjians, and it ties in to Duhamel. I'm not thinking so straight these days, and I'm getting to the point where I'm going to fuck you for it."

Exley stepped back. "You're detached to Homicide and in charge of this investigation. You can do anything you want except approach the Kafesjians."

Chimes streetside—ice cream trucks.

34

3rd Street, Bureau bound. A stoplight at Normandie—Plymouths cut me off and boxed me in.

Four cars—Feds piled out aiming shotguns. Radio mike loud: "You are under arrest. Get out with your hands up."

I killed the engine, set the brake, complied. Slooow: grip the roof, arms spread.

Swamped/frisked/cuffed—crew-cut shitbirds loving it.

Milner poked me. "Reuben Ruiz said he saw you dump Johnson."

Three men tossed my car. A skinny hump checked the glove compartment.

"Milner, look. Looks like white horse to me!"

Lying snitch fuck Ruiz.

Heroin jammed in my face.

Downtown—the Fed Building—manhandled upstairs. Shoved into an office—

Four walls paper-draped—graph lines visible underneath.

Noonan and Shipstad waiting.

Milner sat me down; Shipstad took my cuffs off. My dope passed Fed to Fed—whistles all around.

Noonan: "Too bad Junior Stemmons is dead. He could have been your alibi on Johnson."

"You mean you *know* Ruiz is lying? You *know* he was sleeping when Johnson jumped?"

Shipstad: "There's no evidence sticker on this bag of white powder, Lieutenant."

Milner: "I think he's got a habit."

His partner: "Stemmons sure as hell did."

Noonan tugged his necktie—his underlings walked out.

Shipstad: "Do you wish to examine the arrest warrant, Mr. Klein?"

Noonan: "We'll have to amend it to include violation of Federal narcotics statutes."

I threw a guess out: "You rigged the warrant with a friendly judge. You told Ruiz to lie, then recant when you turned me. You told the judge what you were doing. It's a Federal warrant on some trumped-up civil-rights violation, not a California Manslaughter One paper, because no Superior Court judge would sign it."

Noonan: "Well, it got your attention. And of course we have binding evidence."

"Release me."

Noonan: "I said *'binding.'* "

Shipstad: "Shortly after we released you early this morning, Abe Voldrich was released to take care of some personal business. He was found murdered this afternoon. He left a suicide note, which a graphologist examined and said was written under physical duress. Voldrich had agreed to testify as a Federal witness, on all matters pertaining to the Kafesjian family and this perhaps tangential burglary investigation that you and the late Sergeant Stemmons were involved in. An agent went by his house to pick Voldrich up for more questioning and found him."

Noonan: "Agent Milner canvassed the area. A 1956 powder-blue Pontiac coupe was seen parked by his house around the approximate time of his death."

Shipstad: "Did you kill him?"

Noonan: "You own a blue automobile, don't you?"

"You know I didn't kill him. You know it's Tommy and J.C. You know that I own a dark blue '55 Dodge."

Shipstad: "The Kafesjians have an excellent alibi for the time of Voldrich's death."

Noonan: "They were at home, under twenty-four-hour Federal surveillance."

"So they called out a contract."

Shipstad: "No, their phone was tapped."

Noonan: "And *had* been tapped, going back prior to the time we picked up Voldrich."

"What else did they discuss on the phone?"

Shipstad: "Unrelated matters. Nothing pertaining to that Richie you seemed to be so interested in last night."

Scooped—no Herrick update—clueless on the South Arden slaughter.

"Get to it. Get to 'binding evidence.' "

Noonan: "Your appraisal of the situation first, Mr. Klein."

"You want to take three witnesses to the grand jury. I'm one, one just died, one's this so-called major surprise witness. You're short a man, so you're doubling up on me. That's my appraisal, *so let's hear your offer.*"

Noonan: "Immunity on the Johnson killing. Immunity on *all* potential criminal charges that you might accrue. A written guarantee that no Federal tax liens will be filed against you should it be revealed that you have unreported income earned as a direct result of criminal conspiracies that you've engaged in. For this, you agree to enter Federal custody and testify in open court as to your knowledge of the Kafesjian family, their LAPD history and most importantly your own history of dealings with organized crime, *excluding* Mickey Cohen."

Light bulb—Major Witness Mickey.

Reflex jolt—never.

"You bluffed, I call."

Shipstad ripped the draping off the walls. Shredded paper in piles—column graphs underneath.

I stood up. Boldface print—easy to read.

Column one: names and dates—my mob hits.

Column two: my property transactions detailed. Corresponding dates—Real Estate Board kickbacks—five thousand dollars each—my clip fee funneled.

Column three: kickback receivers listed. Detailed: slum dives offered to me lowball cheap. Corresponding dates: escrow and closing.

Column four—Meg's tax returns '51–'57. Her *unreported* cash listed and traced: to appraisers and permit signers bribed.

Column five—witness numbers—sixty-odd bribe takers listed.

Names and numbers—pulsing.

Noonan: "Much of the data regarding you is circumstantial and subject to interpretation. We've listed only the men that the underworld grapevine credits you with killing, and those five-thousand-dollar windfalls that followed are circumstantially seductive and not much more. The important thing is that you and your sister are indictable on seven counts of Federal tax fraud."

Shipstad: "I convinced Mr. Noonan to extend the immunity agreement to cover your sister. If you agree, Margaret Klein Agee will remain exempt from all Federal charges."

Noonan: "What's your answer?"

Shipstad: "Klein?"

Clock ticks, heartbeats—something short-circuiting inside me.

"I want four days' grace before I enter custody, and I want a Federal bank writ to allow me access to Junior Stemmons' safe-deposit boxes."

Shipstad, bait grabber: "Did he owe you money?"

"That's right."

Noonan: "I agree, provided a Federal agent goes with you to the bank."

A contract in my face—fine print pulsing.

I signed it.

"You sound resigned."

"It's all got a life of its own."

"Meaning?"

"Meaning you should tell me things."

"You don't mention certain things. You call me from phone booths so you won't have to."

"I want to put it all together first."

"You said it's sorting itself out."

"It is, but I'm running out of time."

"You or we?"

"Just me."

"Don't start lying to me. Please."

"I'm just trying to put things straight."

"But you still won't tell me what you're doing."

"It's this trouble I got you in. Let it go at that."

"I bought that trouble myself—you told me that."

"Now you sound resigned."

"Those Sheriff's men came by again."

"And?"

"And a cameraman told them we were sleeping together in my trailer."

"Do they know I was hired to tail you?"

"Yes."

"What did you tell them?"

"That I'm free, white and twenty-nine, and I'll sleep with whoever I want to."

"And?"

"And Bradley Milteer told them that you and Miciak had words. I said I met Miciak through Howard, and he was easy to dislike."

"Good, that was smart."

"Does this mean we're suspects?"

"It means they know my reputation."

"What reputation?"

"You know what I mean."

"That?"

"That."

". . . Oh shit, David."

"Yeah, 'oh shit.' "

"Now you sound tired."

"I am tired. Tell me—"

"I knew that was coming."

"And?"

"And my clutch is still on the fritz, and Mickey asked me to marry him. He said he'd 'cut me loose' in five years and make me a star, and he's been behaving as oblique as David Douglas Klein at his most guarded. He's got some kind of strange acting bug, and he keeps talking about his 'cue' and his 'curtain call.' "

"And?"

"How do you know there's more?"

"I can tell."

"Smart man."

"And?"

"And Chick Vecchio's been coming on to me. It's almost like . . ."

"His whole attitude changed overnight."

"Smart man."

"Don't worry, I'll take care of it."

"But you won't tell me what it's about?"

"Just hold on for a few more days."

"Because it's all sorting itself out?"

"Because there's still a chance I can force things our way."

"Suppose you can't?"

"Then at least I'll know."

"You sound resigned again."

"It's dues time. I can feel it."

L.A. *Herald-Express*, 11/21/58:

HANCOCK PARK SLAYINGS SHOCK CITY

The murders of wealthy chemical engineer Phillip Herrick, 52, and his daughters Laura, 24, and Christine, 21, continue to shock the Southland and confound the Los Angeles Police Department with their brazen brutality.

In the mid afternoon hours of November 19th, police surmise that a man invaded the comfortable Tudor style home where widower Phillip Herrick lived with his two daughters. Forensic experts have reconstructed that he gained access through a flimsily locked back door, fatally poisoned the family's two dogs, then shot Phillip Herrick and employed gardening tools found on the premises to hideously mutilate both Mr. Herrick and the animals. Evidence indicates that Laura and Christine returned home at this point and surprised the killer, who similarly butchered them, showered himself free of their blood and donned clothes belonging to Mr. Herrick. He then either walked or drove away, accomplishing the bestial murders in something like near silence. Postal employee Roger Denton, attempting to deliver a special delivery package, saw blood on the inside den windows and immediately called police from a neighboring house.

"I was shocked," Denton told Herald reporters. "Because the Herricks are nice people who had already had their fill of tragedy."

FAMILY NO STRANGER TO TRAGEDY

As police began a house-to-house canvassing for possible witnesses and lab technicians sealed the premises off to search for clues, neighbors congregating outside in a state of horrified confusion told reporter Todd Walbrect of tragic recent turns in the family's affairs.

For many years the Herricks seemed to enjoy a happy life in affluent Hancock Park. Phillip Herrick, a chemist by trade and the owner of a chemical manufacturing business that supplied industrial solvents to Southland machine shops and dry-cleaning establishments, was active in the Lions Club and Rotary; Joan (Renfrew) Herrick did charitable work and headed drives to feed indigent skid row habitués festive Thanksgiving dinners. Laura and Christine matriculated at nearby Marlborough Girls' School and UCLA, and son Richard, now 26, attended public schools and played in their marching bands. But dark clouds were hovering: in August of 1955, "Richie" Herrick, 23, was arrested in Bakersfield: he sold marijuana and heroin-cocaine "goofballs" to an undercover police officer. Convicted of the offense, he was sentenced to four years in Chino Prison, a harsh sentence for a first offender, meted out by a judge anxious to establish a reputation for sternness.

Neighbors state that Richie's imprisonment broke Joan Herrick's heart. She began drinking and neglecting her charity work, and spent many hours alone listening to jazz records that Richie recommended to her in long letters from prison. In 1956 she attempted suicide; in September of 1957 Richie Herrick escaped from minimum-security Chino and remained at large, police believe, without ever contacting his mother. Joan Herrick went into what several acquaintances described as a "fugue state," and on February 14th of this year committed suicide with an overdose of sleeping pills.

Postman Roger Denton: "What a godawful shame that so much awfulness was visited on one nice family. I remember when Mr. Herrick put those heavy leaded windows in. He hated noise, and now the police say those windows helped stifle the noise of that killer fiend doing his work. I'll miss the Herricks and pray for them."

EXPRESSIONS OF SHOCK AS POLICE INVESTIGATION SPREADS OUT

Shock waves have spread through Hancock Park and indeed the entire Southland, and a memorial service for Christine and Laura Herrick drew hundreds at Occidental College, where they were both enrolled in graduate programs. Locksmiths citywide have reported a tremendous business upswing; guard dog sales have doubled locally. Private security patrols for Hancock Park are being considered, and meanwhile police are jealously guarding investigatory information.

The Herrick investigation is being headed by Lieutenant David D. Klein, the commander of the Los Angeles Police Department's Administrative Vice Division, recently in the news when a Federal witness he was guarding committed suicide in his presence. Lieutenant Klein has detached a half dozen men from the Department's Internal Affairs Detail to work under him, along with his aide, Officer Sidney Riegle.

Chief of Detectives Edmund Exley defended his choice of Lieutenant Klein, 42, a 20 year officer with no Homicide Division experience. "Dave Klein is an attorney and a very savvy detective," he said. "He has worked on a burglary case that may be tangentially connected, and he is very good at keeping evidence under wraps. I want this case cleared, and so I have selected the best possible men to achieve that end."

Lieutenant Klein addressed reporters at the LAPD Detective Bureau. "This investigation is proceeding rapidly," he said, "and progress has been made. Many known associates of the Herrick family have been questioned and eliminated as suspects, and extensive canvassing of the area surrounding the murder scene yielded no eyewitnesses to the killer entering or leaving the Herrick home. We have eliminated robbery and revenge against the family as motives, and most importantly eliminated the Herrick's Chino escapee son Richard as a suspect. He had been our initial major suspect, and we had issued an all-points-bulletin to aid in his capture, but we have now lifted that bulletin, although Richard Herrick is an escaped felon and we would very much like to talk to him. We are now centering our search on a sexual psychopath rumored to be seen near Hancock Park shortly before the killings. Although the three victims were not specifically sexually assaulted, the crime has the earmarks of being perpetrated by a sexual deviate. I, personally, am convinced that this man, whose name I cannot reveal, is the killer. We are making every effort to apprehend him."

And, meanwhile, fear besieges the Southland. Police patrols in Hancock Park have been doubled and the current boom in home security measures continues.

A funeral service for Phillip, Laura and Christine Herrick will be held today at St. Basil's Episcopal Church in Brentwood.

L.A. *Times,* 11/21/58:

SOUTHSIDE CRIME WAVE AROUSES SUSPICION

Citing crime statistics and current rumors, U.S. Attorney Welles Noonan stated today that Southside Los Angeles is "boiling over with violent intrigue" that may well be "connected on some as yet undetermined level."

Noonan, heading up a much-publicized Federal rackets probe centered in South Central Los Angeles, spoke to reporters at his office.

"During the past four days eight violent deaths have occurred within a three-mile South Los Angeles radius," he said. "This is *double* the average of any one-month period of any given year going back to 1920. Add on the curious heart attack of a supposedly healthy young policeman at a nightclub later burned down, and count as perhaps curious the mutilated body of an unidentified man found two miles further south on the Compton–Lynwood border. Collectively, you have fodder for much interesting speculation."

Noonan elaborated. "Three nights ago an unexplained shoot-out at an illegal after hours club in Watts occurred," he said. "Two Negro men and three Negro women were killed, although rumors persist that one of the victims was white. The following morning a young LAPD officer named George Stemmons, Jr., was found dead, allegedly of a heart attack, in a back room at the Bido Lito's jazz club. A scant day and a half later Bido Lito's burned to the ground. Federal agents overheard an eyewitness tell LAPD detectives that he heard a Molotov-cocktail–like explosion moments before Bido Lito's caught fire, but the LAPD Arson Squad has now attributed the blaze, which took three lives, to a carelessly tossed cigarette."

Reporters interrupted the impromptu press conference with questions. Repeatedly stressed: the Federal rackets probe is specifically targeted to discredit the Los Angeles Police Department's Southside enforcement measures; isn't the U.S. Attorney taking an adversarial position predicated on incomplete information?

Noonan responded. "Granted," he said, "that unidentified body found in the L.A. County Sheriff's jurisdiction may be a non sequitur, but I ask you to consider the following.

"One, remember what I told you about that eyewitness to the Bido Lito's fire. Two, consider that the father of the young policeman who expired of alleged heart failure at Bido Lito's earlier, himself a high-ranking Los Angeles police officer, stated that he thought his son was murdered. That man has been suspended from duty for his open criticism of Chief Ed Exley's handling of the situation, and is rumored to be resting at home under doctor-ordered sedation."

Reporters pressed: isn't the Federal-LAPD quagmire coming down to a battle waged by two highly respected, nationally known crimefighters: himself and LAPD Chief of Detectives Edmund Exley?

Noonan said, "No. I will not let personalities or political ambitions dictate the thrust of my investigation. What I do know is: after hours clubs are allowed to flourish in Watts under unofficial LAPD sanction. Five Negro citizens died as a result, and despite assigning a dozen officers to the case, Ed Exley has not been able to come up with a single arrest. He has shoved the suspicious death of a Los Angeles policeman under the carpet and has deliberately misrepresented the facts in a triple-homicide arson case."

In related developments, Noonan refused to comment on the persistent rumor that LAPD Narcotics Division officers are soon to be called in for questioning, or whether Abraham Voldrich, a rumored Federal witness recently deceased, was murdered or committed suicide.

"No comments on those questions," he said. "But on the topic of witnesses, let me state that when it comes time to present evidence to the Federal Grand Jury, I will offer a major surprise witness with extraordinary cachet and another witness prepared to give astonishing testimony."

Edmund Exley responded to the U.S. Attorney's accusations: "Welles Noonan is an unscrupulous hack politician with spurious liberal credentials. He has no grasp of the situation in Southside Los Angeles and his smear campaign against the LAPD is based on lies, fatuous rumors and innuendo. The Federal rackets probe is a politically motivated front aimed at establishing Noonan as a viable candidate for State office. It will fail because he has grievously underestimated the moral rectitude of the Los Angeles Police Department."

Dues time/time running out—RUN.

Herrick 187 PC—six IA men and Sid Riegle co-opted. Forty-eight hours in:

No eyewitnesses, no vehicle pegged. No prints, no Richie-to-Mom letters found. Confirmed: the dogs sucked stelfactiznide chloride.

Background check:

Laura and Christine Herrick—nice girls. Good students, square boyfriends—almost Hancock Park wives.

Joan Renfrew Herrick—secret boozer. Suicide attempts, suicide. A neighbor doctor told me:

Joanie burned herself, and begged morphine. Demerol prescribed; self-inflicted burns kept it coming. Zombie matron—all-day jazz on cloud nine.

"She drank Drano, Lieutenant. Her ultimate suicide was inevitable, and a merciful relief for the people who cared about her."

Richie Herrick—shy boy, chump musician. One friend—"This hood Tommy," "Oil and water, him and Tommy—I think Richie had a crush on Tommy's sister." Neighborhood shock expressed: shy Richie the dope peddler. The Bakersfield PD queried: Richie was bagged dead to rights, open-and-shut. No co-defendants, no Tommy involved—three-to-four Chino.

Richie's prison file—missing. Misplaced? Misfiled? Stolen?—possible suspect Dan Wilhite—just a hunch.

Warden's aides searching for it: I wanted to nail Richie's Chino KAs.

Escape reports 9/57—adios, Richie—no details, no leads.

Mike Breuning—no call from him yet—my B&E lead was tapped out.

Phillip Herrick:

No record, no Vice Squad sheets City/County.

Chemist.

Chemical manufacturer.

PH Solvents, Inc.—dry-cleaning supplies.

Stelfactiznide chloride—made in-house.

Distributed statewide—to dry-cleaning shops and industrial plants.

NOT a customer: E-Z Kleen/J.C. Kafesjian.

PH employees alibi-checked—clean straight across.

Cross-family background check:

Phillip Herrick—DOB 5/14/06—Scranton, Pennsylvania.

John Charles Kafesjian—DOB 1/15/03—Scranton, Pennsylvania.

No Pennsylvania criminal records/State Police employment check:

1930–32—Balustrol Chemicals, Scranton. Phillip Herrick: solvent analyst; J.C. Kafesjian: laborer/mixer.

California DMV check:

6/32—both men glom driver's permits.

Birth record check:

1932–37: Tommy/Lucille, Richie/Laura/Christine born.

Time ticking—RUN—custody looming.

Running separate—Exley and Noonan—chasing bank writs.

Noonan moving east—furtive—petitioning Fed jurists. Exley sticking west—slower, no connections.

Name it ALL: the Kafesjian/Herrick case.

Breaking now—CRAAAZY volition.

Crazy fake press leaks—my idea.

We announced a fake APB, then fake withdrew it. One fake suspect fed to the press: an unnamed psycho. Bait: to calm Richie down and lure Tommy to him.

A help: Richie's mug shot on page one—a bum likeness, peeper sketch imperfect.

A hindrance: Feds dogging THEM.

Exley, page-one tweaks:

"Dave Klein is a very savvy detective."

"He has worked on a burglary case that may be tangentially connected."

Bait: push THEM toward Richie/push THEM toward me.

One glitch: Fed lockstep surveillance on the Kafesjians.

RUN—

Junior's funeral—mandatory Bureau attendance. Exley there for PR, Dudley Smith somber. Stemmons, Sr., still distraught, sedative bombed.

Father-son farewell: Sad-ass Bible readings. Thirty years since First Dutch Lutheran, catch the gist: mercy for the sick and insane.

RUN—Sheriff's Homicide chasers—"routine" questions, two sessions' worth:

Were you hired to tail Glenda Bledsoe?

Did you become intimate with her?

Did she steal from Howard Hughes' guest homes?

Yes, yes, no—one cop smirking.

Did you argue with Harold John Miciak?

Yes—this cop-hater shitbird. Instant empathy, a smirky punch line: don't you think Mr. Hughes might try to fuck you for taking his money and his girlfriend?

Running with me—Sid Riegle/six IA men: background checks/ interviews/shitwork. Meg working on a title search—4980 Spindrift/"Why meet there?" My own sister: searching records, tracing money—Phillip Herrick's fortune, find me filth—

Kafesjian/Herrick—Mom to Richie: "Long history of insanity, both our families."

Killer Richie—no.

Killer Tommy—doubtful.

Leaning toward: Mr. Third Party insane.

Narco men running scared—persistent Bureau rumors. Mass cop divestment: Kafesjian gratuities dumped. Rumors had Dan Wilhite begging Exley: say something, do something.

Exley noncommittal; Fed rumors: nineteen subpoenas headed Narco's way.

My subpoenas on hold—via Fed custody extortion. Key witness Dave Klein, compromisable: if that movie showed up on Noonan's desk. Call "if" wishful thinking—I kept waiting the delivery out—time ticking slow.

Running, thinking:

THEY made the film—Chick Vecchio their point man. Make him snitch: THEY coerced my starring role.

Conspiracy indictments potentially pending—"maybe" one tainted witness skates.

Maybe wishful thinking.

Running, watching:

THEIR house—night surveillance, parked three doors down. SRO: Feds in front, Feds out back. Family tantrums inside—my nostalgia soundtrack—

The Two Tonys—pomade spatter off point-blank head shots. "No, my children"—a clip victim weeping. Rape-o double-header—buckshot tore this nigger faceless.

Silk dresses for Meg—penance gifts. Meg with Jack Woods now—her own killer. Meg holding ten grand—Jack stiffed, Junior otherwise dead. A stray thought: Abe Voldrich snuffed, a car spotted. Jack's car: that make, that model.

Music to watch by: car-radio bop night one. Night two—straight Champ Dineen.

Soft: Richie and Lucille, maybe lovers. Soft: Glenda turning my way off a skid, all this courage.

Champ Dineen—my car radio on low. Echoed out Lucille's window—the same station.

Lucille in her window—no makeup, new hair—Richie's bedroom pictures life-size.

A nightgown on—almost prim.

Feds on the street—family close.

Johnny begging—constant refrains—unshakable.

Two days down, two days left before custody. Two late nights with Glenda.

She said, "We might not walk."

I said, "You will."

She said, "You're tired."

She said, "You want to confess."

IV

MONEY JUNGLE

35

"**W**ell, this writ *does* appear to be in order. But what's this stamp on the bottom?"

Agent Henstell: "It's a routing stamp. The U.S. attorney here sent the paperwork to a judge back east."

"Was there a reason for that?"

To bypass Exley-friendly jurists—open the vault, you officious little shit.

"No, Mr. Noonan simply knew that the Federal judge for this district was too busy to read writ requests."

"I see. Well, I suppose—"

I goosed him: "The writ's valid, so let's move this along."

"There's no need to be brusque. This way, *gentlemen.*"

Teller cages, guard station, walk-in vault. Unlocked—a Pinkerton at parade rest. Henstell: "Before we go in, I want to recap Mr. Noonan's instructions."

"I'm listening."

"One, you're allowed to keep any money you might find. Two, you're allowed to go through any personal papers you might find, alone, in an examination cubicle here on bank property. After you go through them, they are to be turned over to me, for booking as Federal evidence. Three, any contraband items such as narcotics, or firearms, will be seized as evidence immediately."

"Firearms"—icy tingles. "Agreed."

"All right, then. Mr. Welborn, after you."

Quick march—Welborn leading. Gray metal aisles—safe-deposit boxes recessed floor to ceiling. Left turn, right turn, stop.

Welborn, dangling keys: "5290 and 5291. There's an examination room around the corner."

"And you're to leave Agent Henstell and me alone."

"As you wish."

Two boxes knee-high; four key slots. Tingles—I stuck my keys in.

Welborn—master keys in—clicks simultaneous.

Handkerchiefs up my sleeves.

Welborn, prissy: "Good day, Officers."

Quick now—Henstell picking a cuticle, bored—

I cracked the drawers—paper piles bulged the boxes wide. RIGHT THERE on top:

A revolver—evidence bagged. Powder-dusted prints on the grips and barrel housing—protective glazed.

Henstell picking his nose.

Quick:

Unwrap the gun—bury it—paper-pile cover.

Henstell: "What have we got?"

"Folders and paperwork so far."

"Noonan wants it all, and I wouldn't mind being out of here by lunch-time."

I dropped my hands; the handkerchiefs fell out. Block his view—wipe the piece—

Three times—Glenda—make sure.

I handed it over. "Henstell, look at this."

He twirled the gun and snapped quick draws—bad déjà vu.

"Pearl grips—this Stemmons guy must have had a cowboy fetish. And look, no numbers on the barrel plate."

I pulled the drawers out. "Do you want to look through these for narcotics?"

"No, but Noonan wants it all when you're finished. He said I should pat-search you afterwards, but that's not my style."

"Thanks."

"You're going to love Federal custody. Noonan pops for steak lunch every day."

Fake grunts: "You want to give me a hand with this?"

"Come on, they can't be *that* heavy."

Good fake out—I moved on it—over to a catty-corner cubicle. One table, one chair, no inside lock—I jammed the chair under the doorknob.

Dump the drawers, check the contents:

Folders, photos, odd papers—I stacked them on the table.

Four keys on a fob—"Brownell's Locksmiths, 4024 Wabash Ave, East Los Angeles."

Loose newspaper clippings—I smoothed out the crumples.

Go—skim it all:

Typed depositions—Glenda Bledsoe/Dwight Gilette—Murder One. My evidence suppression—detailed in longhand.

Georgie Ainge's statement: a typed original and five carbons.

Photo blow-ups: Glenda's juvie print strip and the gun prints. A fingerprint analysis report; photo glossies with comparison points checked.

Witness Disposition Report:

"Mr. Ainge is currently living under an assumed name at an undisclosed location in the San Francisco area. I have telephone access to him and have given him money so that he might hide out and escape potential reprisals from Lieutenant David D. Klein. He remains available to me should he be called as a witness in the matter of the County of Los Angeles vs. Glenda Louise Bledsoe."

My bullshit detector clicked in—Ainge bugged out on his own—I'd bet money.

Handwritten pages—doodles, scrawls—half-legible hieroglyphics:

(Unreadable)/"I've got a trail worked out on paper"/(unreadable)/ "He's spent a fortune so far"/(unreadable)/ink smears. "So he's spent a fortune operating Officer John Duhamel"—smears—"But of course he's a rich kid policeman whose father died (April 1958) and left him millions."

Scribbles/penis drawings—doped-up homo Junior. "Rich kid" Exley— easy make—working Johnny D.—no huge surprise. Doodles/gun drawings/indecipherable gobbledygook. "Operating this guy whose story you won't believe." Coffee stains/smears/cock drawings/"See file marked Evidence #1."

Check the stack—there—a folder:

Newspaper clippings: mid-April '58. Human-interest schmaltz:

Johnny Duhamel turns pro—his "wealthy" parents died penniless and USC dunned their estate. Johnny: attending grad school, three jobs—no pro fight career plans. USC cracks down: repay your college debt or drop out.

That piece—the L.A. *Times*, 4/18/58. Three recaps—the *Herald/ Examiner/Mirror*—4/24, 5/2, 5/3.

Weird:

Four L.A. dailies/four stories—no new facts exposited, no new angles probed. Gallaudet's file check confirmed: Duhamel's parents died broke.

More "Evidence #1": numbered document photos. I flashed back to Junior's pad—that Minox camera.

Photos 1, 2, 3: Security First National Bank forms. Checking and savings accounts opened: Walton White, 2750 N. Edgemont, Los Angeles. Two thirty-grand deposits coming off hinky: Edgemont stopped at 2400.

Notations on the back:

#1—"Manager described 'Walton White' as 'familiar somehow,' 6'2", 170, blond-gray hair, glasses, late thirties."

#2—"Manager shown magazine photograph of Edmund Exley. Confirms that E.E. opened the 'Walton White' accounts."

#3—"Manager stated that 'Walton White' (E.E.) requested blank bank checks immediately so that he could begin fulfilling transactions."

Hot now—I started sweating.

Photos 4, 5, 6—cancelled "Walton White" checks. Four grand, four grand, five grand—4/23, 4/27, 4/30/58.

Made out to:

Fritzie Huntz, Paul Smitson, Frank Brigantino.

Bingo: the bylines on those copycat articles.

Photo #7—a cancelled check. Eleven grand and change paid out to: the USC Alumni Debt Fund.

"So he's spent a fortune operating Officer John Duhamel."

"Operating this guy whose story you won't believe."

Reporters bribed.

Johnny bought.

Junior glomming bank records—intimidation prowess and charm pre-CRAAAZY.

Sweating—dripping on my file swag:

Duhamel fight clippings.

A deposition—Chuck "the Greek" Chamales—matchmaker, Olympic Auditorium.

"Revealed under the threat to expose his liaison with Lurleen Ruth Cressmeyer, age 14":

Johnny D. tanked his one pro fight.

Ed Exley paid him to do it.

Duhamel told Chamales this—"one night when he was drunk." The Greek to Junior, verbatim: "He didn't get specific. He just told me on the QT that that Exley guy had special work for him."

Odd pages left—gibberish/doodling. One sheet block-printed:

ADDENDUM:

As former Academy evidence instructor I was invited to the October 16th retirement party for Sgt. Dennis Payne. Talked about my recent sergeantcy and transfer to Ad Vice with Capt. Didion, who told me my father had old Dep. Chief Green move Dave Klein up to the Ad Vice command as only a Lieutenant partially to grease things for my ultimately taking a spot there. Capt. Didion told Dave "The Enforcer" stories for half an hour, and I only listened because

I wanted to tap the grapevine for information on Johnny. Capt Didion told me that Exley personally requested that Johnny graduate early (the 7/10/58 cycle) in order to fill a potential Wilshire Patrol vacancy, which made no sense to him. Also, Dennis Payne confirmed what I suspected when Johnny was yanked early from my evidence class: that Exley urged those undercover assignments on him personally, asking Capt. Didion that he be assigned to them while still technically a cadet.

Exley and Duhamel—operating partners—operating WHO?
Suspects:
The Kafesjians.
Narco.
"This guy whose story you won't believe."
"This guy"—*singular.* A semantic fuck-up—maybe, maybe not.
Single-o suspects:
Tommy K.
J.C.
Dan Wilhite.
Skewed—I couldn't link them directly to Johnny.
Crack the door—Henstell on the walkway, pacing. Shove the chair back, jam the knob shut, go—
I lit a match and torched a file page: faggot artwork sizzled. More matches, more pages—a contained blaze right there on the table.
Smoke out the floor crack—
Henstell banged on the door. "Klein, Goddamn it, what the hell are you doing!"
Flames, charred paper, smoke. I kicked the table over, stomped the blaze out.
"Klein, Goddamn it!"
Jerk the door open, shove him back, coughing smoke—
"Tell Noonan it was personal. Tell him I'm still his witness, and now I owe *him* one."

Out to East L.A., light-headed—light smoke inhalation. Custody forty-seven hours off—two days to GET it:
"LONG HISTORY OF INSANITY BOTH OUR FAMILIES."
Olympic east—rain clouds dousing smog. Chasing/chased/partnered up/partner fucked:

Richie's Chino file was still missing—warden's aides were tossing storage bins for it. Sid Riegle was out chasing Richie—Darktown/Hancock Park—no leads.

Six IA men tapped out: no new Herrick/Kafesjian links. Links extant: Pennsylvania/chemical work/L.A. arrivals '31–'32. Late-'31 marriages: Joan Renfrew, Madge Clarkson—no criminal records—their hometowns queried.

Meg chasing real estate: a Spindrift pad title search. Zero so far, Meg persisting.

The Kafesjians at home, cabin-fevered—Feds out front, Feds out back. Partnered-up-family-tight—no way to tell them:

You and the Herricks—filthy together. Liquor bottles smashed/dogs blinded/music trashed—murder/suicide/castration—I can TASTE it. You'll tell me, you'll tell somebody—I'm partnered up strong on my ride down.

Strong and dirty: Exley. Strong/cautious/grasping: Noonan.

Use them both: fight/squirm/lie/beg/ manipulate them.

Exley: Johnny D. as my wedge. The Feds—no lever yet—that fire fried my momentum. Henstell: "You know, Mr. Noonan *was* starting to think you'd be a pretty good witness."

Was/is/could be/would be: DUES TIME. Junior nullified now—Glenda safe—punch my new grief ticket: FEDERAL.

No pre-court testimony taken yet—custody meant interrogation. Noonan—cautious/grasping—shooting me wake-up phone calls:

"You're commanding a homicide case—how odd."

"Would Richard Herrick be the Richie you seem to be so interested in? The man Tommy Kafesjian seems to be rather concerned with? Chief Exley told the *Herald* that you worked on a burglary case that may be tangentially connected to the killings. We *must* discuss this after you enter custody."

"I understand the dilemma you're in, David. You may think that you can dissemble to us and be less than forthcoming vis-à-vis your organized-crime connections, thus sparing yourself a Syndicate death sentence. You will of course be given Federal protection after your grand jury testimony, but you should know now that lies and lies by omission will not be tolerated."

Smart fucker.

Holding back information—bet on it. My big fear: those Fed tails post-Johnson. Long-shot stuff, hard to shake: Abe Voldrich snuffed, a blue Pontiac spotted. Jack Woods—nine contract hits minimum—*my* preferred killer. Jack Woods, proud owner: a powder-blue '56 Pontiac.

Downtown, the 3rd Street Bridge, Boyle Heights. East to Wabash—Brownell's Locksmiths—

A parking-lot drive-up hut.

Four keys—three numbered—maybe traceable.

I pulled up, honked. A man right there, customer smile on. "Help you?"

I flashed my badge and the key fob. "158-32, 159-32, 160-32, and one unstamped. Who did you make them for?"

"I don't even have to check my files, 'cause that 32 coding's from this rent-a-locker storage place I do all the locker keys for."

"So you don't know who rented these individual lockers?"

"Right you are. The unstamped key's for the front door, the number keys are for lockers. And I don't cut no duplicates 'less the manager at the place gives the okay."

"What 'place'?"

"The Lock-Your-Self at 1750 North Echo Park Boulevard, which is open twenty-four hours, case you didn't know."

"You're pretty snappy with your answers."

"Well . . ."

"Come on, tell me."

"Well . . ."

"Well nothing, I'm a police officer."

Whiny, wheedling: "Well, I hate to be a stool pigeon, 'cause I sorta liked the guy."

"What guy?"

"I don't know his name, but he's that little Mex bantam fights at the Olympic all the time."

"Reuben Ruiz?"

"Right you are. He came in yesterday and told me he wanted dupes of the keys with them numbers, like he *saw* the keys but couldn't get his mitts on the two original sets I cut. I told him, 'Ixnay, not even if you was Rocky Marciano himself.' "

"You cut *two* original sets for the Lock-Your-Self place?"

"One customer original, one management original. The manager sent a guy by for a second customer set, 'cause the people who rented those lockers wanted dupes."

Set number one—Junior. Set number two—maybe Johnny D.—Reuben's pal.

"Officer, them locks and keys are being changed continually to thwart theft. So if you talk to Bob, the manager, will you tell him I'm doing my part toward keeping things—"

I hit the gas—the lock man ate exhaust fumes.

Echo Park off Sunset—a big warehouse. A parking lot, no door guard—*my* door key got me in.

Huge: crisscross hallways, locker-lined. A directory/map up front, number-coded.

The 32 codings were tagged "Jumbo." Follow the map—two corridors down, left, stop:

Three floor-to-ceiling lockers six feet wide.

Scratched up—lock-pick marks.

Keys in, crack the doors:

158-32: mink coats hung eight feet deep, six feet wide.

Seven empty hangers.

159-32: stoles and pelts—dumped shoulder-high.

160-32: fox/mink/raccoon coats—fuckloads hung/dumped/piled/folded/tossed.

Johnny/Junior/Reuben.

Dudley Smith, fur-heist boss—scooped/hoodwinked/stiffed.

Exley and Duhamel—operating WHO?

Mink—touch it, smell it. Empty hangers—Lucille's fur strip? Johnny trying to sell Mickey Cohen bulk fur??

Reuben Ruiz: ex–B&E man/burglar brothers.

His direct key approach—no go.

Break-in scratches/no door guard/Lock-Your-Self: open twenty-four hours.

Key clicks/lock clicks/brain clicks—I got my notebook and pen out. Three lockers—I dropped three identical notes inside:

> I want to deal on Johnny Duhamel, Junior Stemmons and whatever or whoever else connects to this. This is for money, independent of Ed Exley.
>
> D. Klein

Lock the doors—lock clicks/brain clicks—get to a phone.
I found a booth across Sunset. Ad Vice, two rings, "Riegle."
"Sid, it's me."
"You mean it's you and you want something."
"You're right."

"So tell me, but I'll tell *you* right now this Homicide work is wearing me thin."

"Meaning?"

"Meaning Richie Herrick is nowhere. First Exley issues an APB, then he rescinds it, and we *still* can't locate one single white man known to frequent Negro areas."

"I know, and our best bet is to let Tommy Kafesjian find him for us."

"Which doesn't seem too likely with those Armenian humps holed up with Fed surveillance outside their house. Jesus . . ."

"Sid, write this down."

"Okay, I'm listening."

"The storage locker place at 1750 North Echo Park."

"All right, I wrote it down. Now what?"

"Now you get your civilian car and stake out the entrance and parking lot. You write down the plate numbers on everyone who walks in. Every five or six hours you call in the stats to the DMV, and you go through until tomorrow morning and call me."

Stage groans. "You'll explain then?"

"That's right."

"It's the Herrick job?"

"It's fucking everything."

36

euben Ruiz—talk, strong-arm—whatever it took.

R&I shot me his address: 229 South Loma. Not that far—a quick run over—brother Ramon on the porch.

"Reuben's at the ravine, bein' a *puto* for the City of Los Angeles."

Another quick run—Chavez Ravine.

Swarming now—evictions pending. "Police Parking"—a dirt lot going in. Cop cars jammed up tail to snout: Sheriff's, LAPD, Feds.

Hills fronting the main drag; Mex kids chucking rocks. Black & whites scratched and dented.

An access road up—narrow, dusty. I walked it, hit the top, caught the view:

Hecklers bucking bluesuit containment—the main road cordoned off. Shack-lined roads/hills/gulleys—eviction notices rife. Camera crews shooting door to door: Feds and a bobbing sombrero.

Dig it: shack dwellers swarming that hat.

I walked down into it; blues juked me through the cordon. Catch the view: Shipstad, Milner, Ruiz in bullfighter garb.

Reuben:

Passing out money, spics swamping him.

"Dinero!"

"El jefe Ruiz!"

Big-time Mex jabber—incomprehensible.

Milner gaga-eyed: what *is* this?

I shoved, waved—Shipstad saw me. Trembly and flushed—Henstell probably blabbed.

He shoved toward me. We collided: hands on suitcoats instinctive.

"Gracias el jefe Reuben!"—Ruiz tossing cash away.

A dirt yard off the road—Shipstad pointed over. I followed him—tree shade, a sign: "Notice to Vacate."

"Justify that firebug routine before Noonan revokes your immunity and has you arrested."

Eyeball magnet: Reuben dishing out greenbacks.

"Look at me, Klein."

At him, lawyer bullshit: "It was nontangential incriminating evidence. It in no way pertained to the Kafesjian family or to any focus of your investigation or my potential grand jury testimony. Noonan has enough on me as it is, and I didn't want to feed him more potential indictable information."

"Attorney to attorney, how can you live the way you do?"

Tongue tied—

"We're trying to help you get out of this alive. I'm developing a plan to relocate you after you testify, and frankly Noonan doesn't think I should be working so hard at it."

"Which means?"

"Which means I dislike him slightly more than I dislike you. Which means he's two seconds away from arresting you and putting you on display as a hostile witness, then releasing you and letting Sam Giancana or whoever have you killed."

Meg jailed/ brutalized/clipped—Technicolor. "Will you relocate my sister?"

"That's impossible. This last escapade has cost you credibility with Noonan, relocation for your sister was not covered in your contract and there is no established precedent for mobsters harming the loved ones of fugitive witnesses."

GET MONEY.

Ruiz throwing it away.

"We're your only hope. I'll square things with Noonan, but you be at the Federal Building by eight A.M. day after tomorrow, or we'll find you, arrest your sister and begin tax-charge proceedings."

Crowd noise, dust. Reuben watching us.

I waved the keys. Sunlight on metal—he nodded.

Shipstad: "Klein . . ."

"I'll be there."

"Eight A.M."

"I heard you."

"It's your only—"

"What's Ruiz doing?"

He looked over. "Expiation of guilt or some such concept. Can you blame him? All this for a baseball stadium?"

Reuben walked up.

"Did you come to see *him?* And what's with those keys?"

"Give me some time with him."

"Is it personal?"

"Yeah, it's personal."

Shipstad walked; Ruiz passed him and winked. Rockabye Reuben: bullfight threads, grin.

"Hey, Lieutenant."

I twirled the keys. "You go first."

"No. First you tell me this is just two witness buddies gabbing, then you tell me popping Mexican bantamweights for robbery don't push your buzzer."

Bulldozers down the road—a shack crashed.

"Keys, Reuben. You saw the originals, memorized the numbers and tried to get that locksmith to cut dupes, and there's tool marks on the lockers at that storage place."

"I didn't hear you say anything like 'This is just two guys who'd like each other to stay out of trouble talking.' "

Gear whine/wood snap/dust—the noise made me flinch. "I'm way past arresting people."

"I sort of thought so, given what the Feds been saying."

"Reuben, spill. I've got this half-assed notion you want to."

"Do penance, maybe. Spill, I don't know."

"Did you boost some furs out of those lockers?"

"As many as me and my righteous B&E buddies could carry. And they're gone, in case you want a mink for your slumlord sister."

Flowers sprouting next to weeds; smog wafting in.

"So you bagged some furs, sold them and gave the money to your poor exploited brethren."

"No, I gave a silver fox pelt to Mrs. Mendoza next door, 'cause I popped her daughter's cherry and never married her, then I sold the furs, then I got drunk and gave the money away."

"Just like that?"

"Yeah, and those stupidos down there'll probably spend it on Dodger tickets."

"Reuben—"

"Fuck it, all right—me, Johnny Duhamel and my brothers took down the Hurwitz fur warehouse. You were maybe pushing that way when I saw you in my dressing room, so now you tell me what you got before I sober up and get bored with this penance routine."

"Let's try Ed Exley operating Johnny."

Smog—Reuben coughed. "You picked a good fucking topic."

"I figured if Johnny talked to anybody, it was you."

"You figured pretty good."

"He told you about it?"

"Most of it, I guess. Look, this is, you know, off the record?"

I nodded—easy now—cut him rope.

Tick tick tick tick.

Jerk the rope: "Reuben—"

"Yeah, okay, I guess it was like this spring, like April or something. Exley, he read this newspaper story about Johnny. You know, a what you call human-interest story, like here's this guy in graduate school working all these jobs, he used to be a comer in the Golden Gloves, but now he's gotta turn pro even though he don't want to, 'cause his parents croaked and stiffed him and his school, and how he's broke. You follow me so far?"

"Keep going."

"Okay, so Exley, he approached Johnny and what you call manipulated him. He gave Johnny money and paid off his college loan, and he paid off these debts Johnny's parents left. Exley, he's like some kind of rich-kid cop with this big inheritance, and he gave Johnny this bonaroo fucking amount of money and paid these reporter guys to write these other, you know, similar-type newspaper stories about him, playing on this angle that he had to turn pro out of, you know, financial necessity."

"And Exley made Johnny tank that one pro fight he had."

"Right."

"And the newspaper pieces and the tank job were to set Johnny up as some sort of hard-luck kid, so it would look realistic when he applied to the LAPD."

"Right."

"And Exley got Johnny eased into the Academy?"

"Right."

"And all this was to set Johnny up to work undercover."

"Right, to get next to some people or something that Exley had this hard-on for, but don't ask me who, 'cause I don't know."

THEM/Dan Wilhite/Narco—mix them, match them—

"Keep going."

Bobs, feints—Reuben oozed sweat. "So Exley, he got Johnny this outside work while he was in the Academy, this gig where he what you call infiltrated these Marine Corps guys who were beating up and robbing all these rich queers. That punk Stemmons, you know, that ex-partner of yours, he was Johnny's teacher at the Academy, and he read this report that Johnny wrote on the fruit-roller gig."

"And?"

"And Stemmons, he was both, you know, attracted to and, what you call it, repelled by homos. He had the hots for Johnny, which embarrassed the shit out of Johnny, 'cause he's a cunt man from the gate. Anyway, Johnny busted up the fruit-roller ring, and the Marine Corps police, they got, you know, convictions against the guys. Johnny graduated from the Academy and got assigned to the Detective Bureau right off, 'cause the queer gig made him look righteous good, and 'cause being a Golden Gloves champ gave him some righteous prestige. Anyway, that Irish guy, you know, Dudley Smith, he took a shine to Johnny and got him assigned to the Mobster Squad, 'cause he wanted an ex-fighter for this strongarm work they do."

Linkage clicking in—no surprises yet.

"And?"

"*And* somehow Stemmons found out that Exley was what you call operating Johnny, *and* he pulled this wild queer number on him, *and* it disgusted Johnny, but he didn't beat that *puto* faggot silly, 'cause Stemmons was this hotshot evidence teacher cop who could screw Johnny on this gig he was fuckin' embroiled in with Exley."

Popping punches, popping sweat—little moves synced to his story.

"And?"

"*And* you cops always pull that 'and' bit to keep people talking."

"Then let's try 'so.' "

"*So* I guess it was about this time that Johnny got tangled up in the fur job. He said he had inside help, and he just hired on me and my brothers to do the hauling work. He was doing these other so-called bad things, and I figured it was strongarm shit on the Mobster Squad, but Johnny said it was lots worse, like so bad he was afraid to tell his good buddy Exley about it. Fucking Stemmons, he was talking all this criminal-mastermind noise up to Johnny, and I don't know, but somehow he found out about Johnny and the fur heist."

Ruiz shit-eater-grinning—punched out, winded.

"When did Johnny tell you all this?"

"After the fur heist, when we put on gloves and he told me to give him this penance beating."

"And around that time Stemmons tried to horn in on Johnny's part of the fur job."

"Right."

"Come on, Reuben. Right, *and?*"

"And Johnny told me the fur job was an Exley setup from the gate. It was part of his what you call cover, and Exley was in with that guy Sol Hurwitz. Hurwitz was some kind of gone-bust gambler, and fuckin' rich-kid Exley, he bought all the furs and told Johnny how to stage the heist."

AUDACIOUS.

Links missing.

Exley's heist/Dudley Smith's investigation—why did Exley assign someone that good?

Linkage chronology—pure guesswork:

Johnny offers Mickey Cohen hot fur.

Dud gloms the Cohen lead and scares Mickey shitless.

Exley intercedes.

Exley operates Mickey—*toward what end?*

Mickey, skewed behavior—movie mogul, Darktown bungler—he *still* won't pull his Southside slots.

Chick Vecchio—Mickey linked.

Chick—finger man—Kafesjian movie time.

Mickey and Chick—linked to:

THEM/Narco/Dan Wilhite.

Links:

Missing/hidden/obscured/twisted CRAAAZY—

Reuben—punched out, grinning: *"So,* I guess all this is just between us witness buddies."

"That's right."

"Is Johnny dead?"

"Yes."

"Too bad he never got married. Mea fucking culpa, I could of dropped a nice mink coat on his widow."

Crash noise—another shack went down.

tone's throw: Chavez Ravine to Silverlake. Over to Jack Woods' place—his car outside.

Powder blue gleaming: Jack's baby.

The front door stood ajar—I knocked first.

"I'm in the shower! It's open!"

I walked in—brazen Jack—phones and bet slips in plain view. A wall photo: Jack, Meg and me—the Mocambo, '49.

"You remember that night? Meg got plowed on brandy alexanders."

Meg sat between us—hard to tell whose girl.

"You're cruising down memory lane pretty steep, partner."

I turned around. "You clipped a guy for Mickey a couple of days before. You were flush, so you picked up the tab."

Jack cinched his robe. "Is this the pot calling the kettle black?"

"Did you pop Abe Voldrich?"

"Yeah, I did. Do you care?"

"Not exactly."

"Then you just came by to rehash old times."

"It's about Meg, but I wouldn't mind an explanation."

Jack lit a cigarette. "Chick Vecchio bought the hit for Mickey. He said Narco and Dan Wilhite wanted it. Voldrich was the Kafesjian family's bagman to the LAPD. Chick said it was Mickey's idea, that the Feds had turned Voldrich as a witness, and Mickey wanted his connections to the Kafesjians snipped. Ten grand, partner. My consolation prize for that hump Stemmons dying on me."

"I'm not so sure I buy it."

"So what? Business is business, and Mickey and those Armenians have got lots of stuff going down in Niggertown."

"Something's missing. Mickey doesn't clip people anymore, and he hasn't got ten grand liquid to save his life."

"So it was the Kafesjians direct, or Dan Wilhite through Chick. Look, what do you care who—"

"Wilhite doesn't know Chick personally, I'd bet on it."

My sister's lover—bored. "Look, Chick played on you and me as friends. He said Voldrich could spill to the Feds on you, so did I want to make ten G's and help a buddy out. *Now,* you want to tell me how you made me for the job?"

Links: obscured/hidden/fucked with—

"Dave—"

"The Feds saw a car like yours near Voldrich's place. They didn't get any plate numbers, or you'd have heard from them by now."

"So it was just an educated guess."

"You're the only clip guy I know with a powder-blue car."

"So what about Meg?"

"First you tell me how it stands with you two."

"It stands that she's thinking about leaving her husband and getting a place with me."

"A phone drop? Some crap-game pad?"

"We ruined her for squarejohn guys years ago, so don't act like she doesn't know the score."

That photo—a woman, two killers.

"The Feds have got me by the shorts. I'm going into custody day after tomorrow, and if they try to screw me on my immunity deal Meg might get hurt. I want you to tell her to pull our money out of the bank, and I want you to stash her some place safe until I call you."

"Okay."

"Just 'okay'?"

"Okay, send postcards from wherever the Feds hide you, and I've had a hunch that you were screwed for a couple of weeks now."

That picture—

Jack smiled. "Meg said she's doing this title search for you, and every time you talk on the phone you sound less like a strongarm guy."

"And more like a lawyer?"

"No, more like a guy trying to buy his way out."

"Look after her."

"Write when you can, Counselor."

A pay-phone call to Homicide. Shit news—no trace on Richie Herrick's Chino file. A message—meet Pete Bondurant—8:00, the Smokehouse, Burbank.

The Vecchio job—looming ugly.

Time to kill. Stone's throw: Silverlake to Griffith Park. I drove up the east road to the Observatory.

Smog clearing, a view: Hollywood, points south. Coin telescopes mounted by the entrance: 180-degree swivels.

Time to kill, pocket change—I aimed one at the set.

Glass blur, asphalt, hills. Parked cars, up, over: the spaceship.

Crank the lens, squint—people.

Sid Frizell and Wylie Bullock talking: maybe their standard gore shtick. Blur, twist the lens: winos sleeping in the weeds.

Look:

A trailer door embrace: Touch and Rock Rockwell. Over right: Mickey C. spieling extras. Metal glare—Glenda's trailer, Glenda.

Sitting on the steps, her legs jammed up. Her vampire gown getting ratty—faded, threadbare.

Glass blur, sun streaks. People walking by—dark obstructions. Hard to see, easy to imagine:

Her breath catching low guiding me in.

Sweat matting her hair a shade darker.

Touching her scars—her eyes implicit: horror gave me the will—and I won't tell you how.

Sun spots, eyestrain. Twist the scope—a wino fistfight—pratfalls, gouging.

The lens clicked off—my time was up. My eyes hurt—I closed them and just stood there. Images hit me rapid-fire:

Dave Klein, strikebreaker—teeth on my truncheon.

Dave Klein, bet enforcer—baseball bat work.

Dave Klein, killer—hung over from cordite and blood stench.

Meg Klein, sobbing: "I don't want you to love me that way."

Joan Herrick: "Long history of insanity both our families."

Somebody, please: give me one last chance to know.

38

"**. . .** so Mr. Hughes is pissed. Some psycho chopped Harold Miciak, and he was hoping it'd be open and shut, but now the Malibu Sheriff's are thinking it's not that Wino Will-o-the-Wisp guy. They're thinking somebody chopped Miciak and strangled him to make it look like the Wisp, and Miciak's ex-wife is bothering Mr. Hughes to put private eyes on the job like he's supposed to spend *money* on this thing. *Then,* on top of all *that,* Bradley Milteer finds out that *you're* porking Glenda Bledsoe and that she's been stealing from Mr. Hughes' fuck pads, but *you* never reported it."

Southbound—Pete's car. Bonus armed: knucks and sap.

"I got you the Glenda gig. Mr. Hughes didn't trust me on it, 'cause he knows I'm susceptible to snatch. I figured, give the job to the old Enforcer, 'cause he's pretty stoical in the woman department."

I stretched—neck kinks, jangly nerves. "I'm paying you seven grand for this."

"Yeah, and you bought me a barbeque beef plate and a beer, which frankly Mr. Hughes never did. What I'm saying is that Mr. Hughes is pissed at you, which is grief you don't need."

Normandie south—Pete smoking—crack the window. Replay: my call to Noonan.

"You burned up potential Federal evidence. You're lucky I haven't revoked your immunity outright, and now you want this rather outsized favor."

"PLEASE."

"I like the tremor in your voice."

"PLEASE. Lift the surveillance on the Kafesjians tomorrow. It's my last full day before custody, and I want to see if I can learn a few things before I go in."

"My guess is that this pertains to the Kafesjians looking for that Richie character, who may be Richard Herrick of that rather outré triple-homicide case you're working."

"You're right."

"Good. I appreciate candor, and I'll do it if you formally depose your Richie information during your pre-grand-jury interviews."

"I agree."

"It's settled, then. Go with God, Brother Klein."

"Brother" Klein—Lutheran choirboy—fists/sap/knucks—

Pete nudged me. "Chick's meeting Joan Crawford at the Lucky Nugget. She'll be camouflaged up, and they're gonna play pokerino or something, then head for the fuck spot from there. I'm gonna snap some pictures on the QT, then Chick's gonna give me the high sign. We'll tail them to the spot, let them get cozy and take it from there."

Cold air, bouncing headlights. A billboard: "Dodger Stadium Is *Your* Dream! Support the Chavez Ravine Bill!"

Pete: "Seven grand for your thoughts."

"I'm thinking Chick must have a money stash someplace."

"If you're thinking take it, it means we have to clip him."

"It's just a thought."

"And as thoughts go, not bad. Jesus, you and some ex-carhop actress. Is she—"

"Yeah, she's worth the trouble."

"I wasn't gonna ask you that."

"I know."

"Like that, huh?"

"Like that."

Straight south—Gardena—Pete talking grapevine:

Fred Turentine, *Hush-Hush* bug man: scandal duty for off-the-books cash. Boozer Freddy, AWOL: from dry-out farms and his jail teaching gig. Fed heat, restless niggers—you couldn't score good ribs or dark poon for shit.

Gardena—poker-palace row pulsing neon. The Lucky Nugget— Chick's Caddy in the lot, top down.

We pulled up behind it—tail ready. Front-seat action—Joan Crawford and Chick necking hot.

Pete said, "Duck down, they'll see you."

I ducked and listened—car doors slammed. Back up—lovebirds on the stroll.

Pete got out. "Take a snooze or something. Don't play the radio, you'll run the battery down."

Tracks inside: movie star, thug, shakedown man. I skimmed the radio dial: news, religious shit, bop.

Memory jog: rolling Gardena drunks back in high school. Bop to ballads, memory lane—zipping Meg's prom gown too slow.

Fuck it—spare the battery—I turned the music off and dozed. Pete at the door: "Wake up, they're leaving."

The Caddy rolled, ragtop up. Pete pulled out—not too close.

East, north—cool air woke me up. Easy tailwork—collusion—Pete drove nonchalant. One arm out her window, oblivious: Joan fucking Crawford.

Due north—Compton, LYNWOOD—spooky turf.

Chick out front: left turn, right turn—Spindrift Drive.

48, 4900—curb plates pulsing weird/nuts/strange. 4980—Johnny D.—"Why meet there?"

Hard to breathe—I rolled the window down.

Left turn, right turn.

Empty courtyards.

Dry-ice chills: hot and cold.

Pete: "Jesus, I never made you for such a fresh-air fiend."

Chick stopped—brake-light taps, signallike.

Memory lane:

Needle stabbed.

Toasty-warm tingly doped up.

Chick and Joanie, walking love-draped:

Into a vacant courtyard, up the RIGHT side walkway.

Then:

Carried, treading air.

RIGHT turn—a skanky room—MOVIE TIME.

Now:

Sucking air—hard to breathe—Johnny replays zinging me.

Pete pulled up curbside. "Chick passed me a note. He knows some guys making smut films here, so he thought Joanie'd like that angle. Movie stars never fail to fucking amaze me."

Memory clicks—brutal late:

Glenda said Sid Frizell was shooting stag films.

"At some abandoned dive."

"Down in LYNWOOD."

"Hey, Klein, are you okay?"

Weapon check: .45, sap, knucks. "Let's go."

Pete loaded his camera. "It's all set. We go in on 'Baby, it's so good.'"

Ready: knuck teeth scraped my law-school ring.

Pete: "Now."

We ran in: stucco cubes, walkways, grass.

Place it then and now: Movie time, Johnny begging: "PLEASE DON'T KILL ME."

Sex grunts—a right-side shack midway down. Tiptoes up, listen:

Smut moans, Chick: "Baby, it's so gooood."

Pete camera ready.

Looks, nods, kicks—we snapped the door clean.

Pitch black half a second.

Flashbulb pops: Joan Crawford gobbling Chick V. tonsil-deep.

Speedo:

Bulb blips—Joanie running out the door bare-ass, shrieking.

Chick pawing at a wall switch—the lights on.

A magnum on the nightstand—I grabbed it and scoped the room:

Mirrored walls.

Linoleum floor—maroon dots—dried blood.

Chick on the bed, zipping his fly.

Knucks/gun butt—quick—

I bashed his face, racked his nuts, cracked his arms. Bone jar up my hands—Chick balled himself tight.

A shadow on the bed—Pete restraining me. *"Ease off.* I gave Crawford some clothes and some money. *We've got time to do this right."*

Chick doubled up, quaking, good cause: two giant fists flexing straight at him.

Canned shtick—Pete gleeful:

"The left one's the hospital, the right one's death. The right one steals your life while the left steals your breath. These hands are bad juju and the bad boogaloo, they're the teeth of the demon as he slides down the flue."

Chick stood up—bloody, trembly. "I am Outfit. I am a made guy. Feature you are both dead for this."

Pete: "Dave, ask the man a question."

I said, "You set me up. I told you I was meeting a 'pretty-boy strongarm cop' in Lynwood. Now, for starters you tell me *who* you told and how they got that home-movie idea."

"Feature I will tell you nothing."

Pete grabbed him by the neck. Flick: two hundred pounds airborne. Chick hit the far wall—mirror glass shattered.

Rag doll Chick—this "huh?" look.

Pete right there—stomp, stomp—fingers cracking under his heels. Chick showed balls: no audible grief.

I knelt down. "You set me up with the Kafesjians."

"Go fuck yourself."

"Chick, we go back. This doesn't have to be ugly."

"Feature you *are* ugly."

"You fingered me to the Kafesjians. Cop to it and go from there."

"I didn't clue nobody you were meeting that cop you told me about. So you got set up, what the fuck, they set you up. Feature I knew they set you up, but feature it was after the goddamn fact."

"You said 'they.' You mean the Kafesjians?"

"I mean it's a figure of goddamn speech. You got set up 'cause you were born for it, all the shit you pulled and walked on. You got set up, but feature I didn't do it."

Pete: "I didn't know you knew the Kafesjians. I thought you were strictly a Mickey guy."

"Fuck you. You're a chump change pimp for Howard Hughes. I fucked your mother. My dog fucked your mother."

Pete laughed.

Chick—broken fingers, shock pale: "Feature I been roughhoused before. Feature I gave you a free introductory answer, but from here on in you get shit."

Blood flecks on the floor—Johnny begging.

"You said 'they.' You mean the Kafesjians? Give me some details I can use."

"You mean feed to the Feds? I know you rolled over for Welles Noonan."

This greaseball thug—sweating off Joan Crawford's perfume.

"Hand the fuckers up. Give me details."

"Detail this"—one smashed middle finger twirling. "Suck on this, you kraut cocksuck—"

I grabbed his hand—a wall socket close—jam that fuck-you finger in—

Sparks/smoke—Chick convulsing—live-wire jolts shaking me.

Pete shook me: "STOP IT, YOU'LL KILL HIM!"

Chick shook free: juiced-up hip-hops on his knees, going green.

Fast:

Pete tossed him on the bed. Pillows, sheets, blankets—one mummified geek inside seconds.

Hip-hops sputtering out, his green tinge fading.

Johnny Duhamel begging—IN THIS ROOM.

I grabbed the magnum and popped the cylinder. Six rounds—I dumped five.

Pete nodded: I *think* he's okay.

Show the gun, show the cylinder—spin it, lock it.

Chick—read his eyes—"You wouldn't."

I aimed point blank—my gun, his head. "You said 'they.' Did you mean the Kafesjian family?"

No response.

I pulled the trigger—*click*—empty chamber.

"How'd you get in with the Kafesjians? I didn't know you knew them."

No response.

I pulled the trigger—*click*—empty chamber.

"I know you gave Jack Woods the contract on Abe Voldrich, and Jack said Mickey ordered it. I don't believe that, so you tell me who really did."

Chick, raspy: "Fuck you."

I pulled the trigger—twice—empty chambers.

Pete whooped: "Mother dog!"

Rainbow Chick turning gray/green/blue.

Cock the hammer, eeeaase the trigger sooo slooow . . .

"Okay, okay PLEASE!"

I pulled the gun back. Chick coughed, spat phlegm and talked:

"I got this order to recruit a hit on Abe Voldrich. Feature they figured I was too well known on the Southside to do it myself, so I thought, 'Dave Klein, he could get burned by this Federal biz,' and 'Jack Woods, he does a job for a price, he's Dave's buddy, he'd want to spare Dave grief,' so I talked him into it that way, not that he didn't jew me up on the ticket."

Raspy working on hoarse: "So, feature—I *talked* to Voldrich. The Feds cut him loose to take care of some stuff for a day or so, and I wanted to know what he knew before I had Jack clip him. Now, now, now"—snitch fever—"you just listen."

Pete popping his knuckles—loud, like hammer clicks.

Chick, thrashing his blankets: "Voldrich said the Feds were hot to turn you as a witness. He said he overheard Welles Noonan and this FBI man Shipstad talking. They said they bugged your pad, and they've got a tape with you talking this amorphous stuff about your mob hits, and Glenda Bledsoe saying she snuffed some nigger pimp named Dwight Gilette. Feature, Davey: Noonan told Shipstad he was going to offer you immunity, get a shitload of information, then violate the agreement unless you testify against Glenda on the murder charge. Shipstad tried to talk Noonan out of crossing you, but Noonan hates you so bad he said he'd never agree."

Feature:

The bed spinning.

The room spinning.

The gun spinning—

"Who are 'they'?"

"Davey, please. I just did you this all-time solid."

"Something's off here. You're not the one the Kafesjians would send to pump Abe Voldrich. Now, who set me up to kill Johnny Duhamel?"

"Davey, *please.*"

Everything spinning—

"Please, Davey . . ."

I hit him—gun-butt shots—his blankets caught the brunt. I pulled them down—ribcage work—the bed spun.

"Who set me up?"

No snitch.

"What's with Mickey? Why are those out-of-town guys working his slots with the Feds right there?"

No snitch.

"You're in with the Kafesjians? You're tight with them? *You fucking tell me what you know about Tommy chasing a guy named Richie Herrick.*"

No snitch—ribcage work—my pistol grips shattered. Pete flashed me a signal: EASY.

I spun the cylinder again. "Is Sid Frizell shooting smut films here?"

No answer.

I pulled the trigger—*click*—empty chamber.

Chick balled up, quaking—

Pull the trigger—*click*—empty chamber.

Quaking/snitch-begging eyes: "They said they needed a strongarm place, so I said take this place, Sid and his crew were editing their stag stuff, so this place was empty."

"Did they tell you they were making their own movie?"

"No! They said 'strongarm spot'! That's all they said!"

"Who developed their film? Did someone on Mickey's movie crew help them out?"

"No! Frizell and his guys are fucking clowns! They don't know anybody except me!"

"Who's been running you?"

"No, Davey, please!"

I put the gun to the mattress—next to his head. "Who are THEY?"

"NO! I CAN'T! I WON'T!"

I pulled the trigger—*click/click/roar*—muzzle flash set his hair on fire. This scream.

This huge hand snuffing flames out—stretching huge to quash that scream.

A whisper:

"We'll stash him at one of your buildings. You do what you have to do, and I'll watchdog him. We'll work an angle on his money, and sooner or later he'll spill."

Smoke. Mattress debris settling.

Chick torched half-bald.

EVERYTHING SPINNING.

39

Back to L.A.—Pete's car solo—
pay-phone stops en route.

I broke it to Glenda: you're
nailed for Dwight Gilette. She
said, "Oh, shit" and hatched a
plan: she'd bus it to Fresno, hide out with an old carhop pal. Phone-tap
panic hit me—I spieled her through the checkout procedure. Glenda pulled
wires and checked diodes—no tap on her line.

Her goodbye: "We're too good-looking to lose."

Jack Woods—three no-answers—Meg ditto. A booth outside the Bureau, luck—Jack just walked in. I told him the Feds fucked me: grab Meg,
grab our money, GO.

"Okay, Dave"—no goodbye.

I ran up to Ad Vice. A clerk's slip on my desk: "Call Meg. Important."

My In box, my Out box—no new Herrick field reports. I checked my
desk—the Kafesjian/Herrick case file was gone.

The phone rang—

"Yeah?"

"Boss, it's Riegle."

"Yeah?"

"Come on, you assigned me to a stakeout, remember? The storage
locker place, you told me—"

"Yeah, I remember. Is this routine, or something good?"

Miffed: "I got you twelve hours of DMV-certified squarejohns and one
interesting bit."

"So tell me."

"So, a guy went in, then ran back to his car looking spooked. *So,* I got
his plate number and checked him out, and I thought he looked sort of familiar. *So,* Richard Carlisle, you know him? He's LAPD, and I think he
works for Dudley Smith."

Soft clicks.

"Boss, are you—"

I cradled the phone down, soft clicks building:

Dick Carlisle—fur-job detective.

Dick Carlisle—Mike Breuning's partner.

11/51—Breuning dead-ends a juvie B&E. Obvious perps: Tommy K., Richie Herrick.

My Kafesjian/Herrick case file—missing.

I walked down the hall to Personnel. File request slips on the clerk's desk—for Division COs only.

I braced the clerk:

Michael Breuning, Richard Carlisle—get me their folders. "Yes, sir," ten minutes, folders out—"not to leave the room."

Carlisle—Previous Employment—no clicks.

Breuning—movie click—Wilshire Film Processing, developing technician—'37–'39—pre-LAPD.

Click—soft, circumstantial.

1:00 A.M.—back to Ad Vice. Stray thoughts: Pete guarding Chick at my El Segundo vacant.

Chick:

"THEY."

Afraid to say "Kafesjian."

Afraid to snitch they/THEM/who?

That message slip: "Call Meg. Important."

Circumstantial—prickles up my short hairs.

Meg at Jack's—worth a try. Three rings—Jack, edgy: "Yes?"

"It's me."

Background noise: high heels tapping. Jack said, "She's here. She's taking it pretty well, maybe just a little bit nervous."

"You're leaving tomorrow?"

"Right. We'll hit the banks early, withdraw the cash and get bank drafts. Then we're going to drive down to Del Mar, open some new accounts and find a place. You want to talk to her?"

Tap tap—Meg pacing—high heels made her stocking seams bunch. "No. Tell her it's just goodbye for now, and ask her what the message was."

Tap, tap, low voices. Footsteps, Jack: "Meg said she's got a partial trace on that building in Lynwood."

"And?"

"She found some property evaluation reports in that storage basement at the City Hall. What she's got is a 1937 report listing Phillip Herrick and a Dudley L. Smith as bidders on 4980 Spindrift. Hey, you think that's *the* Dudley Smith?"

Sweaty hands—I dropped the phone.

Say it:

Ed Exley vs. Dudley Smith.

40

EMERGENCY COMMAND #'s—my desk card. Chief of Detectives (Home)—dial it.

Exley, 1:00 A.M. alert: "Yes? Who is this?"

"It's Klein. I just figured out you're working Dudley Smith."

"Come over now. My address is 432 South McCadden."

A trellised Tudor—lights on, the door ajar. I walked in uninvited.

A showroom living room, catalog perfect. Exley in a suit and knotted tie—2:00 fucking A.M.

"How did you find out?"

"I beat you to a bank writ and hit Junior Stemmons' vault boxes. He had notes on you operating Duhamel, and Reuben Ruiz filled in some blank spots on the fur heist. I found out that Dudley and Phillip Herrick went in on some property together back in '37. Herrick and J.C. Kafesjian came to L.A. a few years before, and I'm betting Dudley was the one who set J.C. up with the LAPD."

Standing there, arms crossed. "Continue."

"It fits. My Kafesjian and Herrick files were stolen, and Richie's prison records are missing. Dudley could have snatched them both easily. He loves developing protégés, so you shoved Johnny Duhamel in his face."

"Continue."

Shock him: "I killed Johnny. Dudley doped me up, provoked me and filmed it. A fucking *movie* exists. I think he's waiting to use me for something."

Exley "shock"—one neck vein pulsing. "When you said Duhamel was dead, I knew it had to be Dudley, but this film business surprises me."

"Surprise *me*. Give me your end of it."

He pulled chairs up. "Give me your take on Dudley Smith."

"He's brilliant and obsessed with order. He's cruel. It's occurred to me a few times that he's capable of anything."

"Beyond your wildest imaginings."

Scalp prickles. "And?"

"And he's been trying to set himself up to control the L.A. rackets for years."

"And?"

"And, in 1950 he acquired some heroin stolen from a Mickey Cohen–Jack Dragna truce meeting. He enlisted a chemist, who spent years developing compounds with it, in order to produce the drug more cheaply. His design was to accrue profit through selling it, to utilize it to keep Negro criminal elements sedated and then branch out into other rackets. His ultimate goal was something along the lines of 'contained' organized crime. He wanted to perpetuate illegal enterprises within specific vice zones, most notably South Los Angeles."

"Get to specifics."

Slow—tantalizing me: "In '53 Dudley became involved in an attempt to take over a pornography racket. A meet was set up at the Nite Owl Coffee Shop. Dudley sent three men in with shotguns. A robbery was faked, and six people were killed. Dudley was instrumental in attempting to frame three Negro thugs for the murders. They escaped from jail and hid out, and as you know, I shot and killed them, along with the man who was hiding them."

The room swirled—

"The case was assumed closed. As you also know, a man came forth later and gave the men I killed a valid Nite Owl alibi, which prompted a reopening. I know you know most of the story, but let two facts suffice: the actual gunmen were killed during the reopened investigation, and they left not one shred of evidence pointing to Dudley Liam Smith."

Swirling—grab for threads:

Dudley—smut fiend?—MOVIE TIME. Sid Frizell shooting stag films in that courtyard—no connection to Smith.

"Dud's got new takeover plans going—strictly Niggertown."

"Bravo, Lieutenant."

"He's running Mickey Cohen?"

"Continue."

"Mickey's been scuffling since he got out of prison. Four of his men disappeared earlier this year—Dudley killed them. All Mickey's got going is that stupid horror movie he's bankrolling, which I don't think ties to any of this."

"Continue."

"Mickey's been acting strange since the Fed business started. He won't dump his Southside coin machines, and I warned him half a dozen times. He's got some out-of-town guys servicing slots in plain sight, with the Feds right there taking pictures. I mentioned it to Chick Vecchio, who handed me a line of shit about Mickey paying off a syndicate loan with his coin percentages. Chick's in with Dudley. Dudley clipped those four Mickey guys and approached Chick. Chick's the liaison between Dud and Mickey. That slot work with the Feds watching is some kind of setup."

Exley fucking *smiled.* "You've put it together exactly as I have."

"Get to Johnny. Tell me how you operated him."

"No, tell me about your Stemmons evidence first."

I ticked points: "I know about those bank accounts you set up. I know how you paid those reporters to write stories about Johnny. I know you paid off his debts, got him to tank that fight and got him into the Academy. You set up the fur heist yourself, so I'm thinking you arranged leads to have Dudley actually *make* Johnny for the heist. You *knew* how Dudley loved developing 'protégés,' so you put a fucking humdinger right in front of his nose."

"Keep going."

"Breuning and Carlisle—they're in with Dudley."

"Correct."

"You got Johnny that Academy undercover job."

"Elaborate on that."

Leading me/pushing me/praising me—this string-pulling weak sister.

"You coached him to overreact. Dudley likes tough boys, so you made damn sure Johnny established some strongarm credentials."

"Bravo, Lieutenant"—toss the dog a bone.

"You like running people as much as Dudley does. It must gall you to know he's better at it."

"You're sure of that?"

"No, you cocksucker, I'm not. But I *know* it must get you to look in the mirror and see Dudley."

Exley "anger"—a tight little grimace.

"Continue."

"No, you give me a chronology. Dudley bit, and got Johnny assigned to the Mobster Squad. He's the Robbery Division CO, so he got the Hurwitz heist pro forma. You planted leads to put Dudley on to Johnny, then what?"

"Then Johnny became an official Mobster Squad goon. It's brutal work, Lieutenant. I always thought you'd be well suited for it."

Tight fists—my knuckles ached. "Reuben Ruiz said Johnny was doing some 'very bad things.' Dudley started working *him* then, right? He made

Johnny for the robbery, and he *liked* it. It impressed him, so he let Johnny in on his plans."

"You're on track. Continue."

"Continue shit—what 'very bad things'?"

"Dudley had Johnny terrorizing out-of-town hoodlums he had plans for. Johnny told me he was having difficulty doing it."

"You should have pulled him then."

"No. I needed more."

"Do you think those out-of-town guys were the guys working Mickey's slots? Do you think it ties into Dud running Mickey?"

"Yes. I'm not entirely sure, but I think it's possible."

His chair—Scotch tape dangling off a slat.

"Wrap it up."

Exley buffed his glasses—his eyes looked soft without them. "Johnny began to lose Dudley's respect. He was too lax with the out-of-town men, and he told me that Carlisle and Breuning were surveilling him sporadically, apparently because Dudley became instinctively suspicious of him. Junior Stemmons came back into Johnny's life then, quite accidentally. Both he and Johnny were working South-Central, and somehow Stemmons got Johnny to admit his participation in the fur robbery. Johnny didn't, apparently, implicate me, but Stemmons sensed that he was being operated. Dudley became aware of how dangerously unstable Stemmons was, and I *think* he suspected him of trying to extort Johnny. I *know* for a fact that Dudley tried to get a bank writ to seize potential Stemmons evidence, and I'm assuming that he tortured Johnny for information on the extent of Junior's knowledge before he had you kill him. I had already gone to a Federal law clerk that I know, and he stalled Dudley's writ while I tried to get one. You got to the vault boxes first, and I'm thinking that Welles Noonan must have assisted you."

That dangling tape—just maybe.

"He did."

"Are you going to be a Federal witness?"

"I'm supposed to be."

"But you're considering not testifying?"

Glenda—potential FED indictments pending.

"Mostly I'm thinking of running."

"What's stopping you?"

"The Kafesjian-Herrick job."

"You're expecting some kind of payoff?"

"No, I just want to know why."

"Is that all you want?"

"No. I want you to get me a cup of coffee, and I want to know why you assigned me to the Kafesjian burglary."

Exley stood up. "Do you think Dudley killed Junior Stemmons?"

"No, he would have ditched the body to buy more time to get at the vault boxes."

"Are you thinking it was a legitimate overdose?"

"No, I'd bet on Tommy K. My guess is that Junior came on strong and Tommy got pissed. It happened *at* Bido Lito's, so Tommy left the body there. The Kafesjians torched the place to destroy evidence."

"You could be right. Wait, I'll get you your coffee."

He walked out. Kitchen sounds—I grabbed the tape.

Safe-combination bingo: 34L–16R–31L. Squarejohn thinking: every rich stupe pulled that chair-reminder bit. I pressed the tape back and scoped the room: cold, expensive.

Exley brought coffee in on a tray. I poured a cup for show.

"You put me on the Kafesjian burglary to bait Dudley."

"Yes. Has he approached you?"

"Indirectly, and I told him flat out that you were using me as some sort of agent provocateur. He let it go at that."

"And he has you compromised with that movie you told me about."

"PLEASE DON'T KILL ME."

"Get to it. Dudley and the Kafesjians."

He sat down. "The burglary itself was just a coincidence, and I simply capitalized on the fact that Dan Wilhite sent you over to smooth things out with J.C. I suspect that the burglary and the Herrick killings, which *are* connected, are connected to Dudley at best tangentially. Essentially, after the Nite Owl reopening, I began querying retired officers about Dudley. I learned that he, not Chief Horrall, suborned the Kafesjians into the LAPD fold twenty-odd years ago. *He* was the one who initiated the notion of contained narcotics peddling in exchange for a certain amount of Southside order and snitch information, and of course many years later he went crazy with the notion of containment in general."

"What about Phillip Herrick?"

"Your property-ownership lead is my first indication of a Smith-Herrick connection. You see, I just wanted Dudley diverted. I knew he had things brewing in South-Central, and I knew he was taking a discreet percentage from J.C. Kafesjian. I wanted the Kafesjians rattled, and I had hoped that your reputation would move Dudley to approach you."

"Then you'd operate me."

"Yes."

Dawn breaking—my last free day. "I burned up Junior's evidence. He had notes, your cancelled checks to those reporters, everything."

"All my dealings with Duhamel were verbal. You've just assured me that there is no evidence on my operation extant."

"It's comforting to know that you'll skate."

"You can, too."

"Don't jerk my chain. Don't offer me protection, and don't mention sparing the Department."

"You consider your situation beyond those things?"

Dawn light—my eyes stung. "I'm fucked, plain and simple."

"Ask a favor then. I'll grant it."

"I got Noonan to lift his surveillance on the Kafesjians. They'll be tail-free today only, and I think they'll go after Richie Herrick. I want a dozen mobile tail men with civilian radio cars, and a special frequency set up to monitor their calls. It's a shot at Dudley, which should please you no fucking end."

"You're assuming Richie can fill in some blanks on Dudley and the Kafesjians?"

"I'm assuming he knows all of it."

Exley stuck a hand out—Dave, my buddy. "I'll set up a radio spot at Newton Station. Be there at ten-thirty, I'll have your men briefed and ready."

That hand, persistent—I ignored it.

"You're letting Narco go. The Department needs a scapegoat, and they're it."

That hand disappeared. "I have extensive dossiers on every Narco officer. At the proper time, I'm going to present them to Welles Noonan, as a way of affecting a rapprochement. And, parenthetically, Dan Wilhite committed suicide last night. He left a note that included a brief mention of the bribes he's taken, and I'm going to send Noonan a memorandum on it before too long. He was obviously afraid of having his more outré secrets exposed, which is something you should consider should you decide to testify against the Department."

Bad morning light—glaring.

"I'm past all that."

"You're not past needing me. I can help satisfy your curiosity regarding those families, so don't forget that your interests are identical to mine."

Bad morning light—one day left.

41

0:30—Newton Street Station. A briefing room—chairs facing me.

No sleep—phone work kept me up. Recap: early-A.M. check-in—the Wagon Wheel Motel.

Those fur-storage notes: Dudley knew I knew/Dudley knew where I lived.

Calls:

Glenda said she was safe in Fresno.

Pete said he had Chick V. stashed, with Fred Turentine guarding him. Safe: *my* slum building, dummy signers, untraceable. "When he heals up a little, I'm gonna lean on him. He's got money tucked away someplace, I can tell."

Implied: rob him, kill him.

Welles Noonan had Kafesjian news:

Per our bargain: all Fed tails were lifted today only. TV misinformation was planted: "Probe surveillance quashed by court injunction."

"I'm hoping our friends will think that an LAPD fix is in, and resume their outside life. Godspeed in this mission of yours, Brother Klein—and tune in Channel 4 or KMPC at two-forty-five this afternoon. Really, you'll be in for quite a treat."

Lying treacherous hump.

Tail men walked in and sat down. Mixed bag: suits and ties, loafer types. Twelve men—eyes on me.

"Gentlemen, I'm Dave Klein. I'm commanding the Herrick homicide job, and per Chief Exley's order, you are to keep a twenty-four rolling surveillance on J.C., Tommy, Lucille and Madge Kafesjian. We are hoping that one of them will lead us to Richard Herrick, who Chief Exley and I want to question as a material witness in the Herrick 187s."

Little nods—Exley pre-briefed them.

"Gentlemen, those folders on your desks contain Intelligence Division photos of the four Kafesjians, along with State Records Bureau mugs of Richard Herrick, and a more recent artist's sketch of him. Know those faces. Memorize them. You'll be stringing three-man tails on each family member, both mobile and on foot, and I don't want you losing them."

Folders open, pix out—pros.

"You're all skilled tail men, or Chief Exley wouldn't have chosen you. You've got radio-equipped civilian cars, and Communications Division has got you hooked up on band 7, which is absolutely Fed-listening-proof. You're hooked up car to car, so you can talk among yourselves or contact me here at the base. You all know how to leapfrog suspects, and there are boom mikes outside the Kafesjian house. There's a man in a point car listening, and once you assume your perimeter posts, he'll tell you when to roll. Questions so far?"

No hands up.

"Gentlemen, if you see Richard Herrick, apprehend him alive. He's a peeper at worst, and both Chief Exley and I believe that a man peeping on him is in fact the Herrick family killer. If approached, I doubt that he'll react violently or resist arrest. He might try to flee, in which case you should pursue him and take him *alive* by any means necessary. *Should you spot one of the Kafesjians, specifically Tommy or J.C., trying to kill or in any way harm Richard Herrick, kill them.* If Tommy himself spots your tail and attempts to flee, chase him. If he makes *any* aggressive moves toward you, *kill him."*

Whistles, smiles.

"Go—you're dismissed."

Bugs in my walls, bugs on my phone. Bugs snooping on Glenda, snooping on Meg. Fred Turentine—the "Bug King"—guarding Chick.

Bugs in my buildings—three hundred units plus. Tenants overheard: fix the roof, kill the rats. Bugs blasting bop—niggers tearing up my slum pads.

"Sir? Lieutenant Klein?"

I woke up aiming—trigger happy.

A bluesuit—scared. "S-s-sir, the point man broadcast in. He said the two Kafesjian guys are mobile, and he said he heard them talking up Richie Herrick."

42

ail reports—band 7, continuous squawk:

11:14: Madge and Lucille at home. J.C. and Tommy driving eastbound—separate cars.

11:43: J.C. at the downtown Public Library. Tail men in foot pursuit—walkie-talkie talkback:

The music room—J.C. rousting winos. "Hey! You know Richie Herrick, he used to read books here! Hey, you seen Richie, you tell me!"

No Richie confirmations.

12:06: J.C. mobile, eastbound.

12:11: Madge and Lucille at home.

Earaches—my headset fit tight.

12:24: J.C. at a skid-row movie house.

"He's shining a flashlight at all these bums sleeping. He's getting nowhere, and he's getting mad."

12:34: J.C. walking—Q&A at the Jesus Saves Mission.

12:49: Tommy walking—skid row.

12:56: Tommy at a skin-book arcade.

12:58: Tommy talking to a clerk.

Linkage?:

Transom magazine—Richie Herrick, author.

1:01: Tommy muscling the clerk. Unit 3-B67, walkie-talkie: "The guy's pleading with Tommy. If Tommy pulls a weapon, I'll go in."

1:01: J.C. at a hot-dog stand.

1:03–1:04: Tommy driving northbound.

1:06: Unit 3-B67, walkie-talkie:

"I talked to the clown Tommy leaned on, and he said that Richie bought dirty magazines there. He said Richie said something about a pad in Lincoln Heights, and he told Tommy about it to get him off his back."

1:11: Tommy—Pasadena Freeway north.

1:14: Tommy—Lincoln Heights off-ramp.

1:19: J.C. eating lunch: five kraut dogs, Bromo Seltzer.

1:21: Lucille heading out in her Ford Vicky.
1:23: Tommy cruising North Broadway, Lincoln Heights.
1:26: Madge at home.
1:34: J.C. scarfing dessert: jelly doughnuts and beer.
1:49: Tommy cruising side streets, Lincoln Heights.
1:53: Lucille—Pasadena Freeway northbound.
1:56: Lucille—Lincoln Heights off-ramp.
1:59: 3-B67/3-B71—crosstalk:
Lucille cruising Lincoln Heights.
Tommy cruising Lincoln Heights.
North/south/east/west zigzags—missing each other.
Educated guess:
Two Richie chasers chasing Richie—cross-purposes.
Maybe Lucille got a phone tip—maybe the skin-mag clerk.
2:00–2:04: All J.C./Tommy/Lucille units:
No Richie Herrick sightings.

Transmitter static. I flipped dials—squelch, odd words: "multiple," "maybe mob stuff," "Watts."

A clerk tapped me. "Sorry, Lieutenant, a Code 3 screwed up the lines."

"What is it?"

"Homicides at the Haverford Wash. Maybe shotguns, maybe gangster stuff."

My hackles jumped. "You monitor band 7, I'm going."

Watts—Code 3, join the crowd: black & whites, lab vans, Fed cars. *Deep* Watts—rural—fields, scattered shacks.

A bluff—cop vehicles at the edge. I skidded up and fishtailed in close.

Men looking down—Feds and LAPD combined. Push through, scope it:

A concrete run-off ditch—twenty feet deep.

Sewage water ankle-high—tech men kicking through it.

Blood streaks down the right-side embankment.

Four garbage-soaked bodies just below.

Steep cement leading down—I skidded all the way. Tech guys snapping pix—bulb light bouncing off bloody water.

I looked up:

Trees lining the embankment—good cover.

I looked down:

Shotgun shells bobbing in the muck.

Call it:

Tree-cover ambush—buckshot blew them down.

I sloshed over—techs swarming—more sirens up top. Four bottom-sucking dead men—their backsides ripped tailbone to ribcage.

Jumbled voices on the bluff: Noonan, Shipstad, Exley. Lab men flipping bodies, getting gore-splashed.

Four stiffs face-up now—two white, two Mex. I made three: goons working Mickey C. coin.

Snap conclusion:

Dudley ambush—NO FACE SHOTS—Darktown slot geek victims.

Snap theory:

Staged killings for the Feds—some onus dropped on out-of-town gangs. A Dudley Smith charade—SOMEHOW.

Look:

Exley kicking up water—his cuffs soaked.

Noonan closer—trousers rolled, fucking garters.

Tech talk, scrambled:

Handguns on the stiffs.

Spent rounds up top—threads attached—the killers wore bulletproof vests.

Lab men swamping Exley, holding him back. Noonan on me, splashing me.

Waving photos—matching dead men—dead panicked.

"Oh God, oh no. We identified these—"

I steered him clear of Exley. Noonan kicked at the water—shotgun shells jumped.

"We identified these men. Mickey Cohen divested his Southside coin machines to them. They're part of a midwestern syndicate. . . . Mickey said they're the ones who killed those men of his who just disappeared a while ago. Mickey's got no stomach for the rackets anymore. . . . He sold them his coin business to get out of it."

Bullshit—actor Mickey—Glenda critiqued his "style."

Noonan: "We turned Mickey as a witness. We granted him immunity and promised him a Federal Service Medal. He thinks it will help him secure a district gambling franchise, which is absurd, since that bill will never pass the State Legislature."

Mr. U.S. Attorney—plaid garters.

"Klein, do *you* know anything about this?"

"Major Witness" Mickey—confirmed. A flash: Bob Gallaudet supported district gambling.

Exley watching us.

"Klein—"

"No, I don't."

"This may hurt us. Mickey was going to testify against those men."

"Us"/"we"—Glenda juked Fed royal.

"I want an extra day before I enter custody."

"Under no circumstances. Don't ask me again, and don't even consider begging additional favors. This is your last day to resolve your curiosity vis-à-vis the Kafesjians, and as of tomorrow those curiosities will become a matter of Federal testimony."

Mr. U.S. Attorney—used rubbers stuck to his ankles.

"Who do you think killed these guys?"

"I would say East Coast mafiosi. I would say the word got out that Mickey divested his coin machines, and some East Coast men are attempting to crash the racket."

Clueless dumbfuck.

"Trust ME, lad"—Dudley Smith in my head.

Shouts up top:

"Mr. Noonan! Mr. Noonan, he's on the radio!"

Noonan splashed up the hill; Exley hooked a finger my way.

Duck him—up to the bluff fighting shivers. Fed cars, Feds: Shipstad, Noonan, Milner et fucking al.

Mickey Cohen on KMPC:

". . . This is a public announcement undertaken in true sincerity, so I will say it now: I am severing my rackets connections. It is a mitzvah and a good deed of atonement, and I am coming forth to aid the Federal rackets probe currently doing business in Nigger—I mean Southside Los Angeles. I do this with great personal tsuris, which is the same as agony to you many Angeleno viewers and listeners who do not understand Yiddish. I am doing this severing because vicious midwestern hoodlums killed four of my men some months ago, and they are now threatening to kill my ex-wife, and let me now state that those rumors of her leaving me for some shvartze calypso singer are false. I am doing this severing because it is the moral thing to do as taught in the Bible, that wonderful perennial bestseller with many wonderful lessons for gentiles and Jews alike. I sold my Nig—I mean Southside vending-machine business to the midwestern hoodlums to save lives. I am now prepared to aid my dear friend U.S. Attorney Welles Noonan and his courageous . . ."

Mickey rambling.

Shipstad grinning.

Noonan trembling—wet feet, rage.

". . . and the Federal rackets probe is undertaken out of principles espoused in the Bible, one of those goyishe chapters that serve as the basis of inspirational movies like *Samson and Delilah* or maybe the scintillating *The Ten Commandments.*"

Noonan: "Mickey's testimony is a bit anticlimactic now. I would like to blame these deaths on the Kafesjians, but vending machines have never been their raison d'être. Eight A.M. tomorrow, Brother Klein. Bring Kafesjian information, and don't even think of asking for an extension."

"Trust ME, lad"—Dudley Smith sweet as Jesus.

43

:09: J.C. and Madge at home.

4:16: Lucille walking—Lincoln Heights—bars, newsstands.

4:23: Tommy walking—Lincoln Heights. Unit 3-B67: "I think he's checking out shooting galleries. He's hit four places the past two hours, and they look like hype pads to me."

4:36: Lucille walking.

4:41: Tommy walking.

3-B67: "I called the Highland Park Squad about those places Tommy hit. They said hype pads affirmative. Him and Lucille haven't run into each other yet, which goddamn amazes me."

4:53–4:59, all units: No Richie Herrick sightings.

5:02: Base to all J.C./Madge units: proceed to Lincoln Heights and saturate for Richie Herrick.

5:09: Lucille at Kwan's Chow Mein Pagoda. 3-B71: "She walked straight to the kitchen, and I *know* this place. Uncle Ace Kwan sells white horse, so I'll bet Lucy didn't stop in for chop suey."

5:16: Lucille exiting the restaurant. 3-B71: "She looks nervous, and she's carrying a brown paper bag."

Weird—hype Lucille?—unlikely.

Junkie Richie—ditto.

Tommy cruising dope pads—????

5:21: Tommy pissing in the street in full view of children. 3-B67: "Jesus, what a whanger! This clown has gotta hold the white man's world record!"

A clerk nudged me; I pulled off my headset. "What is it?"

"High brass to see you. The parking lot, ASAP."

Exley.

Go—past the squadroom—civilian radio blaring: Gangland Slayings! Mickey Cohen Reforms! Outside—Dudley.

Lounging on a prowl car.

Breuning and Carlisle by the fence—out of earshot. Breuning wearing a herringbone coat—MOVIE TIME patterns.

"Hello, lad."

Don't flinch, don't move too sudden, don't tremble.

"I got your notes, lad."

I stepped closer. Smell him: bay rum cologne.

"I hope you availed yourself of a splendid mink stole for that lovely sister of yours. Is she still consorting with Jack Woods?"

"I've got Chick Vecchio stashed. He snitched you on the movie, the furs, you running Mickey and those slot guys you clipped in Watts."

"I would say you're dissembling. I would say Exley hearsay is your sole source of information. You're assuming I told Chick things that indeed I didn't, and frankly I doubt that he would speak indiscreetly, even under the most severe duress."

"Try to find him."

"Is he dead or just temporarily indisposed?"

"He's alive, and he'll talk to stay that way."

Breuning and Carlisle watching us bug-eyed.

"They can't hear us, lad."

Don't blink. Don't tremble—

"Lad, your notes stated that you wished to act independent of Edmund Exley. I found that encouraging, and your mention of money even more so."

"Breuning put that sword in my hand. I'll trade you Vecchio for him, the movie and fifty thousand."

"Mike was hardly the director of your cinema debut."

"Let's just say he pays."

"Lad, you surprise me. I had thought your homicidal tendencies to be strictly profit-motivated."

"I'm afraid you'll just have to accept this new aspect of my personality."

Dudley roared. "Lad, your sense of humor is beyond salutary, and I agree to your offer."

"Tonight then. A public place."

"Yes, my thoughts exactly. Shall we make it eight o'clock, the Hollywood Ranch Market parking lot?"

"Agreed."

"I'll have Mike bring the fifty. He'll think it's a payoff run, and he'll be told to accompany you to fetch Vecchio. Take him with you, and when things are settled, call me at AXminster 6-4031 to tell me where Chick can be found. And, lad? Mike will be wearing a vest—you should know that and aim accordingly."

"I'm surprised—you and Breuning go back."

"Yes, lad, but you and I go forward. And on that topic, how do you assess the extent of Edmund Exley's information?"

Seal it—touch him. That cologne—don't gag.

"Lad . . ."

I draped an arm around his shoulders. "He knows everything that I do and whatever else Johnny Duhamel told him. There's nothing on paper, and his Duhamel evidence is hearsay impossible to corroborate. He ran me against you on the Kafesjian burglary, and my only regret is that he's too big to kill."

"Are you saying our transgressions might go unpunished as a result of his lack of evidence?"

"I'm saying you'll skate—*if* you curtail your plans with Mickey."

"And yourself, lad? Dare I proffer the word 'loyalty'?"

"It's the Feds, Exley or you. You're the only one with cash money."

Embracing me—Dudley Liam Smith. "You've made a wise choice, lad. We'll discuss Exley later, and I won't insult your intelligence with the word 'trust.' "

44

—

6 :16: J.C. and Madge at home.

6:21: Tommy prowling dope pads—Lincoln Heights.

6:27: Lucille prowling bars—Lincoln Heights.

6:34, all units: no Richie Herrick sightings.

6:41: Tommy eating dinner: Kwan's Chow Mein Pagoda.

3-B67, walkie-talkie: "I'm no lip reader, but I can tell Uncle Ace is telling Tommy how Lucille copped some white horse from him. Tommy's goddamn fuming. Oops, he's walking. 3-B67 to base, over and out."

6:50: Tommy cruising Lincoln Heights—random zigzags.

6:54: Lucille walking—Lincoln Park—chatting up bums.

6:55, 6:56, 6:57, 6:58—Mike Breuning pictured dead a hundred ways. NO—

45

"... so I'll cross Dudley. I won't hand over Vecchio—and Dudley thinks I'm going to kill Breuning. *We* nail Breuning for the Duhamel killing, and *I'll* eyewitness Tommy K. popping Steve Wenzel, which gives us a wedge on the Kafesjians. Breuning will fucking shit his pants when I ARREST him, then we'll—"

"Klein, will you calm down—"

"Calm down shit, I'm a lawyer, you listen to me."

"Klein—"

"No, you listen. Breuning snitches Dudley, then Gallaudet convenes a special County grand jury to hear evidence. We upstage the Feds on Narco and the Kafesjians tangential to Dudley, and I testify on the Duhamel killing and all conspiracies extant with the Kafesjians, Dan Wilhite, Narco, Smith, Mickey Cohen, my mob hits, all of it. I'm a cop, I'm an attorney, I'll be the goat, I'll testify when the trials start, the Feds'll be fucked, you'll look so good Welles Noonan'll wither up and die and Gas Chamber Bob'll ride the trials straight to the governorship and—"

"Klein—"

"Exley, PLEASE, let me do this. Dudley knows I'm a killer, and he thinks he's operating *me* on Breuning. Now, if I bring Breuning in, he'll punk out—without Dudley he's got no guts. Exley, PLEASE."

Tick tick tick tick tick—seconds/a minute—

"Do it."

Phone-booth sweats—drenched—I cracked the door for a breeze.

"And no backup men at the Ranch Market—Breuning might spot them."

"Agreed. Do it."

Pay phone to pay phone—bug-fear precautions. Long distance—twenty dimes—Newton Station to Mel's Drive Inn, Fresno.

Glenda talked a blue streak:

Touch told Mickey she drove to T.J. for a scrape. Dig her new stand-in— Rock Rockwell, full drag. Dig Fed witness Mickey on TV—blatant Vampire *plugs.*

Reckless Glenda—tell me everything.

She was carhopping now: roller skates, cowgirl outfits. A Fed fugitive— fuck it—she spilled a malt on the Fresno DA—and he loved it. Good tips, getting gooood on skates—really gooood tray dips. Stylish Glenda, strong Glenda—tell me ANYTHING.

Her blue streak dwindled; her tough-girl shtick tapped out hoarse. Scared Glenda—chain-smoking to tamp down her nerves.

I told her:

You scared me.

You cut me loose from this woman I had no business loving.

46

ollywood Ranch Market—
Fountain and Vine.

Open-air entrance, park-
ing lot. Cars, shoppers, box
boys pushing carts.

8:02 P.M.—standing curbside. Sweaty, chafing—my bulletproof vest fit tight.

Breuning walking toward me—across-the-lot diagonal.

Packing a suitcase.

Fatter than fat—*his* vest bunched up at the hips.

Parking-lot lights: humdrum shoppers lit up. No backup types dawdling.

I cut over. Breuning clenched up—fat neck toady fuck.

"Show me the money."

"Dud said you should hand up Vecchio first."

"Just show me."

He opened the bag—just a crack. Cash stacks—fifty grand easy.

"Satisfied?"

A box boy circled by, hands in his apron. A toupee, familiar—

Breuning eyeballed him—Say what?

Black-and-white-glossy familiar—slot surveillance pix—

Breuning fumbled his piece up—

His suitcase hit the ground.

I snagged my .45 on my vest.

The box boy shot through his apron two-handed—Breuning caught two clean head shots.

Screams.

A breeze—money flying.

I got my piece free; the box boy swung my way—two hands out.

Point blank: three shots slammed my vest and pitched me backward. Muzzle smoke in his eyes—I shot through it.

Point blank—no way to miss—a bloody toupee sheared clean, Jesus fuck—

Screams.

Shoppers grabbing money.

Breuning and the box boy tangled up dead.

Another "box boy"—braced against a car hood, aiming at me.

People running/milling/huddling/eating pavement.

I threw myself prone. Shots—rifle loud.

Roof snipers.

That box boy blending in—human shields bobbing every which way.

Snipers—Exley backup.

Firing at the box boy—missing wide.

Bullhorn amplified: "Cease fire! Hostage!"

I stood up. "Hostage": box boy dragging an old lady backward.

Elbows flailing, clawing at him—resisting mean.

Blade flash—he slit her throat down to the windpipe.

Bullhorn roar: "Get him!"

Rifle shots strafed the old lady—box boy hit the sidewalk hauling dead weight.

Run—

Straight across diagonal—his blind side.

"DON'T SHOOT, HE'S OURS!"—somebody/somewhere.

On him, his shield up—this mouth-gaping, neck-severed thing. I shot through her face and ripped them separate; I matched his face as one more Fed-photo dead man.

47

"T he crime wave that has local authorities baffled continues. A scant hour ago four people were shot and killed at the picturesque Hollywood Ranch Market, two of them identified as Midwest-based criminals posing as market employees. An LAPD officer was also gunned down, as was an innocent woman taken hostage by one of the criminals. Thousands of dollars dropped from a suitcase were scattered in the ensuing pandemonium, and when calculating in the gangland slayings in Watts earlier today that also left four dead, the City of the Angels begins to seem like the City of the Devils."

My motel room, TV news. Call it for *real:*

Exley backup, Smith targets: Breuning and me. A Dudley charade: rogue cops slain, bag cash found. Movie time pending then: my rep even more trashable postmortem.

". . . LAPD Chief of Detectives Edmund J. Exley spoke to reporters at the scene."

Recap—my Newton check-in call:

"Tommy and Lucille are still cruising Lincoln Heights, and they *still* haven't seen each other. And . . . uh . . . sir? Your pal Officer Riegle called in . . . and . . . uh . . . sir, he said to tell you he heard that Chief Exley issued an APB order on you 'cause you left that shooting scene without telling anybody."

Exley on camera: "At this time we are withholding the identities of the victims for legal reasons. I will neither confirm nor refute a rival television station's speculation on the identity of the officer who was killed, and at this time I can only state that he was killed in the line of duty, while attempting to entrap a criminal with marked LAPD money."

Flashback: that slot man eating that old lady's brains.

I called El Segundo. Ring, ring—"Yeah, who's this?"—Pete Bondurant.

"It's me."

"Hey, were you at the Ranch Market? Some news guy said Mike Breuning got it and one cop bugged out."

"Does Chick know about Breuning?"

"Yeah, and it's spooking him no end. Hey, *were you there?*"

"I'll be over in an hour and tell you about it. Is Turentine there?"

"He's here."

"Have him set up a tape recorder and ask him if he's got the equipment to monitor police calls. Tell him I want to tap into band 7 at Newton Street Station."

"Suppose he doesn't have the stuff?"

"Then tell him to get it."

he stash pad—*my* low-rent unit.

Pete, Freddy T.; Chick Vecchio cuffed to a heat pipe. A tape rig and short-wave set—with band 7 pickup.

Mobile units calling in to Newton. Broadcasting base to cars: Exley himself.

Incoming:

Tommy and Lucille cruising separate—Lincoln Heights, Chinatown, moving south.

The point man at the K. house:

"I heard it out the boom mike. It sounded to me like J.C. just slapped the piss out of Madge. To top it off, there's Fed cars driving by on the QT every hour or so."

Unit 3-B71: "Lucille's walking around Chinatown asking questions. She's looking sorta distraught, and that last joint she went into—the Kowloon—it looked like a dope front to me."

Pete—wolfing spareribs.

Fred—nursing a highball.

Chick—purple bruises, half his scalp scorched.

Fred poured himself a refill. "The Kafesjians and you. I don't get it."

"It's a long story."

"Sure, and I wouldn't mind listening to something other than these goddamn radio calls."

Pete said, "Don't tell him shit, it'll end up in *Hush-Hush.*"

"I'm just thinking twelve mobile tail cars and Ed Exley monitoring calls himself means it's some kind of big deal, which maybe Dave should elaborate on. Like for instance, who are these Tommy and Lucille chumps looking for?"

Light bulb:

Richie "Peeper" Herrick—Chino inmate/bugging know-how. Fred Turentine, drunk driver—Chino teaching gigs.

"Freddy, when were you teaching that electronics class up at Chino?"

"Early '57 up till I got bored and hung up my probation maybe six months ago. Why? What's that got to do with—"

"Did a kid named Richie Herrick take the class?"

Light bulb—dim—juicer Freddy. "Riiiight, Richie Herrick. He escaped, and some psycho chopped his family."

"So, did he take your class?"

"Sure did. I remember him, because he was a shy kid and he played these jazz records while the class worked on their projects."

"And?"

"And that's it. There was this other white guy that he palled with, and he took the class with Herrick. He stuck close to him, but I don't think it was a queer thing."

"Do you remember his name?"

"Nooo, I can't place it."

"Description?"

"Shit, I don't know. Just your average white-trash inmate with a duck's-ass haircut. I don't even remember what he was in for."

Something?/nothing?—tough call. Chino files missing—

"Dave, what's this all ab—"

Pete: "Leave Klein alone, you're getting paid for this."

Band 7:

Tommy mobile—Chinatown.

Lucille mobile—Chinatown near Chavez Ravine.

I doused the volume and grabbed a chair. Chick edged his chair back. In his face: "DUDLEY SMITH."

"Davey, please"—raspy dry.

"He's behind all the trouble in Niggertown, and he just sent Mike Breuning out to die. Spill on him, and I'll cut you loose and give you some money."

"Suppose I don't?"

"Then I'll kill you."

"Davey . . ."

Pete signaled me: feed him liquor.

"Davey . . . Davey . . . please."

I handed him Freddy's glass.

"You guys don't know Dudley. You don't know the kind of stuff he'd do to me."

Bonded sour mash—three fingers. "Drink it, you'll feel better."

"Davey . . ."

"Drink."

Chick guzzled it down. Grab the glass, refill it, watch him swill.

Instant booze panache: "So what kind of money are you talking about? I've got expensive tastes, you know."

"Twenty grand"—pure bullshit.

"That plays lowball to me."

Pete said, "Talk to Klein or *I'll* fucking kill you."

"Okay, okay, okay"—refill gestures.

I filled the glass. "Chick, *give.*"

"Okay okay okay"—sipping slow.

I propped the tape rig up by his chair and hit Record.

"Dudley, Chick. The furs, Duhamel, the Kafesjians, the whole takeover story."

"I guess I know most of it. Feature Dudley likes to talk, 'cause he figures everybody's too scared of him to tattle."

"Get to it."

Booze-brave: "I say Domenico 'Chick' Vecchio knows when to talk and when to shut up. I say fuck 'em all except six, and save them for the pallbearers."

Pete said, "Will you *please* fucking give?"

"Okay okay, feature Dudley, he was the boss at Robbery Division. Exley, he had this hard-on for him, because he made Dud for lots of stuff over the years—"

"Like the Nite Owl job?"

"Yeah, like the Nite Owl. Anyway, Dudley always took the most interesting robbery cases for himself, 'cause that's just the way he is. So Exley shot the Hurwitz Fur case to Robbery, and Dud grabbed it, and he got some leads that he later on figured out were planted by Exley, and those fucking leads led him to his very own so-called protégé, Johnny Duhamel."

Freddy and Pete noshing spareribs—rapt.

"Keep going."

"Okay, now Dudley, he'd recruited Schoolboy Johnny for the Mobster Squad. You know how he drools for tough boys, and when Johnny was in the LAPD Academy he showed some meanness that Dud really liked. So he stayed mean on the Mobster Squad, and now Dudley sees that he's a fucking badass heist guy, which, being Dudley, pleases him no fucking end. So, Dud called Johnny on the heist, and Johnny admitted it, but he refused to snitch his partners, which also impressed Dud. So, feature, Dudley gave Johnny a skate on the fur job and confided some of his own crime gigs to him, which meant that so far Exley's trap was working."

Tape hiss. Chick, snitching nice and loose now: "So feature that Dudley bagged Johnny's furs and stored them at a storage locker joint. A couple got out, 'cause Dudley told Johnny to get next to Lucille Kafesjian when Exley assigned you and that punk Stemmons to that burglary job. Johnny, he got a little lightweight boner for Lucille and gave her one."

"Dudley told Johnny to become intimate with Lucille?"

"Yeah, sort of like a safeguard if you started leaning on the Kafesjians too hard."

"Then what?"

"Then that goddamn Stemmons blundered in. He was Johnny's teacher at the Academy, and Johnny made him for a closet fruit back then. So Junior, he saw this striptease that Lucille did with this mink Johnny gave her, I think he was working Bido Lito's on the burglary job. Johnny was there, and him and Junior talked, which resparked this fucking faggot torch Stemmons had for Johnny."

"So at first Junior came on like a pal."

"Right, and feature that all that Mobster Squad strongarm stuff wasn't really Johnny's style, it was just this role Exley had him playing. Anyway, Johnny, he was stretched pretty thin and feeling pretty bad about it, and he told Stemmons about how brutal the work was, and Junior started figuring out that somebody was running him undercover. Johnny never flat-out snitched Dudley to him, but he told him about these 'auditions' Dudley was doing without naming no names."

"What 'auditions'?"

"Dud was bringing these out-of-town guys in. He needed them to work the Southside coin, and he *wanted* the Feds to see them. Dud said later that Johnny figured out the guys were going to get clipped when Mickey went public with his Fed witness bit."

Haverford Wash—four dead. "But Johnny didn't confide *that* to Junior."

"Right."

"And the coin men were just pigeons set up to get clipped later?"

"Right."

"What about the 'auditions' themselves?"

"Dudley told the out-of-town guys they had to earn the right to work for him. He said that meant enduring pain. He paid them money to let Johnny hurt them while he watched and talked this philosophical shit to them. Dick Carlisle said Dud broke their spirits and made them goddamn slaves."

Pete said, "Holy shit."

Freddy said, "I don't believe this."

"Who clipped the slot guys?"

"Carlisle and Breuning. You want to hear a nice Dudley touch? He had them soak their buckshot in rat poison, then repack the shells."

"Get back to Johnny."

Chick stretched—his cuff chain rattled. "Dud had Johnny monitoring the slot guys—you know, watching them service the machines. He was doing that one night or something, and Dick Carlisle saw Junior come up to him and start talking this nutso rebop. Carlisle got this feeling that Johnny might be a plant, so he told Dudley, and Dud had Carlisle and Breuning keep this loose tail on him. Now, I don't know who killed Stemmons—probably Tommy or J.C. Kafesjian—but around the time Carlisle got hinky, J.C. told Dudley that Stemmons was acting crazy, shaking down pushers, shaking down him and Tommy and telling them he could monkey-wrench *your* burglary investigation. So, this nutty faggot Junior, he's talking up his own Niggertown takeover stuff, and in my opinion Dud would have clipped him himself, if he hadn't of OD'd or got snuffed by the Kafesjians."

"Then what?"

"Then Dud got a tip that Johnny called *you* to set up a meet—*and I didn't tell him.* So now he *knew* Johnny was a fucking traitor or decoy or something."

The meet: Chick knew. Bob Gallaudet knew.

"Then what?"

"So Johnny told you to meet him at that pad in Lynwood. Dud used to own it years ago, so I guess Johnny just wanted to meet you someplace close to the bungalow where . . . you know."

Change-up: "Phillip Herrick."

"Who's that?"

"He was murdered in Hancock Park last week. Dudley co-owned 4980 Spindrift with him."

"So?"

Easy call: no Herrick knowledge.

"So Johnny told me to meet him there, and your little movie set was close by. What do you figure he wanted to show me?"

"Maybe the smut-movie setup."

"Maybe, but you told me Sid Frizell wasn't connected to any of Dudley's plans."

"He's not, but Dud *loves* stag stuff, and when he got tight with Mickey, Mickey told him about this batshit horror movie he was bankrolling and how Sid Frizell wanted to shoot smut films, but he couldn't find a spot. Dud told Mickey to tell Frizell to use one of the rooms in that court, so down the line Sid did, but feature I know for a fact that he doesn't even know Dudley."

SOMETHING—some CONNECTION—knifing me.

"Does Dudley own those bungalows?"

"Feature yes he does, through dummy partners. Feature he owns about twenty other abandoned dives, just bought dirt fucking cheap off the Lynwood City Council."

"And?"

Leering at me ugly drunk: "And feature Dudley Liam Smith does not get his rocks off on girls, boys or Airedale terriers. Feature he likes to watch. Feature the mirror walls in that flop where you rousted me and feature he's got a shitload of other flops just like it. Feature he's got this idea to film these on-the-sly smut movies where the fuckers and fuckees don't even know they're being watched. Feature he's got bids in with the Bureau of Land and Way to house the spics evicted from Chavez Ravine in those pads and that dump on Spindrift. Feature Dudley's going to film all these taco benders fucking and sell the movies to geeks like himself who dig all that voyeuristic horseshit."

Rumors:

Sid Frizell shooting LYNWOOD stag films.

LYNWOOD spic relocation maybe looming.

That SOMETHING—click:

Atomic Vampire.

Movie gore: incest/eye poking/blinding.

Kafesjian 459—dogs blinded.

Herrick 187—three victims eye socket blasted.

Sid Frizell—ex-con type.

Non-Dudley-connected—Chick convinced me.

Non-click: SOMETHING missing.

I said, "Dudley and Mickey."

"You mean what's the skinny on Dudley's rackets thing?"

Shortwave sputter: "Chinatown, Chinatown, Chavez Ravine."

"Right."

"Well, feature the word 'containment.' That's Dud's big word, and what he wants to do is build up this empire on the Southside, maybe stretching into Lynwood, where he's got all this property. He'll only sell dope to niggers, and he'll run whores and smut on the QT, and he'll run all the coin hardware that Mickey so-called divested. His big deal is supposed to be district gambling, with Mickey as his front man. Feature he killed all of Mickey's guys except me and Touch, and feature he fucking manipulated Mickey into cozying up to the Feds. The Mick's a hero now, he's a lovable shmuck, and Dud thinks he can buy up more Lynwood property and start so-called 'containing' the economy down there, then set Mickey up to front his district gambling franchise, all nice and legal."

"District gambling won't pass the State Legislature."

"Well, feature Dudley thinks otherwise. Feature he's got a political guy with very large juice in his pocket to make sure it does get passed."

Gas Chamber Bob Gallaudet: district gambling supporter.

Tipped off to the Duhamel meet.

Goosebumps: my dry-ice burns started tickling.

"So Dud found out you were meeting Johnny. Breuning and Carlisle slugged you and doped you up, and Dud tortured Johnny before you sliced him. They got him to admit that Exley was running him as a decoy and that he had these fake bank accounts and this operations cash stashed in a safe at his house. Johnny said he kept trying to pull out of the deal because he knew the slot guys would probably get clipped and lots of other shit would hit the fan, but Exley kept sending him back to find out more."

Radio hum: Tommy mobile, Lucille mobile.

Pete and Freddy dumbstruck—holy shit/mother dog!

"Why did Dudley make that movie? Why didn't he just kill Johnny and me?"

"He said he wanted to compromise you and use you. He said he was going to offer you this job as liaison and bagman to the LAPD. He said he could use you to take Ed Exley down. He said you were probably a pretty good lawyer, and he said you could teach him things about property maintenance."

Chick oozing brainwaves: kowtow to Dudley or die.

Pete oozing brainwaves: kill the wop and grab his money.

Freddy oozing brainwaves: *Hush-Hush* would love THIS.

Atomic Vampire—INCEST/GORE.

"Chick, what do you know about Sid Frizell?"

"Feature I know close to nothing."

"Has he done time?"

"County time for child-support skips. He's no hard-case penitentiary guy, if that's what you're thinking."

To Freddy: *"Sid Frizell.* He's a tall, skinny guy about thirty-five. He's got sort of an Okie drawl."

"No bells. Am I supposed to know him?'

"I thought he might have taken your class at Chino."

"No, I don't think so. I mean, I'm a bug man, so I listen to how people talk. Sorry, but there were no Okie drawls in my class."

SOMETHING MISSING.

I grabbed the phone and got an operator—Chino on the line.

A warden's aide answered. Go, tell him:

Compile a roster for me—cons at Chino Richie Herrick concurrent. Messenger it down?—No, I'll call you back for a verbal.

2:00 A.M.—custody looming. Radio sputter, *pop/pop*—Pete cracking his knuckles. Chick loopy drunk, scorched hair—my damage.

Smells—stale food, smoke. A view out the window: overflowing trashcans. *My* building—nine G's a year net profit.

Think: snitches, deal-outs.

Last-ditch tries.

Welles Noonan—a Gallaudet rival.

Think trades: Glenda for Bob G. and Dudley.

The bedroom phone—shaky hands on the dial. MA 4-0218—Noonan.

"U.S. Attorney's Office, Special Agent Shipstad."

"It's Klein."

"Klein, this call didn't happen."—low, furtive.

"What?"

"Noonan got a film can special-delivery. It's you chopping up some guy, and *I* know it's a setup, but *he* doesn't care. A note said copies go to the press if you testify for us, and Noonan said your immunity agreement is cancelled. He's issued a Federal arrest warrant on you, and *this call did not happen.*"

CLICK—

Chairs/shelves/tables—I threw them and kicked them and dumped them. I punched myself arm-dead on the curtains; exhaustion had me swaying light-headed.

Radio squawk:

"Madge left the house alone. The point car's on her."

"Lucille's entering Chavez Ravine. She's driving erratic, she's side-swiping trees—"

49

Crisscross headlights, dirt roads—Chavez Ravine.

Dark—no streetlights—cop lights only. Roof lights, headlights, flashlights—tail men mobile and on foot.

Bumper crunched upside a tree: Lucille's Ford, abandoned.

APBs out on me—

I ditched my car and sprinted up the access road. Zigzag flashlights down below: a shack-to-shack search.

"Lad."

Dark, just his voice. I aimed at it, half pull triggered.

"Lad, hear me out before you act precipitously."

"You sent that movie to Noonan."

"No, Bob Gallaudet did. I told him you had Chick Vecchio hidden, and Bob assumed that Chick would behave in a cowardly fashion and inform on us. Lad, Bob handed you up to Noonan. He threatened to make public a second copy of the film if you testified as a Federal witness, assuming that your testimony would damn both himself and this aging Irishman who bears quite a grudging fondness for you. Noonan was furious, of course, and Bob quite wisely retreated to a more judicious footing: he said that the film threat stood, but he would not enter the attorney general's race if Noonan promised no open-court mention of him. Noonan, bright lad that he is, agreed."

"Gallaudet ratted *you* to Noonan?"

"No, Allah be praised, he just evinced panic and spoke nebulously of complex criminal conspiracies. I'm sure Noonan considers me just an aging policeman with a gift for language and a stern reputation."

Shouts down below. Stray headlights blipped Dudley smiling benign.

"Who gave Bob that movie copy?"

"Mike Breuning. He was afraid our enterprises were in jeopardy, so he gave Robert a copy to cut a deal for himself. Alas, Mike confessed what he had done before I sent him out to meet you, which is why I set him up so harshly."

"Gallaudet?"

"Ensconced with Allah, lad. Neatly dismembered and unreachable. Kill Vecchio, if you haven't already, and there's just Exley sans hard evidence."

"Chick told me Duhamel snitched Exley."

"Yes, that's true."

"He said Exley kept money in a safe?"

"Yes, Chick is correct."

"Inside his house?"

"Yes, lad, that would be logical."

"Big money?"

"Yes, that's correct. Lad, get to the point, you're tantalizing me."

"I can tap that safe. I'll kill Vecchio and steal Exley's money. We'll split it."

"You're very generous, and I'm surprised that you haven't expressed rancor over my machinations at the Ranch Market."

"I want you to like me. If I run, I don't want you coming after the people I leave here."

"You're perceptive to assume my survival."

"The money?"

"I'll accept half graciously."

Commotion down the hill: cops kicking in shack doors.

"Chick told you the thrust of my plans, did he, lad?"

"Yes."

"Did you infer that I enjoy watching?"

"Yes."

"I view it as a dispensation for the grand work of containment I'll be doing. I view it as a means to touch compelling filth without succumbing to it."

FLASH: Lucille nude.

"You're a watcher, lad. You've touched your own dark capacities, and now you enjoy the surcease of simple watching."

FLASH: whore-pad windows.

"I empathize with your curiosities, lad."

FLASH—peeper tapes—pictures synced to sounds.

"It pleases me that the Kafesjians and Herricks seem to have piqued those curiosities. Lad, I could tell you many grand stories about those two families."

FLASH—bright open windows—TELL ME THINGS.

"Lad, do you feel the basis of an understanding starting to form? Are you beginning to see the two of us as kindred souls, brothers in curious—"

Shouts, flashlights converging—

I ran down—tripping and stumbling. Shacks pressed up tight together—lights fixed in one doorway.

Tail men huddled outside—push through, look:

Lucille and Richie Herrick—DOA.

Tourniquet tied/veins pumped/mouths frozen gasping.

Entwined on a mink coat bed.

H bindles, spikes and Drano on a fox pelt.

50

8:01 A.M.—Federal fugitive.

Fugitive pad, fugitive car—a '51 Chevy bought off a junker lot. Fugitive calls:

Glenda safe—style vs. fear—style winning.

Sid Riegle, panicked—Exley men rousted my men.

Bureau talk: Lucille and Richie died from heroin-Drano cocktails. Sid: "Ray Pinker said she hotshot him, then killed herself. Doc Newbarr said no way was it murder, then suicide—everything was too nice and neat."

More talk:

Tommy and J.C.—Fed-rousted and released at 4:00 A.M. Madge K. gone for parts unknown—the point man lost her.

A call to Pete—find me that woman, she can TELL ME things.

Fugitive wheels: the Cahuenga Pass south. Rearview panic checks—everything looked strange and wrong.

Radio news: Hot L.A. Crime Wave! Mickey Cohen Federal Witness! DA Gallaudet Misses Breakfast Talk—Assembled Scribes Baffled!

Last night—Dudley's farewell:

"I'll require verification on Chick. His right hand should suffice—it bears quite a recognizable tattoo."

Brain teaser:

Vampire gore/the Kafesjian-Herrick case—who?/why?

South: Hollywood, Hancock Park. Left turn—432 South McCadden.

Virgin—no cars curb or driveway.

I walked up and knocked. Nobody watching—knife the keyhole, work the lock.

In.

Close the door, bolt it—lights on, go.

I checked the living room walls: no pictures, no fake panels.

I checked the den—framed photos—Dudley Smith, Bureau toastmaster. Pull them, look behind—

No safe.

Upstairs—three bedrooms—more walls, more pictures:

Dudley Smith as Santa Claus—a polio ward, '53.

Dudley Smith, guest speaker—Christian Anti-Communist Crusade.

Dudley Smith at a crime scene: ogling a dead jigaboo.

Three bedrooms—twenty Dudley Smith pictures—Exley hate fuel. No safe.

Back downstairs—check the kitchen—nothing.

Check the carpets—every one tacked flat. Upstairs—hallway throw rugs—pull them—

A hinged panel under a red Persian.

Inset with a tumbler dial and handle.

Trembly—34L–16R–31L—two run-throughs, snap/thunk—yank the handle.

Drawstring bank bags. Five. Nothing else.

Hundreds, fifties, twenties. Old bills.

I shut the lid, spun the dial and fixed the rugs. Downstairs, the kitchen—

Cutlery right there. I grabbed a cleaver—heebie-jeebies—Chick.

51

"Davey . . . please."

Psychic: begging me two seconds in the door. A tattoo on his right hand: "Sally 4-Ever."

"Davey, please."

683 grand and that cleaver. Pete out chasing Madge, Fred asleep in the bedroom.

Chick, cuffed down—panic spritzing:

We go back, we had laughs, I'm sorry I got fresh with Glenda, but how can you blame me? We had laughs, we made money, Pete wants to kill me, he's a fucking neon sign. . . .

"Davey, please."

Pillow bullet mufflers. Curtains for a makeshift shroud.

"Davey . . . Jesus Christ . . . Davey."

Tired—no stones for it—yet.

Dead man talking:

I'll disappear . . . you can trust me. . . . Glenda's great . . . Sid Frizell says she's star stuff. Frizell . . . what a chump . . . no ideas . . . that camera guy Wylie Bullock's got twice the smarts, and he couldn't direct traffic on Mars. You and Glenda . . . I wish you the best. . . . Davey, I know what you got planned, I can see it in your eyes. . . .

Tired.

No stones for it—yet.

The phone rang—I cradled it up. "Yeah?"

"It's Pete."

"And?"

"And I found Madge Kafesjian."

"*Where?*"

"The Skyliner Motel, Lankershim and Croft in Van Nuys. She's in room 104, and the desk man says she's on a hankie binge."

"You're staking her?"

"I'm on your payroll, and I'm watching that room till you say otherwise."

"Just stay there. I'll be out soon, so—"

"Look, I talked to Mr. Hughes. He said the Sheriff's found a witness who saw Glenda by the Hollywood Hills fuck pad like the approximate night that Miciak bought it. They think she's hinky, and they're looking for her as a suspect. It looks like she blew town, but—"

"Just stick at the motel."

"Your payroll, boss. How's Chick—"

I hung up and dialed Chino direct.

"Deputy Warden Clavell's office."

"Is he in? It's Lieutenant Klein, LAPD."

"Oh, *yes,* sir. Mr. Clavell left me a list of names to read you."

"Read off the released inmates first."

"Current addresses too?"

"The names first, I want to see if something grabs me."

"Yes, sir"—slow, precise:

"Altair, Craig V. . . . Allegretto, Vincent W. . . . Anderson, Samuel NMI. . . . Bassett, William A. . . . Beltrem, Ronald D. . . . Bochner, Kurt NMI. . . . Bonestell, Chester W. . . . Bordenson, Walter S. . . . Bosnitch, Vance B. . . . Bullock, Wylie D.—"

Tilt/click/snap—SOMETHING missing/SOMETHING there:

Wylie Bullock.

Vampire cameraman.

Idea man—pressing gore on Sid Frizell.

"Burdsall, John C. . . . Cantrell, Martin NMI—"

"Go back to Wylie Bullock. Give me his parole date and his last known address."

"Um . . . he was paroled on November 9, 1957, and his parole disposition address is the Larkview Trailer Court, Arroyo and Brand in Glendale."

Freddy in the hallway—yawning.

"Sir, do you want the rest of these names?"

I put the phone down. "Was there a guy named Wylie Bullock in your class at Chino?"

"Yeah . . . riiight . . . he was that guy following Richie Herrick around." Adrenaline—*zoooom.*

Chick: "Hail Mary full of grace the Lord is with thee."

Stay of execution: dumb guinea luck.

52

R

&I/DMV:

Bullock, Wylie Davis—DOB 7/16/25. Brown/brown, 5'10", 165. Popped 3/56—pornography beefs—3 to 5, Chino.

Occupation: photographer-cameraman. Vehicle: '54 Packard Clipper, white & salmon, Cal. GHX 617.

Freeways out to Glendale—my rat's-ass car belched smoke. Wylie/Madge/Dudley—TELL ME THINGS.

Arroyo off-ramp, south to Brand—the Larkview Trailer Court.

Parking slots: and no two-tone Packard tucked in. A map out front: "W. Bullock"—three rows over, six trailers down.

Rock gardens, jacked-up trailers, white trash wives out sunning. My SOMETHING MISSING:

Frizell-Bullock confabs—Wylie assertive: Incest! Poke the vampire's eyes out!

Three over, six down—a chromium Airstream. My .45 out surreptitious—knock.

No answer—no surprise—no Packard. I tried the door—locked—too many squarejohns around for a break-in.

The set—go.

Freeways back—my clunker wheezed. Griffith Park, the set—no Bullock vehicle in sight.

Mickey by the spaceship—wearing a Jew beanie.

"The Feds and LAPD were here chasing your tush. The Malibu Sheriff's were looking for my erstwhile star Glenda Bledsoe, who I understand you are playing Bury the Brisket with. You break my heart, you handsome snatch bandit."

No "crew"—just Mickey. "Where is everybody?"

"Shmuckface, *Attack of the Atomic Vampire* is in show-biz parlance a 'wrap.' Glenda may look a bit muscular in her concluding moments, given that Rock Rockwell portrayed her in long shots, but that aside I consider my movie a cinema landmark."

"Where's Wylie Bullock?"

"I should know? I should care?"

"Sid Frizell?"

"Paid off and on the night boat to Nowheresville for all I care."

Beanie, flag lapel pin—hero Mickey. "You look happy."

"I have a movie in the can, and I have made friends of the Federal persuasion. And do not judge me as a snitch fuck, because a certain U.S. attorney told me you have those tendencies yourself."

Dudley's lovable shmuck. "I'll miss you, Mickey."

"Run, David. The tsuris you have caused seeks retribution. Run to Galapagos and watch turtles fuck in the sun."

The Cahuenga Pass—back over coughing fumes. Lankershim and Croft—the Skyliner Motel.

Horseshoe-shaped—cut-rate pool-view cabanas. Pete staked out curbside—snoozing with the seat back.

I parked behind him. Tell-me money in the trunk—I stuffed my pockets.

Skirt the pool over—room 104. I knocked—Madge opened up quick.

Haggard—heavy makeup made it worse. "You're that policeman. Our house was broken into . . . you came over. . . ."

"Hankie binge"—wet eyes, tear tracks.

"I'm sorry about your daughter."

"It was a merciful death for both of them. Did you come to arrest me?"

"No. Why should I—"

"If you don't know, I won't tell you."

"I just wanted to talk to you."

"So you filled your pockets with money."

C-notes spilling out. "I figured it couldn't hurt."

"Did Dan Wilhite send you?"

"He's dead. He killed himself."

"Poor Dan"—one short sigh.

"Mrs. Kafesjian . . ."

"Come in. I'll answer your questions if you promise not to slander the children."

"Whose children?"

"Ours. Whoever's. Just exactly what did you . . . ?"

I sat her down. "Your family and the Herricks."

"What do you want to know?"

"Tell me everything."

1932—Scranton, Pennsylvania.

J.C. Kafesjian and Phillip Herrick work at Balustrol Chemicals. J.C. is a laborer, Phillip a solvent analyst. J.C. is crude, Phil is cultured—they are friends—nobody knows why.

1932: the friends move to Los Angeles together. They court women and marry them: J.C. and Madge Clarkson, Phil and Joan Renfrew.

Five years pass: the men toil at boring chemical jobs. Five children are born: Tommy and Lucille Kafesjian; Richard, Laura and Christine Herrick.

J.C. and Phil are bored, angry and poor. Their chemistry knowledge inspires a scheme: brew homemade liquor.

They do it—and thrive.

The Depression continues; poor people *need* cut-rate spirits. J.C. and Phil sell it cheap—work-camp workers their chief clientele. They accrue profits and hoard their shares.

J.C. and Phil—friends and partners.

J.C. and Phil—cuckolding each other.

Neither man knows:

Two affairs predate their weddings. Lovers: J.C. and Joan, Phillip and Madge. The adultery continues—five children are born—their patrimony inconclusive.

J.C. opens a dry-cleaning shop; Phil invests in a chemical plant. They continue their home liquor business.

J.C. pushes Phil to cut costs: lower-quality alcohol solvents mean greater profits.

Phil agrees.

They sell a batch to some CCC workers—a dozen men go permanently blind.

June 22, 1937:

A blind man carries a pump shotgun into a tavern.

He fires the weapon at random—three people are killed.

He sticks the barrel in his mouth and blows his own head off.

Sergeant Dudley Smith investigates. He learns the source of the shotgun man's blinding; he tracks the liquor to Phil and J.C. He makes them an offer: his silence for a percentage of their holdings.

They agree.

Dudley recognizes J.C.'s mean streak—and cultivates it. He believes that Negroes could be kept dope-sedated; he urges J.C. to sell them drugs.

He urges Chief Davis to let J.C. "serve" them: as a sanctioned dope peddler and informant to the fledgling Narcotics Squad.

Dudley hides his role—few know that he is J.C.'s recruiter. Chief Davis retires in '39; Chief Horrall takes over. He assumes credit for the Kafesjian recruitment—and taps Officer Dan Wilhite to serve as J.C.'s contact.

Years pass; Dudley continues to extract his business percentage. J.C.'s dry-cleaning shops flourish; he builds up a Southside dope kingdom. Phil Herrick earns legitimate wealth: PH Solvents is hugely successful.

The adultery goes on: J.C. and Joan, Phillip and Madge.

Both women have assured their lovers that birth control precautions have been taken. Both have lied—they loathe their husbands, but will not leave them. Madge knows J.C. would kill her; Joan needs Phillip's money and newly developed social connections.

Five children.

Inconclusive patrimony.

No dangerous resemblances emerging.

Joan *wanted* J.C.'s baby: he treated her atypically tender. Madge wanted Phillip's: she despised her vicious husband. Guesswork fathers softens things—both women believe it.

Post–World War II:

Major Dudley Smith, OSS, sells black-market penicillin to escaped Nazis. Phil Herrick, naval officer, serves in the Pacific; J.C. Kafesjian runs his dry-cleaning shops and dope racket. Dudley returns to L.A. late in '45; Herrick, fourteen months at sea, comes home unexpectedly.

He finds Joan nine months pregnant. He beats her—and learns that J.C. has been her lover throughout their marriage. She had planned to put the child up for adoption; Phil's surprise return prevented her. She hid her pregnancy with long indoor sojourns; Laura, Christine and Richie—away at boarding school—do not know what happened.

Joan runs to J.C.

Madge hears them talking and confronts them.

J.C. brutally beats both women.

Madge admits her long affair with Phil Herrick.

Cuckold husbands, cuckold wives. Enraged men—two women beaten and raped. Terrible chaos. Abe Voldrich calls in Dudley Smith.

He has the five children blood-tested—the results are ambiguous. Joan Herrick delivers her baby; Dudley strangles it three days old.

Laura and Christine never learn the facts of their lineage.

Tommy, Lucille and Richie do—several years later.

The boys grow up friends—maybe brothers—whose father is whose?

They burglarize houses and play jazz; Richie falls in love with Lucille. He comforts her with Champ Dineen—he didn't know his bloodlines either.

Tommy emulates his "name" father J.C.—selling dope while still in high school. He's always lusted after Lucille—now there's a chance she *isn't* his sister. He rapes her—and makes her his personal whore.

Richie finds out—and swears to kill Tommy.

Tommy relishes the vow—he considers Richie a weakling.

Richie drives to Bakersfield and buys a gun. He gets caught selling dope; Dudley Smith intercedes, but cannot convince the DA to drop charges. Richie Herrick, sentenced to Chino: 1955.

Tommy swears he'll kill him when he's released—he knows his personal whore Lucille deeply loves him. Richie swears to kill Tommy—he has debased the maybe sister he loves chastely.

Lucille runs wild—prostitute, window dancer, taunter of men. Phil Herrick seeks her out—his maybe daughter. Their first coupling is a street assignation. Lucille agrees just to taunt him.

His gentleness surprised her—this maybe daddy more like Richie than Tommy. They continued to meet: always talking, always playing games. Phil Herrick and Lucille: maybe daddy-daughter lovers, maybe just a whore and a john.

And Madge and Joan became friends. They hid from the madness together—fugitive time spent simply talking. Confidantes: years of partial shelter.

Richie escaped from Chino—fit only to voyeur-watch Lucille. Joan and Richie exchanged letters; Richie said a friend soon to be paroled would avenge him painlessly. This man seemed to have a hold on Richie: Richie never even said his name.

Joan killed herself nine months ago; the insanity peaked all at once. Lucille did not know Richie was watching her; Tommy read Junior Stemmons' reports and assumed that Richie was the voyeur. He vowed to kill him—afraid that Exley-linked men would find him first. Lucille found him—their ticket to shelter in a needle.

Tissues on the floor—Madge fretted a whole box to shreds.

"Would you call that 'everything,' Lieutenant?"

"I don't know."

"Then you're a very curious man."

"Do you know the name Wylie Bullock?"

"No."

"Who killed Junior Stemmons?"

"I did. He was browbeating Abe Voldrich at one of our cleaning shops. I was afraid he'd find out the truth about Richie and Lucille, and I wanted to protect them. I attacked him rather foolishly, and Abe subdued him. We knew Dudley would protect us if we killed him, and Abe knew he was an addict."

"So Abe shot him up and dumped him at Bido Lito's."

"Yes."

"And you told Tommy, and he burned the place down. He hung out there, and he was afraid we'd find evidence on him."

"Yes. And I don't feel bad about that young man Stemmons. I think he was in as much pain as Richie and Lucille were."

I emptied my pockets—big wads of cash.

"You're naive, Lieutenant. Money won't make J.C. and Tommy go away."

53

"**E**VERYTHING" = "MORE" = "BULLOCK."

Back to the trailer dump— a two-tone Packard in the lot. I jammed up behind it, spewing smoke.

Voices, feet kicking gravel.

Thick fumes—I got out coughing. Exley and two IA men—packing shotguns.

"Everything" means "more" means—

Fumes, gravel dust. Shotgun flankers, Exley sweating up a custom-made suit.

"Bullock killed the Herricks and trashed the Kafesjian place. How did you know—"

"I called Chino to get my own roster. That woman in the warden's office told me you went crazy over Bullock."

"Let's take him. And get those guys out of here—I *know* he's got stuff on Dudley."

"You men wait here. Fenner, give the lieutenant your shotgun."

Fenner tossed it—I pumped a shell home.

Exley said, "All right then."

Now:

We ran three rows over, six trailers down—civilians watched us slack-jawed. That Airstream—radio hum, the door open—

I stepped in aiming; Exley squeezed in behind me. Two feet away: Wylie Bullock in a lawn chair.

This bland geek:

Smiling.

Raising his hands cop-wise slow.

Spreading ten fingers wide—no harm meant.

I jammed the shotgun barrel under his chin.

Exley cuffed his hands behind his back.

Radio hum: Starfire 88's at Yeakel Olds.

"Mr. Bullock, you're under arrest for the murders of Phillip, Laura and

Christine Herrick. I'm the LAPD chief of detectives, and I'd like to question you here first."

Monster's den: *Playboy* pinups, mattress. Bullock: Dodger T-shirt, calm brown eyes.

I goosed him: "I know about you and Richie Herrick. I know you told him you'd get him revenge on the Kafesjians, and I'll bet you know the name Dudley Smith."

"I want a cell by myself and pancakes for breakfast. If you say that's okay, I'll talk to you here."

I said, "Make like you're telling us a story."

"Why? Cops like to ask questions."

"This is different."

"Pancakes and *sausage*?"

"Sure, every day."

Chairs circled up, the door shut. No Q&A/no notebooks—Maniac speaks:

June, 1937—Wylie Bullock, almost twelve—"I was just a kid, you dig me?"

An only child, nice parents—but poor. "Our flop was as small as this trailer, and we ate at this gin mill every night, because you got free seconds on the cold cuts."

June 22:

A crazy blind man enters the tavern. Random shotgun blasts: his parents get vaporized.

"I got hospitalized, 'cause I was in some kind of shock."

Foster homes then—"some nice, some not so hot"—revenge dreams minus a bad guy—the shotgun man killed himself. Trade schools—a knack for cameras—"Old Wylie's a born shutterbug." Camera jobs, curiosity: 6/22/37—why?

Amateur detective Wylie—he kept pestering the cops. The brush-off: "They kept saying the case file was lost." Newspaper study: Sergeant Dudley Smith, investigating officer. Calls to now-Lieutenant Smith—none returned.

He haunted that tavern. Rumors haunted the place itself: bad bootleg trashed the shotgun man's eyes. He chased rumors: who sold bootleg whiskey back in '37?

Bad leads—years' worth—"like impossible to verify, you know?" Two rumors persistent: "dry-cleaning-cut hooch," "this Armenian guy—J.C."

He made a logical jump: the E-Z Kleen shops/J.C. Kafesjian. "I didn't have any proof—it just felt right. I kept a scrapbook on the blind man case, and I had this picture of Sergeant Smith from '37."

"It was becoming like an obsession."

Supporting that obsession: camera work. Illegal: "I took snatch pictures and sold them to sailors and Marines up from Diego."

Obsession focus: the Kafesjians.

"I sort of circled around them. I found out J.C. and Tommy pushed dope and had these police connections. Lucille was a floozy, and Tommy was vicious. It was sort of like they were my pretend family. Tommy had this buddy Richie, and the two of them played this jazz music really lousy. I used to follow them, and I watched them get into some kind of big falling-out over Lucille. Richie got popped selling dope up in Bakersfield. He got sentenced to Chino, and I was in an E-Z Kleen shop one day, and I heard Tommy tell Abe Voldrich that when he got out Richie was dead meat."

Early '56—two bombshells hit him simultaneous:

One—he's outside a Southside E-Z Kleen. Huddled up: J.C. Kafesjian and Dudley Smith—nineteen years older than that news pic.

Two—he gets popped selling snatch photos.

"I figured Dudley Smith and the Kafesjians were dirty together. I couldn't *prove* anything, but I thought maybe Smith gave J.C. a skate on that poison liquor he sold. After a while I just believed it."

He started hatching revenge plots—this Eyeball Man inside him fed him plans. He pleaded guilty to selling pornography—his lawyer said beg for mercy.

"At the County Jail this guy told me about the X-ray lab at Chino— what a good job it was. I figured I could get a job there if I got sentenced to State time, 'cause I knew so much about photography. See, I had a real plan now, and I wanted to do a Chino hitch so I could get next to Richie."

The judge hit him with three-to-five State. They bought his X-ray experience snow job: Wylie Davis Bullock, go to Chino.

"So I went to Chino and got next to Richie. He was a lonely kid, so I befriended him, and he told me this AMAZING goddamn story."

Amazing:

The Kafesjians, the Herricks—who fathered whose children? Phil Herrick and J.C.—bootleg dealers back in the '30s. The blind man killings—Richie said yes, maybe—it might be Dudley Smith's wedge. Incest: maybe/quasi/brother/father perv stuff.

"I guarantee you you have never heard *nothing* to compare to the stuff Richie told me."

Richie, sissy/voyeur:

"He told me he was in love with Lucille, but he wouldn't touch her because she might be his half-sister. He said he loved spying on her."

Richie, compulsive talker:

"He put things together for me. I figured out enough about Dudley Smith to know that he met up with Herrick and Kafesjian some time right after the killings. I figured Smith got cozy with them and took bribes not to snitch that they brewed that liquor. I knew now. I knew these two crazy families killed my family."

Richie, talking vengeance on Tommy:

"I knew he didn't have the balls for it. I said just wait—I'll get you your revenge if you promise not to bother the Kafesjians."

Richie promised.

"Then his mother wrote him and went through this sob-sister suicide routine. Richie walked Chino—fucking minimum security, he just *walked.*"

Richie stayed loose.

He got paroled two months later.

"I tried to find Richie. I staked out the Kafesjian and Herrick houses, but I never saw him."

"That Lucille, though—wow. I used to watch her do the shimmy-shimmy naked."

Months ticked by. "One day right before she killed herself I saw Old Lady Herrick leave a letter in her box for the postman. I snuck up and grabbed it, and it was addressed to Champ Dineen, this jazz clown that Richie worshipped. There was a PO box address, so I figured Moms and Richie were working a mail-drop thing. I sent Richie a note at his box: 'Dig Lucille do the shimmy shimmy in her window. Now you be patient and I'll get you your revenge.' "

The note worked—months ticked by—he peeped Richie peeping Lucille. AMAZING: peeper Richie, amateur bug man—that electronics class did him solid. He walked the straight and narrow himself—movie jobs, parole confabs—nobody knew the Eyeball Man kept his dick hard—

"I started getting these wild ideas.

"The Eyeball Man said I should follow the Kafesjian guys and Dudley Smith around just for kicks.

"I was dogging Smith one day. He had lunch with Mickey Cohen, and I grabbed a booth next to them. Cohen said he was fronting this horror movie shooting in Griffith Park, and this Sid Frizell guy who was directing it shot stag films on the side. Smith said he loved naughty movies, and that Cohen should tell Frizell he had a nice sound stage he could use. Cohen said Frizell was skanky enough to take him up on it."

He hit the *Vampire* set—"Man, was this flick from hunger." He offered his camera services cut-rate; Cohen hired him; he gamed dumbfuck Sid Frizell—strapped for ideas. "I fed him these incestuous-type bits and all this blinding stuff, 'cause I figured one day I'd show Richie the finished-up movie. I told Frizell I had smut experience, and he pestered this Cohen guy Chick Vecchio into talking to Smith. Smith gave the okay, so Frizell got to shoot his stuff at this dive down in Lynwood.

"So I got cozy close to things, but I still didn't have *the* fucking plan worked out. Then the Eyeball Man came through."

He said tweak the Kafesjians with a voodoo B&E. Put the onus on Richie—keep him scared—keep him hiding.

"So I did it. I guess it's like symbolism, 'cause the Eyeball Man told me exactly how to do things. I tried to blind the dogs with this dry-cleaning chemical, but that didn't work, so I pulled their eyes out. I broke liquor bottles to goose them on their bootleg gig, and I broke Tommy's records up 'cause the Eyeball Man said that would symbolize how Richie hated Tommy. Richie always hated Lucille whoring, so I cut her pedal pushers up and shot a load on them."

Wicked fun.

"The Eyeball Man said make Richie squirm, so I scoped him out at these motels, getting all weepy over Lucille, and I cut up his bed with this silverware I stole to spook him. There was lots of heat around the Kafesjians because of the B&E and the Fed thing, so the Eyeball Man told me to kill Phil Herrick early. The daughters came home unexpected, and the Eyeball Man said snuff them too. I figured Richie was a fucking escapee, so the cops would think he did it and snuff him on the spot."

Then?

"The Eyeball Man said kill Tommy and J.C. slow. He said rip Dudley Smith's eyes out and eat them."

Now?

"Pancakes and sausage, daddy-o. A nice safe cell for me and the Eyeball Man."

Licking his chops.

Flapjack batter on a shelf.

EVERYTHING.

Chest pings/headache/dry mouth—Dudley Smith meets the Eyeball Man.

Exley pointing at the door.

I followed him outside. Spooky sunlight—trailer-park geeks watching us.

"What's your assessment?"

Juke him/fuck him—LIE:

"I want to take Bullock in to Welles Noonan. I'm dodging custody, and he can help me smooth things out. He's a key witness on Dudley and the Kafesjians, and if we cooperate with the Feds we can cut their probe off at the knees, especially with you giving them Narco."

"He's insane. He's not a valid witness."

"Yeah, but all he is to *us* is a psycho. He's not even fit to stand trial."

"Gallaudet will get indictments. He'll prosecute him himself."

"Bob's dead. He was in with Dudley on some district gambling scheme. Dudley killed him."

Weak knees—I steadied him—Edmund Jennings Exley popping cold sweat.

"I've got Chick Vecchio stashed. He begged me for Federal custody, and Madge Kafesjian filled in some of Bullock's story and told me how Dudley hooked J.C. up with the Department. Exley, it's all *contained.* Vecchio, Bullock, Madge—*they* rat Dudley and only Narco gets hurt. It's *your* basic plan, and all you have to do is cut me some slack before I take Bullock in."

"Specifically?"

"Call Noonan. Tell him you're handing your Narco dossiers over. Tell him to retract his warrant on me until I bring our witnesses in."

Do it—grab the bait—I'll run with *your* money—

"Exley . . ."

"Yes. Move Bullock some place safe after dark, then call me."

"You'll call Noonan?"

"Yes, I'll call him now."

"I'm surprised you're trusting me."

"I've betrayed your trust before, and I'm running out of strategies. Just keep the shotgun and try not to kill him."

I settled in.

Bullock talked pancakes and the Eyeball Man.

EVERYTHING spun me crazy—backward, forward—back to Meg, up to Glenda.

Escape plans. Buyouts. Schemes—nothing jelled.

Dusk came on—I kept the lights off. Music somewhere—EVERYTHING spun me fresh.

Nothing jelled.

Bullock fell asleep cuffed to his chair.

Nothing jelled.

Bullock muttered gibberish in his sleep.

Shakes, shudders—something like a whimper ripping through me.

I braced myself against the wall—

Killings, beatings, bribes, payoffs, kickbacks, shakedowns. Rent coercion, muscle jobs, strikebreaker work. Lies, intimidation, vows trashed, oaths broken, duties scorned. Thievery, duplicity, greed, lies, killings, beatings, bribes, payoffs, Meg—

That whimper got loose—Bullock cocked his head to hear it better. Sobs then—choking back tears, sobs racking through me so hard the trailer shook.

EVERYTHING.

Spinning, falling, confessing.

I don't know how long it lasted.

I came out of it thinking:

NOT ENOUGH.

I made the call.

54

T he Sears & Roebuck parking lot: wide open, empty. A block off: *my* Eastside building.

Early. Arclights on asphalt—he'd see us.

683 grand stuffed in four attaché cases.

My .45 taped to my ankle.

Wylie Bullock in the front seat—cuffed with his hands in his lap.

Exley's cleaver beside him.

Headlights coming.

I laid the money bags on the hood. No suitcoat, no holster—frisk me.

Headlights up, brakes, lights off. Dudley Smith stepped out, smiling.

Coatless, empty holster—frisk *me*.

"Lad, you're early."

"I'm cautious."

"Given your circumstances, I would be, too. And that man I glimpse in your car?"

"He's a pilot. He's flying me south."

He looked in—the passenger window half down. Bullock stayed calm, my suitcoat draped over his cuffs.

"What grand briefcases! Have you tallied the amount?"

"Almost seven hundred thousand."

"Is this my share?"

"It's yours."

"In exchange for?"

"The safety of the people I leave here."

"You used the plural, lad. Have you loved ones beyond your sister?"

"Not really."

"Aah, grand. And Vecchio?"

"He's dead."

"Have you brought the verification I requested?"

"It's in with the money."

"Well, then given that Edmund Exley is unapproachable and some-what compromised, I would say this is goodbye."

I stepped closer—blocking his view—cover for Bullock.

"I've still got those curiosities."

"Such as?"

Louder—*barely*—don't rile him yet:

"Madge Kafesjian told me about the blind man killings. I wondered how you cut your deal with J.C. and Phil Herrick."

Dudley roared—huge stage laughs.

I reached back and freed the door.

"I was brazen then, lad. I understood the metaphors of greed and blind rage, and the absurdity of a sightless man wielding a ten-gauge did not escape me."

"I wish I could have seen you cut the deal."

"It was fairly prosaic, lad. I simply told Mr. Kafesjian and Mr. Herrick that their thriftily brewed liquor caused four deaths and assorted untold suffering. I informed them that in exchange for a percentage of their business holdings that suffering would remain strictly a point of contention between them and God."

"Just like that?"

Bullock mumbling.

"I also offered visual persuasion. A coroner's photograph of a young couple rendered headless expressed a certain shock value."

Mumbling louder—I coughed to cover the noise.

"Lad, is your pilot confrere talking to himself?"

Getting hinky—watch his hands.

"Lad, will you open the briefcase that contains my verification?"

I stepped closer.

Dudley flexed his hands one single beat too quick.

I pivoted to slam a knee shot; he sidestepped me.

Shivs dropping out his shirt cuffs—grab a briefcase, swing it—

Two stilettos palmed deft.

Stabbing at me—ripping leather—two blades stuck.

I dropped the briefcase.

Dudley stood wide open.

Bullock piled out, hands on the cleaver.

"EYEBALL MAN! EYEBALL MAN!"

I slammed a knee shot.

Dudley went down.

Bullock went at him cleaver-first.

Wild swings—the handcuffs fucked his grip up—the blade ripped Dudley's mouth ear to ear. Roundhouse coup de grace—the cleaver hit asphalt.

"EYEBALL MAN!"—Bullock on Dudley:

Biting.

Clawing.

Ripping at his eyes.

Look:

One gushing red socket.

"NO!"—*my* scream/my gun out/aiming at them tangled up together.

I fired twice—two misses—ricochets off the pavement.

Two more shots braced against the hood—Bullock's face exploded.

Bone spray in my eyes.

Firing blind—ricochet zings, a jammed slide.

Dudley on Bullock—prying at his hands.

Dudley weaving, screaming exultant—his eye cupped back to his face.

I grabbed the money and ran. Echoes boomed behind me: "EYEBALL MAN! EYEBALL MAN!"

A week—backtrack it:

I ran that one block to my building. Old bookie stash holes in the basement—I tucked the money away.

Calls from the janitor's phone:

Glenda, long distance: come down, grab the cash, hide. Pete in El Segundo: cut Chick loose—Glenda's got twenty grand for you.

Pandemonium at Sears—prowl cars responding to shots. Bullock dead, Dudley rushed to Queen of Angels. My explanation: ask Chief Exley.

I was arrested—bagged on Exley's APB. I was allowed one phone call—I buzzed Noonan.

A custody battle ensued—LAPD vs. Feds—Noonan victorious.

Material witness protection—no charges filed on me yet.

A Statler Hilton suite, friendly guards: Jim Henstell and Will Shipstad.

A TV in my room—dig the news:

Mickey Cohen—solid-citizen Fed helper.

Gas Chamber Bob G.—nine days missing, where's the DA?

Frequent visits from Welles Noonan.

My tack: total silence.

His tack: threats, lawyer logic.

Exley called him the day we glommed Bullock; dig the deal he offered:

A joint LAPD/Fed effort—Narco swings and Dave Klein brings in four witnesses. Cooperation assured; Exley quoted verbatim: "Let's bury the hatchet and work together. One of the witnesses will be a high-ranking LAPD man, more like a hostile interrogatee. He has intimate knowledge on the Kafesjian family, and I would call him federally indictable on at least a half-dozen charges. I think he will more than make up for the loss of Dan Wilhite, who regrettably committed suicide last week. Mr. Noonan, this officer is very dirty. All I ask is that he be portrayed as a contained, totally autonomous entity within the LAPD, just as you've agreed to portray the Narcotics Division."

Coming up: an LAPD/Fed press conference.

My "witnesses":

Wylie Bullock—dead.

Chick V.—probably hiding.

Madge—grieving somewhere.

Dudley Smith—on the critical list.

"Critical" PR—Exley press manipulation—no word on the Bullock thing issued. No City charges filed on me; Bullock cremated.

No "witnesses"—and Noonan was furious.

Threats:

"I'll prosecute your sister on tax charges."

"I'll give the DA's Office my bugging tapes—Glenda Bledsoe goddamn admitted she killed Dwight Gilette."

"I have you on tape telling a man named Jack to 'kill him.' If you refuse to talk to me, I'll have Federal agents comb a list of your known associates for that man."

My tack: total silence.

My ace: sole-witness status—I knew EVERYTHING.

Days dragged. No more L.A. "crime wave" news—Noonan and Exley put the fix in. Tommy and J.C.—under Fed surveillance, untouchable.

A visit from Ed Exley.

"I think you stole money from me. Cooperate with Noonan and I'll let you keep it. You'll need money—and I won't miss it."

"Without your testimony Dudley can't be touched."

"If this agreement with the Feds falls through, the Department will look disgracefully ineffectual."

My tack: total silence.

A visit from Pete B. Whispers: Glenda's got the money—and she paid me my cut. Word's out you're a Fed snitch—Sam Giancana just issued a contract.

A visit from two Sheriff's dicks: "We like Glenda Bledsoe for the Miciak job."

My tack—confession—I killed him solo. I dropped knife wound details— they bought it—they said they'd file Murder One on me.

Noonan right there: "I will use the full power of the Federal Government to keep this man in my sole custody."

A phone call—Jack Woods checking in:

"Meg's okay. Sam G. put the word out—you're dead."

Stale news.

Long days—playing cards with Will Shipstad killed time. Instincts: he hates Fed work, he hates Noonan. I threw out a bribe flyer: erase the Glenda tape for thirty grand.

He agreed.

Noonan confirmed it the next day: "Incompetent technicians!"—a huge tantrum.

Long nights—bad dreams—killings, beatings, bribes, shakedowns, lies. Bad sleep, no sleep.

Afraid to sleep, nightmares on call: Johnny begging, one-eyed Dudley. Glenda—hard to conjure—easy to hear:

"You want to confess."

Two nights, six legal pads—Dave "the Enforcer" Klein confesses—

Killings, beatings, bribes, payoffs, shakedowns—my police career up to Wylie Bullock. Lies, intimidation, vows trashed, oaths broken. Exley and Smith—my accessories—tell the world.

Ninety-four pages—Shipstad leaked it to Pete B.

Conduit Pete, copies to: Hush-Hush, *the L.A.* Times, *the State AG.*

Time ticking, Noonan crazed: the press conference is pending, I need you to talk.

Threats, offers, threats—

I talked:

"Give me two days of freedom under Federal guard. When I return to custody we'll prepare my testimony."

Noonan—reluctant, half crazy: "Yes."

L.A. *Herald-Express,* 12/6/58:

LAPD–FEDERAL PRESS CONFERENCE CANCELLED

The announcement last week surprised everybody: the Los Angeles Police Department and the U.S. Attorney's Office, Southern California District, were holding a joint press conference. Adversaries during U.S. Attorney Welles Noonan's still ongoing Southside rackets probe, the two law enforcement agencies had recently come across as anything but friendly. Federal officers charged the LAPD with allowing vice to rage in South-Central Los Angeles, while LAPD Chief of Detectives Edmund Exley accused Mr. Noonan of mounting a politically motivated smear campaign against his Department. That dissention ended last week when both men issued identical statements to reporters. Now, tomorrow's press conference has been precipitously called off, leaving many members of the Southern California law enforcement community baffled.

Last week's press release was carefully worded; it hinted only that a cooperative Federal-LAPD effort had been mounted, one perhaps aimed at securing indictments against members of the LAPD's Narcotics Division. Much more was to have been revealed tomorrow, and an anonymous source within the U.S. Attorney's Office stated that he thought the joint effort was scotched due to breach of official promises. Queried as to exactly what "promises," the source stated: "A Los Angeles police officer skipped Federal custody. He was to have testified against members of the LAPD Narcotics Squad and a criminal family they have long been allied with, and he was also to have induced a total of four other potential witnesses into testifying. He did not deliver those witnesses, and when allowed two days out of custody to take care of personal matters, he attacked his guard and escaped. Frankly, without him the Federal Government has only Mickey Cohen, a former gangster, to offer testimony."

CRIME WAVE SPECULATION

This situation occurs in the middle of a statistically staggering Los Angeles crime wave, much of it Southside based. The City homicide rate for the past month soared 1600%, and although neither the LAPD nor U.S. Attorney's Office will confirm it, speculation has linked last week's gangland killings in Watts to the Hollywood Ranch Market shootout that also left four dead. Add on the mysterious disappearance of Los Angeles District Attorney Robert Gallaudet and the November 19 Herrick family slayings, still unsolved, and you have what Governor Goodwin J. Knight has called "a powder keg situation. I have every confidence in the ability of Chief Parker and Deputy Chief Exley to maintain order, but you still have to wonder what could cause such a drastic upsweep in crime."

Asked to comment on the press conference cancellation, Chief Exley refused. Queried on the recent crime wave, he stated: "It was simply coincidental and non-tangential, and now it's over."

L.A. *Mirror,* 12/8/58:

LAPD PRE-EMPTS FEDS IN DARING MOVE

The Los Angeles Police Department's famously stern Chief of Detectives Edmund J. Exley called an impromptu press conference this morning. He was expected to digress on the recent Federal Southside crime investigation and offer comments on why the LAPD and local U.S. Attorney's Office have apparently abandoned their short-lived "cooperative venture" into probing both Southside malfeasance and the Los Angeles Police Department's own Narcotics Division.

He did neither. Instead, in a terse prepared statement, he blasted the Narcotics Division himself and said that he would personally deliver incriminating evidence to a specially convened County grand jury, then offer tax fraud information unilaterally to the U.S. Attorney's Office.

Describing "Narco" as a "police unit autonomously run amok," Exley stated that he was certain its "long-standing tradition of graft" did not extend to other LAPD divisions, but Internal Affairs Division, under his supervision, was going to "comb this police department like a bloodhound sniffing out graft to make sure."

Stunned reporters asked questions; Exley refused to answer them. He did state that the commanding officer of Narcotics Division, Captain Daniel Wilhite, 44, recently committed suicide, and that Internal Affairs detectives were currently interviewing various "Narco" officers with an eye toward securing voluntary grand jury testimony.

Asked just how "dirty" "Narco" was, Chief Exley said, "Very. I am personally stating that it has been in collusion with a vicious dope-pushing family for over twenty years. It is my desire to reform the Narcotics Division from the ground up and take that family down. I will be passing pertinent Federal venue information on to U.S. Attorney Welles Noonan, but he should know that I am taking the primary responsibility for cleaning my own house."

Hush-Hush Magazine, 12/11/58:

FREEDOM OF SPEECH GAGGED!!!!! J'ACCUSE! J'ACCUSE!

Journalistic nitroglycerine—that's the only way to describe it. 94 pages that arrived at *Hush-Hush* ten days ago, atom bomb accusations that were also sent to a Los Angeles newspaper and the State Attorney General's Office.

They chose to ignore it; we chose to print it. The confidential source that transmitted this literary A-bomb verified its authenticity—and we believed him. 94 pages: scorching, scalding, burning hot revelations, the confessions of a crooked Los Angeles policeman on the run from the mob, the cops and his own violent past. You *would have seen it here* on December 18th—but something happened.

Kats and kittens, we're on dicey legal ground here. We can describe the "legal" machinations that have censored us; our lawyers tell us that the vague description of the material covered in the preceding paragraph does not violate the "legal" injunction filed against us by the Los Angeles Police Department.

And we'll go just a tad further in our description: those 94 pages would have brought the LAPD to its knees. Our (regrettably) anonymous author, unflinching in his portrayal of his own corruption, also charged celebrated Los Angeles policemen with felony malfeasance on a spectacular scale and claimed that LAPD officials covered up a complex web of circumstances surrounding the recent L.A. crime wave. Scalding, scorching hot revelations— verifiably true—and we can't print them.

That's as much as our attorneys will permit us to tell you about those 94 pages. Is your appetite whetted? Good, now let us stoke your rage.

An employee of ours, a man charged with gathering electronic information, has a drinking problem. He saw those 94 pages, recognized them as dynamite and called an LAPD acquaintance. Our employee, a probation absconder ducking drunk driving warrants, leaked those pages to his acquaintance. Word spread to the LAPD hierarchy; a restraining order was secured. Our employee was rewarded: his warrants were rendered null and void. Those scalding 94 pages were seized; we cannot print any portion of them under threat of "legal" injunction.

The newspaper? The State Attorney General's Office?

They discarded their 94 pages. They ridiculed them as hogwash. The monstrous facts were too ugly to believe.

The author? He's out there among the night blooming fiends in the City of the Fallen Angels.

The upshot? You decide. Decry this fascistic censorship. Write to us. Write to the LAPD. Express your rage. Send one up for a rogue cop whose mea culpa read too explosive to print.

BANNERS:

L.A. *Times*, 12/14/58:

GRAND JURY CONVENED; "NARCO" COPS TESTIFY

L.A. *Mirror*, 12/15/58:

HUSH-HUSH "CENSORSHIP" BLAST MEETS DEAF EARS

L.A. *Herald-Express*, 12/16/58:

LAPD DERIDES HUSH-HUSH INVECTIVE

L.A. *Times*, 12/19/58:

NARCOTICS OFFICERS INDICTED

L.A. *Mirror*, 12/21/58:

EXLEY: HUSH-HUSH ACCUSATIONS "NONSENSE"

L.A. *Mirror*, 12/22/58:

REPUTED DOPE KINGPINS FACE GRAND JURY

L.A. *Herald-Express*, 12/23/58:

GRAND JURY SHOCKER: NO KAFESJIAN INDICTMENTS—ACTING DA SAYS NARCO TESTIMONY COMPROMISED

L.A. *Examiner*, 12/26/58:

GALLAUDET STILL MISSING; SEARCH CONTINUES

L.A. *Mirror*, 12/27/58:

MAYOR POULSON: HUSH-HUSH ACCUSATIONS LAUGHABLE

L.A. *Mirror*, 12/28/58:

FEDERAL RACKETS PROBE DISBANDS

L.A. *Herald-Express,* 1/3/59:

TOASTMASTER POLICEMAN VOTED SPECIAL PENSION

The scene was sad, touching, antithetical to recent police headlines: Narcotics officers indicted on graft charges. That scene: a grossly injured Los Angeles policeman fighting for his life in a hospital bed.

Dudley L. Smith, Captain, LAPD. Dublin born, Los Angeles raised, a World War II OSS spymaster. 53 years old, thirty years a policeman. A wife, five daughters. Numerous commendations for bravery, LAPD toastmaster, lay chaplain. Dudley L. Smith: stabbed in an altercation with a robber five weeks ago—now fighting for his life.

He's winning that fight so far: he lost an eye, he's paralyzed, he's sustained brain damage, he'll probably never walk again. When he's lucid he charms nurses with his brogue and jokes that he'll do advertisements like the eye patch man who hucksters Hathaway Shirts. He's not lucid most of the time, and that's a heartbreaker.

The LAPD will not release details on the altercation that earned Dudley Smith his wounds; they know he would prefer to spare the family of the robber he killed the ignominy of public recognition. That's a heartbreaker, as is the fact that Dudley Smith will require intensive sanitarium care for the rest of his life.

His police pension and savings won't cover it. He's too proud to accept police charity contributions. He's a legendary policeman, much beloved, a cop who has killed eight men in the line of duty. Knowing these things, LAPD Chief of Detectives Edmund Exley asked the Los Angeles City Council to exercise a rarely used option and vote him a special pension: an amount to sustain his care in a comprehensively equipped sanitarium indefinitely.

The City Council agreed and voted in Dudley Smith's pension unanimously. Chief Exley told reporters: "It's important that Captain Smith remains contained and receives the care he deserves. He'll be safe and secure, and he'll be able to live out his days free of the taxing problems of police work."

Dudley L. Smith, hero. May those days stretch long and peacefully.

V

HUSHABYE

55

ake-out cartons, newspaper stacks—Pete's hole-up a month in.

A tract house outside San Diego. Safe—his ex-wife was touring Europe for six weeks. Rent pirate Pete: two grand a week.

Newspapers—the story dispersed:

My confession quashed by legal injunction.

Dudley half-dead.

The Fed probe blitzed.

Narco destroyed—Exley triumphant.

Time to think.

Phone time—outside conduit Pete reporting in:

Warrants out on me—State and Fed—nine indictments total. "They've got you on Miciak, tax charges, two State and three Federal conspiracy statutes. There's national APBs out on you, plus Fed bulletins up the wazoo. You can keep the house until January 27th, but that's it."

Pete—January 13:

"Glenda's still in Fresno. The Feds have got her under surveillance, but I think I can sneak her down for a visit before you take off."

January 14:

"I called Jack Woods. He said Meg's okay, and I checked with a Fed guy I know. He said Noonan's not going to file tax charges on her—he's too busy cooking up some new probe gig to give a shit."

January 15.

January 16.

January 17.

Tired, sludgy—chink take-out five weeks straight.

January 18:

"Dave, I can't get you a passport. I've got no legit contacts, and I heard the mob fronts aren't selling them, 'cause they figure *you're* buying."

January 19—blind run fever.

Nightmares—EVERYTHING swirling.

January 20:

"Glenda thinks they lifted the surveillance on her. She's going to bring your money down in a couple of days."

January 21—Pete, fucking scared:

"Mr. Hughes found out I've been hiding you. He's pissed that Glenda skated on Miciak and . . . shit, you know, you and her. He wants some personal payback, and he said he won't turn you in if you cooperate. Dave, I'll try to go easy."

56

O n my knees—woozy. Shock waves up my spine—one punch in.

The backyard—Howard Hughes watching.

I stood up groggy—loose teeth, split lips. Left-right/left-right/left-right—my nose somewhere down my throat. Propped up—eyebrow flaps shredded loose, shading my eyes.

Howard Hughes in a business suit and wing tips.

Kicked prone—"No, use your fists."

Jerked upright—left hook/left hook—spitting gums, no nose, hard to breathe. Left hook/left hook—bones cracking.

No legs, no face—signet ring rips jaw to hairline.

"A few more."

"He can't take any more."

"Don't contradict me."

No legs, no face. Eyes to the sun—burning red—please don't blind me. Left-right/left-right—"Leave him for the doctor."

Fading somewhere—don't take my eyes.

Spinning, falling.

Music.

Darkness/light/pain—arm jabs, crazy bliss. Light = sight—don't take my eyes.

Spinning, falling—EVERYTHING synced to bop. Champ Dineen riffs—Lucille and Richie waved down from heaven.

Sweating—cold swipes at my face. Somebody's face—an old man.

Needle jabs eating up pain.

Arm pops = craaaazy bliss.

EVERYTHING—spinning, falling.

Cheek rubs half blissed—thick beard stubble.

Time—light into dark, light into dark, light into dark.

A man wearing glasses—maybe a dream. Voices—dreamy, half real.

Music.

57

Four days sedated.

The doctor, walking out: "I left you some morphine Syrettes. You're healing up nicely, but you'll need to get some bones set within a month or so. Oh, and a friend of yours left you a package."

Numb throbs chin to forehead. Fresh newspapers—check the dates—January 22 to 25.

Mirror check:

My nose—smashed flat.

My jaw—bent sideways.

No eyebrows—scar tissue instead.

A raised hairline—scalp cuts ripped me balding.

Two new ears.

One eye squinty, one eye normal.

Dark brown hair gone pure gray inside a week.

Call it:

A new face.

Healing—bruises fading, sutures out.

I checked the package:

One blank passport.

One .38 revolver, silencer fitted.

A note, unsigned:

Klein—

IA found you, and I've decided to let you go. You served me very well and you deserve the chance I'm giving you.

Keep the money you took. I'm not optimistic, but I hope the passport helps. I won't apologize for the way I used you, since I believe the Smith situation justified it. He's neutralized now, but if you consider the justice you meted out less than absolute, you have my permission to follow it up more thoroughly. Frankly, I'm through with him. He's cost me enough as it is.

Indirect order: kill him.
Not HIM—THEM.

58

"We used to be a great-looking pair."

"That part's all on you now"—loose teeth, painful.

"You're different, David."

"Sure, look at me."

"No, it's that we've been together for five minutes and you haven't asked me to tell you things."

Glenda: carhop suntan, close to gaunt. "I just want to look at you."

"I've looked better."

"No, you haven't."

She touched my face. "Was I worth it?"

"Whatever it cost, whatever it took."

"Just like that?"

"Yeah, just like that."

"You should have grabbed that movie contract way back when."

Money bags by the door—time closing in.

Glenda said, "Tell *me* things."

Back to then, up to always—I told her EVERYTHING.

I faltered sometimes—pure horror jolted me silent. That silence, implicit: *you*—tell *me.*

Light kisses said no.

I told her all of it. Glenda listened, short of spellbound—like she knew. The story hung between us. Kissing her hurt—her hands said let me. She undressed me.

She slid out of her clothes just past my reach.

I roused slow—just let me look. Persistent Glenda, soft hands—inside her half-crazy just from looking.

She moved above me—propped up off my bruises. Just watching her felt wrong—I pulled her down.

Her weight on me hurt—I kissed her hard to rip through the pain. She started peaking—my hurt ebbed—I came blending into her spasms.

Sleep—day into night. Up startled—a clock by the bed—1:14.

January 26.

A camera on the dresser—Pete's ex-wife's. I checked the film—six exposures remaining.

Glenda stirred.

I walked into the bathroom. Morphine Syrettes in a dish—I popped one and mixed it with water.

I got dressed.

I stuffed two hundred grand in Glenda's purse.

The bedroom—

Glenda yawning, hands out, thirsty—I gave her the glass.

She gulped the water down. Stretches, little tucks—back to sleep.

Look:

A half-smile brushing her pillow. One shoulder outside the covers, old scars going tan.

I snapped pictures:

Her face—eyes closed—dreams she'd never tell me. Lamp light, flashbulb light: blond hair on white linen.

I sealed the film.

I picked up the money bags—heavy, obscene.

I walked out the door bracing back sobs.

asy:

I took a bus to L.A. and got a hotel room. I had a type-writer sent up—one blank passport rendered valid.

My new name: Edmund L. Smith.

Picture valid: photo-booth snapshots, glue.

My ticket out: Pan Am, L.A. to Rio.

My wounds were healing up.

My new face was holding: no handsome Dave Klein showing through.

Morphine pops kept me calm and crazy exultant. This crazy notion: you walked.

Not yet.

60

bought a new clunker—two hundred dollars cash. I took a detour airport-bound: 1684 South Tremaine.

8:00 A.M.—quiet, peaceful.

Voices inside—bellicose male.

I walked back, tried the rear door—unlocked. Laundry room, kitchen door—yank it.

J.C. and Tommy at the table, guzzling beer.

Say what?

What the—

J.C. first—silencer THWAP—brains out his ears. Tommy, beer bottle raised—THWAP—glass in his eyes.

He screamed: "DADDY!"

EYEBALL MAN! EYEBALL MAN!—I shot them both faceless blind.

61

Airport heat: Feds, Sheriff's men, mob lookouts. Right through them—no blinks—up to the counter.

Friendly service, a glance at my passport. I checked my money bags through—"Have a pleasant flight, Mr. Smith."

Gone—just like that.

The will to remember.

Fever dreams—that time burning.

Old now—a gringo exile rich off real estate. My confession complete—but still not enough.

Postscripts:

Will Shipstad—private practice from '59 up.

Reuben Ruiz—Bantam champ, '61–'62.

Chick Vecchio—shot and killed robbing a liquor store.

Touch V.—managing drag-queen acts in Vegas.

Fred Turentine—dead—cirrhosis. Lester Lake—dead—cancer.

The place lost/the time burning/close to them somehow.

Madge Kafesjian—alone—that house, those ghosts.

Welles Noonan—convicted of jury tampering—1974. Sentenced to three to five Fed—a Seconal OD suicide en route to Leavenworth.

Meg—old, a widow—my conduit there to here. Wealthy—our slum pads traded up for condos.

Spinning, falling—afraid I'll forget:

Mickey Cohen—perpetual scuffler—two prison jolts. Dead—heart attack, '76.

Jack Woods, Pete B.—old, in failing health.

Dick Carlisle:

Retired from the LAPD—never charged as a Dudley Smith accomplice. "Dick the Fur King"—the Hurwitz stash expanded legit. Dry-cleaning mogul—the E-Z Kleen chain purchased from Madge.

Dudley Smith—still half-lucid, still a charmer: Gaelic songs for the girls who wet-nurse him.

Edmund Exley:

Chief of Detectives, Chief of Police. Congressman, Lieutenant Governor, current gubernatorial candidate.

Acknowledged Dudley Smith admirer—politically expedient, smart.

Dudley—rakish in his eye patch. Pundit when sane: snappy quotes on "containment," always good for a news retrospective. A reminder: men were men then.

Glenda:

Movie star, TV star. Sixtyish—the matriarch on a long-running series.

Glenda:

Thirty-odd years famous. Always with me—those pictures held close. Ageless—every movie, every printed photo shunned.

In my dreams—spinning, falling.

Like Exley and Dudley and Carlisle.

Exiled from me, things to tell me—prosaic horrors that define their long survival. Words to update this confession to free me.

Dreams: spinning, falling—

I'm going back. I'm going to make Exley confess every monstrous deal he ever cut with the same candor I have. I'm going to kill Carlisle, and make Dudley fill in every moment of his life—to eclipse my guilt with the sheer weight of his evil. I'm going to kill him in the name of our victims, find Glenda and say:

Tell me anything.

Tell me everything.

Revoke our time apart.

Love me fierce in danger.

A NOTE ON THE TYPE

The text of this book was set in a face called Cheltenham,
designed by the architect Bertram Grosvenor Goodhue
in collaboration with Ingalls Kimball of the Cheltenham
Press of New York. Cheltenham was introduced in the
early twentieth century, a period of remarkable
achievement in type design. The idea of creating a
"family" of types by making variations on the basic
type design was originated by Goodhue and Kimball
in the design of the Cheltenham series.

Composed by Creative Graphics, Inc.,
Allentown, Pennsylvania
Printed and bound by Fairfield Graphics,
Fairfield, Pennsylvania
Designed by Virginia Tan